MW00668484

The Calm

Kendra White

Copyright © 2017 Kendra White

All rights reserved. No part of this book may be reproduced or transmitted in any form or by any means, electronic or mechanical, including photocopying, recording or by any information storage and retrieval system, without permission in writing from the publisher.

Publisher: Saffire Sun Publishing –Lake Stevens, WA
ISBN 978-0-692-98463-5
Library of Congress Card Catalogue Number 2017918203
White, Kendra
The Calm
Available Formats: eBook | Paperback distribution

ABOUT THE AUTHOR

Kendra White has written short stories and poems since she was young, and has always loved a good story. She grew up on a South Dakota farm where her imagination was often her sole resource to keeping herself busy. Although this is her first public literary presence, she is currently hard at work creating more enjoyable pieces. She lives in beautiful Washington State, with her husband and young daughter.

CHAPTER 1

There was an eerie calm about the small, dark room, but there should not have been. What had just happened would not warrant peacefulness in most situations.

The old wooden chair creaked as Drake slowly stood from it and walked to the nearby window. He peered out at the darkness, unsure of where was more comfortable to be, out there, where they had just struggled so hard to get to, or where he was, where it all had happened. After several long minutes of unfamiliar silence, the almost inaudible creak of the chair relieved some of the suffocating confusion for the three of them. It was almost impossible to know what to say, where to start. As much as they had been through together, not one of them had ever experienced something quite this life-changing in their seventeen short years. And never before had there been remotely this much unease between them, ever. Fortunately, the small, innocent sound somehow gave them permission to speak.

With his head bent down, looking into his hands that lay in his lap, Joe's voice cracked as he said, soft and low, "I don't want to be here anymore." As simple and as weak as he was sure that sounded, he couldn't help expressing his initial feeling.

He was relieved when Cal finally found his voice as well and confirmed the same notion, "Me neither, this is just too much. But how…? What…?" Shaking his head, Cal couldn't find any words to answer, or even ask, what should have been simple questions. He was at a loss as to what to say or what to do next. This was, naturally, similar to his best friends as they usually shared the same thoughts. They were all very grateful it was over, but the fear of how close it had come to something disastrous was still very much in the forefront of their minds. The unknown might just haunt them forever.

Joe Hart, Drake Briggs, and Cal Parker had been friends since before grade school. They could barely remember a time when they hadn't known each other, and they had shared so much of their lives right beside one another. Their childhoods were not unlike most young boys, getting into trouble whenever they could, scaring their parents both with injuries and bringing home all kinds of wild creatures. With an unspoken protectiveness, the trio always, always had each other's backs. Other friends came and went, but these three always stuck together with a bond like no other.

Once, when they were eleven years old, after watching a commercial on television, Cal got the idea in his head to build a rocket for his skateboard. Drake's sandy-colored hair, usually a bit too long and unkempt, bounced around on his head while he nodded enthusiastically and expressed comments like, "This is going to be so cool!" and "What a great idea, Cal!" He hardly had a drop of patience until it was done. Being a bit shorter and stockier than other kids his age, he always felt he had something to prove. Freckle-cheeked Joe, with a hint of red in his short cut hair, was more hesitant. He was a realistic thinker and more cautious when it came to the reckless ideas the other two consistently came up with. This tendency had probably saved Drake and Cal's lives more than once. But all three were completely committed to making the best rocket skateboard ever.

Day and night, whenever their parents would "get off their cases" about doing their chores and when they weren't in school, they were in Cal's basement working on their project. Even with Drake's constant persistence that "it was done," the mechanical undertaking went through many revisions, tests, and failures before they achieved, what they all agreed, was the ultimate racecar of skateboards. There were a lot of cuts and scrapes, and thrilling fun more often than not, but it wasn't until Joe broke his arm doing a dangerous stunt that they finally gave up on the risky contraption idea and moved on to something else. This was mostly due to the fact that Drake and Cal were a bit protective of Joe, though they would never really admit it for fear of being made fun of. But this collaborative experience of success was theirs, no one else's, and always would be.

The small rural town was the kind where everyone knew everyone, so when a new family moved in, it was not a secret. Cal's dad, Richard, got a new job as town sheriff when Cal was five years old, and they just happened to move into Drake and Joe's neighborhood. Small town neighbors being what they are, Cal's family got to know everyone pretty quickly. It also didn't take the boys long to form a lifelong bond.

Carol pulled up in front of the new neighbor's house, ready to share her family's special dish of Creamy Hamburger Bean Casserole. She knew it would be a hit; she liked being known for her good cooking. She always hoped her fine-tuned culinary skills would overshadow being known for her unlucky-in-love past of bad men. Despite her small, slender frame, she could be an intimidating presence. The usually grown-out blonde highlights in her hair had become more of a habit than a fashion statement, so she had forgotten what kind of image it could portray.

As she was trying to encourage a whining Drake, her oldest son at six years old, to get out of their little two door Honda Civic and help her carry her precious hot dish to the house, she faintly heard Joe's mom Gail call a hello to the pair of them. They found Gail walking up the sidewalk from the direction of her house, pushing Joe's little brother Sammy in a stroller with his older brother Ryan ambling along behind her holding Joe's hand. It looked like she herself had a few goodies to share to give a good first impression as well. Taller than Carol by four inches, heavier by a few more pounds, and older by a few years, Gail did not allow rudeness or disrespect from her children.

Like a dramatic thunderstorm turning instantly to sunshine, Drake's face lit up when he spotted his buddy behind his mom and the stroller. Waving his whole right arm in giant arcs above his head in fear somehow Joe wouldn't see him, he called, "Hiya, Joey!" and started toward him almost at a run. He couldn't wait to tell his friend what treasures he had found the other day in the woods and stream, especially the ones he'd slipped past his mom when she'd said, "*No, those don't belong in the house*"; those were clearly the most valuable.

The two moms stopped for a minute on the sidewalk to catch up.

Facing away from the house, head bent slightly down, Carol asked, "Have you heard anything about them yet? I know it's just been a few days."

"Apparently, they're from Connecticut and just have one young son our boys' age. I'm curious to find out more of their story," responded Gail in a quieter voice, as if they could hear them through the walls of the house. She didn't want to be pegged for a gossip first thing.

"Did you bring your famous casserole? When are you going

to share that recipe with me anyway?" Gail asked with a smirk.

"Yes, indeed. When you share some of your secret recipes with me," answered Carol with a quite similar grin and teasing look in her eye. All the while, Drake and Joe were trying to conjure up a way they wouldn't have to join the adults in the house in a looming few minutes. They were just sure it was going to be the most boring thing they had ever gone through. The women's curiosity was overwhelming them, so with their passports to the new family's story and their children, they started toward the house to meet the latest transplants.

Just when the boys figured their efforts were futile and were ready to surrender, a dark-haired boy who looked to be about their age came running in a zigzag pattern from behind the two-story house with a toy airplane in hand above his head and making flying noises. He was barefoot running through the grass, wearing clean, nicely pressed shorts and a white polo shirt. Once he spotted the gathering people, he stopped, and a questioning, rather shy look came to his face. He spotted Drake and Joe and stood there eying the two other boys who were staring back at him. He fidgeted with the airplane in his hands, now no longer flying through the air. Right away, he had a feeling he'd never had before, like everything was going to be fine here. It was such an unknown feeling, that it frightened him, and he slowly turned around and jogged back behind the house with his now silent toy airplane upside-down at his side. He didn't look back.

Joe and Drake shifted their attention from the new boy to each other with wide eyes. This sure piqued their curiosity; never had a boy their age moved to town before. The boy seemed normal enough, but apparently, he was shy. Completely forgetting any prior excuse to get out of going in the house, they beat their moms to the front door.

5

Once inside, they immediately started glancing around for the peculiar boy, as if drawn to him. After not spotting him right away, and not being the least bit shy, Drake asked where "the other boy" was to the first adult he saw in the entryway of the house. The woman looked like she had come right out of a 1950s Home Living magazine: beauty-salon brunette hair and painted red nails, an old-fashioned-looking dress with an apron, wearing pumps with an inch heel, she stood at 5'9", with a slender-average physique. With an almost robotic smile, she introduced herself as Diane, welcomed her guests exuberantly, and motioned to take their jackets from them. Then she thanked them for coming and bringing food that "smells so good." Acknowledging Drake's question, she replied, "Oh, Cal, yes, he is… somewhere around here," looking a bit perplexed that he wouldn't be right behind her. "Why don't you check the backyard? Just through the kitchen there," she said as she pointed behind herself to the right. Not much could have stopped Joe and Drake from getting to that backyard to continue their investigative mission.

A change had appeared in the new boy, probably because there were just two boys in front of him now instead of what seemed like a crowd of people including adults he didn't know.

Not seeming shy at all now, Cal smiled and asked, "Want to see my new airplane?" He looked very proud of the toy and excited to show it off. "My dad got it for me because I was scared to move here," he added, as if the new information would increase the toy's value and intrigue. Being five years old and having an older brother, Joe was very interested and asked a lot of questions, but Drake acted like it was not out of the ordinary to have a toy airplane, even though he had never seen one in person. He was much harder to please, and Cal picked up on that right away.

The first day of second grade was as exciting as it was scary. The three young boys had a few years' experience under their belts now to get the hang of this school thing, but there were still elements of the unknown. As they just passed the halfway point of the mile walk to their school, a group of boys a few years older emerged from a cluster of trees across the street. The three buddies knew right away that this might turn hairy if they weren't careful; there was not an adult in sight.

"Where are you little girls scurrying off to?" yelled one of the bigger kids, even though they all seemed bigger than the next, and before the three boys knew it, they were surrounded.

"What's your name?" the same boy relentlessly continued, directing his question at Cal.

Drake went to answer, but Cal beat him to it, wanting to speak for himself or it would be an undesirable start of a weak reputation, "I'm Cal." He intended to say more, but his voice elected on its own to stop there once the bullies got closer.

Now Drake stepped in. "What's it to ya?"

"Just trying to be friendly," said the same boy, with a sinister emphasis on "friendly." Drake motioned to Joe and Cal to follow him and tried to break through the barrier of boys, but he should've known getting away unscathed wouldn't be that easy.

"Oh, we'll let you go, but first we want to see what your mommies packed us for lunch," said another boy while grabbing at Joe's backpack.

Cal tried to shove him right before another boy decided to shove Cal in return. Cal went down solo, and while Drake was fending off a few others, Joe's backpack got rummaged through, leaving everything on the ground but his lunch, which they seized for themselves, and they took off toward the school, laughing and high-fiving each other. The trio was all thinking the same thing: luckily the bullies had settled for just one of their lunches; they could still share two lunches between the three of them easy enough, but they were worried about the days to come. As they put themselves back together and continued to school, they discussed their plan.

Drake was angry. "There is no way we're going to let them keep doing this to us."

"Maybe we could find a different route to school," suggested Cal.

Looking down the road towards the school, Joe noted, "This is the shortest, easiest way, though."

"How 'bout we head out earlier?" Cal tried again.

Drake decided, "We shouldn't be scared of them, there has to be another way they won't bother us." They couldn't tell their parents or teachers; the protection of adults would only make their situation worse.

"I know!" exclaimed Joe. "We need a pretend lunch that they won't like. If they only got food that was yucky or made them sick, they would stop taking it!"

It only took one time, and they stopped seeing the bullies for good. This concept worked throughout their primary education. Not very often did they have to worry about standing up for themselves for long; bullies just stopped being interested and found other kids to torment. Between the three of them, they quickly became very skilled at finding solutions to any problem they encountered—every time.

CHAPTER 2

The rugged, shadowy man slowly glanced back at the inferno, not out of fear as most people would, but with satisfaction. Well, mostly satisfaction, for as hard as he tried, there had never been an event that fully quenched his desires. Nothing was ever quite enough for him.

His first event, as lame as it was looking back now, was probably the most exciting due to it being a brand-new experience with sensations he had never previously felt, only dreamed about. Most people would call those nightmares… but not John Hackett; he loved sleeping. His imagination was very generous in allowing him to act with endless possibilities in his slumber, unlike the too-real world where he was constricted by laws of both science and society. Even as a child, back when people still called him Johnny, he never feared a nightmare, and he never had to be told to take a nap or go to bed like most children. It was his pleasure.

It was raining when Johnny awoke on the morning of his first event. He heard the irritating sound of rain and a distant roll of thunder before he even opened his eyes. Being eight years old, he wasn't normally upset by the sound of rain, but today, the pelting wetness not only stole him of more peaceful oblivion but also threatened his long, carefully thought-out plan. As exciting as it was in the beginning, he was done playing with Sodium and water, he needed something on a much grander scale. He liked a challenge, but he had planned today very prudently, overlooking not a single minor detail to avoid making a mistake. He didn't make mistakes. It wasn't supposed to rain today; he'd made sure to check that, and more than once.

He gingerly opened his eyes and looked up at his bedroom ceiling, muttering to himself, *"It better stop,"* as if making an entitled demand to Mother Nature. Though his stomach now growled, alerting him to the smell of bacon frying, he lay there a few minutes longer; the ill-fitting weather stifled his motivation. Besides the clouds parting, bacon might be the only thing that would change his profound grouchy mood, so he eventually arose from his bed, glanced around the room to ensure everything was in its proper place, opened the door of his bedroom, and ventured down the hall to the kitchen in his pajamas.

Since it was Saturday, upon reaching the kitchen, Johnny found his dad, John Sr., at the kitchen table reading the morning newspaper. Without looking up from reading, his father barely acknowledged Johnny with a quiet, "Good morning." Johnny observed that his dad looked very tired and a little under the weather, actually. As usual, Johnny found himself not finding a single part of him that felt bad or worried; the concern was just not there. He never asked his father how he was doing, nor was he asked by his dad about his own well-being. After his mom died, they simply co-existed, which was fine with Johnny; he preferred being left alone, and he didn't need watching over.

"Now that you're up, you need to finish breakfast," said Sr. to his son.

Johnny's mom was just starting to teach him how to cook when she died, but since her passing, if he wanted anything decent to eat, he learned pretty quickly to provide for himself where his dad lacked. After only a year, he felt very comfortable for an eight-year-old in the kitchen. The bacon was all that his dad had started, so he got eggs out of the refrigerator and some bread for toast from the pantry and started making another meal for the two of them that wasn't the first and wouldn't be the last. His dad was lucky; if it hadn't been raining, he wouldn't have had time to make all this food for him, he had so much to do. Breaking an egg in the skillet, he wondered, could he postpone everything until tomorrow? Of course, he knew he could, but he didn't want to; he didn't have all the time in the world either.

Now that he was more awake, while scrambling the eggs, he went over all the details again in his head, concluding with an image of pure heaven... to him anyway. This instantly put a smile on his face, which he made sure his dad could not see, and reignited his enthusiasm once again, almost making him disappointed in himself for being gloomy about the unfortunate weather at all.

The toast popped out of the toaster just as the eggs and bacon were done, so he served everything, sat down at the table, and ate the warm, energy-inducing meal in record time. No word was spoken between the father and son throughout the meal, which was customary. Unfortunately, the clean-up was now his captor, but after ensuring no evidence of breakfast was to be found in the kitchen, he practically ran back to his bedroom to get ready for a momentous day that was sure to go down in history. He could only hope.

By the time Johnny had gotten dressed, double-checked the contents of his backpack, which he had put together the night before, and stepped outside of the house, the rain had slowed to barely a drizzle, and he was sure he could see slivers of the sun trying to peek through the parting clouds. Things were looking up. With newfound enthusiasm, he swung his backpack around his back, put his arms in the shoulder straps, and fastened it around him. He could feel the contents of his backpack jostle around as he hopped on his bicycle: a couple of books of matches, a lock pick set, some string, his camera, a bag of sunflower seeds, a small knife, a flashlight, some gloves, and his bike lock.

First stop – his school's chemistry lab. He didn't need much, but a worthwhile event couldn't happen without the right accelerant. After his mom died, Johnny spent every spare moment he could extensively researching flammables and explosives, among other things, at the town library. The information he could find there was endless, and the more he learned about fire, the more he was addicted to it. How just the right combination of heat and energy could cause such a reaction was stimulating to him; he learned about endothermic and exothermic reactions – the absorbing and releasing of heat. Discovering how to predict an outcome from various equations for ultimate success became his life. He absolutely loved how something so simple and beautiful could be so complex, dangerous, and destructive. Fire had so many qualities and uses but could be so easily misused and almost impossibly hard to control at times.

When he arrived at the school, Johnny made his way around to the back of the old brick three-story building and found the basement window he had previously, barely noticeably, propped open with a tiny stone. Easy entry, just like he planned it, and just how he liked it. Nobody was in sight, so he put on a pair of gloves and slowly lowered himself down through the window to the floor of the basement. It was dark in the cool room, so he fumbled around in his backpack for his flashlight to guide his way through the shadowy halls of the school. Even though the high-school area of the school was in a different part of the building than the elementary, he knew where the chemistry lab was, and he could have made it there blindfolded if he had to.

The door to the lab was locked; he was expecting that. As he pulled his lock pick out of his backpack, he found himself smiling. He was excited to be using it for something real for once. He had practiced so many times at home that he got the knob unlocked in seconds. It was odd being in the school outside normal school hours, so he found himself a little apprehensive opening the door at first. He was used to people being in the classrooms, so he had to remind himself he was alone, even with the unnerving silence surrounding him like the building knew he was up to no good.

Johnny immediately noticed two cabinets on the far wall of the chemistry lab that had variously sized bottles and jars with ominous-looking labels on them. Jackpot. The lock on one of the cabinets was even easier to pick than the doorknob. He opened the doors, and the chemicals were standing before him like a well-behaved army. So many fun options, but for now, he just grabbed a bottle of Butyl Acetate, put it in his pack, and headed out. He was careful to put everything back the way he found it and made sure nobody was outside the building before he emerged from the basement window and continued to the second stop on his itinerary.

The second-hand store on Lotter Street had a drop-off area on the side of their building. The nice people of town donated a lot of things to the store, and Johnny guessed the employees didn't make enough money to be very productive because there was always a pile of used goods outside waiting their turn to be sold – just what he needed. It should be a quick trip, as he just required a couple of plastic bags of old clothes. As he approached the building, he saw he was in luck; there was plenty of loot to help himself to. After taking only a few seconds to glance around the pile, he noticed two grocery sacks with cloth material inside, so he hastily snared them and proceeded to the rear of the building for his next preparatory step.

Once he was safely behind the building, and he'd checked to make sure no one was around and ensured there were no security cameras, he put his gloves back on, got the Butyl Acetate out of his backpack, and poured it into both sacks of clothes to fully saturate them, careful not to spill a drop on himself. Good thing the last stop on his carefully planned out itinerary wasn't too far away, as the bags got pretty heavy with all the liquid. He tied them securely to his bike and rode off feeling very excited all of the sudden. He had been so focused and concerned about the little things that he had forgotten about the end result. It just occurred to him that all his prep work was done, that everything had gone as planned, and that this was actually going to work. Even a little sprinkle from the skies at this point could not wipe the smile off his face as he peddled toward his destination.

A big metal garbage dumpster sat next to the 7-11 on Haney Street that was peculiarly interesting to Johnny. When he would get hankerings for snacks and such, that was his convenience store of choice, and he would often notice quite an awful smell coming from the direction of that dumpster. Also, there was usually extra trash littering the ground outside the bin, and the laziness of people irritated Johnny. As he peddled closer and closer to the target, he got more and more upset and excited at the same time. When he got there, the setup was just as he'd anticipated: the lid was closed and the building overhang had prevented much rain from interfering with his special objective.

It was imperative that Johnny be as careful as possible now. He did not want to draw any attention to himself; he *would not* be remembered. He rode past the dumpster to the back of the store and untied the bags from his bike. There were only woods behind the store; this was partly why he'd chosen this location, as he knew the higher privacy level lowered the chance of anyone seeing him, resulting in insinuating questions. He hated questions. Looking around carefully, as nonchalantly as he could, so as to not draw the slightest suspicion, Johnny walked by the dumpster, throwing one soaked bag inside and the other underneath. He was just throwing away garbage, nothing to see folks. Then he went to park his bike next door at the little strip mall. Taking his bike lock out of his backpack, he securely fastened his bike to the rack. He was probably going to be gone for a bit, enjoying the show. Before putting his backpack back on, he withdrew a book of matches from within.

Making his way back behind the convenience store again, Johnny just waited there, leaning up against the building for a good ten minutes to make it easier for anyone who might have noticed him forget that he was there. He didn't want to risk lingering any longer than that, though, in case an employee decided to take a break. Plus, he was anxious to finally get his reward for all his hard work and patience.

While he waited, he fidgeted with the matchbook in his hands; he couldn't help thinking how innocent it looked contrasting the possibilities of mass destruction one little match could generate. Just the right balance and amount of the right combination of ingredients and *poof*!

It was time, finally. He checked if the coast was clear, lit one match, cupped his hand around the tiny flame to prevent it from extinguishing, and walked around the corner of the building to the dumpster. Just before getting there, he held the one lit match to the whole matchbook until it caught on fire well enough for his satisfaction, opened the lid of the dumpster, and dropped the flaming matchbook over where he had released the flammable, liquid-soaked bag of clothes. He resisted the urge to look in the garbage container to ensure the two had united.

Nothing happened. He got all the way around the front of the convenience store, and still, nothing happened. He thought for a second that he hadn't done something right because nothing happened for what seemed like an hour. If he had known he would have had more time, he would've walked away slower so as to not draw attention. Just as he started to get utterly disappointed, the biggest boom he had ever heard went off around the corner. It worked. Better than he imagined. All that planning and preparing had more than paid off. People started coming out of surrounding buildings looking wide-eyed and lost, so he played the part as well by putting his hand to his agape mouth and looking as surprised as possible. Plus, it concealed his smile. Small pieces of burned garbage fell from the sky, along with some ashes. The smoke was a thing of beauty, only second to the flames. Magnificent flames were spilling out of everywhere they could from the burning dumpster. Johnny deposited a handful of sunflower seeds in his mouth, and without seeming too obvious and enthusiastic, he pulled his camera out of his backpack and started discreetly shooting pictures of the gloriousness of his first event.

CHAPTER 3

It was a perfect summer day, and Joe was en route to Drake's house to see if he could hang out. He was so bored that he begged and begged his mom Gail until she relented. It had only been a few days since the last day of their sixth-grade year of school together, and he was not used to all this time on his hands alone. Drake always knew how to make things exciting, so Joe sure hoped he was home and bored as well.

As he approached the small, two-story craftsman style house, memories of the many hours playing in the yard together invaded his mind. He remembered how, once, when they were running around outside the house, as boys do, he'd tripped on the sidewalk and cut his knee. Drake's grandma Helen had gotten him all cleaned up and had put a Spiderman Band-Aid on the wound, after which they'd gotten ice cream to help ease the pain. The injury had sure been worth all that love and attention. Joe walked up the sidewalk to the front door, as he'd done countless times before; Helen opened the door a few moments after he knocked.

She smiled upon seeing him, and in her naturally soft grandma voice, said, "Come in, son. Drake is in his room. Go on up if you'd like." They were used to seeing each other since Drake's mom worked a lot and needed help watching the kids; his little brother Huck was a year and a half younger than Drake, and his sister Alexis was three years younger. Joe thought Helen was just what a grandma should be, mostly because she baked the best cookies he'd ever had, and that was saying a lot because his own mom was a good cook.

"Thank you, ma'am," responded Joe, smiling back, and he headed upstairs.

Upon arriving at Drake's room, Joe knocked and let himself in. "Hey Drake, I'm bored, what are you doing?"

"I'm so glad you're here," whispered Drake. "I'm trying to trap this fly, but I can't get it." Joe witnessed what he assumed wasn't the first miss of an effort to snag a fly with a plastic cup. Drake held the cup out to Joe, who grabbed it, located the culprit after looking a bit like Stevie Wonder swaying his head around for a minute, and started to sneak up on the little winged insect. A swipe and a miss. Then another swipe, another miss, not even close.

Looking defeated, Drake slouched back on his bed. "Let's go get Cal and dig up worms by the creek," he suggested.

Joe smiled. "Just what I was thinking!" he replied. "And maybe catch some frogs too!" Drake grabbed his backpack and some essentials, deciding to throw the cup that was not a good fly catcher in his pack too, and they headed downstairs to ask his grandma if he could go out. She approved, made sure she knew where they would be, and told Drake not to stay out too long. After they both got a couple of good grandma hugs and some snacks, they were out in the sunshine on their way to Cal's house. They rode along in silence; they were both excited thinking about what kind of creatures they were going to come across today and how dirty they might get in the process of capturing them.

The creek, filled with so many intriguing unknowns for young boys, was usually not more than twenty feet across and a few feet deep as it wound through the trees, rocks, and shrubbery. A bit hidden in the woods on the outskirts of town, they didn't have to worry about cars or many other people. It was like a whole other world to them, where they were free to do as they pleased and be their own little cub scouts, learning what they could and showing each other new skills. Every time they went to the creek and woods, they found or experienced something new. Sometimes, they would go to the library afterwards and research what they found – plants, animals, insects, rocks, fish – the area was completely fascinating to them, and it was somewhat of a challenge and game to be the one to find something rare.

Cal was riding his bike in front of his house when they approached. The bored duo was happy he was home and not doing anything either, and both assumed he'd for sure be able to go with them. They noticed a small ramp built out of boards that Cal must've been doing stunts on. For a minute, they almost changed their minds to stunt ride too, but when they made it to their friend, he looked as bored as they had been just a bit ago, and they hadn't been to the creek in a long time, so it was back to their original plan. When they mentioned their idea to Cal, he was off his bike in a second, running into the house to seek parental clearance to end his dull afternoon.

Back outside a few minutes later, Cal exclaimed, "I'm good to go, guys! I'm going to wear my new mud boots," he informed them, looking down at his feet. At first, Drake and Joe both felt a little twinge of jealousy, but then realized actually getting dirty and wet was more fun anyway. Or so they told themselves. "I also made this fishin' pole out of stuff my dad said I could have. If we find any worms, I might catch a fish!" It was just a four-foot-long dowel stick and some string with a bobby pin, but to the boys, it was something you would pay a lot for in a fancy sporting-goods store.

They left Cal's house and set out for the edge of town, laughing and chatting about nonsense things. This was the life, not a care in the world and so many things to discover. As usual, there were no people in sight when they reached the woods, and they all hoped it would stay that way while they explored. They dumped their bikes when the trees got too thick and the ground was too soft. Once they neared the water, Drake retrieved a little shovel he had brought, and Joe and Cal grabbed some digging sticks to find worms. It wasn't hard to find some since they had done this before, and they decided to use the not-so-good-for-catching-flies cup Drake had brought along to store them in.

Once the boys reckoned they had enough bait, they wandered on further down the creek to a deeper spot better for fishing. Cal baited his "hook," threw his line in, and waited, basking in the sun. The other two decided to do some more digging and see what else they could find besides worms. None of them realized they wouldn't really know what to do if a fish was actually caught.

After about ten minutes of scavenging, Joe exclaimed, "Look at this, it's huge!" He had found a centipede and was in awe of all its legs and how the crusty bug scurried along. He picked it up and brought it over to the rock Cal was sitting on so they could all have a closer look. It was hard to contain, but the three of them had no intention of letting it out of their sight.

Drake was intrigued. "Are they always that big?" he asked. "I wonder if fish like those things."

"Great idea, let's do it!" said Cal, figuring all that wiggling might catch a fish's attention better, so he pulled his line in and traded up.

"If you catch one, it's mine because I thought of it, Cal," said Drake with a smile on his face. "Course I'll share with you guys."

Joe, being the more logical of the three, asked, "How are we

20

going to cook it? We could build a fire while we wait so then we'll be ready." He and Drake started gathering some wood and putting the pieces in a pile on the sandy, muddy ground. Drake got out his lighter and tried to start a stick on fire. After that didn't work, he got some grass and tried that instead. Starting to feel like he did when he couldn't catch the fly, he sat back and pondered; he had never tried to start a fire before, none of them had, and he hadn't realized how hard it could be. Joe quickly concluded that, in order for anything to burn, it needed to be dry, and as they were right near the water and everything was kind of damp, the plan was not going to be successful.

"There isn't much dry stuff around here to make this work very well," Joe explained, disappointed. "Maybe we should do something else."

Drake was just as discouraged, so it didn't take much to convince him there were other fun things to do out there today. He proposed they head down the creek some more. Cal pulled in his line. The centipede looked almost exactly like it had when they'd caught it, except for being drenched and motionless; nothing had taken a bite out of it. And they commenced exploring further down the creek.

Maybe it was because they had been cooped up in a classroom for months, or maybe it was the particularly interesting conversation that day stealing their attention, or it could have been from the disappointment of failure at fire-building, but they ended up down the creek well beyond where they had ever previously gone before realizing how far they'd walked.

Joe was alerted that he had to relieve himself, so he headed in towards the woods for a bit of privacy. Not long after he was gone, Cal and Drake heard Joe call out, "You guys, come here, this is so cool!" They started in the direction of Joe's voice and noticed the old building before relocating Joe.

It was a rough abandoned dwelling, overgrown by the woods, but it looked so inviting to the boys. Their curiosity led them to peer in the windows to ensure the room was vacant of both people and animals.

"This would make an awesome fort!" said Cal enthusiastically. "We could have so much fun here." He continued to investigate the dwelling.

Joe went up the three front steps to the door, opened it easily, and examined the contents; he wanted to make sure it was safe before letting his friends in. If he saw any number of things, including broken glass, worn-through flooring, or the possibility of the ceiling caving in, he would deter his friends from entering. Or at least try to so they wouldn't get hurt. Luckily, the establishment seemed to be in decent enough shape to not worry about their safety being in jeopardy.

Once they were all inside, they found the place to be more than acceptable for a hideout for boys and were so happy no one had beaten them to it. All but one of the windows were intact, the floor didn't have any holes or weak spots, and three old wooden chairs sat underneath a rickety old table with another chair in the far corner. Everything was dusty and dirty, but that didn't matter one bit to the boys. They kind of preferred it that way.

It was just one big room with a support pole in the middle of it, a back door straight across the room from the front door, and a window on each side wall, with two on the front door wall. The v-shaped ceiling was open, no attic, but with rafters across it, much like a barn; they imagined they could tie things up and/or store things up there. A rectangular rustic wooden counter occupied the right side wall near the back of the abode with two square cabinet doors underneath. It looked like it might have been used for preparing food, and they reckoned the crude rock fireplace on the opposite wall was used for cooking and heating. There was a little dirty ash in the bottom of it, but it was clear it hadn't been used in a long while.

"I wonder if we could get some old sheets to put up on the windows so we could camp out here at night," Joe said. He was a little more concerned with giving it a homey feel than the other boys, but they agreed with the logical idea.

"We would need a light. More than just flashlights would be nice," Cal proposed. He wondered if his dad had an old lantern he could borrow or if his parents would ask too many questions and squash this whole new adventure for them with one word. "Maybe we could put our allowances together and go to the second-hand store and get an old lantern."

Drake was just thinking that same thing, but about other essentials too. "That's a great idea, Cal. I can go there tomorrow and scout it out. They probably have other things that would be handy out here too, or the dollar store, and then we can see how much money we need. We might have to do some extra chores, but it would be so worth it."

Splitting up, the boys continued to inspect the place. Cal found some dead bugs underneath the counter, along with some very dirty old rags that were stiff to the touch and a tin bucket big enough to hold about three gallons. Drake inspected the old wooden table and chairs to see if they needed any fixing but found they would suffice; it wasn't like they would be entertaining guests. Some of the rocks on the fireplace hearth had crumbled away, but similar to the table and chairs, it would more than serve their needs. Joe inspected it closer, and remembering their failed attempt at building a fire earlier, he suggested they go gather some wood and bring it inside to start drying. Cal grabbed the bucket from underneath the counter for kindling, and they headed back out of their new awesome retreat.

The supply of wood outside was not lacking, and they didn't need any kind of axe or hatchet yet, as there was plenty of down and dead wood on the ground. In their search, they also noticed a lot of big logs they could eventually chop up if they got an axe. They made quite a few trips back and forth without having to go very far before they had a nice pile accumulated in the corner between the back door and fireplace. A bit tired, they all sat down on the old chairs that had been lonely too long and admired their hard work. Somehow, the simplicity of the overflowing bucket of kindling Cal set beside the fireplace made the house feel like a home.

When the boys weren't making money doing whatever jobs they could for their parents or neighbors, they made many trips to their sanctuary through the summer, and the boys had created surprisingly cozy vacation quarters. When they were more than content with their efforts, and once they had acquired sufficient provisions, they all felt secure enough to make a camping trip out of it and stay overnight in their fixed-up house. They had sure spent enough time there together to feel safe.

Some of the items they wanted or needed at their new place one or more of them had gotten as birthday or Christmas gifts, but for other necessities, they had worked hard to buy them. From mowing lawns to washing cars, scrubbing bathrooms to walking dogs, they had accumulated enough money to buy an assortment of items: utility knives, some rope, a lantern, some matches, a few candles, a pan for cooking fish, dining supplies, dish soap and a scrubber to wash their pan and dining supplies in the creek, paper towels, toilet paper, buckets for bait and caught fish, and fishing poles. Everything was as cheap as they could find but more than adequate and much better than just tent camping, anyway. Cal's mom had some old sheets in a box in the garage, which they hung over the windows with thumbtacks for curtains. The boys always made sure to have snacks and drinking water along because sometimes they were out there for most of the day before they would realize how long it had been. Joe's parents had gotten a little too curious a few times; maybe he just wasn't as good at lying or distracting his parents as the other two were.

The day had finally come. Each boy had told their parents they were staying at another boy's house for the night, but they were planning to meet on the edge of town just before the woods at 6 pm. They could hardly walk from the heaviness of so much packed into each of their backpacks, with more than the usual amount of food and drink and extra clothes. Each of them had remembered to bring their sleeping bag. There was no way they would forget that; that was what made it exciting more than any of the other things. Joe and Drake met up with each other before getting to the meeting point, and they noticed Cal was waiting for them when they approached.

"Hey guys. This is gonna be epic! I can't wait to get there," Cal said with a huge smile on his face when he spotted his friends. He was pretty excited to get out from under his dad's strict thumb for a night and be a real man fending for himself for once like he knew he could.

The other two boys were just as thrilled, "Yeah! We are going to have an awesome time out there for sure!" yelled Drake.

When they reached Cal, Joe asked, "So do we have everything we need? We've been gathering our supplies for quite a while. I think we're good, but can you guys think of anything we might have forgotten before we leave town?"

Both Cal and Drake shook their heads. "I think we're quite prepared," answered Drake excitedly, and he motioned to start heading into the woods. He wasn't known for his patience.

"I agree," said Cal, and he followed his impatient friend, with Joe sidling up next to him in a couple of steps. The sooner they got there, the sooner the fun would start. Walking along the creek to their lodging for the evening, the conversation was light-hearted, and nothing could bring them down now. Even if the weather turned foul, it didn't matter.

"You guys' parents were good with this? They bought it?" asked Drake.

"Heck yeah. They didn't question me at all," responded Cal. "And when they brought up the idea of calling your mom, I just said that she was working and your grandma doesn't hear so well on the phone. I said it would probably just be a bother and reminded them they can call me any time I'm there anyway. Dad was watching the news, and mom was turning down a pot that was boiling over, so they weren't paying much attention anyway. It helps we've stayed with each other so many times already. I think they like the alone time when I'm not there too."

Joe agreed, "Same here, my parents have known your mom and grandma for so long they don't even question anything anymore. It's not like we get into trouble all the time anyway. One less kid to worry about too, in my house."

"I waited until Grandma was making a pie, and I calmly mentioned to her that Cal and I were thinking of staying at Joe's house, and she just said, 'That is a good idea. Those are such nice boys,' and that was it!" Drake laughed at the end of his explanation. "I wonder if it will always be this easy to come out here. I sure hope so."

Cal agreed, "The older we get, the less they will want to keep track of us anyway." That was a good feeling for all three of the boys, growing up and becoming men responsible for their own lives.

The boys arrived at their fort quicker than they ever had before because they were so anxious to start their overnight adventure. They had fun unpacking and settling in, and each of them picked a spot on the floor for their own sleeping area. Drake started to get a fire going so it would be ready when they caught some fish for dinner; they were sure hungry after their trek to get there with their heavy packs on. "Do you guys want to get some bait while I get this fire going? Then we can get to fishing and eat soon. I'm starving."

Joe and Cal headed for the door. "Sounds great," they pretty much said in unison and laughed at the coincidence.

"I'll get the bait bucket if you want to grab the fish one," Cal told Joe, and they headed outside, eager to put the fire that Drake was building to good use. It wasn't long before they had plenty of bait and their lines in the water, anticipating a bite at any moment. Drake joined them shortly after with some Gatorade and potato chips for each of them, and the three friends sat relaxing and immensely enjoying the start of their camping trip. It was ideal weather, seventy degrees and not a cloud in the sky, though a little rain wouldn't dampen their spirits since they had awesome shelter to sleep in instead of just a tent.

"Summer is the best, huh? ... What did you guys think of Mrs. Tomlin last year? I don't think she liked me, she graded my homework so hard," said Cal. "I didn't feel like I could do anything right. I passed my tests ok, but she didn't seem very fair in grading. I hope we get a good teacher next year."

Drake thought about it for a second. He didn't usually think much about his grades, and once a school year was over, he didn't look back. "She was ok, I guess, I didn't notice any difference in her grading compared to Mr. Ginner last year. I finished with the same grades. How did yours compare?" he asked Joe.

"I think she was tough," Joe replied. "I was surprised in the beginning of the year, but when I realized how strict she was, I just tried harder. Plus, since my dad's a teacher too, he'd kill me if I failed anything. But if I need help, he's good to ask questions to anyway."

"I hope we get a good teacher next year too, but I'm just glad we're not there right now. I don't want to talk about school anymore, though, it's summer!" stated Drake, doing a little celebratory dance.

"Oh my gosh, remember when Bobby North had a cold and sneezed in the middle of his speech, and he sprayed snot and spit all over the people in the front row?!" recalled Cal, laughing. "That was so gross it was awesome. I'm just glad I wasn't sitting up there."

"Yeah! And then the snot was running down his face, and he tried to wipe it off, but it stuck so there was a snot string between his nose and arm!" Drake joined in mimicking what their classmate had done. "His face was so beet red, I would've been too, and the teacher made him keep going after he got a tissue and cleaned it up. I would've probably run out of the room and not come back with everyone laughing at me."

Joe was laughing too but not as hard, "I just wish people would've left him alone after that. It was bad enough, but people can be so mean. I don't ever want that to happen to me."

"We'd just kick their butts if they made fun of you anyway, Joe," said Drake.

Joe nodded, "I know, but it would still stink."

"Whoever made fun of any of us would stink because we'd

give 'em a swirly for sure," confirmed Cal. That made them all chuckle just thinking about it.

Just then, Joe's pole jerked. He grabbed it carefully and waited a second to feel a nibble... and sure enough, there was something interested in his bait, so he gave a quick jerk and started reeling in his line. "We got one!" yelled Joe. "It feels like a good size too." He had just got done saying that when Cal jumped up and started reeling his line in too. They had both caught a fish, and they were both around eight inches each, so the boys were close to having a good dinner now. With the snacks they'd brought and, hopefully, a few more fish, they'd be eating well tonight. The fun commotion was over, the fish were in the bucket, their lines were re-baited, and they sat waiting again, hopefully not too long as the snacks Drake had brought out were long gone and they were hungry again.

"That was fun. Drake, it's your turn, come on," Cal egged him on. "Didn't you wear your lucky underwear today?" he said with a smirk.

"Yes, they're always on, but I'll chance taking them off to put them on your head if you keep it up!" snickered Drake. Joe laughed too. He rolled back in his little camp chair a little too far and went toppling over backwards. "You're going to scare the fish away, Joe. Stop laughing at my stupid jokes," said Drake, carrying on as long as his friends were amused by him. He got up and tackled Joe just as he was about to get back up, sending him back to the ground again. They wrestled around, not minding one bit that they were getting dirty. Still chuckling a little and breathing hard, Drake sat back down, and Joe went into the cabin to grab some more snacks and drinks while they waited for the second round of fish to bite.

"I think I got a bug in my ear," said Joe as he returned, sharing food and drink with his friends. "I feel like something's crawling around in there." He went over to have Cal examine it, but no creepy crawly was discovered.

"It's just your imagination. Catch another fish for us so we can eat," ordered Cal playfully. They all sat and watched their lines in silence. Just before sundown, as they were hoping, Drake and Cal each caught another fish, so they cleaned the four of them up and went inside. Joe had gotten the pan out and ready while he was in there earlier, so it was ready to go into the fireplace. The fish sizzled and fried, and before long, the little place smelled like yummy cooked fish instead of slimy raw fish. They were proud of themselves for the meal they made and were all well satiated by the end of it.

"Let's play cards," suggested Joe after they had eaten. The sky had grown dark, and with their bellies full and all that fresh air, they weren't far from going to bed, so they weren't up for much more than that. He got a deck of cards out of his backpack, and they all pulled up to the table for a rousing game of Crazy Eights.

The next morning, Joe woke to see Drake was not in his sleeping bag. Before getting too worried, he realized he needed to relieve himself, so he went outside the back door, did his business, and went around the front to see Drake sitting on a rock down by the water, chewing on a piece of jerky. They greeted each other and enjoyed the peacefulness of the morning with the sun shining through the trees, the birds chirping, and the gurgling of the creek. Once Cal joined them, they consumed a breakfast, which consisted of granola bars and dry cereal, but it was more than just fine with all of them that it wasn't a hot cooked meal.

"Did you guys sleep good?" asked Joe. "I slept a lot better than I thought I would on the hard ground and hearing different sounds." He was pleased with the first night of hopefully many out there.

Cal agreed, "Yes, it was fun. I wasn't scared at all, course, I didn't hear anything too bad either. Being out here by myself would be different, but the three of us could handle just about anything, I think."

"Me too. I woke up a few times, but I didn't miss my bed at all," confirmed Drake. "It's already getting hot. Maybe we can go swimming later since we won't be here for dinner and have to worry about scaring the fish away." The other two boys approved of the excellent idea. They knew they could dry off before having to head back home, preventing any questions from their parents they didn't want to answer.

They spent the rest of the morning exploring up the creek even further. Now that they had a home base, it wasn't so far to wander as having to go all the way back into town. They found numerous different and very interesting critters and rocks and such to keep them occupied for a few hours. By the time they got back to the fort, they were hungry again and ate some apples and peanut butter and jelly sandwiches for lunch, with Grandma Helen's molasses cookies for dessert. Just like the other meals they had prepared for themselves, it all tasted amazing.

"Last one in is a loser!" yelled Cal suddenly, and he stood up from his chair at the table and raced out the front door toward the creek, but he tripped on his shorts as he was not very intelligently attempting to discard them while running, and did a somersault down the front steps. Drake and Joe quickly made sure he was uninjured before they ran past him laughing, also shedding their own clothing as they ran but with much better luck than Cal had had. So, for the rest of the day, they referred to him as "Loser" and didn't call him Cal even once.

There were some big rocks on the other side of the creek with a deep enough pool for cannonballs, so they had fun jumping in and splashing around. Cal tried to earn his good name back by doing the coolest stunts he could think of, but to no avail; his friends wouldn't let this one go too soon. He wondered what would last longer, the teasing or the bruise and scrape on his knee from the hitting the ground after his tumble. Either way, it was a memorable time for sure.

Once they were finally all tired out, they lay in the sun until they were dry, and even longer than they had to in order to eliminate any evidence of being wet, as they were not ready to go back to real life yet at all. Although it helped that they knew this was not a one-time thing, they couldn't wait to get back out there as soon as their parents would let them have another "sleep over." They packed up only what they needed to take back, leaving items that would be handy next time and not missed at home. Saying a temporary goodbye to their hideaway, the boys headed back to town.

CHAPTER 4

He smelled smoke. That would have been a strange sensation just in itself, but since he was awoken by the awful, bitter odor in the dark in the middle of the night, it was even harder to comprehend what was going on and what action to take. Feeling very disoriented, Johnny opened his eyes and blinked several times, striving to focus; he couldn't tell if it was just the darkness or if the smoke was filling up his room and clouding his vision. He rubbed his eyes in an attempt to make things more clear, but that only seemed to make his vision worse.

Sitting up in his bed, he squinted toward where his bedroom door should be and barely made out a very thin sliver of yellow light near the floor. He rolled off his bed and crawled toward the light, since it was the only thing that made any sense in that moment. Hearing faint commotion once he reached the door, he half expected the door to open and to see his mom or dad standing on the other side to rescue him, or at least assure him things were ok and somehow it was all a misunderstanding or possibly a bad dream. After a minute, he became aware that no one was in the hallway and that the sounds weren't of a human nature; they were more like odd rushing roars and some loud crackling. Confusion would not yet release him. Closing his eyes, because they burned a little now, he turned his head and placed his ear closer to the door to get a better listen. It felt hot against his cheek, and the situation became clear at that point that the house was on fire, Johnny panicked, grabbing the doorknob and pulling the door open with a quick jerk, expecting to stand up and run out. Instead, a very hot, suffocating whoosh knocked him off his feet and backwards into his room.

Now he heard indistinct yelling. Feeling a bit dazed from being thrown, it still seemed like a dream, but he slowly recognized that the voice was his dad's. However, he couldn't make out what was being said. Sitting up from the floor, Johnny felt his face. It was hot and grainy; his rear end throbbed with pain, reminding him of his hard fall, and his hand that he tried to open the door with stung quite awfully. Like a switch, fear became a peculiar curiosity. He needed to see what was happening to their house, so he crawled toward his now open bedroom door again and glanced left. The walls were ablaze near the ceiling, and his parents' bedroom door was closed, but the doors to the bathroom and his dad's office were open. To the right, toward the living room and kitchen, countless flames from the walls and ceiling were incessantly licking the air as if it was water and they were dreadfully thirsty.

Where were the sirens and firefighters, he wondered, feeling more clear-headed. There should be some kind of help coming. Instead of assistance, he barely heard his dad's voice again and realized the sound was coming from outside the house. Johnny crawled toward the living room where the front door was. Upon arriving, he noticed that the big front window had been blown out and glass was all over the floor. From low on the floor, he could see people had gathered in the street in front of their house.

Now that he was in sight of his dad, he could make out what he was saying. "They're still in there!" his dad's lips played out in slow motion while his face showed utter disbelief of what he was looking at. Johnny stopped. *Oh no, Mom is still in here too?* He had to get to her. That was why their bedroom door was still closed!

Scrambling on his hands and knees with hurried intent back to their closed bedroom door, even lower now for the smoke was filling the house more and more as the short minutes passed, Johnny put his ear to the door as before but heard nothing.

"Mom! Are you in there?" he cried as loud as he could.

It was nearly impossible for little Johnny to hear anything with the sound of the raging fire engulfing everything it could, so he reached out to grab the doorknob. His hand stopped just short of the knob, though, as he noticed his hand for the first time since being in his bedroom, and he discovered why it was hurting so badly. The skin on his hand was bright red and blistering a bit. He needed something to open his parent's bedroom door with; he wasn't going to make that mistake again. He struggled to think what protection he could use to shield his hand from additional damage, but the stress of the situation was halting his thought process.

An oven mitt would be ideal, he determined, and he hoped the fire hadn't destroyed the kitchen just yet. Keeping his body as low as he could, Johnny partly crawled, partly "army-manned" it back out toward the living room and kitchen area of the house. His short journey disclosed to him that the whole house was a war zone. However, the fire must've started in this end of the house as it was worse than near the bedrooms, and retrieving an oven mitt from a top drawer next to the stove was nearly an impossible and tremendously risky mission. The smoke was thicker, pieces of ceiling had fallen to the floor, and flames surrounded him on all sides.

The heat was exceedingly intense, with a seemingly constant determination to burn his flesh, but there was no way Johnny was leaving this house without his mother. He battled the kitchen obstacles and came out mostly unscathed; so with a flowery patterned oven mitt secured in his clenched jaw, he cautiously crawled back down the hall to his parents' closed bedroom door.

Without wanting to get blown away again, he protected his body behind the wall and reached up with as little of his arm as possible, and closing his eyes, he quickly turned the doorknob and opened the door, pulling his arm back in a split second. Another loud whoosh and a mass of heat came rushing out of the room, making him lurch back and instinctively throw his arms up to protect his head. After the intense blast was over, he ventured a peek around the doorjamb, fearing what he might see.

Their eyes locked. He located his mom huddled in the corner of the bedroom on the floor, her knees pulled up to her chest with a terrified, helpless look on her face. He cocked his head to the side with disbelief; she looked so weak and cowardly. She could have saved herself; she'd had had plenty of time and options – for one, they were in a one-story house, and the window was right above her head for goodness sake. Instead, he was risking his life for hers, which seemed greatly immaterial now.

Not really understanding why, but having it feel very oddly natural to him suddenly, Johnny smiled at her. It wasn't a friendly, comforting grin, as his mother would have expected. It was something his mother had never remotely seen in her son's face before. It was malice.

This broke her out of her trance like a slap to her face, and she unsurely called to him, "Johnny, come here. Help me!" her arm outstretched to him.

But his reason for being there had completely changed, and he found himself greatly anticipating what was inevitably going to happen to her. No longer did he feel the need to save her. He no longer *wanted* to save her; he preferred to watch what he felt she now deserved. He sat against the doorjamb and nibbled on his thumbnail like it was popcorn and he was watching a good movie.

Again, she tried coaxing him to her with her arm outstretched towards him. "I love you. Why are you not coming to your mom? You are my sweet boy. I love you. I need your help."

Looking lost and confused, she feebly pulled her arm back into her chest when she realized her son was not going to come to her aide, and a dazed look swept over her face. The fire alone, with its power and intense heat, was enough to overwhelm her, but the fact that her good son would not help her as well, put her into shock. It seemed to Johnny she actually stopped being aware of her life-threatening surroundings, and it was captivating to him to observe her odd demeanor in such a clear situation.

Just then, a big chunk of flaming ceiling gave way and landed with a loud thud a few feet from her. The flames easily and willingly jumped to her, and she started screaming and trying to smother her now burning robe with her hands. Johnny almost laughed out loud. He could not believe what he was seeing: she still had a fairly easy escape, enough to save her life anyway, but she chose to act like an idiot, thinking putting out her robe was her biggest threat. The screaming was louder now, and as the walls around her were ablaze as well, she had nowhere to go.

Johnny found himself diligently studying how the fire was consuming her body. He took note of how the fire moved from her clothes to her skin and how the thin outer layer of her body morphed into goo, and he especially paid attention to the moment she stopped screaming and then moving at all. It was fascinating to him how the process happened. When the entertainment was all over, he was saddened and felt the whole episode had expired way too fleetingly. He had been so engrossed in what had happened to his mom, he'd forgotten that he himself was actually still in great peril. With the enthusiasm of what he'd just witnessed burning through him, his crawl out of the house was like a cheetah, and he was far from the danger and out in the street with his dad and the others in no time.

Looking back at his house now consumed with flames and smoke, Johnny had to hold back from clapping and cheering. He was still on a high from the show he'd just beheld inside and the narrow escape, but the magnificent sight of all that destruction and power was almost more than he could handle. Tears of joy uncontrollably formed in his eyes and then streamed down his cheeks, and it worked perfectly to mask his true feelings of pure happiness.

CHAPTER 5

"Don't you dare come in the house with all that mud on you," Cal's mom threatened. "Your dad will have a fit. And make sure all your pockets are empty. I'm not washing any more frogs… or anything else… on accident."

Diane shuddered just thinking about such disgusting things going through her washing machine. Cal had just about walked in the back door before being pre-scolded by his mother; he was pretty dirty, and he did have some treasures in his pockets. She's just taking all the fun out of it, he thought, but it had been worth it.

Cal and his two buddies had been playing catch with the football at the park in the rain. The field was soaked and muddy, so it was all they could do to get as soiled as possible rolling around it, jumping for catches, and tackling each other to ensure they were covered head to toe. When that was over, they decided it still wasn't enough and got into a mud-throwing fight too, so when Cal got home, it wasn't hard for his mom to see she wanted no part of all that dirtying up the house. And it wasn't until his mom reminded him, that Cal thought of what his dad would say if he saw him. Instead of asking what kind of boyish fun they must've had and asking how he did playing football, he would probably get after him about something, or most likely, all of it. Cal should've thought of that before heading home all messy like that. He could just hear his dad, "How irresponsible of you to not consider cleaning yourself up. This house does not clean itself…" and on and on until he would feel like he couldn't do anything right. Again. Although he knew his dad was right; why couldn't he think of these things before being told? It seemed common sense once he was aware. But if only his dad could've seen the great catches and throws with the football he had done. He really was getting so much better, even though his dad had no idea of his progress because he'd never seen him in action.

"Yes, Mom. What should I do to clean up?" Cal inquired, not sure how to proceed so he'd be clean before getting into serious trouble.

Diane thought for a moment. "I guess you'll have to hose yourself off outside. I'll bring you some old towels for when you've gotten the muck all off of you. Don't forget your hair, it's caked in there. You boys must have had a pretty good time out there," she said with a wink and a smile. She understood how hard her husband was on their son sometimes, and she knew Cal understood for the most part too.

Cal uncoiled the hose from the side of the house and turned the handle on the spigot until he judged there was ample flow of water to eliminate dried mud. He then proceeded to spray himself all over until he could see more of the actual colors of his clothing and skin instead of blackish-brown. It took a while to get the now-dried mud completely out of his hair; it reminded him of the somersault he'd done over Drake to catch one of Joe's passes, landing him with his head in a big mud puddle. He was a little embarrassed at first, but once they were all laughing hard at how comical the incident was, his self-consciousness was forgotten; it helped that the color of his flushed face was hidden by the muck covering it. That, and it was an epic catch too.

"Wow, Cal, I can't believe you actually caught that," exclaimed Joe. "Nice one!"

"Seriously?" questioned Drake as he recovered from his own fall to the wet, dirty ground. "You caught that? It was supposed to be mine!" Drake proceeded to pick up some more mud and rub it in Cal's hair. "There. Your crown, your Majesty." And they all laughed even harder.

Cal suggested, "Maybe I should go out for the team," hinting for more praise.

"Well, I don't know. That was awesome, but those guys are big," said Drake. "But I guess it's not all about size. Playing catch out here is a lot different than actual practice and games, though."

"Yeah, you're probably right," slurred Cal disappointedly.

"Why not give it a shot," encouraged Joe. "It will give us something to do coming to your games. But we'll be bored without you during practices."

"Let's not get carried away. I probably wouldn't even make the team. You guys should try out too," urged Cal. Drake didn't say anything, and Joe just nodded his head. Cal never really considered himself very athletic, but he did have fun when they played sports together. With every catch or tumble or pass for the rest of the day, Cal got more and more excited to tell his dad his novel idea about being a football star. Now he'd show his dad; he would be a son his dad could be proud of.

"What are all these wet, dirty clothes doing on the laundry room floor?" was the first thing Cal's dad, Richard, said when he walked in the door of their home. He was a big man, just how a sheriff would look in the movies, gruff and tough. This time of day, his five o'clock shadow was in full force, making him look even meaner. Not only was he tall, but he exercised a lot to ensure he could do his job to his utmost capability.

His deep, strong voice seemed to shake the whole house as he said, "This is just a mess. Cal, what happened here?" Cal could hear some banging around downstairs. "I'm working hard all day, coming home tired as all get-out, and this is what I have to deal with? Boy!"

Oh no, thought Cal, trying to remember what he'd forgotten to do. His mom had told him to go take a shower, but he'd forgotten to make sure all his dirty, wet clothes were in the wash. He'd been getting cold, and he'd presumed his mom would take care of it. Slowly he emerged from his bedroom and gingerly started walking down the steps. Holding the banister like it was going to save him, he wondered what he going to say. He had to think of something, but he couldn't; it was clear what had happened, how he utterly lacked in judgment. He decided to just be honest. His father would respect the truth, and Cal believed that when he told him how good he'd done playing football today, his dad would forget the mess anyway!

Once he was in view of his dad, he said as clearly as he could muster, but with dreadful feelings mounting inside of him, "Sorry, Dad. I forgot to put them in the wash. Drake, Joe, and I were playing ball at the park, and you should've seen…" Cal started.

"What do you mean, 'forgot'?!" Richard abruptly cut off his son. "This is not acceptable. I don't care what you were doing, there is no reason for this mess," he sternly stated. "It was raining out anyway. You could catch cold out there," he added.

Cal quickly grabbed up the clothes and solemnly started the wash. He couldn't look his dad in the eyes for his own were quickly filling up with tears despite how hard he tried to prevent his emotions from showing through. Even if he wanted to, or had some reason or excuse to give to stick up for himself, the lump that had formed in his throat prevented him from saying a word. Why couldn't he just talk to his dad like a man, he wondered.

But the berating just kept coming, "Be sure to apologize to your mother for being so thoughtless and disrespectful of our home. You are more than old enough to clean up after yourself," Richard finally concluded.

What was worse was Cal knew his dad was right; he should've made sure the clothes were taken care of before he went upstairs. So much for being a football star, Cal thought miserably.

Richard moved on into the living room and clicked on the television. Besides the thrum of the inner gears of the washing machine, all was silent in the washroom. Cal decided to set the table for dinner. Maybe he could regain a little respect by taking initiative. His mom was in the kitchen cooking, and she gave him such a comforting look when he walked into the room that he almost lost his composure again after doing so well calming himself down once he'd gotten the laundry started.

"Sorry, Mom, I should've thought better," Cal said with his head down, walking to the cupboard where the dinner plates were kept.

"It's ok, sweetie. I'll help you remember next time," she replied, "and I'll talk to him tonight too. Thank you for setting the table; here, can you take these beans to the table for me?" She handed Cal a bowl of the long, green vegetables. The warm butter she had put on them wafted up to his nostrils.

He was more than happy to have been asked to help out, and it lifted his spirits a bit that she acknowledged his forward-thinking of putting dinner dishes on the table before being asked. He really liked helping her in the kitchen, and he told himself to remember to ask more often if she needed any help – maybe that would keep him out of trouble too. If only his dad knew the thoughts in his head. He never tried to cause problems, and he didn't look for ways to upset him. Something unfortunate would just happen before he could see it coming. He knew his dad dealt with trouble-makers all day long; he shouldn't have to worry about coming home to one too. Cal had to be a better son. He had to focus and make his dad proud.

His revitalized plan made him feel even better, so when dinner was finally ready and his dad came to the table, he had almost forgotten the dirty clothes incident altogether. He was very relieved to find his dad seemed a lot more relaxed too; his parents were just talking about their day like nothing was amiss. Thank goodness, because Cal didn't know if he could sit through a whole dinner with his dad upset with him. His confidence grew the more light-hearted his parents' conversation was, so Cal thought it might be a good time to bring up trying out for the football team after all.

Once he found an opening in their conversation, Cal excitedly proposed, "Hey, Mom and Dad, can I try out for the football team? I did really well today playing with Drake and Joe. That's why I was so dirty, because I really got after it. And they even said I was doing good." Cal looked back and forth between his mom and dad, smiling and nodding.

Cal's mom spoke first, "That is kind of dangerous, don't you think?"

"Mom, you wear pads and a helmet and stuff," Cal answered.

"You can still get hurt, Cal," advised Richard. "I'm not sure that's the sport for you."

Cal eagerly continued, sensing their comments were not necessarily conversation-ending, "Maybe the coach could tell me if it's right for me or not. I promise I would do my best."

"We're not concerned about you doing your best, Cal, we're worried for your safety. We don't want you getting hurt," explained Diane. "Is there another activity you're interested in?"

Richard added, "It costs a lot to fix broken bones, and there could be long-term effects of getting hit really hard. I've just seen it too many times." He shook his head and provided himself another bite of dinner.

"What about all those other kids who get to play? That's not fair," pouted Cal. "If you think of all the players who get hurt compared to the ones who don't, my chances are pretty good that I would be ok. I might not even make the team anyway. Can I at least just try out?" He just couldn't give up yet.

Richard and Diane fell silent, looking at each other warily.

"I promise to be more responsible here, and I will still do my chores," prompted Cal.

Diane felt she needed to say something before Richard gave Cal a solid 'no' just yet. "Let us talk it over and make a decision. Finish your dinner and get to your homework. Monday will be here before you know it."

"Thanks, Mom." Cal couldn't hide the smile that surfaced on his face and spread from ear to ear. He wasn't sure he was going to be able to concentrate on schoolwork, but he ate quickly, asked to be excused once he was done, cleaned up his dishes, and went to his room to celebrate the fact that he must have put up a good argument for them to be considering letting him try out after they'd seemed pretty against it to begin with. Maybe he could talk to his dad man to man for once.

Just as he was actually getting into his math work, there was a knock on his door. After verbally granting the unknown visitor access, his dad walked into his room and sat on his single bed. It was disheveled from Cal sleeping in it the night before. Cal anxiously turned in his desk chair, away from the desk where his math problems lay, to face his dad.

"This will have to end if we give you permission to do

something you are excited about," his dad said, motioning to the messy bed he was sitting on. "There is no reason for your bed to not be neatly made, especially after we have told you plenty of times. Making your bed is just the start of an organized life. One thing affects the next. Maybe football could teach you to be more responsible, I guess."

Cal had been getting pretty disappointed in the conversation until that last sentence from his dad.

Richard continued, "You did alright today, huh?" he said with a look in his eyes Cal didn't remember seeing before.

"Yes, and they weren't just trying to be nice either, I swear. I made a really awesome catch that Drake couldn't even get, and my passing is pretty good too," answered Cal excitedly.

"Well, your mom and I have decided you can try out, and we'll go from there. I think I'll go talk to the coach too," a convinced Richard stated, almost not talking directly to his son anymore. "I need to make sure everything will be run correctly on the field."

Cal couldn't believe his ears. "Really, Dad?! Oh, thank you, you won't regret it, I promise!" He jumped up from his desk chair and threw his arms around his dad's neck, almost flattening him on the untidy bed.

Laughing, his dad hugged him back, if a bit awkwardly, while trying to sit back up straight. "You are welcome, but like I said, one sign of irresponsibility in your chores or schoolwork or anything, and it's over," he settled.

His dad couldn't have left the room fast enough for Cal, who exploded in celebration once he was alone again, punching the air with his fist and jumping up and down, but not loud enough to get in trouble. No way, no more getting in trouble, he would make sure of it. He felt so good; he and his dad had had a great, adult-like conversation for once, he wasn't getting scolded for anything, and he was given the chance to prove he was responsible and didn't always do everything wrong. The way the evening had started, he could not have imagined it would end so well. He could even foresee his dad coming to watch him play, maybe, if he made the team, of course. Then his dad would be proud of him. He just knew it.

CHAPTER 6

The back door of the fort quickly swung open, and Drake clumsily entered with his arms full of a new supply of firewood.

"This should do us for this weekend," he supposed with a smile on his face to his two buddies, who were busy re-associating themselves with their little weekend home.

Cal was unpacking the food they'd brought, and Joe felt the place needed a little tidying up before they completely settled in.

The boys had been going out there for a few years now, so they had quite a system down. They had a particular place for everything, their own separate sleeping quarters, and what food they needed and supplies that required restocking each time; their quaint home was very comfortable for the trio.

Joe rushed over to Drake to help him lower the firewood into and next to the wood bucket, as there was more than was going to fit; he had hardly made it through the back door with the size of the load he'd been carrying.

"Nice haul, Drake, thanks! I think you're right, there's plenty here, and it's not that cold out. It just means we have less to gather next time," agreed Joe encouragingly. Together, they made a nice pile by the fireplace, but it was early enough in the day that they didn't need to get a fire going just yet. "I'm going to go scrounge up some insects or worms for bait. Be right back!" advised Joe.

"Ok," replied Drake excitedly, "I'll get our fishing rods ready and come out in a bit too." The poles were leaning up in the corner nearest the front door, and he carried them to the table to evaluate their lines, reels, and hooks. He knew it was essential that they were in tip-top shape to be able to snare the best fish in good time.

"Great, see you out there," a grinning Joe replied. Humming to himself, he grabbed the bait bucket and a shovel and practically skipped out the front door of the shack on a mission. The soil near the creek was perfect for finding the best creepy crawlers, and was easiest to dig so that's where he started. The babbling of the creek flowing over rocks and against the shore allowed his mind to drift off as he dug and pulled insects out of the rich soil.

His humming reminded him of when he'd left the house that afternoon. His mom had been in bed sleeping even though it was the middle of the day; he couldn't remember the last time she had taken a nap. Between her part-time job at the dentist and all the chores around the house, she was always up and doing things. It seemed to him she always had a piece of clothing she was folding or dish she was drying, or she was at the stove cooking something – softly and melodically humming to herself the whole time. Even though she was more than happy to, he always had to beg her to sit and watch a movie or show with him, or sometimes play a board game. He assumed being busy all the time must have finally caught up with her.

Drake's emergence from the shack broke Joe out of his trance, and he eagerly showed him all the great bugs he had gathered that were going to provide them a delicious, hearty meal later.

"Cal's getting things ready to cook up the fish we *are* going to catch," stated Drake after seeing the variety of bait Joe had acquired. "Great, Joe, thanks!"

"You bet, man. Oh, good, I'm going to be hungry soon. I'm

ready for the fresh catch of the day," replied Joe with an enthusiastic grin.

He took his pole from Drake and set down the bucket for both of them to grab their choice of bait. Once they both were set up, they each found a lucky spot near the water and started casting their lines in, ready to tug the moment they felt a nibble. They kept silent, mostly not wanting to scare any fish away but also enjoying the outdoors and their freedom, as they were more than pleased to be out of the house and on their own. The day was so peaceful, and the sky was mostly cloudy, but the temperature was just right, and they didn't want to be anywhere else.

A short five or so minutes later, Drake noticed Cal approaching to join them in fishing, and he suddenly felt a little vibration in his fishing pole, so he quickly looked at both of them, slowly put up his hand and then his index finger to his closed lips, in an effort to prevent either of them from saying anything loudly that would foil his possible catch.

He stood there as still as he could, staring where his line entered the water, waiting for another, stronger pull, urging the forces of all things angling for one more good tug. Joe and Cal followed suit and didn't move a muscle, as if the fish would be able to feel them even breathe. Then he got it! Not just a nibble, but a good bite. Drake yanked his line up hard and reeled it in with about four rotations. Then he stopped and dropped the tip of his rod back down to feel for a sign of weight again. And there it was. Sure enough, he had hooked one good! As he started reeling in again, he yelled for someone to grab the water bucket, but no one had remembered to do that yet, so Cal ran back to the hut to grab it while Drake labored to get his catch on land. Finally, the fish was safe in the bucket, writhing in the shallow water, and the three friends were back to seeking to duplicate the incident while enjoying the tranquility of their surroundings.

With one fish down now, it wasn't as imperative to keep completely quiet, so the boys were able to chat a bit while waiting for a chance at more food. Cal excitedly began telling his buddies about the night of their muddy football fun and how he talked his parents into letting him try out for football. He purposely avoided getting into too much depth describing the things his dad said to him while scolding him, but he emphasized how adult-like he acted and conversed with his parents to convince them he was good enough to try out. The last thing he wanted to look like to his friends was a frail, dumb child.

"So when are tryouts? Can we come watch?" inquired Joe delightedly. He was so proud of Cal. He knew, maybe a little more than Drake did, how hard Cal's dad was on him and his need to prove himself. Joe sure hoped Cal would make the team; the failure might be disastrous to his ego if he didn't.

Cal smiled. "In two weeks. I've been trying to get in shape ever since they approved. I'm anxious to show them I'm capable of being a good sport and responsible. But I'm nervous too."

"That's awesome, Cal, good job," stated Drake, throwing a stone into the stream, forgetting about the fish. "Anything we can do to help, just ask. You have to make the team. That would be so fun. I wish I could try out too, but my mom needs help at home with Huck and Alexis. Grandma can't be there all the time, so I have to help out," he stated, feeling melancholy for being forced to be responsible.

"Thanks, guys, it's still kind of sinking in. I never thought they would even let me, or that I would be any good. I've never had a goal like this before. It feels good," opened up Cal as he gazed off into the trees across the creek. Drake and Joe could tell this was something Cal really needed, so they were more than supportive. They all sat quietly for a while until a deer slowly emerged from behind a big boulder on the other side of the creek. The slender animal had its head down and grazed closer and closer to them, unaware of their presence though its ears were swiveling to catch any threatening sound and its nose was twitching for any peculiar smell.

"Hey," whispered Cal, "guys, look. Be quiet." He pointed across the water at the four-legged creature, amazed at how close it was to them. "The stream must be concealing any noise we have made," he concluded.

Drake looked out into the trees, located the deer, and instinctively wished he had a bow and arrow. Joe's first thought was how much more serene the area instantly became with the animal's presence. It was so graceful and calm, minding its own business. They sat absolutely still, quietly watching it for a few more minutes before the wind changed direction and it looked up, straight at the trio. They could see surprise and then fear in its eyes, like it was disappointed in itself for letting its guard down. Then, after considering its surroundings, the graceful, furry animal seemed to grasp there was a barrier of water between them, so it chose to flee before waiting to see if it was going to have to defend itself from the odd beings. With this new insight, it swiftly turned on its heel and ran in the opposite direction they were in, and with the cover of trees and brush, it was out of view in a matter of seconds.

"That was so cool!" exclaimed Cal. "I can't believe it was so close to us." All three were still amazed.

Joe stated logically, "Yeah, but I hope that's the worst of the wild animals we ever see out here. I can handle deer and rabbits, but I don't need to meet a bear or anything else big and

52

mean." The others agreed, temporarily bringing down the excitement of their close encounter to nature by making it more real how alone they were. "Maybe we should be more careful when we're out here, be more on a lookout."

"I suppose. We've been lucky so far, I guess," agreed Cal. "Maybe having some kinds of weapons would be a good idea, each of us carry something, just in case. I'm not so sure about my middle-of-the-night bathroom breaks anymore," he finished, looking a little scared and unprepared.

Drake nodded in agreement, since that had been his initial thought, not only for protection, but for something to eat other than fish all the time. "Yes, I'd rather eat food than be the food. We could eat deer, or rabbit, or other things besides fish; our weapons would come in handy for that too."

"I didn't even think of that," said Joe. "Fish would get old fast if we are out here enough, but we will need to know how to prepare animals to eat; I don't want us getting sick all the way out here."

Cal sat pondering all this new information. "That's kind of a lot to think about. Maybe we should just focus on protection for now and worry about killing things out here when or if that ever comes up," he suggested.

"Yeah, maybe there aren't worse things than deer anyway," hoped Joe.

"Well, I'm hungry," Drake informed his friends as his stomach growled; he made a mental note that he needed to see about getting a bow and arrow out here somehow, no matter what his friends were saying. He had lost interest in fish for now. "Let's just go make what we have caught already. How 'bout it, guys?" He started reeling in his line to head in for dinner. After the safety talk, Cal and Joe were all for going inside as well, and they quickly pulled in their lines too. They gathered their poles, bait, and fish bucket and headed toward the shack, chatting more about the wilderness experience they had just encountered.

Arriving at their shelter, Drake and Joe stayed outside to clean the fish while Cal continued with the kitchen tasks that had to be done before the food was actually present. By the time Cal was done, Joe entered with the cleaned fish ready for frying.

"We're going back to the creek to wash up and discard the entrails so there is no smell around the house," he informed Cal.

Cal nodded. "Yes, please, I don't need anything more to worry me about sleeping soundly tonight. Thanks, Joe. I'll get this going right away." As the front door closed behind Joe, Cal placed the fish in the pan that he had previously prepared with some oil and secured it above the low flames in the fireplace. Then he shook on some seasoned salt and lemon pepper. Even though he had just gotten the fire going, he could hear some sizzling already, and he knew that, by the time the guys got back, the fish would be half done and ready to be flipped. While the fish cooked, he rifled through the food bags and pulled out some bread, butter packets, three apples, and a gallon jug of drinking water and set it all on the table. He returned to the frying pan to check on the progress of the fish and, as he suspected, found it wasn't quite time to flip yet.

The sun was sinking behind the trees, and the room was growing darker. Cal had just enough time to start the lantern and hang it on the designated lantern-hanging rafter before hearing his friends outside again.

"Glad that's done. What do you need us to do?" asked Joe when they returned. Cal notified them that the fish wouldn't be too much longer and then reminded Joe of the paper plates, cups, and plastic cutlery in the cupboard under the corner cabinet, so Joe proceeded to amass the supplies and put them on the table. Drake grabbed some paper towels. His hands were still wet from the creek, so he used one and set the rest on the table for dinner. Then he sat down on one of the old chairs. The fire was really going now, so Cal reckoned the fish were ready to be flipped.

"Thanks, guys. I think we're about ready. I'm so hungry. I'm glad it doesn't take fish long to cook," said Cal impatiently.

Joe responded, "You bet, thanks for cooking this round. That smells amazing; maybe I'm just really hungry."

"You guys didn't see or hear anything on your way to the creek and back, did you?" asked Cal, looking a little concerned.

Drake shook his head. "Nope, nothing; I think that's the way it's going to be usually. I haven't seen many droppings of any kind. I think we just got ourselves worked up."

"I hope you're right," said Joe. "That would sure take the fun out of being out here. I don't want to have to just stay indoors; I can do that at home. I mean, we are here together, but still, things can go wrong."

"I'll feel a lot better once we get some weapons, but I'm sure we will just have good stories to tell, if anything," Drake said with a comforting smile to calm his companions.

By the time their meal was over, the conversation subject had changed multiple times, and they found themselves laughing and carrying on again. With no more talk of danger, the boys were feeling a lot more secure again. They had cleaned up the dinner clutter, and Cal decided to relieve himself. He got one step out the backdoor and then stopped. It had gotten completely dark out during the mealtime. He retreated to grab a flashlight and then proceeded on his mission without another thought of his safety being risked outside. Their makeshift bathroom wasn't more than twenty feet from the hut, but a flashlight was definitely needed in the brush after dark. Standing quietly in the dark by himself, Cal could hear a lot of interesting noises; scary thoughts then easily crept back into his imagination, and he found himself walking a lot more briskly back to the fort once he was finished. He stood at the back door for a few minutes, feeling safe enough, but not wanting to enter out of breath for fear of being teased. He could hear them conversing inside but not what was being said until he opened the door once his breathing was under control.

"Well, at least your dad is around. I'd give anything to not have to be so depended on by my mom," Drake was saying, obviously in a defensive mood all of the sudden. He was standing at the fire stoking it, maybe a little more than it truly needed. Cal supposed Joe had inadvertently said something without thinking it through first.

"I feel like I never have a minute to myself," Drake continued. "Thank goodness Grandma comes a lot. My little brother and sister are a stinkin' handful sometimes. I still shouldn't have to look after them so much. And my mom always asks me if I have a dollar or so for things. It's not like I have a real job. Just wait until we're old enough to work. I bet I have to share what I make then," he finished, looking quite depressed.

Joe looked a bit sheepish. "I'm sorry, Drake, I wasn't thinking. It's just tough having a teacher for a dad. I never get away with anything. He knows all the tricks. I have to stay on top of everything because he will find out. I do alright in school, it's not too hard, but I can't ever let my guard down. But I guess I'd miss him if he wasn't around. Do you ever wonder where your dad is?" inquired Joe, who was still sitting at the table from dinner.

"Yes, all the time. I used to ask my mom a lot, but she would just get upset, so I've stopped bringing up the subject very much. Sometimes, I can't help it and I ask her, but I always regret it after," replied Drake. "She either doesn't know or the memories hurt her too much to talk about it. I'm sure it's hard on her, but I think we deserve to know about him."

Cal sat on his bedroll and joined in, "Maybe it's better you don't know. Even though your mom should let you decide that, have you ever thought she's just trying to protect you? What would it fix if you knew anyway?"

"She once said she would tell me more when I'm older," answered Drake, "but it's so hard waiting. And when is 'older' anyway? If I have to be the man in the house, I should get some answers. I want to find him and ask him why he left and why he stuck me with taking care of *his* family." Drake was getting more and more worked up.

They all sat in silence for a few minutes. Cal and Joe felt increasing sympathy for their friend.

In a supportive tone, Cal spoke, "I just finally had an adult-like conversation with my dad. Maybe yours is coming soon. I think you're definitely due."

"Maybe you could just ask her when she thinks you're going to be old enough. Then it would be easier waiting," Joe logically supposed.

"Yeah, that's a good idea," said Drake with a nod. "I think I will. It has been a while since I've bugged her about it."

"And maybe catch her when she's not doing something else, and definitely not after a long day. If she's in a good mood, your chances of getting answers will be better," suggested Cal.

Joe added, "If that doesn't work, you could at least remind her about all the stuff you do around the house and with your brother and sister and at least get some credit for all your help. She probably gets too busy to notice and doesn't realize. That would make you feel better getting that off your chest. No wonder you like coming out here so much!"

Drake smiled and remembered where he was. He had no added responsibilities out here; he didn't have to worry about taking care of anyone but himself for another day. Well, besides his friends, but that was different. He was glad to be their protector, partly because he wasn't expected to be responsible for their well-being, but mostly because they were his guardians too. The unspoken agreement was equal, not one-sided. He stopped poking the fire and lay down on his bedroll to relax. He felt encouraged to try the ideas his friends had recommended, but he was still a little worked up.

Lying on his back with his hands behind his head, he muttered, "Thanks guys," to his friends, took a few deep breaths, and closed his eyes.

CHAPTER 7

John had everything planned out perfectly, as usual, and he was extremely impatient for this next event to take place. He was pacing back and forth between his living room and dining room, going over details in his head. Each time he felt he was completely prepared, and there was nothing more to go over, he would take a seat on the couch and start flipping television channels only to pop back up and start pacing again without even realizing what he was doing until he was halfway to the kitchen table once again. The anticipation felt stronger than previous times, but with every event, he seemed more excited than the last one. It was going to be a Hackett original, something he had never tried before, a luxury-car dealership lot. Unfortunately, there probably wouldn't be any lives lost unless a lone salesperson was working late, but he trusted the vast multiple explosions would be worth the sacrifice.

John was waiting for the cover of night since the location he'd chosen was an outdoor public place; there was just no way of carrying out his plan during the business day, and he had brainstormed any possible way but with no success. The lucky car lot in danger was half a city block in size, full of Cadillacs, Bentleys, Hummers, Lexuses, Porsches, and then some. With minimal investigation, he'd attained specific detail on which days the vehicles' gas tanks were topped off too. Even better.

Since he couldn't calm down, John rechecked his supplies for probably the hundredth time. This event was going to be more difficult than previous ones, as he was going to have to set up multiple explosion points, instead of just one or two, and then link them together. It would be more time-consuming and risky for sure. Once he hacked into and altered the video monitoring feed on the grounds, he would only have to worry about passersby and police, whose presences both greatly diminished as the night ticked on. John also planned on eliminating some of the street lights with his hacking skills, but not all of them, as that could very well draw curiosity and attention to his location instead of the opposite.

By the time dusk arrived, John could not wait any longer, and he decided that he could at least load up his truck in the garage, which might help his patience, at least for the time being. His trusty old backpack contained all the usual emergency and/or useful essentials so that was loaded into the truck. Next, he carried ten detonation boxes filled with lead azide, two at a time, out to his truck bed. Then, it was the almost mile-long electrical wire, blasting caps, and remote detonator's turn to be loaded. Lastly, he filled up a couple of water bottles, grabbed his laptop and camera, and finished his packing by placing those on the truck's passenger seat.

A fully checked-off supply list confirmed he was done, so he lowered the truck bed cover and secured it. He pictured the setup of the car lot. Once he had the boxes in position and wire strung out, the rest would be easy; he would just have to be on high alert for witnesses while he was busy setting up. To his dismay, there would be no opportunity where he could prepare any part of the site in advance either.

The night was going to be longer than his usual events, so John decided that it would be a good idea to eat something hearty before he started. He would need sustenance and suitable hydration to endure the physical activity this event was going to require; not only were the boxes heavy, but he would be working swiftly and in a larger area than he was used to.

He journeyed to the kitchen and opened the refrigerator; he had plenty of time to prepare himself a nice meal, so he pulled a pork chop out of the meat drawer, a potato from one of the crisper drawers, and a bag of mixed greens from the other crisper drawer. After taking a second to choose blue cheese dressing over Italian, he started warming up a skillet with some olive oil in it on a stove burner. He seasoned both sides of the pork chop and let it sit on the countertop to await its fate of being chemically altered by increased temperature.

Then, on to the doomed potato. It too needed to be prepared for cooking, so he washed it up, carefully poked holes in it with a knife, and placed it in the microwave with a plastic bowl covering it to catch the moisture. He set the cook time to 2:22 and proceeded to prepare his salad to eat while waiting for his entrée. He was finished with his salad before the skillet had reached the appropriate chop-cooking temperature, so in the meantime, he focused on the spud in the electromagnetic radiation box, turning it over and cooking it an extra few minutes. The potato had to only wait alone in the microwave for ten minutes for its protein meal partner to be primed.

John sat at his kitchen table and savored every bite of the warm, buttery, fluffy baked potato and tender, juicy, flavorful pork chop. The blend of their differing flavors and textures together in his mouth was absolute perfection. Washing that down with cool, smooth milk almost put him over the edge. The meal really wasn't anything special, but he was enjoying it so much that he seriously wondered if he should change careers.

It was only 10 pm when he was through cleaning up his dinner mess in the kitchen. John stood gazing at the green digital clock on the oven while wiping dry his final clean dish. He was aiming for about 2 am, so he still had way too many agonizing hours to wait, and staring at the blinking dots of the oven clock would only make the minutes drag on. Maybe a full belly of food would allow him to relax enough to get a nap in. That would pass the time the quickest and replenish some energy for later. Attempting the channel surfing again, he lay on the couch with every effort to temporarily put tonight's itinerary out of his head.

John was sharply broken out of his deep slumber by an *As Seen on TV* salesperson with the most annoying voice and dynamism. Quickly, his high irritation was replaced by panic – what time was it!? How long had he been asleep?? He hadn't even considered setting an alarm, as he was sure he would not have fallen asleep.

After finding a reliable timepiece and coming to the conclusion that his event was not ruined, his displeasure with the flamboyant television personality also swiftly transformed to immense gratitude, for he might have slept right through his go-time window, and that would have been vastly unacceptable. He didn't have time to scold himself, as he was one and a half hours late getting out the door; he was off the couch and in his bedroom changing into full black attire in a matter of seconds. In the bathroom, he quickly applied black face paint to his face, neck, and the backs of his hands, the only places his clothing did not cover. He was ready; and after recalling that he had already thoughtfully packed his gear in his truck, his disappointment in himself was nearly forgotten.

The luxury-car lot was twenty minutes from his house, but in his rush, it seemed to take at least twice that, even with so few cars on the road to prohibit his progress due to the early morning hour. John approached the lot carefully, analyzing the surroundings, and parked a block away. He plopped a handful of sunflower seeds in his mouth, pulled out his laptop, and got to work hacking into the accurate virtual spots to take care of the building's cameras and slowly, one-at-a-time, doing away with extra, unneeded artificial lighting.

Once the lot was better concealed by additional darkness, and he had waited long enough to be sure the sudden lack of lighting hadn't caught anyone's attention, he continued onto the dealership grounds and parked in the darkest area he could find, somewhat blending his truck in with the other vehicles, seeing as how it was not a luxury vehicle.

Then, like a conditioned athlete, he positioned one detonation box with blasting cap under whatever vehicle was in each of the four corners of the lot, then four more underneath cars in each compass direction, and the last two beside the business building in the center of the lot. On the lookout at all times, John listened intently for any threat, along with using random vehicles' windows to spy through for any potential spectators who might spoil his fun, before reemerging from behind or underneath vehicles. Once the boxes were all precisely situated, he took a short break to guzzle half of one of the water bottles. Even with the chill of the evening, the thirst-quenching liquid was quite refreshing and necessary after lifting and hauling all the boxes, besides all the scurrying and crouching around the lot.

Next, the electrical wire needed to be attached to each blasting cap, run underneath as many vehicles as possible, and linked to the next detonation box. While doing this, again, John was more than vigilant of any unfavorable visitor to his newly and beautifully renovated car lot.

He was on the ground, halfway under a Volvo, securing the

electrical wire to the final detonation box, when he heard an engine, closer to him than the street. He stopped. His breath was heavy, and beads of sweat were forming on his brow and at the nape of his neck. Desperately listening and mentally attempting to influence the vehicle to move along, John scooched a little further underneath the vehicle just in case his mind trick didn't work.

Soon, he could see brighter and brighter headlights directed his way; the vehicle was moving very slowly, too slowly for just a prospective car buyer getting a head start for weekend shopping. His truck was across the parking lot; there was no way he could escape unnoticed if the intruder didn't vacate the property – he was stuck until they left. And if they lingered too long, they would soon notice the electrical wire all over the pavement.

The hard, cold ground was digging into his back when the vehicle arrived at his position; the car didn't stop but didn't increase its speed either. Once it passed him enough for the headlights to cease blinding him, he got just enough of a glimpse to see it was, in fact, a police car. This was not good. A simple civilian might not care enough to question the wire or detonation boxes out in the open by the offices and showroom, but for cops, it's their job; their detection and suspicion was guaranteed.

John didn't have any type of weapon. He felt like a caged animal and foolish for not hearing the vehicle in time, arming himself, or at the very least providing himself with a foolproof getaway plan. He was going to have to add that to his checklist first thing, if he got home.

Even if he didn't care about sacrificing his truck, the remote detonator was still in it, so he couldn't even initiate the explosions from where he was if he'd wanted to. He waited, but with an almost irresistible curiosity and urge to get out from under the car and see how bad his fate was. Then the car stopped, just what he was fearing. His gut told him it was near the office building, the riskiest place it could be. A few long minutes ticked by, and he couldn't take the unknowing any longer. He was either caught or not, and staying there wouldn't change that now. He slowly crept out from underneath the car, looked all around him first, and then peered over the roof of his hideout in the direction the cop car had gone. He discovered it was indeed parked near the office building, but facing away from it pointed toward the street. Odd, and he presumed the officer would've gotten out of the vehicle by now if he was intrigued by something, but the parking lights were still lit up. Maybe he had a chance after all.

His back was starting to hurt from being crouched over so long. John attempted the Jedi-mind trick again, wishing with all his might. *Why won't you move along?* he thought, abstractly and mentally fighting with the inanimate object. He'd had enough. The night was dark enough, and he had plenty of vehicles to conceal his movements, so he slowly snuck closer to the squad car. When he was about four cars away, he could hear faint music playing from inside the vehicle. Then, squinting to discern the movements in the side mirror, he eventually discovered that the officer was on his lunch break, as he was eating a sandwich and slurping a drink from a straw. So the cop was just looking for a quiet, dark place to take a breather. *Me too, buddy. Now get back to work; there are criminals out there who need to be apprehended,* thought John, with a huge sigh of relief. No wonder he hadn't noticed John's handiwork; he was off duty for the moment. Now to get him off the property before he did notice.

John figured that since the cop car was facing away from the dealership, his chances were pretty good that he was going to be able to finish his assignment. And since he was able to sit against one of the cars for sale instead of lie or crouch, the waiting wasn't near as bad; still bad, but not as bad. He still had a few hours before sunrise, and he reminded himself that patience is a virtue. He closed his eyes and breathed slowly and deeply. He guessed his wait time shouldn't be more than another fifteen minutes, but hopefully less as he was so close to the end result. He couldn't tell if he was catching the smell of sweet success or the exhaust from the police car.

At long last, John heard the change in transmission in the cop car from "P" to "D," and it slowly rolled off the lot and down the street. All was quiet again. Before allowing any more rude interruptions, he ran to his truck, started it up, and moved it two blocks away; he was not going to get trapped there again. He grabbed the remote detonator and his camera, got out of the truck, and moved to half a block away from the lot, behind some trees. This was it, no more waiting; he happily flipped up the safety cap, grabbed the switch, looked up at the car lot, and flipped it.

Instantly, the vehicle in the corner closest to him exploded. Up into the air it flew, and before it could come down to allow John to hear the catastrophic crash of metal and glass on pavement, more and more vehicles followed suit. There was at least twenty seconds of continuous explosions; this was the best idea he had ever had! He smiled and remembered that he needed to get his camera out and document the stunning sight. The noise was almost unbearable, but the immeasurable amount of smoke and flames more than made up for any possible hearing loss. With the grand finale of the office/showroom building blowing up, it proved this event was going to be hard to top. His eyes were glistening, the flames dancing in his dark pupils, and he almost felt emotional, as if he was not worthy of such a grand spectacle. He never imagined he could enjoy an event this much when no one was injured or killed. It had worked exactly like he wanted. No vehicle went undamaged, and he felt his need for seeing fire tragically destroying things was temporarily met.

CHAPTER 8

With renewed optimism to getting some straightforward answers from his mom, Drake concocted a plan so he would be ready for the first possible moment he sensed she was in a relaxed and fairly tranquil state of mind. He had done some research on how to sound more mature and grown-up in a conversation. The best online resource he found provided him with tips on keeping his voice level down, knowing when to speak versus listen, and being sincere by staying away from snide comments. Another valuable tip was to increase his vocabulary to utilize more formal words and phrases. Drake was pretty sure he wasn't going to learn too many big words before he would get a chance to initiate the conversation with his mom, and he didn't want to risk using them incorrectly, so he focused on the prior tips. Besides, this was way more research than he was used to anyway. He did not allocate near this much time towards his schoolwork. These new ideas were surprising and intriguing to him, as he had never been remotely aware of alternative ways to communicate, so he felt even better about a more favorable outcome.

Surprisingly, again unlike any previous schoolwork effort, he had also written out a game plan of sorts so he would have his thoughts in order to prevent getting overwhelmed or confused. This also provided him with possible counter arguments to further convince her he was ready for the truth.

Friday night had arrived, and Drake figured, since it was the end of the week, his mom should be capable of bearing the heavy conversation he would be laying on her. From up in his room, he could hear her car pull up outside, then the front door open and close, and her keys being dropped on the little table in the entryway. He crept to his bedroom door and opened it just enough to hear better; he needed to get a sense of her attitude before making the delicate decision of whether the mission was a go or not. His mom and grandma were talking from what sounded like the kitchen; he sensed lighthearted conversation, so he ventured downstairs to see about helping dinner get going. That wasn't out of the norm, but he knew his initiative would be just another influence to enhance the possibility of his plan going his way.

"Hi, Mom, welcome home," Drake cheerfully, but not over-doing it, greeted his mom when he arrived in the kitchen. Carol was leaning against the kitchen counter, while his grandma sat at the kitchen table.

Carol smiled. "Thank you, Son, it's good to be home finally." She lightly tussled his hair and kissed his head when he approached her. Drake noticed she didn't look or sound worn out.

"Do you want me to get something started for dinner?" he asked. "Grandma, are you staying to eat with us?"

They both looked at him, pleased that he was taking some burden off of them again, and Helen answered first, "Depends on what you're making," she teased, but then more seriously, "I would love to, no matter what. Thank you, Drake."

"How about we do something easy, maybe pizza or grilled cheese?" his mom suggested. "Do we have a pizza in the freezer?"

Drake checked for pizza and returned a negative result. "Grilled cheese it is. I know we do have cheese and bread."

"You slice up the cheese, and I'll butter the bread. Sound

good?" Carol proposed. Drake agreed, appreciating the help, even though it was an easy meal to prepare. Maybe spending a little time together would ease the probable edgy conversation later as well.

Helen slowly arose from her chair. "Well, it looks like you two have it under control. I'll go get the kids ready for dinner." And she left the room.

As they worked together, Drake noticed another opportunity to grease his possible sticky plan. He wanted to ask about her day but also realized that, if she'd had a bad day, that idea could foil everything. He decided to chance it, figuring there would always be another time to bring up his dad, and letting her vent would be a value to her.

He grabbed the cheese slicer from the utensil drawer and asked, "How's work, Mom?" He tried to sound consoling and supportive instead of it being just a question to fill silence.

"Oh. Work is work, Drake," she started to say, and he immediately regretted asking, but he then looked at her inquisitively, so she conceded. "I just wish I could do more than waiting tables to provide for you guys, but I'm kind of stuck where I'm at. The girls are great to work with, but we really rely on our tips, so slow days can be frustrating. There are some interesting customers who come in for sure," she said, ending on a lighter note.

Drake was actually intrigued by this last statement. "Tell me about some of them," he encouraged as he placed a slice of cheese on the pile of others.

"Well, we have some regulars, of course; there is a group of about ten old men that come in for their coffee in the morning and sit and talk for hours. It is so cute." Carol's eyes lit up a bit as she pictured them and what they might discuss. "I think some of their conversations get a little heated sometimes; I can't

70

imagine what is so important at their age," she said with a giggle. "But mostly it's a lot of laughing and teasing each other."

Carol continued, seeming somewhat lost in thought and maybe even enjoying herself as she analyzed her customers, "Then we have new customers come in now and then. Sometimes you can tell they're just passing through, and others seem like they have just moved to town. I like working when we're busy, but not too busy to sometimes ask people about themselves. Some have pretty fascinating stories."

"That's cool." Drake was even more curious. He was done slicing the cheese, so he turned to give her his full attention. "Which is your favorite?"

Carol thought for a minute until Drake could see in her eyes the answer coming to her. "As much as I love hearing about the people's stories who are just passing through on exciting adventures, it has to be Mrs. Olson."

"Who's that?" pressed Drake, growing even more captivated.

"Margaret Olson has been coming in almost every day for years," Carol recollected. "The weather is the only reason she sometimes doesn't make it. I almost forgot about her because she is so quietly consistent she's unnoticeable, but all the girls know our day would not be complete without preparing her order and being blessed by her comforting aura when she arrives at the same time every day. She gives our job meaning.

"She is this sweet, tiny, elderly lady, with the heart of a lion. She always walks, never without her cane and scarf, from her home every day she can; the weather has to be pretty bad to prevent her daily errand. Her husband is an injured military veteran, and he relies solely on her. The one thing he missed the most when he was overseas was her sweet, buttery, homemade

71

cherry pie. Unfortunately, Margaret can't bake anymore, so once she discovered our diner makes the pie as close to her recipe as she's ever found, she gets him a slice for his daily afternoon tea. Sometimes, she'll get herself something, but usually it's just for him, probably because they don't have a lot of extra spending money. I think it's what keeps her going in life."

His mom stopped for a second to ponder, so Drake got a skillet out, placed it on the stove, and turned the burner on to medium-high heat. They were both done with their initial tasks, so Carol grabbed some plates and glasses, and then they set the kitchen table and took seats. Drake listened to her story with his full attention.

"One day, she was all set with her to-go container of pie, and she reached in her pocket for payment only to realize, to her embarrassment and utter disappointment, she had forgotten her wallet. She had never before forgotten her wallet, and she looked crushed. Her once-a-day round-trip walk was just enough for her frail body; there was no way she would be able to make a second trip. Well, pie being one of the least expensive items on our menu, I was about to tell her that it was no problem, the slice was on us today, which gave me such a happy feeling inside to help out, when a younger gentleman sitting at the counter, who had been seemingly minding his own business and completely unaware of the little old lady, insisted we add the slice of pie to his bill.

"Margaret turned to him, and before she could even get a thank you or 'you don't have to do that' out of her mouth, he gently instructed her to take a look at the menu and order anything she fancied for herself as well. He told her she deserved it and that he would be honored for them to enjoy themselves on his dime for once."

Drake couldn't help but notice his mom's voice cracking a bit at the end of her last sentence. She was about to tear-up. "That is such an awesome story, Mom. So did she order more? How did the guy know about them?"

"I've seen him in there now and then. He must know their story somehow," Carol answered. "At first, she tried to decline his offer, but he more firmly insisted by reminding her it would be his honor for everything her husband had done for our nation, and she ended up getting a couple of small meals, just light enough for her to carry." She blotted the corner of her eyes with her index finger knuckle.

Drake stood up from his chair, walked over to his mom, and gave her as much of a hug as he could while she was sitting. "That's so cool, Mom. That makes me want to work there too!"

"Oh, no you don't. You are going to do something with your life, young man," she ordered, smiling at him and gladly returning his hug. "It is a rewarding job sometimes, but I wish the reward was something I could use to pay the bills with.

"I suppose we should get these sandwiches going before grandma and the kids get in here," Carol said. She felt good sharing that wonderful story with her son and told herself she needed to remember to make more time for just them.

They had gotten a couple of sandwiches made before they could hear Helen and the kids nearing the kitchen, ready to enjoy the cheesy goodness. It was a fun meal, better than Drake could remember them having in a long while. There was teasing and a lot of giggling and laughing; he really enjoyed his little brother and sister having a carefree time, and with both his mom and grandma there, he felt a little more "off duty" for the night, not having to be as concerned about their immediate welfare. This freeing feeling allowed him to worry about just himself for once.

After dinner, Carol went to read to the kids, and Helen needed to get home, so Drake found himself cleaning up the kitchen alone. It was fine with him; he needed some quiet time to mentally go over his plan again. The more he thought about it, the more nervous he got, and when he heard his mom coming back, he almost chickened out, but then he remembered their great talk and supposed he might not get another night like this one.

"Mom, can I talk to you?" Drake began.

Carol almost looked worried but agreed, "Of course, honey. Let's go sit in the living room."

Once settled in, Drake in an armchair and Carol on the sofa across from him, he took a deep breath, looked his mom in the eyes, and slowly and calmly started, "I know you're so busy and you have a lot to take care of. I want you to know I can't imagine raising a family without a husband, so I appreciate you being such a good mom to us. But I do a lot around here too. I'm always here when you need me, sometimes cancelling other plans, and I'm very responsible with my chores and sometimes do extra so you don't have to. And Huck and Alexis are quite a handful sometimes, and they don't always listen to me." He realized he was unintentionally speaking faster and faster and dragging on, and he needed to take another breath. Before his mom could respond, he quickly continued so he wouldn't lose his chance, "I think I'm old enough, and more than deserving, to get some straight answers about Dad finally." His heart was pounding in his chest as he waited for her reply.

Carol sighed deeply and looked instantly exhausted but yet still calm. "First, it's not that I think you're not old enough to know, it's that you knowing about your father will have no benefit to your life, trust me," she softly explained. "Having anything to do with your father is not going to bring you happiness or peace. Seeking closure does not always bring contentment; many times, it simply creates more confusion and animosity."

This concept took Drake by surprise. He hadn't even thought of that, and he suddenly felt slightly foolish for believing he was grown-up enough to talk about this with his mom. He'd been so proud of himself for securing every avenue of defeat, or so he thought. Darn it, she'd gotten one over on him already.

"Second," she continued, "you are absolutely right; I have not given you the credit you deserve. You have been taking on responsibilities similar to that of a husband and father for years now, and I have taken it for granted, at least to you anyway. I don't know how many times a day I am relieved that Huck and Alexis are in good hands when I'm not here because I can count on you."

Drake felt a lump growing in his throat, and he had to look away from her gaze as he fought away tears; he almost felt bad for putting his mom on the spot. He couldn't believe how much she actually appreciated being able to rely on him.

Carol gently continued, "Regardless of your maturity and your support of filling in when I'm not here, I am still your mother, and my daily decisions regarding my children are first and foremost of protection and safety. For the most part, you will have to trust that my knowledge of your father gives me the insight of how much you need to know. However, since you have come to me with such poise and respect, I will tell you enough, hopefully, to appease you."

Upon hearing this excellent news, Drake's throat lump dissolved, and he sat up even straighter in his armchair. Not even a bomb could have distracted his attention away from his mom at that moment.

Carol stood up, went to the kitchen, poured herself some

75

whiskey on the rocks, and returned to the couch. She wasn't sure she wanted to dredge up these feelings, but her son was right; she needed to give him something, and if she could get over the sadness and fear once, she could again.

Taking a big gulp of the cool, bitter liquor, she proceeded, "Your father left one month after Alexis was born, and I haven't heard from him since. Not a word." She shook her head.

Drake was almost sure she was going to stop right there, her sentence was so final, and she didn't look happy.

But she continued, "You were three years old. He was never affectionate with any of you. I thought maybe once we had a girl that it would change something in him, but he didn't give it time for me to see. He was gone, without warning. He had emptied both his closet and our bank account and never looked back. I really don't think it was hard for him. If I knew him at all, it was ultimate freedom for him finally. He probably thought he should've gotten an award for the years he did put in. Having a family was never his plan. He always talked about going places and seeing things, and it wasn't in the plural tense, it was always just him by himself. He didn't worry one bit about how guilty that made me feel for 'making' him settle down. I didn't trap him, believe me."

Even though he didn't deserve it, Carol took a little time to think about how to explain the type of person Drake's dad was without completely trash-talking him, but there was only so much she could do. She took another sip of her drink and decided that just telling the truth, objectively, was the way to proceed.

"At first, your dad was so charming that it wasn't hard to fall for him instantly, especially since I was so young and inexperienced. But then he became sly; when he wanted something, he knew how to get it, and how to keep it. Once he realized I had fallen for him and would foolishly satisfy his every wish, he changed. I think his way of keeping me was to put me down, make me feel like I wasn't worth anyone else's time or consideration. I finally managed to see how poorly he treated his friends and family and realized that it wasn't just me, and that's when I decided I'd try to help him overcome his mean side."

Carol took another big swig of whiskey and sat quietly until the burn in her throat subsided. "Only, there was no solution, no fix to make him happy. So I lived on edge every day, always trying to foresee anything that would set him off, to catch things before they happened, but I wasn't always successful...," she let her sentence trail off, knowing she was entering an area her son need not know.

She looked straight in Drake's eyes now and firmly stated, "I know for a fact he was solely in my life to give me you three. You kids are my life, and I have actually thanked him in my mind for giving you to me, many times.

"I hope that more than satisfies your curiosity and that you believe me when I tell you that we are much better off without him," Carol finished and hoped she wouldn't have to explain any more.

Drake sat quietly for some time. The terrible information he had just heard was a lot to take in. He'd guessed the truth wasn't going to be good, but he couldn't fathom how someone who'd helped create him, and his brother and sister, could be that immoral and cruel.

"I'm sorry you had it so bad, Mom, and that I just made you remember it all," he apologized. "Now I see why you didn't want to tell me."

"Well, it was my fault for making the decisions I made, but thank you for understanding Drake," she replied, finishing her drink.

Sitting back in the armchair now, Drake said, "I can't promise I won't have more questions once I remember more of what you said, but for now, I think I've had enough. I have to agree, we are a pretty happy family by ourselves, and it sounds like he would only bring sadness. I just wish you had someone to make you happy and to help you out with us. And selfishly, for me too."

That just about broke Carol's heart. She got up and went to him, pulled him close, and it was her turn to apologize to him.

They talked a bit more, about how life can be so unfair sometimes, and how it probably wouldn't get any easier for either of them, but now they had a better understanding of each other and more support for each other. The night had been definitely more productive than Drake could have planned, as he now knew how much his mom appreciated him, and additionally, he got the truth he had been yearning for, even though it was maybe more than he wanted to know. He fully understood why his mom was hesitant to tell him the truth about his dad, for now he felt the heavy burden of keeping the truth from his brother and sister.

CHAPTER 9

"I've got it!" confirmed Drake loudly as he held up the newest car racing video game. Joe had just opened the front door of his house to allow his good buddy to enter.

Joe smiled exuberantly but then shushed his friend, "Quiet, my mom is sleeping."

"Sorry. I've got it...," he whispered and handed the game over to Joe.

"Cal is downstairs already. He's playing a war game right now. Let's go stop him so we can play this," Joe stated.

Drake nodded "Cool," he said, and he beat him to the stairs.

In the fairly dark, cool basement, it was easier playing two at a time, which worked just fine for each of them to get breaks now and then for the bathroom or snacks. Besides, it was enjoyable watching the techniques of their friends too. While Cal and Joe were taking their turn, Cal sitting in the gaming chair and Joe laying on a bean bag, Drake crunched on some pretzels while lounging on an old couch that the family had moved to the game room when they'd gotten a new one a few years ago, and explained how the talk with his mom had gone. He didn't have their full attention, but that was ok; they got the gist enough. He chuckled a little when he told them how he had actually done some research on how to have adult conversations. The pair of buddies didn't miss a beat by teasing him, knowing full well he never did research with his schoolwork, so he must've been pretty adamant to get answers about his dad.

Joe's little brother Sammy emerged at the bottom of the stairs and stared at them for a minute, waiting for a scolding to leave them alone, likely followed by name calling. At eleven years old, he could really be a pest to boys three years older than him. After acquiring a silent clearance, he joined Drake on the couch to watch the racing game.

Drake continued, telling them how he had taken their advice and picked the best time to find his mom in the right mood and how the plan actually worked. The he told them how he didn't get the news he had been hoping for, that his dad was as bad a loser as he feared after all. He told his friends that he was glad he now knew, but also not glad; he used to picture his dad being some important businessman or busy doctor doing the world some good and imagined that was why he left. He didn't go into all the detail, partly because they were a little preoccupied, but mostly he didn't want them knowing what kind of person he was created from. He ended with describing how he and his mom had a better relationship now and thanked them for being there for him.

Joe paused the game and turned to Drake. "That's so awesome, buddy. You really needed that time and talk with your mom, huh?"

Cal agreed, "Too bad about your dad. But it's his loss. If he only knew the cool guy you are, he'd come back and be a good dad to you and Huck and Alexis for sure."

Suddenly, they all looked over at Sammy on the opposite end of the couch from Drake and wondered how and when he had gotten there.

"You little sneak, what are you doing? You're ruining everything," cried Joe.

"I'm not doing anything. I'm just sitting here watching you guys," pleaded Sammy. "Come on, I won't bug you."

Cal wanted to get back to the game instead of listening to Joe and Sammy argue, so he suggested, "Let's leave him be. I'm unpausing it." With that, he turned back toward the television.

"Fine, but don't bother us, you little punk," Joe stated firmly to his brother, turning back to face the television just in time to catch his virtual car being released from its frozen state.

A while later, it was time to change up players. Drake took Cal's spot, so Cal headed upstairs for a much needed restroom break.

The other three boys, being engrossed in the video game, naturally hadn't taken note of how long he had been gone, but when he finally came back, he had a quite concerned look on his face. Joe, having a more sensitive personality, and it being his house, knew right away the reason wasn't just that he'd seen a mouse or something immaterial.

"What's wrong?" Joe inquired.

Cal shook his head. "Maybe nothing, but when I was in the bathroom upstairs, I could hear your mom puking in your parent's bathroom. It did not sound good. Is she ok?"

Sammy and Joe glanced at each other with solemn and worried looks; both Drake and Cal caught the ominous feeling and looked at each other with piqued curiosity and concern. The paused video game's peppy melody suddenly seemed very out of place. Joe knew he'd have to come up with something to appease them, but he wasn't sure if he was ready for the truth. He was still dealing with the recent news himself.

"She hasn't been feeling well," he started to say, trying to play it off. "I think she's on the mend, though. You know, that nasty flu that's been going around. I hope I don't get it."

Cal and Drake weren't sure they believed him, but what options did they have. He was either telling the truth or didn't want to say, and they didn't want to make him tell them if he wasn't comfortable. The feel in the small room had heavily shifted from carefree to discomfort.

"Well, I hope she gets better soon, and yeah, I hope we don't get it too." Cal questioned whether he wanted to stay there overnight after all now. But why would Joe invite them over if his mom was very ill? He figured whatever the discreet illness was, it must not be contagious, which didn't make him feel any better.

Drake was feeling the same way and proposed, "Maybe we should go. If she isn't well, she probably doesn't want us here."

"Nah, we can just be quiet. It won't bother her. You guys know she likes it when you're over," countered Joe. His close friends being there helped make life seem more like normal, how it used to be, before his mom got sick. He needed them to take his mind off his mom, so he insisted they stay. "Should we watch a movie?" he asked, in an obvious attempt to bribe them.

Drake and Cal both cautiously relented, especially after seeing Joe had a couple of really good new releases neither of them had seen yet. Joe talked Sammy into making them popcorn, saying he could stay and watch the flick too if he did. While they waited for their salty treat, the three boys chatted about how anxious they were to see the movie they had decided on and what reviews they had each heard about it. Sammy had been gone longer than expected, so Joe went to hurry him up.

Knowing he had to be quiet, and time was of the essence, Cal just had to see what Drake thought about the peculiarity of Gail's health, and more so, Joe's indecisive behavior, so he initiated a whispered conversation.

"What the heck? Tell me you're catching the weird vibe too," he said.

Drake nodded gingerly, not really wanting to talk about it. "Yes, I caught that. What do you think is going on?"

"Well, I assume she must not be contagious, or they wouldn't have us over," Cal stated, glancing at the stairwell. "So it must be something worse than a cold or the flu. I sure hope I'm wrong, but what else could it be?"

"I really don't want to assume anything, Cal. I guess he will tell us when he's ready. He obviously doesn't want us to know yet," answered Drake simply. He thought if he started speculating, it would make it real, if he denied the possibility, everything would be ok. He just couldn't imagine Joe's perfect family having a "flaw."

Cal felt a little defeated. It wasn't the response he was expecting, but realizing his expectations were too high, as Drake would not know more than he did, he didn't go on. Besides, they could hear someone approaching, so their time was up anyway. Once Joe emerged, Cal glanced at Drake to see how he would react to Joe after their little uneasy talk, but he was either not worried or a good actor because he just greeted Joe by taking one of the bowls of popcorn, thanking him, and teasing about getting the movie started already, like nothing was amiss. Joe playfully retorted by slugging him one in the shoulder and promising they could start now.

At first, Cal was irked by Drake's behavior, and he wondered why Drake wasn't more concerned for their friend and giving Joe a little more considerate attention. But then realized most of the heaviness of the room had lifted due to the others leaving the unease behind, so he might as well too and enjoy the rest of their time together. Nothing good would come, at this point, from not letting it go. And treating Joe differently would only make things more uncomfortable, so he put a couple of freshly popped corn pieces into his mouth and settled in to watch the movie.

Only ten short minutes into the action flick, Joe's older

brother Ryan came home, with three of his burly friends, and demanded the basement for themselves. Joe fought back, telling his brother that he knew Joe was having his friends over and that the basement was off limits. Ryan had no comeback, but he didn't need one; they were outnumbered, out-sized, and out-aged. Joe knew very well not to bother their mom about their unfair situation, and complaining to their dad, Henry, would make them look weak, and being a teacher, he always told them to find a solution to their problems on their own anyway. The day was too late, and the weather was too cold to go outside and do something, so it was, grudgingly, up to Joe's bedroom for the three of them. At least they were safe there, he supposed, from Ryan as well as Sammy.

On the way there, they passed by the bedroom of Joe's sister Leslie, who was older by a year and a half. Drake had recently been seeing her a little differently now that they were in their teens. Before, she was a cootie-carrying, whiney girl, but lately he found himself drawn by what she was wearing, by what words came out of her lip-glossed mouth, and by her cute little giggle. Her door was ajar enough for him to peer in quickly without it being too creepy. Her room smelled like flowers, and there were a lot of pink and purple fluffy things all over. Confusion overcame Drake, it all seemed so silly, but the urge to go in was apparent, which made him very nervous at the same time. Breaking himself out of the semi-trance, he quickly moved on to Joe's room before they got suspicious why he wasn't right behind them. He wondered if his friends had similar emotions towards the opposite sex or if he was the only weird one.

The original plan was to sleep downstairs in the rec room, but they knew they wouldn't be getting the room back any time soon, so they laid out their sleeping bags and got cozy.

Boredom soon set in. They were sure not tired yet, and with the unexpected absence of electronics to entertain themselves, they were forced to resort to old-fashioned fun.

Joe had just gotten a "Super" Erector set for Christmas, so Drake proposed they hold a contest to see who could build the best vehicle; it could be anything they wanted, for movement on land, sea, or air. They laid out all the parts on Joe's bed and took turns selecting just the right pieces for their personal arsenal. It took some quick strategizing due to none of them knowing at that point what kind of unique means of transportation they were going to create. Once all the pieces had been spoken for, they laid out some ground rules:

- What pieces they had was what they got. Nothing other than erector set pieces (i.e. paperclips, glue, rubber bands, etc.) were allowed.

- No internet researching. They had to come up with ideas relying solely on their own imagination.

- They could use blank paper and a pencil to brainstorm possible designs and configurations.

- Each vehicle's end result was to physically carry out some useful action.

The boys gathered their assortments of nuts, bolts, gears, wheels, and various sizes and shapes of metal parts and relocated them to separate corners of the room and got to work. Cal imagined that the more futuristic the design the better, so as to awe them he started drawing up unusual, yet functional, ways to hold the body of a craft together. Eventually, his ideas culminated into a starship that could attach any type of space object to its underside and transfer it to other locations, eliminating the need to load it aboard the craft itself, especially if it was too large an item. He was proud of himself for thinking this up and grinned as he imagined the reaction he was going to get from his buddies.

Drake, no doubt, wanted something big and brawny, so it had to be a tough, massive truck of some kind. His drawings consisted of big wheels, a big engine, and a big truck bed to haul big, heavy things. Big was the undeniable goal. The idea wasn't very creative, but he was counting on the great size and power of the vehicle to win him the challenge. There wasn't a lot for him to sketch, so he was on his way and assembling his vehicle before the other two boys were. *Too bad there isn't a time limit*, he thought, or he'd win for sure.

Building things wasn't really Joe's forte (he hadn't asked for this erector set for Christmas and thus believed his parents must've been hinting for him to try new things), so he opted for a more realistic approach and just decided on a four-wheeler that was the ultimate in off-road specimens. Its function was going to be to pull other vehicles out of thick, deep mud and the like.

An hour into their contest, Drake noticed the other two had caught up to him. His lack of preparation in well-thought-out sketches proved to be a detriment after all. He was having a hard time using the pieces he had: too many of certain ones and not enough of others. He wondered if his friends were having the same issue.

"How are you guys coming along?" he inquired, desperate to hear some equal frustration.

Joe answered first, "I think coming up with what type of vehicle I wanted was the easy part. I don't think I have the right pieces for what I want to make."

"Me too," added Cal with a sigh. "Maybe we could start a trade system. Each of us put what pieces we can't use back on the bed, and we can trade."

Drake smiled. "Yes, that's an excellent idea! I was starting to lose interest in this whole game, but you just revived me. Let's see what you guys have." He rubbed his hands together and grinned wryly like a thief about to get his hands on some precious loot.

They converged back at Joe's bed with their unwanted parts and inspected what each other had. Some pieces were larger or more functional; therefore, they were more valuable than others, so sometimes, a couple of parts for one was considered fair barter. When they were all satisfied, once again, they resumed their task, and aside from tiny construction noises, all was quiet in Joe's bedroom once more.

A half an hour's time went by this time, and Joe suddenly announced he was done. Cal and Drake quickly turned their heads out of natural curiosity and reflex, but Joe had thought ahead and draped a pillowcase over his creative invention. He was pleased with himself for finishing first and at how awesome his creation turned out as well. Maybe his parents knew what they were doing after all.

"I'm going to the bathroom. No peeking at my project!" Joe announced. The other two were still working when he returned, so he took another fresh look at his handiwork to see if it needed any revising or if he'd missed something. "How much more time do you guys think you'll need?" he asked.

Drake divulged, "Just one more minute. I'm almost done too." He was quickly putting on the finishing touches and testing out the vehicle's functionality.

"I've got about five more minutes, but I'm right there," replied Cal. "Besides, I've got to go to the bathroom too, and I'm going cross-eyed from staring at this thing for so long now," he said, chuckling a bit.

They had each finished, taken a "break," and reconvened.

No one had thought far enough ahead to question how the

judging was going to go, so Joe asked, "Who's going to decide who won? How are we going to do this? We're each obviously partial to our own."

"How about your brother or sister? Well, maybe not since all those guys are down there and they will probably tell us to get lost," concluded Cal.

Joe contemplated for a minute. "We can't vote for our own. There are three of us, so we could each write down 1st, 2nd and 3rd and see which gets two votes each."

"Sounds fair enough," said Drake. "Now that that's settled, who's presenting first. Can I?" he asked excitedly.

Cal and Joe accepted his proposal and they sat down to watch Drake amaze them with his creativity and assembling talents. They could tell he used every last one of his pieces to make his truck as big as possible. As impressively massive as it was, its useful function of hauling items in its bed was barely remarkable to Cal or Joe, but they kept quiet about it and nodded and smiled at his creation.

Next it was Cal's turn; he unveiled his flying spacecraft with flamboyant vim and vigor in an effort to promote wonder and amazement in his friends. Joe and Drake noted Cal's attention to detail and how he hadn't copied the style of anything they'd ever seen before on space shows and movies. They were quite captivated, and once Cal explained how the craft could attach any size or shape of outer space object, they were even more impressed by the imagination their friend possessed to think that up.

Joe was hesitant to show his vehicle, knowing he couldn't compete with his friends in this area of skill, especially after Cal's marvel. As long as he didn't get laughed at, he would be ok, and his friends were never so mean to him as to make him feel bad anyway. Besides, he was proud of his work, so he just went with it. Without near as much showiness as Cal, but still with bated breath, he revealed his machine to his pals. He finished his demonstration by explaining the way his four-wheeler was a rescuer by getting other vehicles out of trouble, and he used a ruffled up blanket to pull Drake's enormous truck out of a sticky spot. He actually got some oohs and aaahs until he unintentionally suggested Drake's perfect truck would ever need help.

"All right, let's vote," urged Cal. The feel that he got from all the reveals made him confident about his chances of winning. Joe got out some makeshift ballots and pencils and emptied a bowl of odds and ends from his desk for depositing them into. The only sound in the bedroom for 30 seconds was scribbling. It was time for the results.

"What does the winner get?" asked Drake. He really wanted to win, or at least beat Joe for making his truck look weak. He wanted to go smash up the four-wheeler and show how it wasn't tough at all.

Cal quickly thought and then answered, "The winner doesn't have to cook at the fort next time we're there."

"Awesome! Works for me," agreed Joe. He did most of the cooking anyway, so it wouldn't matter if he lost. He gathered the ballots and tallied them up to announce that Cal and his spaceship had won, his three-wheeler had come in second, and Drake's truck was third. All of a sudden, Drake stood up from the floor beside the bed and stormed out of the room. Cal and Joe looked at each other, puzzled.

"I didn't think he'd be upset," said Cal. "What's gotten into him?"

Joe thought back. "I wonder if I shouldn't have used his truck in my demonstration," he sadly reasoned. "I didn't even think. I was nervous, but I would be upset too."

"Well that didn't alter my vote, so what does it matter?" supposed Cal.

Joe shrugged. "I don't think he sees it that way. I better go talk to him."

"Let's just wait for him to come back, and we can explain," offered Cal. "You made an awesome three-wheeler, dude. I'm impressed. You deserve second place." He smiled at Joe and patted him on the back.

That made Joe feel a lot better, and he thanked Cal for the compliment. "I wish I had thought of a spaceship. You rock at building things, Cal," Joe praised him back, "and thinking up creative ideas."

It didn't take long for Drake to reemerge, as he didn't have many places to go to sulk for long. He repositioned himself in his previous spot on the floor at the end of the bed. Joe was very relieved Drake didn't look as upset as he was afraid he was going to be. He wanted to forget about the whole silly thing, but he didn't want the discomfort hanging over them, so he decided to get the apology over with.

"I'm sorry, Drake, for using your awesome truck in my demonstration," Joe said. "I wasn't thinking."

Before Drake could say anything, from Joe's desk chair, Cal added, "It wasn't a factor in my vote if that makes a difference. I just really liked Joe's three-wheeler."

The look on Drake's face made Joe unsure if Cal's support was going to help or hurt his efforts of peace, but Drake didn't speak right away. Joe sat on his bed in agony waiting for Drake's forgiveness for his thoughtlessness.

Finally, Drake, looking down at the floor, muttered, "It was just a stupid contest anyway, no big deal." Joe wasn't completely convinced, but it was a start. At least Drake hadn't yelled at him like he had imagined, and maybe even deserved.

"I guess you didn't mean any harm by it. You did make a cool three-wheeler... and you didn't get out of making food." He gave in and actually smiled, giving Joe a quick look but then staring back down at the floor.

The argument was over. Joe wasn't going to be punished with silence or worse. "Believe me, I won't do it again," Joe confirmed. He tried to make it as light-hearted a comment as possible in an attempt to return the atmosphere back to positive and fun.

"Well, I'll beat both of you next time," Drake said confidently, realizing he didn't like the negativity in the room either. "You're going down!" he exclaimed as he jumped up from the floor and tackled Joe on the bed, sending him on his back. Drake put him in a headlock and rifled his reddish hair a bit before letting go. That was just what they all needed, some rough-housing. Cal joined them on the bed and got some playful punches in before they all made themselves tired enough to settle in for the night. Drifting off to oblivion was much easier being in a peaceful disposition rather than a tense one. They congratulated Cal once more on his win and, before long, were all sound asleep.

CHAPTER 10

This was his most dreaded part of his school day, turning from the end of the lunch line toward the other kids and walking through the tables, much like dangerous landmines, to find a safe haven of an open seat to dine peacefully. Johnny wished there were assigned seats. Then there would be no confusion, only consistency. He craved constants in his life. However, almost every single day, someone, for whatever reason, would make a rude comment or try to trip him or shove him all while he was just longing to be left alone. In the halls, he could at least protect himself, but with a tray of food and drink, his chances of being unnoticed and coming out unscathed dropped significantly, and his fellow classmates knew it. One constant he could count on was, once he finally claimed a secluded spot to enjoy his meal, they would forget about him. But it never failed, something always happened, and the effort it took to reach refuge was exasperating. Even on the very rare good day he was left alone, he could still feel their eyes on him, judging, watching, waiting for their next move.

Today, Johnny turned just in time to see a tableful of boys just finishing their lunch and getting up from their table. It was his chance. Feeling lucky, he timed his pace just right to where they didn't see him coming, and no one claimed the table before he did. Success. He sat down quickly without looking up, secured his backpack between his legs under the table, and opened his single-serve milk carton. The smell of the mac 'n cheese under his nose helped him forget his surroundings, and as he shoveled a big forkful into his mouth, the warm creaminess took over his taste buds. He countered that with a bite of lightly seasoned broccoli. After his cup of applesauce was extinguished, he finished with the sweet mini blueberry muffin, which paired perfectly with the last gulp of his milk. The enjoyment he was experiencing in his mouth was second to the fact that there was no drama or commotion made at his expense during his time in the lunchroom.

Now came the next to worst dreaded part of his school day – leaving the lunchroom. Johnny didn't have a tray full of food anymore, but his hands were still occupied. For the first time since he'd sat down, he gingerly looked up to survey how risky the environment was. Today might just be one of the good days, as his fellow classmates looked to be busy minding their own business for once, which actually seemed a bit odd, but he was so relieved he didn't think much of it. He re-secured his backpack on his back and rose from the table. After removing his legs from behind the bench, he grabbed his tray and started toward the trash and exit.

Out of the blue, he heard a girl loudly shouting, though in a contented belly daze he didn't hear what she was saying. He didn't look back; their drama was never his business, so he kept walking, not caring what her problem was. Before he could empty his tray's refuse into the trash, a teacher approached him and grabbed at his backpack. Johnny instinctively twisted his body to release the teacher's hand on his property. He wanted very badly to scold him for touching his things but thought better of the reaction until he knew what was going on.

"Come with me, young man," said the male teacher sternly, "right now." And he grasped Johnny's arm this time instead of the pack, brusquely leading him out of the lunchroom. Too soon, they arrived at the principal's office. Johnny didn't say a word along the way; he didn't want to unintentionally falsely incriminate himself more than was obviously already happening. His lunch was so uneventful that he couldn't imagine what the issue was.

The balding, slightly overweight principal opened his office door, instructed Johnny to take a seat in one of the two chairs across from his desk, thanked the teacher who'd led the boy there, and sat down behind his desk. The teacher left the room, shutting the door behind him. Johnny deposited his backpack in the second chair as he sat down and turned his attention back from the now shut door to Principal Hunter with wide, puzzled eyes. The principal appeared tired but not upset, so Johnny felt a little more at ease and able to express himself.

"Why am I here, Mr. Hunter?" he asked. He wanted to sound even more bewildered than he was; it would be more believable because he feared he wasn't going to be heard in the end.

The principal shook his head. "You tell me. You know what you've done," he answered.

A bit shocked, Johnny replied, "But I don't, I have no idea. I was just eating, and I got up to leave the lunchroom. That's it," Johnny explained. He couldn't think of anything that could have gone wrong in that short of time.

"Well, now you're just being defiant and lying. I can see the item in question in your backpack myself," the principal claimed and motioned to Johnny's backpack next to him. Johnny's head just about spun off his neck he looked over so quickly. There was a pink notebook sticking out of the front pocket. Johnny couldn't believe it. How did that happen? He'd secured his pack between his feet. He must have been too engrossed in his meal to have felt or heard someone messing with his stuff. His stomach churned, and he felt flushed; sickness and anger consumed him. Why?? Why do they choose

94

him? He never bothered anyone. What did they have to gain by doing this to him? He had no idea who had framed him, or why, and that was infuriating. The more time that passed, the angrier he became.

Johnny spouted off, "I didn't take it, I was just eating, minding my own business. They're always, every single day, in my business and doing mean things to me!" He snatched the foreign object out of his pack and threw it on the desk. "I don't even want it. Why would I take it?" he finished.

"How can you say you didn't take it? You were caught red-handed, Johnny," maintained a calm Mr. Hunter. He was not getting worked up at all, and Johnny was not sure how to take that. "It looks like you were trying to read a girl's diary, is what it looks like to me. Is that how you get your kicks, Johnny?" he asked without expecting a response.

"Sounds like you have a reason too," Mr. Hunter reasoned, "since they're always bugging you apparently."

Johnny thought quickly. "Don't you think I would've hid it better if I knew it was there?" A just argument indeed, he reasoned.

"Now you're just making it worse," the principal stated calmly. "Why don't you just admit you took the poor girl's notebook so I can suspend you and get on with my day? Come on, you're already at a week, do you want more? Lie to me again, and I'll be glad to lengthen the suspension," he said. Principal Hunter's unfaltering, heated stare pierced Johnny's eyes.

He couldn't believe what was happening, Johnny didn't have a choice. It was like they were all in on it, even the teachers, who were supposed to be understanding and impartial. He realized how the situation looked, but there are always other reasons for the way things happen. Not only was he being outright accused, but he was being forced to actually confess to something he didn't do! He was not even being allowed to be heard. Nothing he said was making a difference, only getting him deeper into trouble. This was against all his ideals; not that he was perfect, far from it, but the belittling was crushing to the insignificant self-esteem he had left. He just couldn't confess, so he sat there looking at the floor.

"Well? I'm growing impatient," pressed the principal, sitting back in his chair and looking at his watch with a huff.

Johnny wouldn't budge; he physically couldn't. Every piece of anatomy in his body used for the production of speech was striking. The only thing he could do was look up from the floor, as confidently as he could, back to the principal in hopes his poised expression would portray the slightest bit of his complete innocence in an effort to be respectful.

The final attempt was either misunderstood or never had a chance because Mr. Hunter's eyes turned even angrier and his face reddened with the apparent non-compliance of his request from the delinquent boy in front of him ruining his day.

"Two weeks!" he shouted, throwing his right arm into the air like a victory decision. He didn't look away from Johnny. "And you had better learn from this experience while you're gone, think about what you did, stealing from an innocent young lady, and how you have lied, because when you come back, I expect to see a different boy. Or else."

The empty threat sounded so silly to Johnny. Or else what? What could he do to him that his classmates didn't do every single day? It was done, his fate so unfairly sealed, so with no more efforts to prove his innocence, he shook his head and smirked. He couldn't help it. Even if his reaction to his punishment gave him another week's suspension, that would just be more time he had to prepare his next event, one that had so willingly just fallen into his lap.

The only unfortunate thing about being absent from school was that it prevented Johnny from investigating who framed him for stealing the stupid notebook. He couldn't care less about a girl's notebook; why couldn't they have at least framed him for something interesting, for goodness sakes?! Because retaliation would be a long time coming since he couldn't pinpoint who was actually responsible and no one had come forward to clear his name, Johnny decided everyone would just have to pay. It would be easier and more fun that way anyway.

Luckily, John Sr. normally left for work before Johnny left for school and got home after Johnny did. And since Johnny would be home by himself for two weeks, he would get the letter the school sent to the parents of such felonious children informing them of suspensions and the like. Neither was he the least bit worried about the call the school would make to his father, for his father did not concern himself with such frivolousness. They would not be able to reach him, and he would not call them back; John Sr. considered anything to do with his son a serious waste of his time, and Johnny knew this. With such freedom, he had uninterrupted time to work on his plan.

Initially, Johnny focused his current mission around the lunchroom; it seemed the obvious next location for an event as it was the place he hated the most, especially after the recent incident. But after a day of planning, he realized that a lunchroom event would be too complex and risky for him to pull off with his current level of experience. He turned his attention to the principal's office and, though potentially difficult to gain access to, hoped it might be a better fit for his current skill level.

Just gaining access to the principal's office wouldn't actually be that hard. If his presence was not requested by Mr. Hunter upon his return to analyze if he'd learned his lesson, he could easily be called in again, gladly, for some reason or another that was of his actual doing. However, being in Mr. Hunter's office was one thing, but leaving his mark while retaining ambiguity was another. Thanks to his classmates, two weeks was plenty of time to figure out the puzzle.

Johnny sat at the library, his second home, researching school arson cases for ideas. Unsurprisingly, he found that most successful school building fires were started on the weekends or at night in the façade of the building. This made the most sense from a risk standpoint, but he was disappointed that he would most likely have to sacrifice causing injury and/or death to retain a clear name. However, this plan would make the whole operation a lot easier. He also read that arson crimes were difficult to solve as long as the arsonist was careful; too many of the stories ended with how the crafty criminal came, one way or another, to his unfortunate demise.

This was the point in Johnny's life where he created his number one rule: eliminating risk is the most important aspect of any event. Period. No matter how grand his scheme would be. No matter how long he had been working on any plan. Any time he felt his anonymity was threatened, he would alter his plan, no matter how long it took to change; it just wasn't worth getting caught and not being able to play anymore. It was too easy to get carried away with the excitement of it all and forget the repercussions that could arise, so this was the absolute utmost principle to never overlook.

After realizing his entertainment could come to a crashing halt with the slightest of errors, Johnny decided to play it safe and have the school building be his only victim. The new plan would still cause mass damage and extend his two-week vacation. With his extra time, he could create another event somewhere else; it was almost like a buy-one-get-one-free, and this restored his positive attitude from the disappointment of his wholly gratifying original plans being stifled.

The night of the weekend before his scheduled return to school, Johnny devotedly lit the mass amount of gasoline he had just dispensed surrounding the outside of the school building with a match. Watching from the wings, with camera in hand, he smiled at the delightful red-orange flames, and as he intently listened to the tremendous low roar and loud crackling, he almost felt content. Almost.

CHAPTER 11

Cal had been training any way he could, by himself, with friends, at home, or at school, and interrogating coaches for the most beneficial workouts to ensure he would make the football team. He worked on plyometrics, agility and speed training drills, as well as strength training in the school weight room. Before every workout, he would check his daily schedule of chores, homework, and training so as to not let anything slip by him and give his parents a reason to prevent him from reaching his goal. At this point, he didn't even care if he played; he just wanted to prove to himself, and his dad, that he was at least good enough to be on a team.

The daily schedule was Cal's idea, not his parent's, and he found that, the more time that went by, his organized program was less and less a dictator but more a reassurance in his life. Other things fell into place and became easier as well: his grades were the highest they'd ever been, and it wasn't even a struggle to keep them there either. He seemed to actually have more time to devote to schoolwork, even with the added training and chores. He even figured out the best time for his mom to take him to get his physical so as not to inconvenience her, even though she was glad to do it and spend time with her son. He was feeling good.

So when tryout day came, he was nervous, but not overly so to where it would affect his performance. All week, and especially on tryout day, he restricted his diet to mostly protein, but with a few carbohydrates to keep his energy up. Cal knew he wasn't the biggest kid around, so he guessed the positions of either offensive or defensive lineman were probably out for him. He believed he was pretty fast and agile, so being either a wide receiver or cornerback would be suitable if he was asked his preference. Otherwise, he would take any position they saw fit for him, gladly.

Doing his best and making the football team was all Cal could think about through the whole school day; he was surprised he didn't get scolded at all for not being mentally present in any of his classes. And he was grateful there were no tests or quizzes; he would've failed for sure. At lunch, Joe and Drake gave him a hard time but also highly respected his focus and drive. They were pretty eager as well to hear the outcome; giving up a lot of quality time with their friend had better not have been for naught.

The final school bell rang, and Cal hurried to the locker room to get ready. There were tons of boys getting changed from their school clothes to sports attire and chatting excitedly about anything football; he became discouraged and felt foolish. He hadn't counted on this much competition, and he was sure they had all done as much, if not more, training as he had. He heard too many terms and phrases he was not familiar with; he hoped it was just the boyish stink of early testosterone that filled the locker room that made him uneasy and forgetful.

Cal endeavored to raise his self-confidence by reminding himself of how many long, hard hours he had put in to prepare for performing to the best of his ability. Maybe there was still a chance. At least he would go out there and show them his best. Some of his competition would beat him hands-down, but he doubted all these boys had what he had.

When he arrived at the football field, Cal observed some boys standing around talking, some stretching, and others taking slow laps around the track. At this point, he was feeling so unsure that he hoped his dad, his mom, and his friends weren't there, just in case things didn't go as he planned; he didn't even glance at the bleachers to see if they were there or not. Not wanting to exert himself too much, but knowing he was too hyped up to just stand around, Cal decided to join the boys on the track to loosen up.

Before long, there was a long, sharp whistle, and from his jogging location on the track Cal looked hastily in the direction it came from to see a cluster of men dressed in coach-like attire, with one looking much more in charge than the others. He hurried over to the men without a second thought; he wanted to show them his respect and full attention. Eventually, after a few more whistle blows, all the boys were huddled around the coaches, and the head coach introduced himself and his staff.

"Good afternoon, boys, thank you for coming. I'm head coach Rick Steed, and this is my staff…," he said as he pointed to each fellow coach and stated their names and positions. But Coach Steed was all that Cal caught for now; he was too mesmerized by the man in charge. Cal could tell right away he was a man to respect, learn from, and adhere to. He broke himself out of his trance just in time to catch some instructions.

"We're going to split you up into four circuit sections: 40-yard dash, bench press for one-rep max, vertical jump, and shuttle run. We'll be timing and recording each of your scores," he advised. "When you are done with each circuit, you are free to leave. We hope to have the team roster decided by this Friday. The position lists will be posted outside the locker room door. We're anxious to see what you gentlemen can do," he finished, rubbing his hands together and looking at the other coaches.

Then the boys were told to line up, and one of the coaches

counted them off one to four and sent each of the four teams off to the four separate sections of the field. Cal was confident about all the circuits because he had been working on these exact drills a lot, as well as others.

His first designated section was the shuttle run, and he hurried over to be one of the first in line. His nerves would only get worse watching his teammates-to-be, who were currently his competitors, either blow it or blow it out of the water. He visualized how to move quickly but not slip on the grass when he reached to the ground for the blocks, and he made sure to remember to sprint through the finish line. He watched four other boys take their turns first, and then it was his time to shine. He stepped up to the first line and crouched over in a ready stance with his eyes on the parallel line thirty feet ahead of him. The two blocks sat awaiting their transport. Two short whistles and then the long one for "GO," and he was off like a shot, sprinting as fast as he could, slowing just enough to plant his right foot sideways, bend over and grab the first block, and then he was off again, back to the starting line to drop it off. The second block went just as the first, and he found himself crossing the finish line before he knew it. He was breathing hard, and it felt good as he grabbed the first block and jogged back to the far line to take the blocks back.

As he turned back to the starting line, he noticed the coach with the stopwatch looking at him curiously. As Cal approached him to see if he could know his time, the man smiled and said, "Well, thank you, young man. Your initiative resetting up the course is appreciated."

Cal shrugged his shoulders and smiled back. The concept was nothing to him but common sense. "You bet. Can we know our times?" he inquired.

"Only being the fifth one to go, it's hard to say, but I think you did well, son," answered the stopwatch coach, and he lightly patted Cal on the back.

Cal smiled again; the coach thought he did well! "Thanks! I've been practicing really hard. I just hope it shows," he said and hurried to the next part of the circuit. One down, three to go.

The next drill was the bench press. This was probably going to be his worst circuit section. He just wasn't brawny; he knew it, but he planned on making that up in other areas, and he knew the roster took a variety of guys to fill all the positions a football team required, so he wasn't too discouraged. The worst that could happen here would be overdoing it and making a fool of, or hurting, himself, so he was careful and only lifted as much as he had in training, no reason to try to even compete with the big, muscular guys. Besides, they didn't compare to his best skills anyway, so the playing field evened out, hopefully more in his favor, though.

The vertical jump and 40-yard dash were straightforward and nothing to worry about; he completed both near his usual training scores. Cal really felt he was in a good position to make the team. After observing his competition and seeing what the coaches were expecting, he was feeling quite confident. Now that it was over, his nerves allowed him to inquire into whether he had any fans in the bleachers, and to his surprise, he spotted his dad. Drake and Joe were sitting a couple of rows up from him. Richard was looking straight at him, and once he saw that his son noticed he was there, he clapped his hands a few times and motioned for him to come over. Cal jogged up to his dad, and once he reached him, Richard put up his hand for a high-five from his son.

"Cal, I'm so proud of you. You really impressed me today," Richard said with a gleam in his eye. "You told me you had it in you, and I didn't believe you at first. I'm glad you kept on me about it. This was really fun to watch you perform. And the coaches seem competent enough." He had to get that last part in there, of course.

"Thanks, Dad. I'm so glad you made it to watch me." Cal's smile was so wide it almost wrapped around his head. "I was nervous, though."

"Well, I couldn't tell." Richard put his hand on his son's shoulder and asked, "So when do you find out if you made the squad?"

"They said hopefully this Friday. I sure hope they don't make me wait through the weekend," Cal declared. "It's going to be hard enough to be patient as it is."

Richard laughed at his son's eagerness and recalled himself having those same feelings at different times in his own life. "It's good for you, Cal. It will be here before you know it. Need a lift home?" he offered.

"That would be great, thanks, Dad," Cal accepted. "Can I just quickly say hi to Drake and Joe and thank them for coming? Then I'll get my things from the locker room and be right back."

Joe and Drake presented Cal with more high-fives and praises. As they walked him back up to the school, Cal expressed how appreciative he was that they were there supporting him and told them he would see them in school the next day and tell them more of how it went on the field.

The ride home was only fifteen minutes, and Cal and his dad talked nonstop about football and putting oneself out there to try new things. And they shared examples of how hard work pays off every time, one way or another. Richard even commended him on how he noticed his chores were always done and his grades hadn't suffered. Usually, his dad was all about the hard lessons and, probably unintentionally, made Cal feel like a young child. But this time, they were actually swapping stories and ideas. It was such an uplifting conversation for Cal that he was disappointed to see their driveway come into view. He sure was seeing his strict dad in a new light, and he hoped the inspirational conversation would continue through dinner as he shared his story with his mom too.

Every day, Cal checked the posting board by the locker room door just in case they had made their decisions earlier than expected. And every day, he was disappointed. Friday finally came, and he was hesitant to look and risk being let down yet again, because if the results were still not posted, it was going to be a very long weekend. The final bell of the day sounded, and Cal rushed, once again, to the locker room. The crowd of boys gathered near the locker room facing the wall revealed the fact that he was going to be finding out his fate today, no more waiting. Again, even though having his dad at tryouts had already changed their relationship for the better, he was still scared he would end up disappointing him after all.

Cal approached the crowd and eventually, as the other boys either found their names, or not, and moved on, made his way to the front and searched for *Cal Parker* anywhere on the sheets. Up and down, back and forth, his eyes scanned, he looked through each sheet of paper and didn't see his name. He told himself to look again, start over, and go slower; the other boys could wait their turn. *Cal Parker… Cal Parker…* come on… there it was! He saw his name on the paper to make the football team. He couldn't believe it. It was there! He did it! What a day this was; all he could think about now was the look in his dad's eyes when he told him.

Richard was never home before Cal, so he knew there was no

reason to rush home. His mom would be so proud of him too, but nothing like his dad; girls just don't understand. But that was ok; his mom has been there for everything else in his life.

"Calm down, silly, your pacing won't bring your father home any earlier," Diane said, trying to reason with her son. She was, as usual, moving efficiently around the kitchen from the sink to the stove to the counter, back and forth, always busy taking care of things.

Cal stopped walking around the kitchen table and took a seat. "I know, I've just never been this excited to share something with him, ever," Cal replied. After only a few seconds, he got back up and walked to the front window of the house to peer outside.

"I thought I heard his truck," Cal explained on his way back to the kitchen while his mom chuckled.

Diane placed a large bowl of cookie dough on the table and asked Cal to stir the chocolate chips in for her while he waited. "It will help keep your hands busy," she suggested.

After the cookie dough was stirred to oblivion, Diane asked Cal to wipe down the counters and table with cleaner. When he was done with that, while he had so much energy, she had him empty the dishwasher and then take some trash out to the street. He hadn't complained once, or even made a face or noise suggesting he was being put out; he was too focused on the wonderful news he was going to be sharing with his dad.

Unfortunately for her, Diane's fun with her preoccupied son's mind finally came to an end when they both heard the garage door jolt open. Cal ran through the house towards the door that joined the house with the garage, but then halted just before grabbing the doorknob. He didn't want to bombard him; if he had had a bad day, the news would be wasted and turned into something negative. He also thought quickly if he had left anything unattended that he should've known better not to; with all his attention on one thing, it wouldn't have surprised him if he had been forgetful about something. That would ruin what was supposed to be a great night as well.

The garage to house door flung open, and Cal could tell his dad was in a hurry. Richard looked intently at his son as soon as he spotted him. *Was he really in a hurry to see me?* Cal wondered.

"So? Did you find out?" Richard probed. "I've been wondering all day." He looked like he had ants in his pants.

Cal couldn't believe it. He'd been on his dad's mind *all day*! He had never heard those words before and had never seen his dad so impatient like this. He couldn't imagine now, if he'd had to tell him bad news, how awful that would have been.

"I made it, Dad!" Cal exclaimed, and he flung his arms around his dad's neck.

Richard returned his son's hug with a solid fierceness and picked him up off the ground, though he wasn't a little boy anymore. He let Cal down, put a hand on each of his son's shoulders, bent down a bit to look more directly in his eyes, and smiled.

"Son, I'm so proud of you. Both your mom and I are," Richard said. "You've put on some weight too. I can tell you've been hitting the gym hard." Standing back up straight, he squeezed Cal's bicep and roughly patted his arm the way a father would to a son. Cal flexed his arms playfully for his dad to confirm his hard work.

The three of them talked enthusiastically through dinner about his game schedule, again about how his chores and schoolwork hadn't suffered, and about other interests he had for his future. Cal was also thoughtful enough to inquire about each of their days as well, and surprisingly, he found himself truly interested and even asked additional questions. He learned interesting things about his parents that he never knew before, and hadn't thought to ask.

Unsurprisingly, he was so pumped up, Cal had a hard time falling asleep that night.

CHAPTER 12

Joe and Cal were leaning on their bicycles at the edge of town, waiting on Drake to head out to their fort. Joe was pestering Cal to give up the news if he had made the football team or not, but Cal resisted. He thought it only fair to tell them at the same time, so he changed the subject.

"I brought a surprise," he hinted to Joe while squinting down the street in hopes of seeing a tiny version of Drake appearing at any moment.

Joe's eyes widened, and he smiled at Cal. "What is it?" he inquired. "Or do I have to wait for Drake for that too?"

Cal pulled some firecrackers out of his backpack that sat on the ground next to his front bike tire. "What do you think of these?"

"Oh, man, that's so awesome. How'd you get those?" Joe asked, putting out a hand to grab them from his friend.

Pulling them back, Cal denied his friend access to them just yet. "I was in the garage with my dad the other day, helping him clean some stuff out, and we found these. Well, things have been going so good between us lately, he said I could have them. He didn't even tell me to be careful," answered Cal before returning them to his backpack.

"Drake is going to pee his pants; he's going to want to blow up everything in sight," said Joe with a laugh. "Well, even though your dad didn't warn you, those are dangerous, so we are going to have to be careful, especially with Drake, who doesn't always think things through." He looked at Cal warily, maybe with a little jealousy too because he wouldn't let him touch them.

Cal nodded his head. "Yeah, I know. There isn't much to wreck out there, outside of the shack, so we should be good. And as long as we don't start a forest fire either. Good thing it's been rainy lately. The trees and grass aren't too dry."

"Good thinking. So the only thing we really need to worry about is hurting ourselves," added Joe. He took off his baseball cap, ran his hand through his hair, and then returned his cap to his head. "I think we've all dealt with enough fireworks over the years that we know how to handle them, though."

"There he is," stated Cal, pointing down the street. Joe looked, and sure enough, he saw his friend cycling toward them and growing larger with every second.

As soon as Drake was within shouting distance, he yelled, "So did you make the team?"

Cal smiled, and he couldn't wait one more second. He nodded his head and yelled back, "Yep, I did it! I'm on the football team, guys."

Drake punched his fist up in the air, but it was just at the wrong time as he hit a large enough stone to put him off balance, and he went hurling sideways off his bicycle to the rough pavement, rolling a few times after he hit. The other two hurriedly peddled toward him to see if he was ok. It had looked like a major crash, but before they reached him, Drake was already back on his feet and examining his bike for damage.

"Are you ok?" asked Joe once he and Cal reached Drake. They stopped their bikes and examined him as much as he was looking over his bike.

Drake took a second to answer; he was too concerned about the condition of his bike. Joe took this as a good thing. If he were truly hurt, the pain would be breaking his concentration on the inanimate object.

"This was not a good way to start our weekend. Yes, I think I'm good, and luckily, my bike seems alright too, just a couple scratches." He brushed some pebbles off his knees and elbows while looking for blood. Then, remembering what caused the accident in the first place, he exclaimed to Cal, "You made the team!" and almost tackled him with a hug. "Nice work, man!"

"What did your dad say?" asked Joe, smiling and then taking his turn to hug his friend after gently laying his bike down. "No wonder you got fireworks."

Drake's head almost swiveled off his neck as he turned quickly to Cal. "What?! You brought fireworks?! No way! Woohoo!" he yelled, jumping in the air. "Let me see them," he commanded.

"Let's wait until we're out there. Let's go," Cal said, and he got back on his bike. He started peddling quickly to prevent being stopped and they wouldn't waste more time. He just wanted to get to out in the woods and start their weekend instead of standing in the middle of the street. He was glad he had only showed them the firecrackers and not the bottle rockets and fountains; they would've been standing there forever. He looked behind him after a minute to confirm Drake and Joe were, of course, following and trying to catch him.

The terrain turned from pavement to gravel, then to dirt, and finally to grass before they made it close to their hideout. That steady ground change always made them feel a bit like time was going backwards and like the world was becoming more just theirs. Upon reaching their destination, they unpacked their belongings first thing, like always, but this time they were in an extra hurry, especially Drake. He wanted to get his hands on those little explosives. He was respectful enough to wait until all the chores were done before asking to see the fireworks again, so once the firewood bin was full and the food was stored, he inquired about them.

"Cal, are we finally ready to have some fun yet?" he practically begged. "Come on."

"Sounds awesome to me. I've been itching to get into those too," Cal replied while just finishing putting his bedroll out. "Joe, do you know where the lighter is?" he inquired.

A grinning Joe grabbed the little plastic flame generator from the counter and motioned to head outside. Cal grabbed his backpack and followed him through the front door with Drake quick on their heels. They walked some ways from the building, nearer the creek for safety. Hunching on the ground, Cal dug into his bag and pulled out the firecrackers, and then he revealed the bottle rockets and fountains.

"We need to save these," he said, holding up the fountains, "for later, when it's dark."

Drake made a squealing sound like a little girl. "You've got more than firecrackers?! Oh my gosh, I'm so excited!" When realizing he was being overdramatic, he toned down his enthusiasm. "Do we only have one lighter? I guess we'll just have to take turns," he finished in a deeper, gruff voice.

Clueless to Drake's emotional recovery, Joe concluded, "That will make them last longer, but we really should have more than one lighter out here. I didn't think of that." He made a mental note to get a couple more for next time. He was also a little disappointed in himself for not thinking of it before. If the lighter broke or was used up, the mishap could really change their weekend with the limited options available. Of course it wouldn't be a matter of life and death, but fire was definitely close to a necessity, giving them both warm meals and beds.

"Me first," said Cal excitedly, "since they are mine and all," he teased. Joe handed him the lighter, and he separated the bundles of firecrackers to get singles; if they blew up multiples, the fun would be over way too quickly. Cal took a few steps away from his friends and the rest of the fireworks, held one firecracker in his left hand, flicked the lighter with his right hand, and joined the two together, lighting the thin fuse. He held it for a few seconds, and just before it was about to explode, he threw it into the air with the intent of it blowing up before it hit the ground. Sure enough, the little explosive produced a sharp, loud pop midair, causing the boys to cheer and holler.

Drake was chuckling at the anticipation of himself causing such a ruckus, so he helped himself to the stash of firecrackers and asked for the lighter from Cal. He had grabbed two of the little explosives, and he twisted their fuses together while taking a few steps away from his friends and lit them. He paused, holding the smoldering firecrackers in his hand, and then hastily threw them into the air, higher than Cal had. *Pop, pop* went the loud noisemakers, and they all cheered again.

It was Joe's turn. He enthusiastically closed in on Cal's pile of dangerous fun, took one single firecracker, and walked to the spot the other two had lit theirs. Drake and Cal watched as Joe dug a little hole in the ground, stuck the firecracker in the hole, standing it on end, and lightly pushed the dirt back around it so just the fuse was sticking out of the ground. He lit it and joined his friends in the "safe" area ten feet away. Shortly after being lit, the little mine exploded and threw dirt and smoke up into the air, causing a lot more cheering, clapping, and laughing between the buddies.

The three young men enjoyed finding new ways to blow up a few more before deciding they should save the rest for later that night and the next day. They were getting hungry, as boys often do, so it was time to see about catching their dinner again.

After gathering up their fishing poles, bait, and a snack they found themselves at the creek performing a much quieter activity.

"So you didn't answer me earlier when I asked what your dad said when you told him you made the football team," Joe said while they waited for their dinner to bite.

Cal smiled. "He was so happy. He said he had been wondering all day. Crazy huh? I was sure glad I could give him good news, not bad."

"Don't you think he would've been happy either way?" Drake asked.

Cal nodded, beaming. "Yeah, but this was way better!" he answered with an emphasis on the word *way*. He talked a bit about his game and practice schedules. Joe and Drake congratulated him again and voiced how excited they were to see him in action.

"I'm too antsy to fish today. I'm going to shoot off a couple bottle rockets," Joe announced, and he reeled in his line.

Cal shook his head. "It's only been fifteen minutes, man."

"I know, I'm just not feeling it," Joe informed them. "I'll go a ways off, so I don't spoil your chances of catching fish, though."

"Ok, well, don't shoot them all, save some for us," Cal ordered and then focused his attention back on his line in the water.

Joe snatched four bottle rockets out of the supply, along with the lighter, and proceeded to the jar designated for such activity. He steadied the first one into the tall, slender glass container, making sure it was pointing in the right direction, and carefully lit the fuse. Hurrying to what he figured was a safe but short distance away, he turned to see the results of his actions. Nothing. It should have gone off by now. He waited. There was no smoke coming from the fuse area.

115

Well, that was anticlimactic, Joe thought. Cautiously, he approached the jar and rocket, and as he reached down to inspect the dud bottle rocket, he almost inaudibly heard Drake say something, so he turned his head to see what he was saying, and just before he was able to seize the firework, it suddenly exploded. He jumped back in surprise; there was a loud ringing in his right ear, and he smelled smoke. *Oh no,* he thought, *how bad is this going to be?* Instinctively, he gently touched his right hand to his right ear, but the sensation in both body parts was abnormal. He couldn't discern anything and feared that couldn't be good. He slowly pulled his hand back down in front of his face to examine it, and there wasn't any blood, so he dropped to the ground in relief and exhaustion. However, his hand was badly burned; he found char marks on his palm and red splotches on the tips of his fingers. Joe sat on the ground a bit bewildered; he was in disbelief that the accident even happened, that he hadn't been careful enough, besides trying to recover from the shock of the unexpected blast.

Drake was the first to reach him, with Cal only a few steps behind as he did not see what happened. They inspected Joe and reassured him that his "ringing ear," besides being a little red, was just fine. His right hand had taken the brunt of the explosion. Luckily, he hadn't actually grabbed the firework due to being distracted by Drake. Since the injury was a burn, Cal decided dunking it in the cold stream would be helpful before applying any type of first aid; this would clean it up a bit too and get any shrapnel off the wound. Afterwards, they led the dazed Joe inside the shack, and Cal quickly retrieved the first aid kit while Drake sat him down at the table.

Taking a clean dishrag from the corner counter, Drake very gently dried Joe's hand so that Cal could apply antibiotic cream, gauze, and a bandage to keep the damaged area clean.

Joe was extremely glad when they were done fussing with his hand because it was really starting to hurt.

"Is there pain medication in there," Joe asked, pointing to the first aid kit.

Cal quickly rummaged through the kit and found a couple of packets of medicine. "Yes. Here you go. I'll get you some water."

"How are you?" asked Drake. "What else do you need?" He felt helpless watching his friend suffer.

Joe took a second to answer, looking puzzled. "I think I'm fine. It just hurts pretty bad. I think I'm still in shock a little," he concluded.

"Should we go back to town?" asked Cal.

"Oh, I don't think it's that bad. Let's wait to see how it feels once the medicine kicks in; I don't really want to leave," answered Joe.

Drake added sternly, "We'll keep an eye on it. And at the first sign of infection, I'm putting you on my back and carrying you into town if I have to. No arguments."

Well, that image made Joe laugh and eased the pain. "I'm lucky to have you two to take care of me. I bet I'll be almost as good as new by tomorrow, though, thanks to you guys." He was quiet for a second, reflecting. "It's so crazy, the stupid thing wasn't even smoking. I have no idea how it blew me up."

"I think we'll leave those fireworks alone for a while," said Cal. "And be even more careful next time we shoot them off too."

The day had grown dark during the mock emergency room visit, so they decided to just eat the dry food they had brought. With a third of them out of commission, they were prevented from doing some of their usual after-dinner activities, so they sat around telling jokes and funny bonding stories until they

117

crashed for the night. As tired as they were from the commotion, none of them slept very well that night, Joe from the pain and Drake and Cal from worry.

In the morning, they examined Joe's hand again and found it to be looking worse. It wasn't infected; it just looked worse. It was redder and oozing puss, but they had all had enough injuries in the past to know that this was the healing process. Joe made a mental note to replenish the first aid kit the next time they came – he had been lucky they'd had one in the first place – and maybe even add some items to it to be ready for if anything worse ever happened.

CHAPTER 13

A few of John's co-workers invited him out on the town with them. It was a Friday afternoon, and three women and two men were irritatingly gabbing in the hallway near the restrooms about making plans to see a live band at a little bar downtown that evening. John was just grabbing a quick snack from the office vending machine when he overheard the conversation they were having. He wished he was aware of what he did to look pathetic enough for them to think he wanted to be invited because he would be sure to not replicate the error. He hadn't even looked at them, neither as he passed nor while he was deciding on which snack to enjoy; it was just the wrong timing apparently, and his bad luck. This is what he got for being so absentminded to run out of his trusty sunflower seeds and have to look for a salty alternative. John quickly but cordially declined but made a mental note as to which nightclub they were to be patronizing. Maybe he could turn his bad luck to his advantage.

When he got back to his desk, he opened his new bag of chips, inserted one into his mouth, enjoyed the crunchy saltiness, and accessed the particular nightclub building's blueprints online. There were two exits, one single-door exit on the side of the building near where the stage would be and a double-door main entrance/exit at the other end of the room. A little more research returned to him that the maximum occupancy of the establishment was 250 people. John sat back in his office chair and smiled as he put another potato chip into

119

his watering mouth. He now understood the fate of his whereabouts, being exactly where he was when he was, for his co-worker's night out conversation and unexpected invitation. He was definitely no longer annoyed; quite the contrary. The only unfortunate element now was time. There was little of it to properly and safely organize a successful event, but his mind was already formulating various options.

Because the locale was a public place as well as public event, John being there would not be out of the ordinary or suspicious. For once, he wouldn't have to be nearly as discreet as usual, and he welcomed that aspect of his plan. Another easy component would be the accelerant; if he knew anything about mass crowds in small places looking to have a good time, there would be plenty flammable liquid spilled at everyone's feet. One dire side effect was that he'd have to wait through too much of the show, which was most likely horrible music and awful entertainment, before there would be ample liquid to cause the uproar he desired. And showing up late would be a suspicion-causing move, so that wasn't an option. However, he could help the condition along and donate some drinks to the cause; there would be plenty of alcohol in stock.

Another convenient aspect to this event was, if he felt anything could go wrong, he would just leave without completing his task. Since there should be no setup preparation, he wouldn't be leaving anything behind. The only supplies he needed was a lit cigarette or matchbook and his own drinks to spill to activate the fire. It would be disappointing to have to leave without an exquisite end result, but he wouldn't be suspected of any wrongdoing, and that was his number one rule. Period.

John felt he had a very good head-start on his event by the time his workday, which had transformed into a play day, was over. He really wanted to scope out the joint on his way home, but he just couldn't risk the individual attention that might bring. The whole event idea was exciting him more and more the closer it got and the more preparation he did; it was such a small space with such a large crowd and limited access to saving your own life by either not being burned or trampled. The comparison between the chance of success of the event to the time he would spend planning was unbelievable; he'd never experienced such a contrast. Little work with big reward, he couldn't be happier with that equation.

Now John got impatient. This was ironic because he had initially been concerned about the lack of sufficient time to plan, but now he sat home, bored, waiting. The show didn't start for another three hours, but he was ready, more than ready. Then he started thinking about how he was going to get good photos. Quite regretfully, he couldn't quite stand outside the place with his personal camera and playfully take pictures; that would seem rude and inhumane. And that behavior equaled risk – not smart. Fantasizing now, he visualized the chaos and panic that would be ensuing inside the venue, but capturing that footage wasn't going to be an option. He would have to settle for just hearing the screams and witnessing the aftermath outside the building.

John's solution to getting decent photos for his collection was to use his professional photo equipment with much greater zoom capability. He could certainly capture adequate snapshots from a less risky distance. He realized this allowed him limited time to get to his truck before too much action happened; he didn't want to miss one moment of the fabulous cataclysm. He also wouldn't be able to hear the screams and panicked voices as well, but that was a sacrifice he was willing to make to adhere to his number one rule. Once he had gotten sufficient pictures, he might just wander up on the scene and try to get his fill of the wicked smells and sounds of distress.

Getting his photography equipment together would gladly eat up some time. John sat on his couch with his gear all over the coffee table and used the extra hours completing some past-due upkeep on his camera paraphernalia. He gently employed a blower and a microfiber cloth with lens cleaning fluid to get any smudges, lint, or dust off his lenses. A simple pencil eraser cleaned up his flash system. He put his camera in sensor-cleaning mode and carefully worked on the body sensor, eliminating any rare dust that might have accumulated there. And finally, once it was all put back together, he meticulously applied a soft cloth to wipe down the exterior from fingerprints, dust, and any other unwanted crud in the creases and cracks. The renewing sense of the spring cleaning feeling John had acquired trumped his impatience, for a little while.

John then reasoned he should probably look presentable, as someone going to a nightclub might dress, since the goal was to blend in like he was just another fan or groupie for the band. So he showered and put on some cologne and a change of clothes. A nice grey button-up shirt, as stylish a jeans as he owned, and a pair of casual loafers would do just fine. He didn't want to be uncomfortable, but he sure didn't want to stand out. He put some gel in his hair to give it a lift, took a look at the finished product, and was pleased. His attractive appearance made him wonder why he didn't go out more often, but just for a second.

It was time to go, so John swapped out his real driver's license for one of his fake ones, loaded up his equipment into his truck, and headed out in search of just the right parking spot near, but not too near, the venue. On the way, he stopped at a cash machine. One rookie mistake would be to leave an easy trail for authorities to track him down; he wasn't going to use a bank card to purchase drinks. Well, more like purchasing provisions. Not one sip of those cocktails would be passing his lips, even if being buzzed would help him get through the unbearable prelude of awful music and irritating company to his very own Armageddon.

Upon arriving to his "Destination for Fun," he found there was an empty lot across the street kitty-corner from the club; he assumed it might have held playground equipment at one time. John could easily shoot pictures through that area; besides a few trees, it was without obstacles, so he parked across the lot on the street next to another building facing the club. It was the best location, as from it, he had full view of both the side door as well as the front doors.

Munching on sunflower seeds, he eyed the building; he could see people were already lining up at the door, but as far as he could tell, none of them were his co-workers. John needed to time it just right to avoid running into them; his plan was to wait until there was no line and sneak in and keep to himself. He would also round the block and approach from the other direction so as not to be seen walking from the direction of his truck. While he waited, he ran the plans through his head one more time. He had a few ideas, any of which would work perfectly; he just had to get in and see the layout to get a sense for which would be the right strategy.

Ten minutes later, when the line was dwindling, John started his scenic-route trek to the nightclub entrance, keeping diligent watch of his surroundings, in particular for anyone who would recognize him and thwart his fun. Or at least alter his fun; he could always create a quick mini blaze-by somewhere, somehow, to make up for the loss. He would not go home empty-handed, or… empty-evented… as risky as that could be.

Just before he made it to the door, he got his ID and cover fee ready; the mustached heavy-set man in a motorcycle club t-shirt and cowboy boots accepted both without question and allowed John access to the building. *If they only knew what they had just done*, he snickered to himself.

Once inside, John moseyed off to the left side of the room in a dark corner to assess his options and tuck his faux ID securely away. The band started playing their first song after a quick monologue by the lead singer, and except for a few small tables at the rear of the room, it was standing/dancing room only. The room was customarily dark. He had been hoping for that; less light would make it much easier to nonchalantly dispense drinks to the floor. He was pleased the establishment was complying with his wishes already – yes, inadvertently, but still complying. His next deduction was that there was no smoking; utilizing a simple lit cigarette to initiate the inferno was not going to be an option. However, the floor was wood. He couldn't have been more delighted about that; the porous material would easily soak up the liquid and aid in his efforts to burn the place to the ground quickly.

Then he spotted his co-workers; they were standing huddled by a small, round table laughing and enjoying fancy, colorful cocktails. John wasn't sure if they were wearing their best attire as they didn't look too flashy to him, but it wouldn't matter; what they were wearing would be the least of their concerns by the end of the evening. Completely per his liking, they seemed too engrossed in themselves to notice he was there, but he planned to keep steady track of their movements and keep his distance from them, just in case. He assumed, after a few drinks, they would be joining the rest of the crowd on the dance floor and he could lessen his watch on them.

John journeyed to the bar and ordered a stiff drink, the

harder the better; he was anxious to start the floor soaking. There were two bartenders, and he planned to alternate between them so they wouldn't keep track of how many he'd gotten or how often he ordered them, seeing as how he wouldn't be taking the customary time to dispense of the liquid as it would be promptly dumped on the floor instead of leisurely down his gullet.

Unfortunately, he was going to have to meander his way in and out of the crowd to get the fullest saturation of the floor as he could. John set the traps in a variety of locations around the room. The first, and most important, was the puddle he made by the single rear-side door that was going to be the beginning of the blaze. The more he distributed, the easier his task became, that is until he felt a tap on his shoulder when he found what he thought was his next ideal spot to drop a liquid package. His co-workers had found him after all; he thought he had been careful, but apparently, he had not been careful enough. He slowly turned, expecting to see one of their ugly, smiling faces, and he geared up to feign niceness and surprise when, to his actual surprise, he saw that it was a large, rough-looking man he didn't know.

"Hello," John uttered warily, trying to eke out a smile.

The man did not smile back. "You're in my spot."

John replied, "Oh, sorry, man, I just wanted a better view. This band rocks."

The man only glared at John.

"You're right, I'm moving along," John quickly said, all the while slowly tipping his cup at his side and releasing the bitter fluid to the floor.

"That's right you'll be moving along. Git!" the man didn't stop moving toward John, and his eyebrows narrowed. His girl beside him took his arm; he was obviously trying to impress her. Depending on how many drinks the burly man had consumed, John was afraid the guy might follow him and attempt a fight, so he apologized again before making his move and offered to buy him a drink. The longer he stayed there causing a scene, the more likely he would be remembered, so before the guy answered, he was gone. He didn't look back until he was at the bar; he had not been followed, but the beefy guy would probably be expecting a drink, so John ordered two straight away and considered them the floor's last call for the night. It was now or nothing. Hopefully not nothing.

The band was going hard and loud, and the whole crowd was into the music, dancing and carrying on like fools. John glanced at the bouncers, who were preoccupied by a drunk couple, one of whom who didn't look like he was going to hold his dinner down much longer. John slipped into the corridor leading to the restrooms. He was alone, so he lit a match and then lit the matchbook itself. He dropped the whole book into one of the cups he had just relieved the liquid from, and after verifying the flame would not extinguish, he walked back to the dancefloor as quickly, but calmly and coolly, as he could.

No one was the wiser of his presence. John returned to the first area he'd laid liquor, towards the side/rear door, dropped to his feet as if meaninglessly attending to his shoe that may or may not have come untied, and turned the cup over onto the puddle. As much as he wanted to see the reaction of the fire to the accelerant, he quickly exited the building before he could get caught up in the devastation himself.

Once outside, John simulated the act of smoking a cigarette. That was all he was out there for as far as anyone else was concerned, nothing for them to see or assume. He pulled one out of his pocket, put it to his lips, and cupped his hands in front of his face, pretending to light it. During the time he was in the club, the daylight had receded, and he welcomed the dark cover of night. He walked slowly enough at first so as not to draw attention from anyone else outside; in that time, he was able to hear the loud music stop and catch some commotion from where he had emerged from. Then, as he discerned all the interest was on the building and not him, he dropped the cigarette and hurried back to his truck.

By the time John had gotten his camera prepared for his personal entertainment, there were already too many people than he preferred gathered outside. Some had escaped his handiwork. But then again, if no one emerged, he wouldn't have much to take pictures of, so he cheered up. The looks on their faces were not quite what he had been anticipating, but he presumed they were still more confused than comprehending the true tragedy of the situation. He clicked away anyway. There was no sign of flames yet, let alone much smoke. Worry set in that his plan had gone awry. He waited.

Quicker and quicker, with more and more urgency, the nightclub-goers emerged, stumbling out and coughing, more at the main entrance than the side. John wondered, as he'd anticipated, if there were blockages at the doors as they really weren't running out like they would with a known emergency. He wished he could be inside, beholding the panic and chaos, seeing people trampling others to save themselves, the selfish pushing and shoving and pathetic sense of superiority.

Finally, John saw the inevitable dark smoke rapidly billowing out of the building through every escape it could find and the sharp orange flames seeking the fresh oxygen of the night air. Now he heard louder screams and running, and he smiled and released a pent up breath. He stopped taking pictures for a moment to watch the happenings with his naked eye. He found that sometimes looking through the camera's viewfinder made events seem too surreal for actual reality, and he could get that just by staying home and watching the television, which he would do later once the news crews arrived and helped him with some of his footage.

Just as John started to catch the sweet aroma of smoke, he heard the fateful, disheartening sound of fire trucks coming to save the day. Even though the building was near collapse, the sign of the beginning of the end was still way too soon for his liking; of course, his liking would be them not coming at all. Happily, John could tell that all of the people from inside were not outside. He couldn't wait to hear the death toll on the news later, and he subconsciously made a prediction to see how close he would be. He fired off a few more impressive shots with his camera, put it away, and headed home feeling particularly successful. His evening had turned out to be especially fun and enjoyable for him, just what his co-workers and the other partiers had expected for themselves.

CHAPTER 14

"You have to finish your homework before you can play video games," Drake insisted to his little brother. This was the third time now he had told Huck, but his brother just wasn't listening. Drake was exhausted and getting impatient with him, so it was time to bring in the big guns.

"If Mom finds out…," he started.

Huck interrupted him, "She won't find out, not unless you tell her." He wasn't worried about getting into trouble one bit.

"Yeah, well, what am I supposed to say when she asks? And you know she'll ask," Drake responded logically.

Not once looking up from his game in session, Huck countered, "Just lie. It wouldn't be the first time. Nothing will happen."

"What do you mean nothing will happen? She'll see your grades, dummy," stated Drake blatantly.

"And I'll say the teacher didn't grade me right, dummy. Besides, she's usually too busy to even notice," Huck said without a care.

Drake had had enough. "She's gotten better lately, and besides that, I notice, and I'll tell her the truth. It matters to me and Mom." He went over to the game console and shut it off, right in the middle of Huck's game.

"Hey, what the heck? You're such a jerk!" Huck yelled at his brother. He stood up from the couch, walked up to Drake, and punched him in the gut. "That was not cool! I was in the middle of a game!"

Drake took a second to recover before hitting him back, but softer, and he said, "If you had listened in the first place, you wouldn't have lost your place in the game. You'd be done with your schoolwork and playing peacefully." Drake thought this was a very reasonable argument.

"And I probably wouldn't have asked you to help with dinner either, but now I'm going to. (He wasn't sure he was, but he wanted to get his point across.) Next time, listen to me, and I might let you do your own thing," Drake reasoned further. "Anyway, now that you're a teenager, you need to do more around here. I can't be the only one doing chores when Mom and Grandma are busy. Even Alexis helps more than you do. I'd like to sit and play games too, but you two would go hungry and fail classes in school if I did. Then where would we be?"

Huck resentfully conceded by stomping his feet with as much power as he could while leaving the living room, and the sound of his slamming bedroom door from above also confirmed his anger toward his brother, as if there was any doubt.

"It's your own fault!" Drake yelled up the stairs. He was ready to give up; he didn't need this. He shouldn't have to raise his brother and sister and, on top of that, not be respected by them.

Alexis was another issue. He really, really wanted to let their mom handle her confusing and draining girl problems, but Carol would be coming home too late, and Drake knew she would not come down to dinner, nor help with chores until she had a good cry to someone who would listen.

He knocked quietly on her bedroom door to receive the answer of a quiet, "Go away," and a sniffle. He sure wished he could. Against his better judgment, he tried again.

"Lex, its Drake. Can I come in?" he urged with as much sincerity as he could muster. Silence. *Why did she have to be so difficult,* he wondered. *Why am I trying so hard?*

"Talk to me, sis... I'm coming in," Drake grabbed the doorknob with enough motion to rattle it slightly in an effort to announce that he would be entering. He hesitated to give her time to strongly object, but no protest emanated from within, so he proceeded into her room. She was lying on her bed, on her stomach, with some sort of squashed stuffed animal underneath her and her head buried in it. When she looked up, Drake noticed her eyes were red and puffy, and teardrops had made her cheeks soggy and glistening. It suddenly broke his heart to see her that way, and he was glad he'd persisted in being her shoulder to cry on for once. The thought formed in his mind if her unhappiness might be because of a boy, and he had to stop his imagination from thinking horrible things as he found himself wanting to beat someone up. He hoped it was the usual insignificant drama that had her in a fit.

"Alright, talk to me. What's up?" Drake asked softly as he leaned up against her dresser. He wanted this to go as quickly as possible, so he got right to the point.

"You wouldn't understand," Alexis cried.

Drake thought quickly. "Well, even so, at least talking about it might help."

"You're just as bad as the rest of them." She would not give up.

"What do you mean by that? What did I do?" Drake almost got angry with her; his nerves were already at their breaking point from dealing with Huck's attitude.

Alexis looked as though she wanted to retract her statement, but she felt he deserved an explanation. "You tease people and bully people."

131

"Who teased or bullied you?" Drake demanded, feeling suddenly protective. Maybe the reason she was upset was going to be as bad as he imagined after all. He hadn't caused a fight in a long time; he might be overdue.

She didn't answer but threw her head back into the soggy stuffed animal and sobbed. He waited, watching her actions, and wondered how long she was going to take to re-acknowledge his presence. Meanwhile, he glanced around her room: she had posters of the most recent boy bands up on the walls, there was a flowery-scented candle burning on her desk, a mass of stuffed animals that didn't make the drama squad in one corner of her room, and clothes all over the floor. Girls... he sure didn't understand them.

Drake was tired of waiting. He tried a little comedy to lighten the air. "Tell me who, and I'll beat them up." Then, in the voice of the Cowardly Lion from *The Wizard of Oz*, he growled, "Put 'em up, put 'em up," while jumping around the room like a boxer. "I can take 'em," and he roared like a lion.

Alexis peeked from her hiding spot to see the show and couldn't help but smile at her brother being silly.

"You can't beat up girls, Drake!" she exclaimed.

"Oh, so there are girls giving you a hard time. I was worried it was a boy," Drake said, emphasizing the word boy and winking at her to try to take her mind off the mean girls that had caused her foul mood.

Alexis finally caved, but she still refrained from full disclosure. "Oh my gosh, no. Not a boy!" She giggled. "Just girls. They can sure say some mean things that make me feel bad. It makes it really hard to go to class, that's for sure." She sat up on the bed, hoping to see more of her brother's imitation of more characters.

"Well, they're just jealous of how pretty and smart you are, I know it," Drake proposed, aiming for a certain desired outcome that led to him gaining an exit.

Alexis blushed and shook her head. Changing the subject, she coaxed him, "Do Dorothy, do Dorothy." She bounced up and down on the bed with her legs bent at the knees underneath her. Drake granted her wish by dredging up his best girly voice and tiptoeing around her bedroom, talking about wanting to go home over and over. This was ironic because he really did want to be elsewhere, so he hoped his strategy would actually work, one way or another. When she started giggling, he gratefully figured he had succeeded.

"Try not to let them get to you. They're stupid. Now, I need your expert help with dinner. Come on," he said, playfully motioning to the door in hopes of keeping her from falling back into her depressed mood. Drake was awfully relieved when he saw she was following him. Her eyes were still puffy, but there was no trace of salty liquid on her cheeks, and her lips were now turned upwards instead of down. He had been successful and didn't even have to hear the details... perfect.

Carol had left easy meal instructions for Drake: tonight he only had to warm up leftovers. Not that he was ever required to prepare a gourmet meal in her absence, quite the contrary, but it was a nice change as it was still easier and quicker than actually making something. Besides, he had used up a lot of time in his sister's room tonight, so he especially didn't have time to chop, stir, mix, etc.

Alexis got out place settings for three while Drake heated up lasagna in the microwave. She filled each of their glasses with milk; their mom insisted they get their calcium. Plus, milk and Italian food went together splendidly; the cool, creaminess of milk perfectly countered the salty spiciness of the pasta sauce and cheese. Drake yelled up the stairs to notify Huck that dinner was ready.

"Aren't we having garlic bread too?" Huck asked as soon as he appeared in the kitchen.

Drake shook his head. "If you wanted garlic bread, you should've come down and made it yourself. Your sister and I did our share." He felt he was being a bit harsh. The preparation they did to get the meal ready wasn't all that much, nor was making garlic bread, but since his brother had been such a jerk earlier, he wasn't going to let him forget it just yet. That and he had asked in such a rude way; there was no thank you, just a negative, snide comment. Drake needed to show him he wasn't going to allow his disrespect, or it would just get worse.

"Actually, you don't have to eat what we prepared at all, since it's not up to your standards," Drake debated. "You are more than welcome to make your own food."

Huck could only grumble; he didn't have much ammunition left for the battle. With a grim frown, he slumped into his seat at the kitchen table. Drake and Alexis joined him, and they ate peacefully most of the meal, until Alexis had enough of the silence and asked if she could turn the television on. Drake was only too obliging, as absent of any other noise, the sound of chewing and plates being scraped with utensils was growing louder and louder with every tense minute.

"Huck, will you please clean up the kitchen when we're all done?" Drake asked cordially. He figured being pleasant was the best way to get what he wanted; there wasn't a lot to tidy up, but he sure didn't want to do it, and he wasn't going to leave it a mess for when his mom got home. She didn't need to deal with that after a long day at work. Huck only nodded; he still wasn't in a mature enough mood to verbally acknowledge and affirm his brother's request that he knew was actually an order. He resented any time Drake thought he could tell him what to do. He was a teenager after all; he didn't need a babysitter. He also noticed there wasn't a lot to clean up. Otherwise, he would've made a stink about being ordered around for sure. Next time.

Drake and Alexis had made themselves comfortable in the family room watching a funny home video show on television. Just as the man on the television screen, who was precariously teetering on a ladder leaned up against a house, took a misstep to the inevitable awkward and most likely painful tumble to the ground, Drake heard a toy foam bullet whiz past his head, narrowly missing his left ear. He instantly turned just to see the last of his brother disappear around the corner of the room. Huck had a foam dart blaster gun and was initiating war – game on. The bad thing was Drake did not know where the other gun was, so his mission to avoid bullets while searching for it was going to be a difficult one.

Alexis took cover behind an armchair and cheered Drake on to go get Huck back even though he had missed both of them. Drake advised her he didn't have a weapon, so she quickly informed him of the last known whereabouts, that she was aware of, of the other blaster gun.

"I'll try to get his attention so you can get out of the room to find the other gun," she whispered, and she cautiously started out of the room, expecting to get hit at any moment. Drake slipped out as he heard another cock of the gun and release of a bullet. He heard his sister squeal, followed by her announcement that he had missed her again, and then running footsteps down the hall. He hurried his pace toward where the other gun might be located and found it unharmed. Ensuring he was loaded up with bullets, he crept back towards the action to teach his brother a lesson. He wasn't sure if Huck was trying to be a nuisance or starting a fun game, but either way, he would get some shots in himself, if only to defend their sister. He stopped in the hallway just before the family room, listening for any sound that would give away Huck's location.

Just when he wanted, Alexis revealed Drake's adversary's locale, so his first shot was an easy one and right in Huck's gut, making him groan and get a shot off in Drake's direction. The foam bullet bounced off the wall behind Drake and dropped at his feet, so he picked it up for stock ammunition as he swiftly ducked into the kitchen.

"Dude, you keep missing me. You sure you want to continue waging this war?" Drake baited his brother from behind the center island. "Plus, I've got more bullets than you do."

Huck didn't answer, causing Drake to assume he didn't want to give up his location and that he was nearing him. He realized he wasn't in the best setting, as he had to look to both ends of the island to preempt an attack.

"I will get one of you once at least. I'm not giving up. One of you is going down tonight," Huck finally declared with a playful yet sinister laugh. Drake was glad he wasn't still in a foul mood; the game must've lightened his spirits.

"By my count, you only have three bullets left. Better make good use of them," Drake badgered, and then he stopped to listen intently for closing-in footsteps, but he heard nothing. He had to make his own move, if only to achieve a better vantage point. Alexis must've been hiding too well now to aid in their combat, as she was silent too. He decided to quickly stand with his gun at the ready and shoot anything that moved as soon as he could, hoping to throw off Huck. *One… two… three!* and up he hurriedly stood and sped out of the kitchen, finding Huck in the hallway where he had been previously peering in the other direction, so he quickly shot off two rounds before Huck was

136

able to turn. Drake believed he got one hit and one miss, and just as he was ducking for cover again as Huck now started to return the barrage, he felt a slight sting in his right shoulder. He'd been hit, so he dramatized it, acting like he was dying. He'd sacrifice the win to make his brother happy and feel victorious, and possibly end his foul attitude. He slowly fell to the floor and onto his back, groaning and whining in pretend pain.

Both Alexis and Huck came running to see if Drake really was hurt, but once they determined it was just an act, Huck put down his gun and held up his arms in triumph. His reaction was just what Drake was anticipating, as he still had four bullets since he'd shot off three and had an extra he'd reloaded. Once Huck's attention was completely diverted, Drake unloaded the remaining bullets at him, laughing while Alexis cheered.

"Aw man!" Huck yelled as he quickly shied away from the onslaught, trying to protect his most sensitive parts with his hands. "Nicely played, brother, nicely played," he pronounced once the gunshots were over. He went to help Drake up off the floor but tricked him back and decided to tackle him instead. They wrestled around good-naturedly until they were both breathing heavy and tired.

Once Huck regained his breath, he suggested, "Ice cream sounds good. Do you guys want some?" He proceeded to get some bowls and spoons out. Drake realized he was going to serve them and was pleased to see that maybe something had clicked with Huck, or at least, that this was his way of apologizing. Whatever the reason, he gladly accepted it because this was a much better way to end the evening than the miserable way it had started.

CHAPTER 15

"Well, maybe before we get too carried away, we should research what type of dangers we may need protection *from,*" Joe suggested as he worriedly eyed the ever-growing items in their shopping cart. The three young lads were at the local hardware store filling a cart with various tools that they supposed would be suitable defense weapons against the somewhat fictitious threatening creatures of the forest around their getaway home. "I don't think we can afford all of this anyway. Or even get everything into our backpacks."

From behind the cart, Drake broke out of his "kill or be killed" mentality and sized up the overflowing cart as well; then he looked at the mighty sledgehammer in his right hand that he was barely able to even pick up off the rack and broke out laughing. With each addition to their artillery, an even greater dangerous beast was imagined, and they easily lost track of the real purpose of the weapons.

"I don't even think I can wield this!" he finally was able to express once his giggling subsided, and he carefully returned the heavy metal-headed stick to its resting place on the wall of the shopping aisle. "I guess we better get to returning more of these things as well, as much as it saddens me." The gleam in his eyes had disappeared with the newfound realization they would not be leaving the store with all the fun toys they wanted.

Their haul currently consisted of a shovel, hammers, a screwdriver set, saws, a pry bar, and a large and small axe, besides restocking items such as some more rope, flashlights, matches and lighters, duct tape, and nails, along with other odds and ends. They argued with their pocketbooks that these items were not merely for fun or protection. They could come in very handy in multiple other situations as well; fixing up things in the cabin and work outside were never-ending. However, their funds were indeed limited and could not be budged or bribed, so for now, they put back most of the items, leaving only the essentials like matches and a few small weapon-like items for emergencies. The shovel, pry bar, saws, and large axe had to be left behind, very regrettably as they had each already envisioned plans for the items.

His friends' gloomy faces told tales of great disappointment and squashed dreams, so Cal attempted to restore their excitement by suggesting they all check their own homes and garages for replacements of the unfortunately rejected items, as long as their parents wouldn't notice them missing and commence with ill-fated interrogations.

"Also, not getting everything we want right now will give us something to look forward to when we've made more money," Cal continued, trying to appease them. Being a naturally logical thinker, Joe agreed and nodded, but Drake was harder to satisfy, and they had a hard time encouraging him to leave the store without the irresistible gadgets he desired.

Once outside, in the chilly breeze and under a cloud-covered sky, they divvyed up their cool new gear to stuff it into each of their backpacks, straddled their bicycles, and rode off towards Cal's house to assess their new supplies and update their stock list. It was too late in the day to transport everything to its new home now, but they were hoping to make a quick trip tomorrow. Joe's family was having a birthday party for his little brother Sammy, so they couldn't stay out there all day, but he hoped he could sneak away for a little bit and not have to spend the whole day helping prepare the house for guests.

Upon reaching Cal's house, they found his dad, Richard, in the backyard sprucing things up, and no sign of his mom, Diane, so the mission was quite effortless to sneak their new loot to Cal's bedroom without suspicion. Hopefully, they would be able to remove the evidence from the premises as soon as tomorrow, but it still seemed like a long time to wait with the threat of being found out and, subsequently, their freedom abruptly ending. Joe had brought up a few times over the last few years the idea of just telling their parents about their fort, but the other two didn't want to risk it.

The boys emptied the treasure from their backpacks onto Cal's bed and started unwrapping ties, opening boxes, and removing items from plastic packaging containers. It was like Christmas, except they did this on their own; they had each worked hard doing odd jobs to be able to acquire these tools and weapons so that they could take care of themselves at their own place. It was a very liberating feeling, not needing their parents or having to ask permission.

"I think we picked out a very good axe here," Drake commented as he inspected it with a grin. "We should be able to cut up some of those big branches that are too big for the fireplace now." He proceeded to motion as if chopping something on the floor. "It fits my hand like a glove," he finished.

Cal replied, "Great, you can do the chopping then." He winked at Joe, expecting some retaliatory comment from Drake. He had just gotten the package of screwdrivers open and was inspecting them as the smooth, shiny silver metal glistened in his hands.

"Oh, come on, I'm sure you two would love to get your

hands on this too," Drake retorted, "but sure, if that means I get to use it most of the time, I'm game." He dramatized his earlier chopping action. "Maybe I'll be the axe superhero," he said with a laugh.

Joe quickly stated, "Be careful, Drake. As fun as these are, they are not toys."

"Joe, the ever-careful party pooper," said Drake, feeling deflated. He rubbed his thumb sideways against the sharp edge of the axe.

"Hey, I'm not trying to take the fun out of it. It's just that I'm always the one who gets hurt," Joe defended himself. "That is a sharp, serious tool you have. Thanks for understanding that I just want us all safe," he finished with a bitter tone.

Cal added, "Getting hurt would be a lot more of a downer than us just being a little more careful with riskier tools, Drake."

Drake ignored them, feeling a bit like he was being scolded. He was being careful; they didn't need to tell him that, so he changed the subject.

"So we're planning on heading out there tomorrow? When can you guys go?" he inquired, trying to cover up what he felt was a blatant insult with excitement.

Cal answered first, "I think, first thing, the sooner we get these things out of here, the better." He glanced at their loot, looking a bit worried about being found out.

"I agree," Joe confirmed, "and less of a chance of me getting stuck doing stupid party stuff; I'll try to get out before my mom gives me stuff to do, but I probably can't stay gone too long, or she'll be mad."

The three boys repacked their backpacks with their new belongings, placed them in the bedroom closet, and covered them with a few clothes and a blanket to disguise the heap. Cal ensured the pile didn't look too messy, or not only would their fort adventures cease to exist, but his chances of continuing his football career would as well. He was glad their parent-unapproved loot wouldn't be in there for long.

Drake showed up at Cal's just after dawn, which very much surprised Cal, and his parents, who were still in bed themselves, because Drake loved his sleep. There wasn't much he would get out of bed for, especially that early; it was usually Cal and Joe dragging him out of bed for whatever important plans they had on a certain day. Cal hoped the change wasn't due to some drama at home.

"Hey Cal, are we ready to go? Is Joe here?" he asked. "Is the stash secure?" he followed up with a whisper.

Cal shook his head and responded quietly, "No, Joe hasn't showed up yet. We should go get him. Between the two of us, we should be able to carry his pack, I'm sure." While Cal distracted his parents by telling them goodbye, promising to not be gone all day, and grabbed his jacket after his mother reminded him to, Drake snuck up to his room to obtain the three backpacks, and they were on their bikes heading to Joe's in no time.

The crisp morning air dusted their faces with a fresh, cool breeze as they peddled. The peacefulness was the perfect addition to their sense of freedom, compelling them to peddle even faster, and they grinned at each other as they rode. Cal had taken the extra load of Joe's pack, but with his strenuous football workouts, it wasn't hard to keep up with Drake.

There was an extra car parked outside Joe's house, which caused the two arrivals concern that the birthday party preparation had already begun. Drake put on a rather pouty face.

"Don't tell me I got up early for nothing," he scowled.

Cal remained optimistic, saying, "Maybe they came last

night and are still in bed." But the front door opened before they were even off the street, and Joe came sulking out with slumped shoulders and an even more pouty face than Drake's. Cal and Drake didn't need explanation; they just knew by the look in Joe's eyes that he was already a hostage for the day.

"At least it isn't a weekend that you're missing; we won't be out there long, Joe," Cal persisted, trying to maintain the upbeat energy however hard it was becoming.

Drake wasn't giving up that easily. "We're not even going to be out there that long. You can't just get away for a bit?"

"Sorry guys, believe me, I tried everything. My mom just can't do it all by herself anyway…" Joe trailed off, looking tired and something the other two hadn't seen in him before. His worn appearance seemed as if he had aged a few years since last night. "It's ok, you guys go. Get us set up for next time."

Drake fought back even though he knew it was useless to combat the inevitable. "We've just never been out there without all three of us before; I don't like it." He stared at the ground beside his bicycle and kicked the dirt with the toe of his shoe. "Maybe we should wait until we can all go."

"I'm not keeping this stuff in my bedroom any longer than I have to," Cal protested. "If we get found out, I'm off the football team, and I won't be happy."

"Alright, alright," Drake said, shaking his head. "You're right. I just don't like it."

Joe felt a little relieved that his friends were giving in and not making his absence a big deal as he felt bad he was causing a bit of a riff. On the other hand, it sure made him feel good that Drake was so disappointed by it.

"It won't be long, and we'll all be out there again having a weekend of it," Joe promised. "I should probably get back inside before they realize I'm not helping." As cheerfully as he could pretend, he gave his friends high fives and sauntered back behind the front screen door of his prison for the day. As much as he knew his mom needed his help, he wasn't mature enough to not feel the invisible heavy shackles around his ankles. Joe watched his friends until they turned the corner and were out of his sight; then he took another minute of feeling sorry for himself that he was not on his bicycle as well and enjoying some relaxing fun before regretfully returning to his tasks.

Cal and Drake took turns carrying Joe's backpack on the way to their fort. They weren't in near as much of a hurry anymore since neither of them had anything to get back to, so the extra load wasn't noticeably slowing them down. However, Joe's absence practically yelled at them with every minute that ticked by, and once they had reached the area where they had to ditch their bicycles, Cal conveyed his disappointment.

"You're right, I don't like this either," Cal finally professed. "It is so weird with just the two of us." He was trotting along beside his friend, halfway to the shack.

Drake nodded. "Such BS that he couldn't come, just for a bit. I seriously don't think they have *that* much party stuff to do. Really?!" He didn't look up from his feet as he hiked, in fear he'd trip over a branch or rock or the like. "There is no way I'll ever stay out here without one of you. It has to be all three of us or nothing," he concluded, feeling very "Musketeerish."

"Here, here!" added Cal, sensing the same feeling. The agreement between them helped lighten their sullen, bitter moods, and once they reached their hideaway a short time after, they actually enjoyed themselves finding homes for their new gear.

CHAPTER 16

The waiting room stunk like antiseptic, and it turned Joe's stomach. The soft classical music coming from the ceiling seemed out of place. Of course, the reason they were there didn't help. He was nervous and unsure. As much as his parents had explained everything and reassured him and his brothers and sister, the communication hadn't helped. They were still there. It was a reality that his mom was sick. And it wasn't just a cold or flu that she was going to get over soon either. As much as he wanted to get out of that uncomfortable waiting room, being called back behind that big swinging door beside the reception desk looked even more ominous to him.

Gail had asked her son to accompany her to her first chemotherapy treatment appointment. Joe was initially more than happy to be asked, but as he sat there with her hand in his while they waited anxiously, he questioned her choice. Ryan would've been able to handle the position better since he was older, or Leslie's feminine side should've been more comforting to their mom, he reasoned. But there he was, not sure of what to do or say to ease the moment for him or his mom.

"Mom," he questioned her quietly, "how are you?" Joe attempted to take his mind off himself to be strong for her.

Gail looked at him apprehensively. "Well, I'm a little scared if you want to know the truth. And a little angry too."

This answer surprised Joe; it was not what he expected. "I'm sorry, Mom. We'll get through this," he said, trying to comfort her but not knowing what else to say. He wanted to share his

147

feelings with her too but supposed it would just add to her stress. She didn't need to be concerned about his emotional state at this time.

"You're not angry with *me*, are you," Joe asked carefully and quietly.

Gail chuckled. "No, son, not with you, with this stupid disease." She finished with a huff, put her arm around him, and pulled him in for a half hug. "But thanks for lightening the mood a bit. I'm so grateful you're here with me, I'm sure it's not easy for you either, so thank you, Joey." She hadn't called him that in years, and it made his throat tighten up. He told himself to think of something else lighthearted before they both lost it, but before he could conjure up a joke, a lady in a white lab coat holding a clipboard emerged from the swinging door and called his mom's name. Joe felt his mom tighten her grip on his hand before rocking forward to stand up, and he followed her lead, a little disappointed in himself for not leading her into it instead.

They followed the petite nurse down a bright, plain hallway to a row of empty infusion chairs with medical equipment surrounding each. The nurse then motioned to a certain chair and politely asked Gail to have a seat, and then she informed Joe that the chair beside his mom's was for him. They both apprehensively took their assigned seats, and the nurse began taking Gail's vitals, explaining what she was doing and how the next hour was going to go. Since it was her first session, the medication part was only going to take 30 minutes, but they needed to stay a while afterwards to ensure she would have no adverse reactions. Then the sessions would more than likely get longer and longer, depending on the results.

While Joe and his mom waited for the medication to work its magic, they chatted about life, and as the minutes ticked by, Joe started appreciating this special, however unfortunate, time they were sharing. Gail let her son in on how she was feeling about her diagnosis, and additionally how she viewed her future. It was an eye-opener for Joe. He had always pictured his parents being so strong, that they didn't worry about anything. Adults were supposed to have everything figured out with the right answer for any situation. The uncertainty in her voice scared him, but at the same time it made him feel closer to her.

"You're old enough to know that life isn't all about sugar and sunshine," Gail said to her son. "No big surprise, huh? So I'm just going to put it all out there because I'd rather you be aware of the truth. It will be easier in the long-run."

Joe was listening intently. Her sentiments made him feel like she trusted him and that she didn't view him as a child, yet he was afraid of what she was leading up to.

"The doctors are pretty certain that this is a fast-advancing type of cancer," she explained, looking from her lap to her son and back again. "They are trying to be helpful and encouraging, but I can tell, I can see it in their eyes, they don't really know how long I have. They're not even sure this chemo is going to do much good. But I have to try. I think of you kids and your dad, and I have to try."

Joe didn't want to be an adult. He wanted her to take the words back and not invite him to go with her today. He felt the tears welling up in his eyes. When Gail saw this, she grabbed a tissue, handed it to him, and then grabbed one for herself as her eyes were glistening now too. They were alone; otherwise, she wouldn't have chosen this time to talk with her son about something so dreadfully unhappy.

"Mom, I don't like this. I don't know if I can do it," Joe said, countering her attack on his emotions. "You have to get over this. I don't have anyone to take care of me like you do." He

149

wanted to stand up and throw things around, but he knew she didn't deserve that and the irrational actions would only upset her. He hung his head down, and a couple tears squeezed by his eyelids to the shiny tile floor.

"Joe, you are growing up so fast," Gail said softly. "You are stronger than you know. I can see it. I need you to be strong for me too because sometimes I'm not sure I can do this." Her voice cracked with the last word.

Joe was shocked at how candid she was being with him. Maybe that's what broke him out of his "poor me" mindset, or maybe the smell finally got to him, or maybe he realized that his mom was not actually immortal, but he suddenly felt tough. Suddenly the words came, and he reassured the both of them.

"Everything is going to be fine, one way or another. It just has to be," he began, nodding. "I'm sure there are lots of options, and aren't there doctors out there working on cancer research constantly?" His eyes had dried out, and the lump in his throat was gone. "We'll just keep a positive attitude and fight through this, together, all of us. I'll help out more at home, and I can get Ryan, Leslie, and Sammy on track too. I can study up on cancer and educate the family. Then it won't seem so scary, because the unknown can be the worst."

Gail's eyes lit up, and she beamed so proudly at her son.

"I knew that was in you," she said. "That's what I needed to hear. Thank you, Joe. We'll still have our scared times, when we feel like giving up, but I already feel better knowing you're on my side."

Joe was ashamed of himself for letting her, for one minute, think he wouldn't be on her side. He'd almost let the cancer get the better of him. Being mad at the disease would only upset his mom, which was not to say that he would never get angry about the situation again; he just won't do it in her presence.

She needed a positive environment if she was going to beat it, and he would make sure their family understood that too.

Just then, the nurse came back. She was not alone but was leading another two people into the chemotherapy room. A woman and what looked like her son, maybe a few years younger than Joe, were guided to their own infusion chairs for the day, next to Joe and his mom, so their intimate conversation was over. Joe felt that was sweet: two sons supporting their moms, but when the boy climbed into the patient's chair instead of the woman, Joe and his mom looked at each other sadly and a bit shocked. It was then that they grasped how thin he was and the dark circles under his bright eyes. Once the nurse left, they introduced themselves.

"Hi there. I'm Gail, and this is my son Joe," she informed them.

The woman smiled at them and graciously responded, "Good afternoon. This is Peter and I'm his mom, Rachel." Joe noticed she looked tired.

"Nice to meet you," Gail said, maybe too passionately. Realizing this was not ideal circumstances to meet people, she wanted to uplift the feeling in the room. She started in about the weather before Joe cut her off.

"How long have you had cancer?" Joe asked Peter bluntly.

"Joe!" Gail tried to correct him. "That's not any of our business. I'm sorry…," she said, starting to apologize to Rachel, who didn't look the least bit fazed.

"Well, we're here aren't we?" Joe explained, shrugging his shoulders. "Why ignore the obvious? Maybe we could help each other."

Peter grinned at Joe and answered him forthwith, "Ever since I can remember. It comes and goes, but mostly I have it every day." He was liking the attention; usually, it was pretty stuffy in this room.

"So you're a pro at this, huh?" Joe asked, nodding and giving Peter a thumbs-up.

Peter's grin grew even brighter. "Yes, I can tell ya anything ya need to know!" He felt famous all of a sudden.

"I don't know how he does it," Rachel said, shaking her head. "He's always in a good mood; I'm exhausted, and I'm not the one in the chair."

"Oh, Mom, stop worrying about me," Peter said. "I'm fine, and now I've got friends." He smiled at Gail and Joe. "Do you come here often? I haven't seen you before. Maybe we'll see you other times now. Do you like chess? My mom's not a fan of it, but I am, but I'm not very good. Maybe we can play next time."

Joe felt like he had pulled the string on a talking toy monkey. Peter was talking so fast he couldn't remember if he'd asked him more than one question. He giggled and answered that he had never played before and suggested Peter teach him how. Well, that was great news to Peter. He'd found not only a new chess opponent, but one he could show how to play too.

The nurse returned just then and advised Gail she was done with her treatment and proceeded to release her arm's vein from being pumped with the vicious drug. They were instructed to stay put for at least fifteen minutes for possible side-effect observation and provided juice and cookies.

This gave Peter time before they left to plan their next visit. He notified Joe that he would bring his chess set next time, and maybe some of his favorite comic books, and they could discuss superheroes, superpowers, and the like. Joe wasn't much into comics, but he didn't let Peter onto that fact. He was just too excited to bring him down at all. Joe rather enjoyed Peter's enthusiasm for life and was looking forward to their next meeting.

Gail and Joe said their goodbyes, and just before reaching the exit, they heard Rachel behind them, so they stopped and turned.

"I just wanted to thank you for being so kind to Peter. You really made his day today," she said, smiling gratefully. She shook both their hands and continued, "I hope to see you two again. I know Peter does too. He needs nice people in his life." Her voice grew thin with the last few words. Gail gave her a comforting look, put her hand on Rachel's arm, gave it a light squeeze, and nodded, wishing she could do more.

In the car on the way home, Joe mentioned to his mom how uplifting that little boy was and how infectious his optimistic attitude was. He had forgotten all about how sad and depressing cancer could be, and it gave him hope.

Gail agreed, "Yes, it sure makes you reevaluate your priorities. I feel silly for being so 'poor me' about all of this. It has been a lot to take in since it's so new, but at least I haven't had to deal with it all my life. I will always have memories of how my life was before I got sick. Little Peter doesn't have that luxury. All he'll likely ever know is living with this, having this cruel illness inside of him, the constant battle." They sat in silence, letting those thoughts sink in while watching the road quickly pass under them.

"I hope we see him again, Mom, I think we need him more than he needs us at this point," Joe stated. All Gail could do was nod her head as her eyes welled up again for the second time that afternoon, but this time it was for a much better reason.

CHAPTER 17

He needed more supplies. Besides depleting his goods when experimenting, what John Jr. had accumulated so far was turning out to be just child's play. He was almost embarrassed at his lack of stock compared to his eagerness to learn. How was he supposed to excel with such limited and novice materials, he wondered. As tired as he was of being called the dreadfully childish name Johnny, he was equally tired and bored of his same old lame chemical combinations. It was beyond time for him to go back to doing some research to reach a more exciting level of excellence.

John Jr. had been so excited last year to finally start high school so he could take chemistry and open up a whole new world. That was his vision and expectation. Unfortunately, the reality was that, not only was the curriculum utterly useless to his goals, what they were teaching was ground-level basics to him. This reality was more than disappointing, and he was forced to resort to relying on himself to be his own teacher again. Unfortunately, he still had to endure class.

First and foremost, the chemistry teacher Mr. Lande instructed the class on safety precautions and how that should always be the first thought whenever handling any chemicals, no matter how harmless they might seem based on their hazard label. Even though they wasted two whole days on the subject, John Jr. recognized it was actually a great reminder: one can never be too safe, in a variety of areas. Safety glasses, protective gloves, and a fire extinguisher were essential. As for himself,

John Jr. had ruined enough articles of clothing to ensure a lab coat was just as vital, and also a mask to prevent himself from inhaling any curious toxic fumes that might arise from his magnificent creations.

Somehow, their first lesson was even less interesting than the safety lecture. When Mr. Lande announced that they would be learning how sweating keeps a person from overheating, John Jr. had to really focus to keep from laughing. He could not believe how nonsensical that was, and why it was so important they needed to know that was beyond him. The only materials needed were an outdoor thermometer, a cotton ball, and some rubbing alcohol; he was going to have to struggle to stay awake to see what those plain ingredients had in store for him and his classmates, for sure. That class period could not have gone any slower.

The day finally came when they were getting a little closer to his style of chemistry. John Jr. was anxious, but judging from the class so far, he didn't hold much value in his expectations of it. The day before, Mr. Lande had actually used the words "chemical reactions" and "explosive" when describing today's lesson; John Jr. sure hoped his own definition of those words corresponded with his teacher's.

The first experiment was hydrogen peroxide mixed with potassium iodide. Since these were not chemicals John Jr. had played around with, he was not sure what to expect. Of course, they couldn't do too much damage, or they wouldn't be allowed in school, but he crossed his fingers that whatever the outcome was supposed to be, it would go wonderfully wrong.

For the first science experiment, Mr. Lande excitedly explained that this demonstration was sometimes called "Elephant's Toothpaste" or the "Marshmallow Experiment." While his classmates laughed and giggled, these childish descriptions were not the least bit intriguing to John Jr., and his hopes for a captivating display were instantly squashed. The teacher went on to educate how the hydrogen peroxide is catalytically decomposed by the iodide ion in the potassium, and how oxygen gas is then quickly formed.

The teacher proceeded to administer a squirt of dish soap and a drop of blue food coloring into fifty milliliters of thirty percent hydrogen peroxide. Seeing the confused look on his student's faces, he explained how the released oxygen gas gets trapped in the soap bubbles. Then, for the final act, he added a couple grams of potassium iodide to the mixture and stepped back. All of the sudden, a huge amount of light blue foamy suds quickly exploded straight up from the tall, glass cylinder, a few feet into the air, and fell to the counter in a foamy mess.

John Jr. was actually more impressed than he thought he would be; he wasn't sure if the fairy-tale like names had thrown him off or if it was the sudden reaction that had caught his attention. Either way, he quickly realized he couldn't use this to demolish anything, so his fascination, even if slight, swiftly faded. Fortunately, there was another presentation coming. He hoped maybe two lame demos would add up to at least a mediocre day of chemistry.

Mr. Lande delegated a couple of students to clean up the mess while he prepared for the next lab test. This gave John Jr. a few minutes to daydream and brainstorm his next event. If they only knew how elementary all of this was to him. He suppressed the urge to let out an evil, comic book villain laugh.

Once the class was gathered around Mr. Lande's next setup, John Jr. took special note of his ingredients and supplies: a ceramic dish over a Bunsen burner, concentrated sulfuric acid, and para-nitroaniline. Mr. Lande described it as an "explosive polymerization of p-nitro aniline" – now that sounded much better to John Jr., and he smiled wryly. The class was then warned that this reaction was also pretty fast-moving, so they should, again, be prepared, and the two ingredients were then quickly combined by the teacher. After a few seconds of the mixture smoking a bit, a black, solid column erupted from the ceramic dish, shot up about four feet into the air, and stopped. The erect, ominous-looking pillar was so unnaturally still after the rapid growth spurt that it awed the class, including the usually skeptical John Jr. They all clapped. Some wanted to touch the oddity and make sure it wasn't a figment of their imagination, while a few of them requested an encore.

John Jr. glanced at Mr. Lande and saw a pleased smile on his face as his students were awed by his cool trick. He rolled his eyes; he could amaze them a lot better, and so easily, if only.

"Is there going to be any type of assignment where we have to research and do one ourselves?" John Jr. asked Mr. Lande while the rest of the class was still mesmerized by the odd black mast.

Mr. Lande quickly responded, "Not in this class, but Senior Chemistry does. Do you have an idea of what you would want to do?" he asked, obviously attempting to be a role-model and mentor and assuming his cool experiments had just turned a student into a chemistry fan.

"Oh yes, a few ideas...," John Jr. trailed off and walked back to his desk. He was through conversing with this foolish man; all he could think about was what kind of award-winning performance he was going to bestow on them in a few years.

When John Jr. searched "chemical mixtures..." at the library's database, he quickly found an article that stated, "...that explode," and he smiled, feeling like the galaxy knew just what he wanted and that it was a sign. He was hunkered down in his favorite corner of the library with a snack of salty sunflower seeds and a peanut butter and honey sandwich. He knew he had all the time in the world. His dad would not be concerned of his whereabouts; he never was. Nor did he have to worry about his dad finding any evidence in his bedroom while he was gone; he doubted it even crossed his dad's mind to look. The only thing better would be if his dad shared his vision and desire to create the perfect event. Nevertheless.

Taking a bite of his gooey, sticky snack, John Jr. dove into the fascinating article. He was quite pleased to find a highly promising list of incompatible chemical mixtures and what the results from each would be, and he quickly surmised his research day might not take near as long as he planned. "Incompatible" became his new favorite word. Paging through the mass assortment, he nearly felt overwhelmed from all the possibilities. The list included various recipes for toxic gases, fire hazards, and possible explosions; he wanted to try them all. However, as tempting as creating some lethal gas sounded, he wasn't sure how he would contain it, and it wasn't really his focus, so he narrowed his search to strictly the fire and explosion compounds.

Since the article stated the mixture was supposed to cause fire and/or explosion, John Jr. chose the combination of the oxidizing agent of nitric acid with the reducing agent of hydrazine for his first experiment and started his shopping list by jotting them down on a piece of scratch paper. Even though the next concoction choice was less likely to serve his overall needs, the description "may explode upon heating" sounded too interesting to ignore, so he added hydrogen peroxide and acetic acid to the ingredient list. His goal was to change the phrase "may explode" to "will explode." He was completely satisfied with his choices and more than pleased that he wouldn't have to do too much hunting to find the fewer than anticipated ingredients.

John Jr. also needed to restock his supplies. Taking the last bite of his sandwich, he joined glass beakers, graduated cylinders, test tubes, and a wickless alcohol lamp along with more accelerant, evaporating dishes, and the ever-important cleaning supplies to the chemicals on his list. All of these items, including some chemicals, could easily be purchased in a store, but with limited funds, John Jr. relied on his thieving skills, which was risky but much more fun anyway.

The trusty high-school lab had been his go-to for years now, and he only took a few things at a time to prevent inquiries and, thus, heightened security measures by the school. John Jr. was unsure of where he would acquire his necessities if forced to look elsewhere, so he didn't take their unawareness and naivety for granted.

John Jr. deposited a handful of sunflower seeds into his mouth and then focused his attention on his good ole backpack to confirm it still stored all the necessary essentials for the normal break-in and movement inside the school building: flashlight, lock pick, gloves, and a knife. Being an actual high schooler now provided him ample time and opportunities to analyze that portion of the building, so resorting to the small, ground-level window in the back of the building was no longer his only point of entry; he was able to access what he needed through a side door instead, but he decided to drop in nearer to dusk for added protection.

Having time before his scavenger hunt, John Jr. ventured home to gather any additional required supplies and maybe have another snack. The kitchen of his home had been left a mess; he assumed his dad had made some sort of meal and hadn't bothered to clean up. The evidence of John Sr.'s presence was two different-sized dirty pans on the stove, various dirty dishes in the sink, and crumbs all over the counter. Not only was the sight and smell of the disorder infuriating, but the fact that Jr. would be the one cleaning it all up, no questions asked, allowed his mind to go places he loved but others didn't understand.

What he couldn't understand was how someone could be so selfish, careless, and messy. He would never leave this sort of mess for his father to deal with and wondered what would happen when he didn't live there anymore. It had been a solid plan of his for years that when the day finally came for him to leave his dad's residence, he would never go back, even to merely visit. There was no reason to. The thought of this helped him calm down a bit while he began cleaning dirty dishes. Being an intelligent human being, John Jr. knew he had it good nonetheless – free room and board, coming and going as he pleased, no curious inquiries regarding any of his activities – so he was content living there in his dad's untidiness for the time being.

While wiping down the counter, John Jr. also remembered how fortunate he was with the setup of the house. The basement was unfinished, so he could perform his science experiments without much worry of ruining the house. After his mom died in the house fire, they moved to a decent enough rambler not too far from their old neighborhood. It didn't take long for John Jr. to realize that his dad was in no hurry to fix anything up, or keep anything up for that matter. The house had definitely deteriorated in the past eight years, which was to Johnny's advantage. He felt absolutely certain that his mom died so that they would have to move so he could have his little dungeon of a science lab; a worthy sacrifice.

John Sr. did venture down to the basement now and then,

but there wasn't much for him to go down there for, so luckily, it wasn't often. However, John Jr. still made sure he kept his lab setup as simple as possible, making it look like he only did novice-type experiments. Anything he really didn't want his dad to find, he'd haul up to his room, which he knew for certain would never be discovered. As much as he appreciated having complete freedom, way more than any other kid out there, he was looking forward to the day he didn't have to hide anything in his own place.

Once John Jr. finally finished cleaning up the kitchen, he still had some extra time before his retrieval mission, so he moseyed to his lab for one last check of his supplies. Passing by the garage, he quickly snuck a peek to see if his dad's car was there. Nope, he was alone, just as he'd supposed and hoped, and he continued his journey downstairs feeling just that much freer. Just before hitting the bottom step, he remembered he hadn't tested or inspected his fire extinguisher in quite a while, and since he would be trying out dangerous new compounds, he'd better make sure it was in proper working order. If he hadn't had such great success in his research, he might not have had the time to remember to check it. Everything just seemed to go his way when doing what he was meant to do in life.

Being in his lab, John Jr. found himself anxious to get started and considered making his move now, before dusk. He knew how to be careful; he could scope the place out for a while before approaching and entering. And he knew when not to make his move, when things looked a little too risky. He had nothing better to do, so he grabbed his backpack and took off for the high school on his bicycle.

Surprisingly, it only took John Jr. an hour between when he left the house to when he returned. Since there were no threats, he entered and exited the building without any trouble. It took him longer to survey the grounds than retrieve the goods, which were safely in his pack, without leaving fingerprints or any evidence of his presence at all. He was sure they would not miss four little bottles and some equipment. Seeing as how the trip went so splendidly, he was pleased with himself for taking the initiative to go earlier than planned; he was unstoppable, and he had so much more time to play… and then plan events.

Back in his lab dungeon, he couldn't decide which of the two combinations to start with; they both sounded intriguing. John Jr. prepared some evaporating dishes and glass cylinders until he made up his mind. Then he lined up the four bottles, labels facing away from him, closed his eyes, and blindly grabbed two; there, that should help him decide. When he opened his eyes and looked in his hands, he held the nitric acid and acetic acid. He cocked his head to one side and quizzically squinted while the wheels turned in his head. Not a combination he had planned but a very interesting idea nevertheless, and he wondered why he hadn't thought of it before, creating his own mixtures. He suddenly felt silly for limiting himself all this time.

John Jr. couldn't put on his safety gloves, goggles and lab coat fast enough; he was too determined to see what these two chemicals would do with each other. But he knew better than to put himself in danger, so not until he was absolutely ready did he approach his workbench with the two acids. Even before opening the bottles, he retrieved the fire extinguisher from the wall and placed it nearer the table, but not too near that it would get caught up in any reaction and explode itself. He took a deep breath, smiled, and slowly and carefully opened each bottle separately, being sure to set them down on a flat surface. Spilling hazardous chemicals, forcing him to make another chancy trip back to the school, would be unacceptable.

He picked up the nitric acid and released a few drops into the small evaporating dish; he was smart enough to realize he needed to start with the least possible dose. It didn't do anything, which he expected, and even though it was only a minute amount, he could detect slight vapors. Thinking and moving quickly but carefully so as not to bump anything, John Jr. stepped away from the workbench to one of his storage bins to grab a mask and place it over his mouth. Then, back at the table, he picked up the acetic acid, slowly opened it, and proceeded to drop an ever-so-small amount into the waiting nitric acid. *Whoosh...* an angry flash fire quickly swept up out of the dish, making John Jr. jump back, but he didn't blink once. He watched the fire dance around a bit and noticed a dark smoke circling above the flames, and he decided to crack open a couple of the windows for fresh air. The less he breathed in, the better. Analyzing the outcome, he was fairly content with this not previously researched combination; it was a very small amount with a quick reaction. He was sure he could concoct an interesting event using it someday.

The glowing orange jumpers evaporated on their own, so John Jr. moved on to the next experiment. He was ready for the promised explosion, so through the still faintly hazy air, he picked out the hydrogen peroxide and acetic acid and readied his area with a large glass beaker.

He double-checked his safety equipment. The fire extinguisher was still nearby, and he had all of his gear on protecting his body. Following the previously researched instructions, John Jr. filled the glass beaker halfway with the hydrogen peroxide. The sizable quantity sure seemed like a lot to him, considering he'd only used a few drops for the last experiment. Once that was safely put away with its lid securely on tight, he picked up the acetic acid and removed its lid.

Anxiously hoping this would be the demonstration he could display to his classmates someday, and more so a concoction that would assist him in creating the perfect event, he slowly started to pour the contents into the beaker to cautiously introduce the two chemicals. He imagined that they would initially attack each other like territorial canines but eventually unite and agree to produce something amazing.

John Jr. was so focused on the clear liquid nearing closer and closer to the lip of the tipped glass container that the unexpected sudden sound of a slamming car door just outside one of the ajar windows caused him to jolt, and before he knew, it all of the acetic acid was swimming in the beaker along with the hydrogen peroxide. Wide-eyed and in disbelief, he quickly began to jump back out of harm's way, but not quickly enough. The mixture exploded so quickly out of the now seemingly very small beaker that a rather large amount already had splattered on his goggles and gloves. More swiftly than he ever remembered moving in his life, he tore off the goggles and gloves and didn't stop disrobing until he was sure there was nothing left on him that had been exposed to the corrosive new substance.

Breathing hard and almost naked, John Jr. glanced back at the blast zone; there stood a completely empty beaker and a large amount of bubbling, smoking gas-liquid covering the workbench and surrounding floor underneath. Careful to avoid the saturated area, he quickly replaced his soiled facemask, as the air was quite intruded with an unknown substance of three different chemicals.

Some of the smoky gas was escaping out of the cracked windows, but not quickly enough for his own safety, so he switched on his floor fan, hoping the forced air would help dissipate the smoke. He also hoped the circulation would lessen the heaviness of the smoke before too much of it at once seeped out of the windows and prevent outside onlooker's inquisitions. That was the last thing he needed, besides his father, now home, breaking his non-interest in the on-goings of his son's life. John Jr. wasn't sure if his facemask was working too well or if there really wasn't a smell to the infected air, but placing his confidence in the latter, he decided that he would not get calls from anyone not minding their own business.

The few minutes that had just ticked by had allowed Jr. to calm down a bit, and he smiled. That was fun and exciting. Now that the danger was over and he could analyze the recent happenings, he was a little disappointed in himself for allowing the startle and consequent over-spillage to threaten his own well-being, but also, and more so, glad for the fate of the recent occurrence because he was usually too overly cautious for fun and exciting things to even occur. New, interesting, fascinating things were, a lot of times, created by accident. He also couldn't help feeling very lucky.

CHAPTER 18

The boys sat in silence. Drake and Cal could not look at their good friend after what he had just told them. The gloom in the small room that was their shack coordinated perfectly with the overcast and drizzly day it was, and the pairing was overwhelming to their senses.

"Come on, guys, I wasn't trying to bring our weekend down," Joe said from his bedroll in an attempt to counter his dreary news. "You both knew something was going on with my mom anyway." He had just filled them in about her prognosis and his day at the chemotherapy place.

Drake was able to speak first, saying, "Well, we had a hunch but were really hoping it wouldn't be this bad. We were hoping for a cold or flu. Just something like that. Something curable." He only looked up from the floor for a brief second, as he could not rely on his eyes to stay dry thinking about what his friend had been going through and about how it would feel if he were in Joe's shoes and had to worry about the possibility of losing his own mom.

"I know you guys need time to let it sink in, but if you take too long I'll start letting it affect me more too," Joe persisted, "and I just can't go backwards." His voice faltered a little at the end. He didn't want to take healing time away from them, but seeing their sad faces wasn't doing him any good. It wasn't their mom who was sick anyway.

Cal still couldn't voice his thoughts, but finally, he was able to at least look up from the floor where he sat beside the rickety table. He realized that Joe was right, that this wasn't supporting him. The wholly unhappy news was quite a shock, but they had to be strong for him. However, he wasn't quite able to keep his emotions in, so instead of letting Joe see how he was feeling, he got up from the chair and quietly walked out the front door. He wasn't sure how his abrupt act would be taken, but it was all he could do at the moment.

Once Cal reached the outdoors and was in the damp, cool air, he let out a big sigh and bent over, putting his hands on his knees. He felt a little sick to his stomach, but he was still too close to the fort just in case. Making his way to the stream, his thoughts wandered. His first thoughts were selfish: what would he do without his mom? How would life be if it were just him and his dad? He felt angry and sad.

After remembering that his parents were just fine and that they would be there when he got home, Cal focused his reflections back on his good friend. Staring at the water flowing over the rocks and lapping the shore, he felt angry again, but for Joe and his family. He picked up a couple of rocks and forcefully threw them into the water. This was not ok; that family needed Gail. Besides, she was like a mom to him too, and he just couldn't imagine her not being around for any of them. He was just going to have to help their family get through it, both before and after she was gone, if she didn't beat the horrible disease. This realization made Cal feel silly for being out in the mist by himself, so he briskly returned to the cabin to ensure Joe knew he would do whatever he could to help out.

"Where did…," Joe started to say, but Cal interrupted.

"I know. I'm sorry, I just needed a minute," Cal replied, and he continued quickly before he could be stopped, either by his friends or his own throat from emotions, "Joe, you have my full support. Whatever you need, I'm here for you guys. I just can't imagine what you've been going through. I wish you would've told us sooner so you wouldn't have had to deal with it alone." His voice cracked at the end, and he slugged Joe in the shoulder, playfully scolding him for keeping it inside and attempting to alleviate the depressed mood and, consequently, remove the emotional blockage from his throat.

Joe nodded. "I knew you guys would feel that way, but I just wasn't sure what to think, and I didn't want to worry you guys. It's not the most fun news to share."

"Yeah, I guess. Well, I second Cal's notion. I'm ready for whatever you need too, for you and your mom and dad and brothers and sister," Drake added. "So, was chemo scary?"

"It was at first," Joe answered. "The place smelled weird and felt cold, but then we met this little boy who had cancer too, Peter. He kind of taught us to be strong and thankful."

"Thankful?!" Cal questioned, sitting back down at the table.

"Yeah. His attitude was so happy. He always had a smile. He just appreciated everything that was good and didn't focus on the bad," Joe answered. He smiled, recalling the boy's infectious positive outlook. "He didn't know anything but having cancer too. At least my mom had many years without it."

Cal noted, "Maybe that's why it's easier for him."

"I guess that's possible, but either way, it helped us break out of our feeling sorry for ourselves mood," Joe reasoned. "And it makes us look forward to going back, in case we get to see him again."

Drake was having a hard time understanding the deep feelings being tossed around so lightly. "I just can't imagine you actually looking forward to going back," he stated, shaking his head and looking confused.

"Maybe that was a little strong. I guess it's more that we

168

won't dread it so badly," Joe explained. "And it's just a great perspective." He smiled thinking how such a little person could have such a great impact on his life in such a short time.

"I guess that's a good thing, but it would be hard for me to have any kind of positive attitude at all," Cal pouted, "especially this early on. I'm not sure I want to ask, but what are her chances? Did they say how long she has?"

This was the part that Joe was not ready to accept, and never would. There was no answer, no time frame that was ok with him, and it angered him that a doctor had the nerve to endeavor a guess to determine when a person's life would end. He was a smart young man, he knew that the patient needed to know, but the idea was still hard for him to grasp. Aside from completely wanting to refuse that his mom was on limited time, his parents had not yet advised the children of that detail; he was not sure if that was a good thing or not, but either way, he was still in denial, so the unknown was ok with him for now.

"Mom and Dad haven't told us," Joe answered almost inaudibly, with a blank look on his face. Like a switch, the influence of Peter's optimistic attitude was completely gone from Joe, and both Drake and Cal knew it was time to change the subject.

Cal stood up from the table and heartily suggested, "Let's go explore! We haven't searched more up the creek much."

"I'm in," Drake agreed. "I'm feeling like getting into some trouble. Or just dirty... or something... I don't know." He laughed, but his forced efforts to eliminate the darkness in the air were too apparent, so to remove the self-inflicted awkwardness from himself, he nervously directed the conversation to Joe. "Are you ready?" he urged unsurely, hoping someone would take over and clean up the emotional mess he was making.

Joe knew his friends were trying to make the best of the circumstances. Therefore, he did his own best to get the awful thoughts out of his head so they could enjoy their weekend. "Yes, I need something to distract me, let's see what we can discover," he said, and he strained the corners of his mouth upward to emulate a smile, but it was strictly apathetic; no blissful emotion was behind the grin.

They each grabbed their raincoats and boots; they anticipated that the damp weather would help their efforts to get dirty, but they did not want to end up uncomfortably soaking wet. Drake put the small axe, some rope, a lighter, and flashlight in his backpack and swung it around his back. He didn't expect to have to use the flashlight or lighter, but he was learning to be prepared just in case.

"This should do it," Drake confirmed, and he started towards the front door with the other two following right behind. They all trusted that the depressing feel in the room would dissipate like smoke through an open window before they returned.

The fresh, crisp air outside was exactly what they needed, and it instantly woke them from their solemn states of mind. No longer was there uncomfortableness or awkwardness, only ease of conversation and playfulness such as normal teenage boys possess. Each of them understood the topic would come back up, that it was necessary for the healing process and that there would be updates in probable changes in Gail's health, but they sure needed a break from the sullen subject.

The trio foraged along the stream further into the forest, away from their shack, stopping here and there when spotting a cool rock, curious droppings, or fun things to chop with the new axe. The sky would not yield to inconsistency when deciding whether to be wet or dry; the day was just wet. However, that did not stifle the boys' adventure one bit; it actually made the exploration more interesting and addicting.

"Oh my goodness, guys, look at that," said Drake, and his pace hastened noticeably. Looking ahead of their friend as he scurried off, away from the stream and deeper into the trees, Cal and Joe quickened their step as well, eager to see what the excitement was about. They quickly noticed some old metal and glass, half covered in nature's debris.

Upon arriving at the large man-made vs. organic united heap, they discovered it was an old car, in very bad condition, but an extremely awesome find nonetheless. It was clear it had been there for years, as the forest was currently in the process of taking it over: grass grew up through the holes in the floorboards; the seats were ripped and worn through, exposing musty yellow foam underneath; there was not an intact piece of glass to be found; wind and dirt had conquered their share of the paint; all of the tires were, of course, flat; and if rust was a hot commodity, the boys would be rich. But it was a gem, now their gem, and all three boys' eyes sparkled as they fervently examined it inside and out.

"Maybe we should go back and get our backpacks so we can take some of this stuff with us," Joe suggested as he unsuccessfully strained to open one of the backseat doors.

Cal was just as motivated but more hesitant. "I'm not sure there's much we are going to need here. It's all kind of waste. But let's keep looking. If we find there is a lot we could use, it would be worth it to make another trip for sure."

"I'm thinking we need to get one of these tires off and make a tree swing back at the fort!" Drake exclaimed as he kicked a tire.

"Maybe there's a spare in the trunk. That would be a lot easier than trying to take a tire off a wheel, especially without a jack," Joe yelled from the backseat; he had eventually found a way back there after the first door he tried wouldn't budge. He looked for the release so he could pop open the backseat and gain access to the trunk. Success of admittance led way to confirmation of the existence of a spare tire, soon to be the seat of a swing, and thus whoops and hollers by his friends, who were impatiently waiting. After the celebration was over, the puzzle of how to free the anticipated toy from the trunk was upon them.

"I'm not sure it will be physically possible to drag this out through the backseat. Do we have something to pry the trunk open with? We don't have to worry about ruining anything," Joe said. His voice was muffled and echoing since the top half of his body was engulfed by the trunk.

This made Drake feel a sense of loss for being forced to leave the pry bar at the hardware store, and he wanted to tell his friends *I told you so* pretty badly, but he resisted, partly because he knew they had been right, that they hadn't had the funds, and partly because he was in such a good mood (passing brief melancholy thought aside) picturing how much fun the tire swing was going to be.

"I didn't pack anything like that; didn't think we'd need it," Drake said, still slightly biting his tongue but thinking maybe he should have thought of it himself.

"How about a tree branch?" suggested Cal as he started looking around for one small enough, but strong enough too.

With his voice still sounding like he had a pillow over his face, Joe shouted, "I'll look for something back here too." And not a minute later, he emerged from the backseat with tire iron in hand and proud smile on his face. "Let's get it outta there!" he anxiously proposed.

Cal eagerly jogged back to the car from his stick hunting as Drake swiped the tool from Joe so he could perform the brute force act himself. This was mostly for selfish reasons, though he tried to convince himself that he simply didn't want his friends to get hurt. The abruptness took Joe a bit by surprise, but he knew his friend well enough to just let it go; besides, the end result of a fun tire swing would be the same anyway no matter who freed it from its prison.

After a lot of loud, awful screeching and metal cracking, and grunting by Drake, the trunk cover was finally open, and the old spare tire was relocated from the trunk to the muddy ground. It was a bit too heavy, and they were too far away from their shack, to simply carry it, but they had the most amusing time taking turns rolling the round rubber object back anyway. The tire was completely dirty and wet when they returned to the fort, not to mention the boys' mud-splattered chests and legs. After they'd all agreed on the perfect tree to swing from, one at an equal distance between the hut and stream, Cal rinsed the tire off in the creek while Joe and Drake prepared the rope.

Cal returned with a shiny "new" tire to find the rope had been successfully thrown up and over a high branch, with one end still dangling about chest high and the other end's extra length coiled on the ground. Drake retrieved the tire from Cal and held it up perpendicular off the ground by the dangling rope, trying to gauge where they'd want it.

"Oh, I guess I was thinking we'd have it parallel to the ground," admitted Joe, seeing where Drake's thoughts were going. "Don't you think that would make more sense? That way, we could sit in it without having to hold on. And that would allow two of us to use it at once; that is, if the rope and tree branch can hold us."

This instantly rendered Drake put off and defensive. This had been his idea from the beginning, so in his opinion, they didn't have much say. They could go get their own tires and rope if they wanted.

"Well, this way," he said, brashly presenting it at a ninety-degree angle to the ground, "one of us can stand on the bottom, and one of us could sit on the top." Drake nodded as if such an argument would easily convince them. "That's how I want it." He didn't really have an equal contra argument, but he'd been struggling with adjusting the way he had been picturing them using it since the idea had come to him.

They all stood in silence for a few minutes, staring at the contraption. Neither Joe nor Drake wanted to budge, and their silent urgings towards Cal to take a side were practically thundering in his ears. He was relieved when Joe spoke up again.

"Maybe, but I still feel its way more functional parallel to the ground." Joe's reasoning hung in the air like the suffocating humidity.

How Joe unintentionally emphasized the word "way" indicated to Drake that his idea was clearly a poorly thought up plan and how stupid of him to even have a theory about it at all, and he scrunched up his face and narrowed his eyebrows. They wouldn't even be doing this if he hadn't suggested it. On top of all that, he felt that, if Cal agreed with him, he'd have spoken up by now.

"*Way* better huh? Fine. You guys do it your way. Apparently, my ideas are stupid," he said, and he dropped the tire on the ground with a huff as his face grew a tint of red. "Just do it, then."

"Come on, Drake, I didn't mean it that way," Joe said, softening his tone. "I'm just trying to be practical. We can do it your way. Both ways are great. It's not really that big of a deal. It will be fun either way." He unfolded his arms from his chest.

Drake stood studying the apparatus for a long while as Cal

and Joe waited nervously for another snide remark. However, Joe giving in was all Drake wanted, besides calming down enough to actually see his point. He went over to the tire and held it parallel to the ground and studied it like it was an expensive purchase that needed long consideration before making such a major decision.

"I *suppose* I see how it could, maybe, be handier this way." He tilted his head from side to side while examining the no-longer-discarded tire. "Alright, let's see how it works."

Once they were in agreement, the painstaking task took all three of them to construct the best way to attach the rope to the tire so it would be level with the ground and at a decent height. They also had to deal with the difficulty of holding the tire securely to get it tied on. Fortunately, the conflicts were over, and before long, they were taking turns swinging high into the air, low at first to try it out, but eventually, being typical boys, testing the limits of both the rope and the tree branch alike.

CHAPTER 19

Cal woke in the morning from an awful night's sleep, his mind full on yesterday. He was surprised he'd slept at all. As disappointed as his dad was in him, he was even more so. He lay in his bed, staring at the ceiling, retracing his steps in order to make sense of where he had made the mistake. Once he figured that out, he could focus on how to regain his position as a reliable, responsible son and, more importantly, prevent anything like it from happening again.

The day-to-day events of his life had been getting harder to control with so many things going on. School, football games and practices, homework, chores, and now, soon to be sixteen, his parents had been pressuring him to have a job lined up for when football was over. Thank goodness he did not have to pencil in dating on his dance card yet; no enticing young lady had caught his eye, nor the reverse. The opposite sex seemed to view him as invisible so far, and that was just fine with Cal. The stress of all of his activities made the worry that much worse that he had ruined everything he had worked so hard to achieve.

So far, he'd been able to keep everything in check. Cal hadn't missed or even been late to any of his football practices, and he'd been glowing in the praise from both his teammates as well as the coaches for how much he had improved. The coaches had been allowing him more and more playing time, and he'd been taking advantage of it by becoming more competent every day. He also really liked how his body was in prime shape too; he'd had no idea he had muscles in some of the places bulges were building up.

His grades were not straight A's, but they were still better than they had been before the distraction of football. Only second to his chores, his parents were greatly pleased and impressed with his success in school, especially considering he was now a junior and his classes were far from elementary anymore.

Not only was Cal consistent with his regular duties around the house, his parents recognized he was taking initiative as well. The more he stepped up, the easier he found it to detect what needed to get done too, and he would accomplish tasks before being asked. Richard and Diane had actually stopped being surprised by their changed son's actions and more expected it than anything, which wasn't all that fair to their son, as their vocal appreciation was equally diminishing.

That's why yesterday was such an enigma to Cal. He could not decipher where his well-tuned locomotive of organization had slipped off track and caused such a chaotic accident. He'd never before had to struggle with making the right decision in a situation, but after yesterday, he learned that sometimes there isn't always a clear choice. Or, better yet… sometimes the clear choice isn't what it seems.

Cal could still taste the tuna salad that had been chosen for that day's entrée by the school's lunch crew while he was getting his English book out of his locker for his first afternoon class. It wasn't that he didn't like tuna; it was that, in his opinion, the school's tuna was definitely not what tuna was supposed to taste like. He had purposely purchased an extra chocolate pudding cup in hopes of cleansing his palate from the distasteful fish dish, but his effort was in vain, aside from getting extra dessert. He couldn't decide which was a worse aftertaste – tuna or chocolate tuna.

Thankfully, the quarterback of his football team interrupted Cal's tuna analyzing when Cal heard him yell his name from down the hallway. He quickly turned to see Brent Jackson eagerly rushing toward him. The star of the team had been Cal's biggest supporter and encourager since the first day of practice, with accolades and great advice alike. Thus, in turn, Cal somewhat idolized his teammate, trusting him implicitly.

Brent had one of those childhoods that all young boys dreamed about. His dad, Dean, was a top lawyer in the big city, just under an hour north of town. His mom, Katherine, owned and operated the fanciest and busiest restaurant around. Both his older and younger brothers were exceedingly talented in their selected sports. Naturally, all three boys had the typical athletic stature: tall, lean, strong, and nimble.

Dean had been a football star too, and not just in high school. He'd started receiving his eventual multiple "full ride" scholarship offers from various prestigious colleges as early as halfway through his freshman year. He had acquired the nickname "The Man" in high school due to his low error rate and magical play-making skills, particularly under pressure. This handle also followed him through his college career, where he was just as unstoppable breaking all kinds of records left and right. The only players who ever came close to his high-school records were his sons, and so they too, in their eras, were each appropriately nicknamed by their teammates as "The Man."

The Jackson family house and property was the largest and most glamorous in their town, and many surrounding towns. They also had a large separate garage full of new and classic cars, as well as all the cool toys and gadgets for boys: dirt bikes,

4-wheelers, golf carts, scooters, buggies, and all sorts of remote control vehicles. Dean and Katherine Jackson originated and hosted the town's annual community picnic and carnival, which grew in popularity every year until it nearly rivaled the big county fair.

They were the town's "perfect" family.

Brent didn't usually acknowledge Cal outside of football, so to be approached by "The Man" in the school corridor, amongst other students, was rather odd but more than welcomed.

"Hey, dude," said a sly, grinning Brent, and he slugged Cal's shoulder upon reaching him. "Whatcha up to?"

Cal was somewhat confused by his nonchalant attitude. "Um… going to my next class. Why?" He didn't want his puzzled look to be misinterpreted as disinterest, so he adjusted his downward-facing eyebrows to a happy-to-see-you smile instead. He realized it was probably a rhetorical question, but it was nonetheless peculiar, as it was clear what he was "up to," just as all their fellow classmates.

"Just seein' how you're doin'," Brent answered, looking around at the other students in the area. He was waiting for the hall to clear out a little.

"I'm good. Thanks." Then, naturally, Cal's politeness overpowered his intrigue. "How are you?"

Brent was ready to reveal his odd behavior and real reason for being there. "Are you going to practice tonight?" he whispered.

"Of course. Why?" inquired Cal, getting slightly impatient. He had his books and had closed his locker, ready to get to class, knowing the second bell would soon be reminding them their time was up, and he did not want to risk any teacher in a foul mood giving him detention for being even a second late to class.

179

"I need you to do something for me. It's not a big deal," Brent informed him, shaking his head. He seemed to be having a hard time verbally communicating his intentions.

Since Brent wasn't getting to the point, Cal started walking in the direction of his English classroom. "Can this wait? I really need to get to class, Brent." Cal hurried away from Brent, who now looked bemused himself.

"Sure, sure, see you after class," he hollered back as Cal was about to turn a corner and away from his sight.

As Cal sat in English class listening to the teacher give detailed instructions about the proper, and improper, way to cite references, he pondered what was so important for Brent to excitedly approach him in the hall as if they were good friends. The unprecedented event made Cal feel honored regardless of the reason, which didn't matter at this point. He felt bad for putting him off, but he just couldn't be late to class; he trusted Brent would understand. Then he realized that if he were sitting there deliberating, Brent might be too, and he might decide to ask someone else for the favor instead. Worried he might have lost his chance to pay back his idol for things he'd done for him, Cal stared at the clock on the wall, urging it to tick tock faster.

When the bell finally rang, Cal had already packed up his book, pen, and notes, so he was ready to just head out the door to find Brent. This time, it was Cal yelling down the hall at Brent once he spotted his teammate.

Cal was out of breath from rushing once he reached the boy prodigy, so it took him a second before he could gasp out, "Hey! Sorry about that earlier. I'm your man, whatever you need." He fully grasped that he was being overly anxious, but he didn't care; he felt his zealousness could only go in his favor.

"So, I have a family thing I have to go to, so I can't make it to practice. Can you tell Coach Steed that I'm not going to be there today?" Brent stated indifferently. The total opposite change in attitude threw Cal off.

"That's it?" he muttered. And to not sound as if the task was too menial for him, he quickly followed his initial reaction with, "You bet! No problem," and smiled.

Brent added, "And if he asks, just say its personal family stuff; that should cease any further investigation." Cal found the choice of words abnormal for what he was being asked to do but not enough to spark his own inquisition on the matter. He was humbly pleased to be the person Brent had asked, even if his request was an extremely simple task to accomplish. He must've really needed help, and Cal was more than happy to oblige.

The first thing Cal did when making it down to the football field after school was to find Coach Steed to deliver his important message. He looked like a fool, grinning ear to ear the whole time, but he didn't care, it was his honor to represent the iconic quarterback.

Once the coach nodded in confirmation of the news, Cal jogged off to the other boys for warmups. Just before he got to the group, he heard a pop and felt his left shoe loosen up greatly. Looking down at his feet quizzically, he saw his shoelace had broken; there was no way he was going to be able to practice like this. Running awkwardly back to the coaches, he soon notified them of his unfortunate situation. One of the assistant coaches informed Cal there were spare shoelaces in the locker room, advised him precisely where to find them, and instructed him to hurry back because they would be starting soon. The young athlete scurried off.

Once in the locker room, Cal heard voices. At first glance, it seemed the locker room was empty, but following the sound of hushed speech and snickering, he discovered he was not alone; not only was he not alone, but it was his now good friend and legend in the making Brent Jackson with another classmate he didn't recognize huddled in a far corner amidst a haze of wispy smoke. And then Cal smelled something.

Upon seeing a curious Cal emerge from behind a row of lockers, Brent became a combination of surprised, alarmed, and then smug.

"I thought you had a family thing?" Cal inquired, instantly feeling duped.

Brent smiled at him. "I do, just not yet." He had one hand behind his back, but Cal was sure he knew why it wasn't in plain view.

"What... are you doing?" Cal asked in a general sense, since he pretty much knew what they were doing literally. He had a feeling he didn't really want to know, but he found himself instinctively craning his neck to see what was behind Brent's back, giving away that he knew the quarterback was withholding something.

"Well, I guess it's pretty clear. Hey, as long as you're here," he presented the source of the smoke from its hiding place and held it out toward Cal, "want a hit?" and grinned even brighter and more proudly.

Cal was dumbfounded; he couldn't believe what he was seeing. This master of the game, the boy who had it all, whom nothing could stop, who didn't have to work for his glory, and who had endless future opportunities was threatening all of that for this absolutely and utterly stupid vice. And he was so easily caught as well; anyone could walk in, and they wouldn't be able to hide it, as had just happened.

"I take that as a no," Brent answered for Cal, seeing that his big eyes and disbelieving expression were not changing.

"Come on, what's the big deal? You're being a baby. Knock it off, Cal," he said as he inhaled another long breath of the bitter substance and handed the joint to his friend, who was too high and absorbed in the activity to join in the senseless discussion.

"Knock it off?!" Cal exclaimed. "Me? *Knock it off?* You have everything…," he said, shaking his head still in disbelief. "People look up to you. I look*ed* up to you. You're going to lose everything."

"Why?" Brent asked, not moving from his leaning position against the wall of lockers. "Because you're going to tell? Who's going to do what, Cal? The team *needs* me. I can do what I want," he said, laughing heartily. "Besides, no one will believe it anyway. I'm the golden boy." Cal couldn't discern whether the chuckle was because he'd fooled him and everyone and could get away with misbehaving, or whether it was from the drugs. Probably both.

Brent was a cocky, selfish boy. This simple conclusion was the complete opposite view of what Cal had experienced thus far in their short relationship, and he still could not even consider it to be true. Two things surprised him: one, that he hadn't seen this malevolence, or stupidity for that matter, in Brent's character all this time; and two, that Brent was willing to ruin his own easy future without concern.

"You want to be like me, Cal, I know that's what you want," Brent continued. "You want to *be* me. Everyone does, and it's pathetic." He took the joint back from his friend and rolled his eyes.

"You're making a big mistake, and if not now, someday, it will matter to someone," Cal advised a disinterested Brent. "Hopefully you'll realize it yourself before someone tries to make you come to your senses, because that will be a lot harder to deal with."

183

Having said his peace, and realizing his efforts were in vain, Cal turned to go just as a deep voice boomed from behind him, "What is going on here?" Once he turned all the way around, Cal stood face-to-neck with the school's vice principal. Even when the man hadn't just caught someone doing something illegal, he was an intimidating presence, standing at six foot four inches in height and being twenty pounds overweight. Mr. Hannover was not well-liked by the students, as he did not let them get away with anything at all, ever. This meant that it was obviously not opportune for Brent and the other student that Mr. Hannover happened to be the one to find them. But it also meant that Cal, who hadn't done anything wrong, was also in deep doo-doo, and he saw his life flash before his eyes. Maybe it was partly due to the second-hand smoke causing a chemical reaction in him too.

Cal quickly stammered, "I was coming in from practice…"

The giant cut him off, "Come with me, all of you." He seemed a bit too relaxed to Cal for what he had just discovered, but then Cal supposed his easiness and soft tone were because he didn't get much resistance from students so he didn't have to raise his voice too often. And he'd probably been on his way home to have a relaxing evening when three students had to irritatingly postpone that.

"I wasn't any part of this. I just walked in," Cal said as he followed the VP out of the locker room. He wanted to clear his name before things got too convoluted.

"We'll see about that," Mr. Hannover replied calmly, making Cal very concerned.

The three boys sat in the waiting room of the principal's office. They could hear the VP on the telephone but couldn't make out what was being said through the closed door.

"Well, this is fun," laughed Brent as he elbowed Cal in the

ribs from the adjacent chair.

Cal frowned. "Don't talk to me. Don't even say a word." He wouldn't look Brent in the eye, half believing his guilt would be contagious through sight.

"Oh, what's the matter Cal-y poo?" the golden boy joked. "Why are you so upset?" Cal didn't answer. The office door opened, and the VP calmly stated that each of their parents would be there soon to pick them up. He also advised them they would be hearing from the school the next day as to what the punishment would be, but that they definitely should not to come to school tomorrow for starters.

The stoner sat up and shouted, "Yes, sleepin' in!" and then slumped back down in his chair with a smile on his face. Cal shook his head. He didn't want a day off. He didn't want any of this. He just wanted to keep to his schedule. Suspension would ruin him, and he felt sick to his stomach when he visualized what was going to happen when next confronted by his dad.

The school authorities didn't give any of them a chance to explain themselves. Cal was uncertain whether he should express that truth or if speaking up again would only make his chances of being found innocent worse, but they (whoever they were, as he assumed the VP didn't make the decision on his own) seemed to be presuming guilt prematurely, even though Cal understood it did look like it was a clear-cut case. All he could do at this point was sit and await his fate, which was an almost unbearable task.

Richard was late getting home, and Cal was not happy about it; it just made the excruciating wait long and drawn out, and he just wanted the talk/lecture and likely punishment over. At the order of his mother, he had a few bites of dinner, more than he wanted as his appetite was non-existent. She hadn't said much to him in the car on the way home; Cal could not read her well enough to know how bad that was.

Cal sat in his room at his desk, staring at page forty-one in his Algebra textbook, but neither the letters nor numbers could outdo his memories of the locker room or, more so, his forthcoming doom.

The garage door was opening, finally, and all of a sudden, he wished for the opposite of what he'd been wanting, more waiting. He sat, heart pounding, listening for yelling, loud footsteps, banging, etc. All quiet. Then there was a loud "What?!" in his dad's voice. Then more quiet; he couldn't stand the seemingly eternal quiet. Beads of sweat were emerging on his forehead as he waited, hardly breathing. Then came a knock on his bedroom door, though not as loud as he expected.

"Come in," Cal's voice cracked.

Richard slowly entered, looking exhausted. He looked at his son with an expression Cal had never seen before in his dad.

"I'm more than disappointed in you, son," he said. "I don't even know where to begin. What were you thinking? How long has this been going on?" He remained standing just inside the bedroom door.

Cal assumed that since his dad was asking questions, it was ok for him to speak and answer and clear this up. "I didn't do anything, Dad, I just walked in…"

"Don't lie to me, Cal. Mr. Hannover said you smelled like pot," Richard said sternly.

"Probably. I was in there for a few minutes, but…" Cal tried again but was again cut off.

Richard continued, "And with Brent Jackson, too?! So you're not just an idiot for doing it yourself, you have to be a bad influence as well?!"

"What?! I didn't…" tried Cal.

"Now *I'll* be in trouble with his parents, do you realize that?" Richard argued. "Do you see what your irresponsible actions will do to our family?"

Cal just couldn't let him think that. "I was *trying* to be responsible. I..."

"I work so hard to give you and your mom everything I can, and now that's all gone," Richard reasoned, shaking his head. "A cop's son engaging in such an illegal act. It's atrocious."

"Why won't you let me tell you what happened?!" Cal screamed, tired of being interrupted and not getting a fair chance. Richard stopped, wide eyed, staring at his son.

"You don't talk to me like that. You have nothing to say, no right to speak. You gave up that privilege," Richard said, setting him straight.

After a minute of silence, Richard folded his arms across his chest, looked straight at his son, and spoke softly, "I don't want to hear any more lies. Your mother and I very apprehensively gave you all this freedom to do what you wanted, and this is how you repay us? This is what you decide to do, throw your life away?"

Richard stood there quietly with his head bent downward. Then, "I just can't..." He shook his head, not looking up from the floor. Cal thought he almost looked like he was getting choked up; he'd never seen his dad like this. He was beyond angry, and that was much worse than his usual just plain mad. Cal was so afraid and lost that he couldn't say another word, even for as unfairly as he'd been treated. Richard slowly turned and walked out of the room, quietly shutting Cal's bedroom door behind him. Even though he was completely innocent, for how utterly disappointed as his dad looked, Cal would've given anything to have the yelling and door slamming back.

CHAPTER 20

"That's outrageous! We need to do something," Drake said when told of Cal's unfortunate story of the locker room/drugs misunderstanding. He was furious that his good friend was in this chance predicament, on top of not being given fair representation.

Joe was just as upset. "How could this happen? I can't believe no one would listen to you. And that Brent, that jerk, wouldn't speak up for you!" He shook his head.

The three boys were sitting in the library after Drake and Joe had gotten out of school. Cal had talked his mom into letting him go, promising that he was strictly there to focus on schoolwork.

"I just don't know how to get myself out of this mess that I didn't even get myself into," Cal said with such a tiredness to his voice and expression. "Now that I'm done with football, I guess I've got time for a job. But who's going to hire a pothead? Oh no, this is terrible." He sat forward in his chair and dropped his forehead to his wrists as they lay crisscrossed flat on the table.

Joe spoke up, "There is no way we're going to let you be punished for something you didn't do and not be able to go to school or be on the football team anymore. Oh jeez, and your dad, he must be pretty upset. That's just not right for him to have that image of you!" He was furious. "We need to get Brent to clear your name, ASAP. We just have to."

"He was such a cocky jerk yesterday, with no concern for

anything, I honestly don't know if he will help," Cal explained with a painful tone to his disappointed voice.

"Well it wouldn't hurt to ask. We have to try," Drake persisted. "Should we just call or go over there?"

Joe evaluated their options, "It's not like we can just knock on their door; the place is gated. But I think we'll have more luck if we're physically there instead of just calling. It will show more sincerity for sure."

"I wonder how much trouble he's in, if he'll be allowed to see us," Cal pondered out loud. "And I'm not sure I should go. I don't want to get myself in deeper. I'm supposed to go straight home when I leave here. I'm lucky to be here in the first place. If I get caught anywhere else, that'll be it for me. Do you think he'd be more inclined to comply if I'm there or not?"

Joe thought about it for a minute. "How about we try, and then if it doesn't work, you can get involved. Better to be safe than sorry. Hopefully, he was just too high to think of clearing your name yesterday."

Drake nodded. "We'll take care of it, don't you worry. The sooner the better… You ready, Joe?"

Drake pushed the buzzer outside the Jackson estate and waited. Joe was about to suggest he push it again when they heard a lady's voice come over the intercom device, "Hello?"

Joe bent toward the speaker and answered before Drake could say anything irrational, "Good afternoon, ma'am. We apologize for the unannounced visit, but we wish to speak with Brent and/or his parents regarding the incident at the school yesterday. Please." Drake gave him a thumbs-up and nod for his professionalism he'd pulled out of a place Drake didn't know existed in his friend.

There was a pause. "Who is this?" the tiny woman in the box inquired.

"Drake Briggs and Joe Hart, ma'am," Joe replied. "It is very important we speak with someone on behalf of our good friend Cal Parker. Please. There's been a grave misunderstanding."

Another pause, longer this time.

"We wouldn't be here if it wasn't extremely important," Drake said, finding it impossible to stand idly by. Then they heard a metallic click at the large black gate, and it started opening slowly inward. Joe and Drake looked at each other and smiled a sigh of relief and success as they started up the long driveway to the main house.

Since the Jackson family was so prevalent in the town's public happenings, the boys recognized Mrs. Jackson right away as she waited for them at the massive double doors that served as the main entrance to their home. She was wearing a smile, a wary one, but a smile nonetheless, and the boys felt more welcome than the sense she thought they were troublemakers by it.

"Please, come in," Katherine said, motioning for them to enter her extravagant home. The boys thanked her graciously and spotted Brent as soon as they stepped through the door. He was perched on the arm of a fancy sofa in a sitting room just beyond the grand, enormous foyer where there was, of course, a majestic crystal chandelier overhead as the main attraction. There was a wonderful, clean scent that reminded them of summer. Eyeing each other nervously, both Drake and Joe suddenly felt quite underdressed and out of place.

"I've called Brent down from his room. Please have a seat," Katherine said, maintaining her stoic courtesy and motioning to the sitting room. "What was it you needed to see him for?"

The boys awkwardly took a seat on a loveseat that matched the sofa Brent had now settled himself onto the cushions in. Drake wasn't sure if any of the furniture was meant to be sat on; they looked like movie props.

"Our friend Cal is in big trouble for something he didn't do, and Brent knows it," Drake blurted out due to his uncomfortableness.

Joe quickly turned the conversation from blaming to asking for help. "Sorry," he said, looking harshly at Drake as if to say, "Shut up!" "We are here to see if Brent can explain to the school and Cal's parents that Cal didn't have anything to do with the drugs yesterday. That he walked in at the wrong time, for a completely different reason, and actually tried to persuade Brent to stop doing it himself."

"I was not aware there was an issue going on," Katherine said, looking sternly at her son.

Joe continued with a very important detail concerning Cal's character, "He would have come himself if he wasn't in so much trouble. He is a very respectful, responsible person. Besides, he was unsure Brent would tell the truth, which has been just as hard on him."

"Brent, what do you have to say?" Mrs. Jackson inquired with an unsure tone of her own.

"The Man" now appeared quite the opposite, resembling a helpless little boy who'd gotten his hand slapped for sneaking a cookie before dinner. This was what Joe was hoping for, some regret; he feared the golden boy would not be compassionate enough, or too smug, to care that someone was suffering because of him. Regardless of his pathetic appearance, he remained quiet for a minute. Joe could not understand what would be holding him up, what he could possibly gain by being dishonest.

"Well yeah, Cal wasn't any part of it. He's a good guy," Brent finally disclosed, and quite willingly. Joe was ecstatic; at least one adult, who seemed trustworthy, had heard the confession.

As long as Mrs. Jackson was not disguising a truly cruel personality, Cal would be cleared before the night was over.

"Thank you, Brent. Now, can we let everyone know so he can get on with his life?" Joe requested. "He deserves it. He's worked so hard to get where he is."

Mrs. Jackson became impressed with Joe. "You are very nice, young gentlemen, and you must care very much for your friend by coming here on his behalf. I appreciate you bringing this to my attention and apologize you even had to." The boys felt her demeanor shift from indifferent and somewhat bothered to personable and remorseful.

"It is our pleasure. Like Joe said, though, Cal didn't want to risk getting into more trouble by coming here himself, or he would have. No one was listening to anything he said," Drake explained, though Katherine had already assumed that. "He believed that if Brent was going to help him, he would've last night, but I guess he wasn't really in good form to do that…"

Katherine frowned, both at what her son did and what Cal was going through. "Oh, poor dear, I bet he had an awful night last night. It's the worst thing being blamed for something you didn't do."

"Yes, and his parents, especially his dad, have been very hard on him. He's a wreck," Drake continued, even though he had already convinced her of Cal's situation. But now, discovering her pleasant and understanding nature, he felt much more comfortable sharing his thoughts.

Brent felt more and more guilty as the conversation went on, as if he wasn't there and wasn't worthy of having anything more to say. He really hadn't given a second thought about Cal, partly because he was feeling so good last night, but now he felt increasingly rotten about being so thoughtless. Now that his head was clear, he was disappointed in himself at not having allowed the idea of clearing Joe's name to even cross his mind. His evening had turned out completely opposite from what he had expected; the cocky boy was not beyond reproach after all and had gotten his share of lecture from his parents. They were going to great, and expensive, lengths to keep the humiliating incident out of the press, but they were ultimately uncertain if it would work.

"We should get going. I want to get this over with so that Cal can be free and I can start forgetting it happened," Brent stated, and after seeing his mom's expression, he humbly corrected himself, "not forget, learn from it."

It had been an hour; the plan was for Drake and Joe to come to Cal's as soon as they were done at the Jacksons. Cal couldn't remember ever being more impatient, especially since his dad would be coming home soon, and he wanted this cleared up before more time with his dad being utterly disappointed in him went by. He wondered if the length of time was a sign things were going well or not.

Cal had his sense of hearing on high alert, so he easily heard the knock on the front door from up in his room. He didn't want to wait downstairs in case his dad got home before his rescue team arrived with victory flags flying high. He bolted down the stairs two at a time and swung open the front door, only to be surprised by twice the number of people he'd expected to see. He too recognized Mrs. Jackson from television, billboards, and social functions, and his confused expression led way to her enlightening him as to what they were all there for.

"Good evening. I'm Katherine Jackson, Brent's mother. Are you Cal?" she asked. Cal gave her a nod of affirmation. "Brent would like to talk to you and your parents if that's ok," Katherine requested of Cal politely.

Cal opened the door wider to let them all in. "Of course,

thank you. Mom!" He was too eager and anticipative to consider that yelling might be uncalled for at the moment. But when he noticed Katherine smile just as she walked by him, he felt it was ok. Better than ok. He had a feeling his nightmare, that he had already dreadfully accepted as his life now, was about to be over. His friends had come through!

As the six of them were getting settled in the living room, the garage door sounded its alert that it was allowing Richard's vehicle entry. For how scared Cal was to hear the sounds of his dad's arrival last night, he was even happier to hear it tonight. It was perfect timing. Diane excused herself to forewarn her husband of their guests and inform him of the situation before he joined them.

Cal's parents didn't know exactly what Mrs. Jackson and Brent were doing there, but they had a hunch, and that hunch provided Richard the sorriest expression when he caught his son's eyes upon arriving in the living room. It was almost surreal to Cal; the thought of his self-made promising life being turned into one of solitude burger-flipping and living paycheck-to-paycheck had been a realization for too long for his mind to quickly switch back to his dad respecting him again. Though Joe and Drake looked mighty pleased with themselves, he couldn't allow himself to get overly confident in the small chance this visit wasn't what he assumed.

Upon returning to the living room, in as formal a gesture as she could represent due to the significant status of their guests, Diane politely offered beverage choices to the tense group. She never imagined the Jacksons would be in her home, especially Katherine, and since it was a surprise visit, not giving her ample time to prepare, she attempted to ensure the memory they had of her house was a pleasant one instead of disagreeable. She wished she had on her fanciest dress and had

had a chance to touch up her makeup, and, moreover, been able to pick up the place a little.

A few moments later, with a glass of lemonade in hand, Mrs. Jackson spoke clearly and articulately, "Thank you for seeing us, I apologize for coming unannounced, but I believe this matter to be an urgent one. I only wish my husband was here. I know he would like to personally apologize for our son's behavior as well. Brent?"

Mrs. Jackson prompted her son that it was his turn by taking a sip of her tart drink and giving him the "you better start talking" eye only moms know how to do. Brent felt relieved and nervous at the same time; it was going to be nice to get this off his chest, but he was worried about how the tardy news would be taken by Cal and his parents.

"Thanks to your friends, Cal, it has come to my attention that I have overlooked an important detail of yesterday's unfortunate event." Brent looked Cal straight in the eye. The Parker's could hear the eloquent speech resemblance between mother and son. "I am truly sorry it required their reminding me that I hadn't cleared your name to do so."

Then to Richard and Diane, he said, "Cal had nothing to do with my senseless extracurricular activity yesterday afternoon when I should have been at football practice with him. I do actually remember him trying to get me to stop and come to my senses. I am, again, sincerely sorry to have put you all through this. And if you can't forgive me, just please, at least, return Cal to his rightful place in your minds to the high regard that I know he deserves." Brent returned his gaze to Cal at the conclusion of his apology.

Katherine smiled at her son. Regardless of what his future now held with likely hardships to overcome, that any parent strives to shield their children from, she was proud of him. It took a lot for a person to admit wrongdoing, especially to strangers.

"We will be talking to the school first thing in the morning. If there's anything else we can do, please don't hesitate. Now we will let you get back to your evening," Katherine concluded with a pleasant consoling smile while she rose to her feet and motioned to return her now empty glass to Mrs. Parker.

"Thank you so much for taking the time to personally clear this all up," Diane answered as she stood and accepted the glass. "Looks like we have a couple of boys to thank and some talking to do with our son." She smiled a very fortunate smile around the room. A lot had happened in the last 24 hours. The worst, for her, had been the strained relationship between her husband and son, and now, thankfully, that was just going to be a good story to laugh about in the future.

Diane and Cal saw Katherine and Brent out. Before the door closed, Brent had one last sentiment he needed to express. "Cal, I hope someday I can regain the level of respect you had for me just a mere day ago. The fact that you tried to help me even as I persisted with criticizing you… that is what will get me through this. I've learned that I should be striving to be like you, not the other way around. I would be honored if you considered me your friend." Brent gestured for a hug, and without a word, Cal gladly received and returned it.

Back in the living room, besides feeling somewhat awkward, Richard felt it best to wait for his wife and son to return before striking up a conversation with Drake and Joe. He was embarrassed that he hadn't believed his son and that Cal had had to rely on his friends instead of his family, who should be his first support, to help him out of a jam. Even if Cal had been guilty, he now knew he should have been more understanding. A lot more. He was ready to thank the boys and get his son to himself.

"Joe and Drake!" Cal shouted once the front door was closed. "You guys are the best!" He couldn't contain himself any longer and was wearing the biggest grin when he returned to the living room. "I can't believe this is over, all thanks to you guys. You didn't doubt me once. I can't thank you guys enough. I have the best friends ever." They were standing by the time he reached them, and it was a mass hug and high-fives all around.

Joe replied, "You would do the same for us. That's just how we do it."

"It was a cinch," Drake added, laughing. "They really are nice people, so that sure helped. I can see some people out there not caring one bit and was kind of worried they would be those kind of people."

"I just can't wait until they tell the school so I can go back, and to football too," Cal spoke excitedly. He rubbed his hands together as if picturing an evil scene, but it was quite the opposite: he just couldn't wait to get back to his normal life.

Diane, regretfully, had to bring them down a bit. "We are very grateful Cal has such good friends in you two. You should probably be getting on home, though, before your parents start wondering where you are." She gave both of them hugs and sent them on their way.

When the little family was once again without house guests, Diane pretended to have things to do in the kitchen to give her husband and son some privacy.

A refreshed but still nervous Cal sat opposite the room from his dad; the perfect setup for a serious heart-to-heart talk. He waited, knowing it wasn't his turn to talk.

"Cal," Richard finally said, his voice full of relief and humility. He hesitated with unfocused eyes, glaring at the wood floor trying to find words that weren't there to help him.

Looking up at his son, he said, "I don't know what to say besides I'm so sorry." His soft tone and demeanor were a complete contrast to his customary authoritative presence. "I was in such a state of shock to hear what you had done that I was overwhelmed by my disbelief... and rage... and denial that I let it get the better of me. I am embarrassed, and I hope you can forgive me."

Unsure if that was an invitation to accept his apology by confirming forgiveness, Cal sat quiet. If his dad had more to say, he did not want to impede his process. This might be his one and only chance to have this kind of conversation with him; he had never seen his dad like this before, and he was rather liking the human side instead of the customary hard-core robot man.

"I have sure learned a lesson," Richard admitted. "I need to be more trusting and fair with you. Not only because it's right, but because you deserve it. You've more than proven that, even before this unfortunate debacle." He shook his head and dropped his eyes back to the floor in an ashamed manner.

"You shouldn't have to rely on your friends, who, thank heavens, were there, to help you through tough times. That's what family is for, first and foremost," Richard added, more scolding himself than speaking to his son. He didn't even look up from the floor, growing increasingly guilty.

Cal reckoned his dad had said his peace, so relieving him of his painful task of an apology was due. He could tell his dad was practically in agony; probably because it was such unfamiliar ground for him, but also because he had really messed up, and the last thing Cal wanted was for his dad to think he hated him.

"Thank you, Dad," he began, "that means the world to me. I understand why you were so angry with me. I'm sure I would've been too in your shoes..."

"Yeah, but you wouldn't have reacted the way I did," Richard interrupted, sounding sorry for himself.

Cal continued, "Well, who knows. But I do know I take it as a sign for how much you love me."

And with that, Richard stopped in his downward spiral of sorry feelings to allow other, somewhat foreign feelings, to emerge from deep within – compassion and love. How could someone who'd gone through such a terrible experience, only magnified by one of the people who should love him unconditionally, be so forgiving and reasonable when he himself, an adult, was so completely the opposite?

Richard sat wide-eyed, beholding his son anew. "You are a remarkable young man," he declared in amazement. "I have really missed out, haven't I?"

"Oh, Dad, we still have time. Even before this happened, we were on a different, better level than we had been before. I'm just so happy you know the truth, that it was all a misunderstanding!" Cal laughed happily.

Richard agreed, "Yes. Thank goodness. I can't imagine how relieved you are, as I am overly ecstatic to have my good son back."

Diane wiped tears from her eyes as she quietly spied on her men from the doorway between the kitchen and living room. They were standing in a warm and cheerful embrace that rivaled the intensely complete joyful feeling in her heart.

CHAPTER 21

The weather had been hot and dry for months. John loved this time of year because everything burned so very nicely. It was almost as if things wanted to be burned, like they were begging for it, to be put out of their sultry misery. And he was only so happy to oblige.

The thing about big, expensive housing developments was that the land owners got a satisfied sense of contributing to the welfare of the planet by planting as much greenery as possible. The great thing for John was that those trees, plants, shrubs, and nice green grass were pleasing to the eye when they got enough water, but in dry periods, even the finished lots were difficult to maintain the plush appearance of a tropical paradise.

Tresson Hill Manor Heights was one of those growing expansions of town with houses in every stage of construction: some properties fully complete with residents occupying them and some just breaking ground. Since half of the development was still in process, the grass and foliage there was especially brown and arid. Not to mention the wide, barren, untouched land adjacent to the new development that would make an excellent starter.

John sat in his parked truck on a side street near one of the construction zones, enjoying his salty, crunchy sunflower seeds. Analysis of the dehydrated area reminded him of the nitric and acetic acids mixture he had played with when he was younger that resulted in a quick reaction of fire. This would not be his typical *boom* of an event. He pictured the blaze gracefully sweeping right across the ground, eating through everything dry, and jumping to each next parched victim as if in a hurry to fill its belly before it got caught. The first good breezy day, blowing in the right direction, would be go-time.

Now that he had found his more than ideal canvas to work with, John moved to the planning stage. He went over details in his mind during his drive home. He figured on needing a fairly large volume of the acid mixture and multiple transport containers to douse that sizable of an area. But the most highly pleasing fact was that there wasn't anything more that this event required. He would easily work by the cover of darkness again, outside the annoying threat of security cameras. There would be no wires to hook up; just a liquid trail from the out-skirting land leading around the houses and open grassy areas would more than do the trick.

Besides absolutely loving his work (not to be confused with the photography job at the magazine), John really felt he was serving society by his good deeds. How many jobs would he be creating once he was done? The firefighters and cops first, then medical professionals, insurance companies, and finally construction workers to rebuild would be a great stimulation to the economy. Not to mention, if the outcome was fully to his liking, an influx of new customers to funeral homes and residents moving into cemeteries. As he unlocked the front door to his home, he felt proud of himself for being such a supporter of the community.

As a rule, John generally ordered his chemicals and supplies over the internet, depending on what and how much. If he only needed a small amount of something that wouldn't cause alarm, he would just buy it locally, but again, to eliminate any risk, the anonymity of online activity was highly preferable –

202

especially since he used an alias and not his home address. The only downside with online purchases was the long wait for them to arrive, but the privacy was more than worth not being identified buying suspicious items in person. Even a couple of days was excruciating sometimes, but for this event, he was sure the dry, windy season would be sticking around for a while.

After a thorough review of his "cart" on his favorite online supply site, John opted for the extra freight charge to receive his order as quickly as possible. He was still feeling energized from his drive home, and the impatience was coming full force. He only needed to click "Submit" for the order to be complete as the site automatically populated his payment information and delivery address from past purchases. Within a few minutes, the confirmation message appeared in his email inbox.

Just as he was closing the lid to his laptop and getting up from the sofa, his cellular phone rang.

"Hello there," John answered. Still on a high from his fun day, John spoke with a zeal he was not accustomed to, so he almost didn't recognize his own voice. He was actually smiling instead of irritated to have gotten a call. He wanted to share the events of his day with whoever was on the line.

"Is this Mr. John Hackett Jr.?" a woman's voice asked in a solemn but polite tone.

John curiously confirmed, "Yes, it is. Who's this?"

"This is Nurse Gibbs at Encompass Hospital. I'm afraid your father, John Hackett Sr., has been admitted here as of this morning, and he has you listed as his sole emergency contact," she disclosed.

John's shoulders slumped. It wasn't that he was sad to hear the news and worried about his father; he was just quite dismayed that the unexpected phone call regarding his least favorite person threatened to fully ruin his splendid state of mind. Of course his dad would do this. He hadn't seen or spoken to him in twenty years, but it was just like him to steal the show and take every bit of happiness right out of him. Damn it.

"Can you tell me his condition?" John asked, solely caring to know to save any scrap of joy from his day by hearing he was in excruciating pain or displeasure.

Nurse Gibbs replied, "It seems he had a stroke and had taken a fall down some stairs. At this time, the doctors are unsure of his prognosis, as it is quite early yet, but they do suggest you come down here as soon as possible."

"My father and I aren't close, so I'd rather just be informed if he passes," John selfishly admitted. Besides, no one was going to tell him what to do. He was too busy for this mess and more than ready to end the depressing phone call and repossess his quickly vanishing elevated attitude.

The nurse fell quiet; it was not what she expected to hear.

"Well, anyway, I know where he is, so if I change my mind…," he wasn't sure exactly what would happen if he did, but John took it upon himself to begin the closing remarks of the conversation. He quickly thanked her as courteously as he could muster and hung up the phone. Unconsciously, he sunk from standing to a seated position on his sofa, a vacant gaze upon his face.

It was too late for the return of joy. He was far beyond that as anger arose from deep within him, and he quickly decided he wasn't going to allow this annoying interruption to his life to happen again. On top of the rude irritation, neither was he going to be stuck with the medical bills from his father being in a hospital day after day, no way. Pacing from his living room to kitchen now, John knew he needed to solve the problem.

And there was only one solution. The inevitable was going to happen eventually, probably soon, but he figured, why not just help it along a little; that would be more than enough to restore his cheerful mood. The more he thought about how to do it, and it being over, the happier he became.

Would a pillow over the face be suspicious? He had stopped wearing the trail in the floor after deciding on the solution to his problem, but he started pacing again when he realized that he had more of the puzzle to solve. Now he regretted letting the nurse in on how he felt about his father, for now, if his father died while he was present, he might be questioned. But it would be hard to prove. Hard enough that he would get away with it, he wondered. He'd never had to weigh this type of risk before. Just to be sure, he decided he would go now, and again tomorrow, with tomorrow being D-day. Dead-day. Dead-dear-daddy-day. This way, he could do his usual analysis of the hospital layout before making a rash move. He was almost more impatient for tomorrow than waiting on his recent chemical order.

The nurse at the central station of the hospital's ICU comfortingly directed John to the room his father now, temporarily, resided in. By chance, he found it far down the hall from the nurse's station, just how he wanted it. However, contrary to his liking, it was not a private suite. There were two beds, and his father was not alone. The risk had just become much higher. He pulled the privacy curtain all the way around the bed for seclusion and stood above his father, observing his motionless body. All kinds of machines were buzzing, whirring, and clicking around him.

He did not recognize John Sr., not at first. Time and recent life-changing events had greatly altered how John Jr. remembered his father looking. It was a good thing the other patient was female, or he'd think he had the wrong person. After a few additional minutes of studying the man's face, John Jr. began to see some familiar features after all. The urge to do the necessary deed right then was immense as the childhood memories started flooding in.

"Mr. Hackett?" A sudden woman's voice just outside the curtain startled him back to the present. *Great. What does she want?* He was busy.

Pulling the curtain back, he acknowledged her, "Yes?" His deeply disappointed demeanor would be easily misconstrued as sadness.

"I just wanted to check in and see how you were doing. Do you need anything?" she asked in a soft, consoling tone.

John Jr. knew he had to feign grief in order for his plan to work. If he got caught killing his father, that would be the end of his destructive fire-making fun, and that was not the way he was going to go out. *Let's get ready for an Oscar-winning performance*, he thought.

"No, thank you," he replied with a tight voice. Tears hadn't graced his cheeks in more years than he could remember, so conjuring up some salty emotions was not happening. He settled for a quivering chin and humbly looking down at the floor.

The young nurse reminded him where she was located if he did need anything and excused herself to leave him to his privacy once more.

John Jr. was unsure how long the suffocation process would take, which was a problem as anyone could walk in on him at any time. He would have to do some research when he got home. Chances were, the hospital staff or the roommate's visitors would announce themselves just as the nurse just had, but his plan was obviously going to be riskier the longer it took to complete. The fact that he most likely wasn't going to have to fend off physical retaliation since his dad was a motionless rag doll was a major plus.

Half of an hour, John Jr. determined, was sufficient time to portray his sorrow, however fake it was. It was not like he could carry on a conversation with his father; he could only sit and stare at him. He doubted the staff would be alarmed at his leaving. But before exiting the room, he plucked a few tissues from the box on the nightstand and, for added dramatic flair, pretended to blot his eyes as he passed the nurse workstation.

John was anxious to get back to Encompass Hospital first thing in the morning. He wanted this dreaded, but happy to perform, task done and off his mind. He hadn't slept well, and anything that disrupted his sleep had to go. At least the tired look it produced would add to his costume of sadness and be just another building block to his caring son character.

He briefly checked in at the magazine and then took off on a fake photo shoot job on the other side of town.

As he walked towards his father's room, he heard louder and louder voices. Sure enough, the roommate had visitors, and he wondered how long he was going to have to wait for them to leave him to his important business. Fortunately, once again, his disappointed expression deceived them into a false impression of woe. He politely nodded to the visiting couple as he quickly pulled the curtain between the beds again to provide him and his father privacy.

He sat. He waited. There were two voices. Nauseating, bothersome, highly obnoxious voices that tested his patience with every word. He hoped that, since their loved one was apparently just as mute as his father, their stay would be limited, but they were in a conversation that, he felt, didn't need to be discussed in this setting. John Jr. was baffled why they insisted on spending their morning here, when it didn't matter one bit to the person lying in the bed before them how rude the waiter was at the restaurant where they had just eaten breakfast. Which then led to other disastrous eatery experience discussions. John Jr. felt sorry for all servers who had to serve these awful people.

He tried clearing his throat a few times to remind them they were not alone but very well overheard and being disrespectful. However, they were completely oblivious to the real world. He considered leaving and coming back, but he really, really didn't want to have to add this back onto his list of things to do today. He needed it crossed off, with heavy black lines.

Then, he reckoned, since they were unashamedly and wholly engrossed in their own perfect world… could he get away with doing it while they were in the room? Maybe this originally adverse, irritating situation would actually work in his favor instead. There was no way anyone would accuse him of killing his father with conscious people in the room, regardless of whether they were in sight or not. This newfound realization intensely excited him. Game on.

John Jr. was in disbelief at how quick and easy it was. Within minutes, he was standing over his father, the pillow was back under the now dead head, and his hand was to his heart to imitate surprise at the now flat lining electrocardiogram machine next to the bed. No sound had come from behind his curtain – the boisterous couple would have drowned out any noise he or his father made anyway – but his father hadn't moved a muscle during the life-taking smothering. No involuntary, muscle-memory, or deep from within adrenaline movement kicked in to try to save his own life. Sr. had either simply accepted the passing to eternal life or was just too far gone already to defend himself.

Soon, a multitude of provoked hospital workers were in the room attempting to discover what went wrong and how to remedy the deadly problem. They hardly noticed John was even there, as they were quite busy striving to bring a dead man back to life. The brazen couple was ushered out of the room, putting up protest the whole way, the evil drama-lovers that they were.

To John Jr.'s distinct satisfaction, his job was done here. He stood back and admired his handiwork that was, in fact, gloriously irreversible. Aside from keeping up appearances of utter despair for a few more minutes, he was ecstatic he had accomplished his task. When the hospital staff was finally done gushing condolences over him, he signed off on the paperwork, and he was gone.

The dependable package had arrived, and John was on his way to pick it up. The weather kindly agreed with the timing of the parcel arrival, so this evening was going to be a party for him. It would be a typical party like anyone would throw – hot and exciting with plenty of toxic liquid and perfect picture-taking opportunities to remember it by.

The next morning, John unintentionally slept in. Not only had it been a late night of grand event-creating, but by the time he got home, he was still on too high of a high to sleep. Once he'd downloaded all the pictures from his camera to his computer, he had spent hours going through them, editing, analyzing, admiring, and, conversely, scrutinizing his work.

Groggily, he climbed out of bed, rubbing his overused eyes. After a quick teeth-brushing, not caring one bit about his tousled hair, he ambled to the living room and switched on the television to the local news.

His event was still the big story. Not a big surprise. The news station played and replayed footage of the raging, multi-acre blaze from last night and the smoky remains of the area this morning; no house was left untouched by the traveling inferno. Some people were scurrying around, carrying out such meaningful duties, while some were shown sobbing and hugging on loved ones. Newscasters searched for any sign of who and why, reporting they had no answers yet but optimistically promising that the authorities were doing their very best to solve the case.

Besides eating and using the restroom, watching the news story was all John did that day. It was by far the best show on television: thrilling drama, puzzling intrigue, mass destruction, and heroic efforts. He was honored to have been the start of it.

CHAPTER 22

"I think it's time for us to start thinking about getting you a driver's license, Drake," Drake's mom, Carol, suddenly announced at the breakfast table one Saturday morning. Neither Huck nor Alexis even looked up from their breakfast. Everyone was still in their pj's or robes, barely showing signs of life yet.

Nothing whatsoever had been previously mentioned about the subject, so Drake's head swiveled so quickly to look at his mom that he about fell off his chair.

"We need to see when the next driver's ed session starts, but it could be your birthday present. How does that sound?" she asked, taking a bite of toast soggy from butter.

"Sounds great to me, but can we afford it?" Drake reasonably questioned, scooping up some cheesy scrambled eggs with his fork.

Carol nodded. "We have to. You'll be on your own soon enough, but it will be very helpful to me when your grandma isn't around. Plus, you need a way to get to your *job*...," she hinted, suggesting he had better find one quick as she was tired of pestering him about it.

Drake blushed a bit. He knew he hadn't been putting much effort in finding a job. The idea of it just sounded way more grown up than he felt. Having spending money would be a great benefit, but it was just so much work.

"I guess I know what I'm doing today," Drake stated, feeling quite melancholy. He hadn't had other plans, but he knew job searching was not a part of anything he wanted to do that day. The sooner he found some options and had a few applications filled out, the better, and maybe he could go see what his friends were up to.

Carol had purchased a used desktop computer a few years back that the whole family used, when it was working. This was another reason why Drake was not looking forward to job hunting; he almost thought it less frustrating to hit the streets on his bicycle, but that wasn't nearly as efficient as he didn't know which places were hiring or not. Besides, he did not want to look like a child either. As he sat down at the makeshift desk in the study/guest room/laundry room, he crossed his fingers that today was a good day for the old computer.

After searching the internet for a while, Drake found his best options to be restaurants, grocery stores, retail shops, the movie theater, and a couple of hardware stores, with the last two being his favorites. Some of them offered online applications, while others required the applicant to inquire at the facility itself.

"Mom, what's my social security number?" Drake requested. This was followed by many other questions a first-time job-seeker didn't know. Carol was happy her son was finally getting on the job-searching task, and the feeling of being needed was welcomed as well.

Drake completed as many applications as he could online before the virtual box could crash, and made a list of the ones he was required to personally visit. He wasn't sure he'd remember some of the things he had questions on, so he printed one of the online applications to have all the right answers while he was out.

Informing his mother that he was leaving, he gathered his bicycle and backpack and took off for the second half of his undesirable chore. This was the first time he disliked being older than Joe and Cal; he pictured them laughing and having a good time somewhere, no worries about a thing. And here he was having to be an adult. His life was over.

"Hi. I saw online that you were hiring," Drake said, feigning interest while putting aside annoyance. "Can I get an application please?" Then he smiled politely, realizing he was nervous and looking like it. The first place on his list was the hardware store where he and his buddies had gotten some of their tools and gadgets for the fort. He was at the customer service desk and the short, energetic lady behind the counter obliged with a form and pen and out-of-the-way counter to use. He made sure to thank her before leaving.

Next he headed to the movie theater. He was hoping one of the benefits of working there would be free movies, or at least at a discount. There must have been a popular matinee starting soon after he arrived, as he had to wait to even inquire about a job. The pretty young girl that helped him caused him to be flustered, so as he left, he wondered if he'd put all the information down correctly on the form.

The little grocery store he pulled up to next on his bike had some produce outside the front door in some bins. The sun shining down on the fruit and vegetables gave the air a sweet smell. While Drake was locking up his bike at the rack, he overheard a couple of boys who looked a little older than him discussing something frantically. He did not recognize them from school. One of them, who was wearing a baseball cap, entered the store while the other stayed outside wringing his hands and looking around nervously.

Drake walked into the store as well and politely asked the first employee he located if they were hiring. A grocery store not being his first pick for place of employment, he was not terribly disappointed when they told him no. As he turned to

213

leave, a commotion broke out in the rear of the store: the cap-wearing young man was yelling at one of the employees. Not wanting to be a part of the drama, he quickened his pace toward the front door.

Just as Drake spotted the nervous boy near one of the cash registers stuffing items into his jacket, the boy hastily zipped it up and ran out the door. *Oh heck no,* thought Drake, and he took off after him in a dead sprint.

It took Drake a couple of blocks to catch the panicky thief, as he was not in good physical shape like Cal, but he tackled the perp to the ground, supposing any broken returned goods were better than no returned goods at all. Some of the wares had fallen out of the zipped jacket during the chase, but the remainder was still bulking up the physique of the shoplifter, who was putting up a good fight. Since Drake was a hefty boy and had had his share of tussles, he quickly won, at least as far as getting the grocery items back, but he had no way of restraining the burglar.

Four store employees were out in front of the store looking in his direction as he ambled back with some of the stolen property. One of them, a short, pudgy grey-haired fellow with a white apron on, had his hands up in the air like he was praising Jesus; Drake assumed he was the store owner.

"Oh, thank heavens you were there," he exclaimed to Drake. "Thank you, thank you."

Drake felt silly carrying the items back from rescue, as some were dirty and damaged, and he was fairly certain he hadn't even recovered all the stolen goods. The possible store owner hugged Drake awkwardly due to the merchandise between them, but he didn't care; a stranger had come to his aid.

"You're welcome. It was not a big deal," Drake replied, handing the items to the other employees.

"I'm Clement Riley, the owner of the store you just saved. What can I get you? Your purchases are free today. What did you need? Anything at all!" the large man said. "You're not injured, are you?"

"I don't think so," Drake answered, introducing himself in return while wiping some dirt off his jeans and inspecting his elbows and knees. "Well, I didn't come in to buy anything; I was looking for a job. They told me you weren't hiring. It's no big deal. I am glad to have helped; just in the right place at the right time." He smiled and motioned toward his bike. He really wanted to get his job search done for the day so he could do something fun.

"You risked your own safety for my store. For that, you must be rewarded. I would be honored if you would work for me," Clement declared. "I need someone like you. Our theft rate is way too high."

"I accept!" Drake consented, smiling. He was not expecting that and was grateful his task for the day was over. He couldn't wait to tell his mom.

Clement led Drake into the store and up some back stairs to his office that overlooked the store to talk business. The two agreed on hours, pay rate, position, and start date. Drake liked his new boss more and more the longer they talked. He found Clement to be soft-hearted but strict, witty but business-serious, accompanied by a perfect balance of intelligence and common sense. Drake knew he had a lot to learn from this man, especially when he struggled with most of Clement's questions that only came with employment experience that Drake didn't yet possess.

The large proprietor had some paperwork to get started before Drake could begin his new position, so in one week's time, he would return ready to learn.

"Drake, is that you?" Carol shouted when she heard the front door of the house open.

"Yes, I got a job," Drake answered searching for his mom after dropping his book bag in the foyer.

Before he could find her, she met him halfway with a big hug and delighted smile.

"Already?!" she exclaimed. "How did that happen? You must've really impressed someone today."

Carol sat in awe, listening to the events of her son's afternoon as they sat at the kitchen table together. Part of her was so proud, while the other part wanted to scold him for endangering his own life. She put on her parent hat and reminded him that it was serious business dealing with crooks, as he might have had a weapon, or a buddy who could overpower him. Drake admitted that those concerns hadn't even cross his mind; he just hadn't wanted the guys to get away with stealing. Carol made sure he knew how proud she was of him and told him how smart this Clement guy was in hiring her good son. She also made a mental note to make a visit to the store to confirm her son would be in good hands.

Drake lay on his bed, mentally reassessing the happenings of the day. It was definitely thought-provoking how one thing led to another to put him right where he was to land him a job. And now that his search was over, he was happy and most comfortable that it was a grocery store instead of the movie theater or hardware store, and that Clement would be his boss. He was excited about this new aspect of his life, growing up and becoming a man, especially since his mom was so proud of him, but he also felt the need to mourn the loss of this carefree era of his childhood.

CHAPTER 23

Drake recounted his recent happenings to Cal and Joe while bicycling their way to their fort for a quick overnighter. They displayed mixed feelings about both him getting a job as well as his risky good deed.

"No way. That is so cool; you caught a crook!" Cal congratulated him, smiling. "What are the odds that would happen? Not many people get a chance to come to the rescue like that. That would have stunk if you hadn't caught him."

"You are so lucky you didn't get hurt... or worse!" Joe angrily rationalized while swerving his bike tire to avoid a pothole in the road.

Ignoring Joe's customary care-taking remark, Cal continued as he peddled on, "And he gave you a job for it, how awesome."

"Yep! He seems like a really cool guy too," Drake chimed back. "I think he's going to be a great boss."

Not giving up his point just yet, Joe added, "Well, just be careful. Next time think about yourself, and us, and your family a little, ok? Hopefully, there won't be a next time, though."

They had reached the edge of town. Looking ahead, the expanse of guaranteed adventure-hiding trees and brush grew increasingly larger until they were past the tree line and the forest fully engulfed them.

"I guess we're all getting busier the older we get, but between your job and Cal's football, this is going to put a damper on our time out here," Joe admitted.

Cal added, "Joe and I will be working soon too, don't you

worry, Drake. But the extra money will be nice. Maybe we can go get some of those tools we had to put back at the hardware store." He jumped his bike off a tree root sticking out of the ground.

Drake's eyes lit up. He hadn't thought of that; he'd just assumed most of his paychecks would go to his family's bills to help out, with some for car expenses and the rest, if any, for him to save. If they too would get jobs, they could buy whatever sweet tools they wanted… Of course, they wouldn't be able to visit the fort as much anymore, though, Drake pessimistically concluded.

"Oh, man, that sounds awesome," Drake agreed, "but I hope we'll still get time to come out here to use the fun new things we buy."

"Yes! We will just have to make time," Cal confirmed. "I can't accept the thought of our time out here coming to an end any time soon."

Joe's ever-logical mind expressed, "And once you get your car, we can get out here quicker and easier too!"

"And haul more stuff," Cal added as he pulled up to the shack with his bike.

The three boys arrived at their hideout in very cheerful moods. The future had revealed some disappointing changes, but also some exciting modifications that provided them more independence. Their backpacks were filled with essential single-night items: food, drinks, and restocking items such as rope, since they'd used it all for the tire swing last time, a change of clothes, and bait, etc. Drake was especially looking to make every minute count this time, wanting to hold on to his childhood and this special time with his buddies for as long as he could.

Once everything was unpacked and stored in their rightful

places, the young trio relaxed and brainstormed the best activities to make the most beneficial and unforgettable use of their limited time. Drake, being the one with the greatest desire to make their time memorable and lasting, mentioned that he was very much appreciating just being out there, doing what they wanted, not thinking about his immediate future filled with responsibility. But, of course, they weren't going to sit around and stare at each other for 24 hours.

"I think we should just go throw some lines in while we think," Joe suggested, glancing out the window. "It's so nice out, so it will be relaxing anyway."

Cal was up from his bedroll and to his fishing rod before Joe was done speaking. The afternoon air and warm sun on his skin had been so refreshing to him on the trek out there that he was all for getting out of their stuffy shelter.

"I'm going to grab some snacks," Drake added. He was slower to get moving from his seat at the table than Cal had been. It wasn't that he didn't like the idea; he just hoped that, if he moved slower, time would too.

The three young men sat quietly by the gurgling stream with their three fishing poles, wiggly bait, crunchy snacks, and refreshing drinks, all wishing time would stop to freeze them in this serene moment. Sometimes, the silent times they spent together just appreciating each other's presence were just as bonding as the times they shared deep thoughts.

Drake thought about their tools they had bought and how most of them hadn't even been used yet.

"Hey, we could throw things at trees!" he declared suddenly and eagerly, smiling and nodding to his buddies.

Both Cal and Joe's heads turned to him quizzically. It was quite an odd and confusing statement, just thrown out there like that. Playfully, Joe picked up a nearby stone and chucked it at the closest tree, acting like it wasn't very fun at all but commenting how exhilarated he now was. Cal enjoyed the tease and laughed at Joe's jokiness.

"What did those poor trees ever do to you, Drake?" Cal said, joining in the razzing.

"Yeah, yeah, whatever. Funny," Drake said, disregarded them. "No, I mean use our tools. Like knife-throwing," he clarified. As he pulled in his fishing line, he grew increasingly motivated. "Let's see, we have screwdrivers, some utility knives... oh, and that small axe. I call the small axe!" He had reeled his line out of the water and was on his way back to the shack before the other two knew what was happening. They were still a bit caught up in their ribbing playfulness.

Relying on their abruptly animated friend to return with the aforementioned tools, the two remained, temporarily waiting for nibbles on their lines, not with the goal of catching a slimy swimmer, since neither was really in the mood for a fish dinner – or, more so, completing the painstaking task of preparing such a meal – they were just too into the laidback atmosphere to be causing the stir Drake had.

However, once they heard some intriguing, intermittent chopping sounds coming from the direction of the cabin, their interest piqued, and soon, Joe and Cal were on their way to the shack, fishing gear and empty food and drink containers in hand. They found Drake pulling the small axe out of a tree while a pile of other tools lay on the ground about twenty feet away; they guessed that the line marked in the dirt was the throwing line.

"We're really going to throw screwdrivers?" Joe asked, looking down at the small pile that lay behind the line in the dirt.

"I don't know," Drake answered as he joined them back at

220

the throw mark. "It's an option anyway. We're not doing anything else with them."

Joe reasoned, "Well, I think we should use them as our *last* option, as we don't want to ruin our hard-earned purchases and literally throw our money away. I wouldn't want to need one only to find it's broken. Same with the utility knives; as fun as this sounds, I don't think they were made to be thrown."

"Yeah, that's fine," Drake replied, hardly hearing him, enthralled at the moment with the axe. Both Cal and Joe were relieved that he hadn't taken offense. "Here, take a turn with this," he said, holding out the axe to neither of them in particular and smiling as if he was presenting a thoughtful gift.

Cal grabbed it before the more apprehensive Joe could. He stepped up to the line, aimed and sized up the tree, lifted the axe above his head, and then swung and released, ending with a quick wrist action. The axe went tumbling to the ground after hitting the tree awkwardly. Cal felt slightly embarrassed.

"I guess that's harder than it looks," Cal stated. "I thought it would just go. I'll have to keep practicing. How many tries before you got it, Drake?"

Drake had picked up a utility knife and was weighing it in his hands, considering how well it would throw. "Just a couple of times," he answered, not looking up from the knife he was holding.

"Ok, can I try again quick?" Cal asked Joe.

Joe nodded. He wanted a try eventually, but this was not his cup of tea, so he wasn't itching to give it a shot.

Cal lined himself up again, took a little longer to aim, feeling the weight of the axe, and finally launched the weapon. This attempt was only a partial revolution from sticking, or at least, the right end contacted the target. He felt better; it was progress. He really wanted to keep at it, but he knew it was

Joe's turn and he would get another chance shortly anyway.

He handed the axe to Joe, who took it with a not-so-strong grip. Joe copied Cal in feeling the weight of the weapon in movement and then lined up to take his turn at war on the tree. The tool flew clumsily through the air and landed with a thud at the base of the tree. Joe laughed so hard; he knew his try at it wasn't going to be pretty, but the way it had happened just made him giggle. Throwing the axe turned out to be more fun than he thought it would be, but not for the same reason.

Seeing that Joe was not upset about the result of his first throw, Cal and Drake joined him in laughing. "You better try that again, Joe," Cal encouraged positively. "You can't leave it like that!"

Joe scurried to the tree, picked up the axe, and quickly returned to the throw line. He jokingly took a few steps toward the tree, past the line, to give himself a better chance, eyed his friends, and laughed some more after they razzed him about cheating. Back at the mark, his second toss did hit the tree but not with the sharp edge, so it bounced off to the ground much like Cal's first throw. He threw his hands up above his head in celebration while jumping up and down. He didn't care; it was just fun being able to hit the tree at all. Drake and Cal joined him in the fun, little rejoicing; they were just pleased at how happy their friend was.

"How about we each keep going until we stick it, and then it's the next person's turn?" Cal suggested. "Unless it takes a while. We can always give up." He winked at Joe, knowing he might not want to just keep failing.

It was Drake's turn again, and with an audience this time, he wanted to be sure to do well. On his first throw, the blade hit the tree straight on but not with enough force to pierce the bark and stay put as he was focusing more on technique than power.

This did not discourage him. The second heave proved trickier as he overcompensated now with the speed of the axe, and it hit flat against the trunk instead. Joe and Cal took the opportunity to root him on, and with a couple of bad throws under his belt, his third throw was precision, with hardly a thud as the blade sunk deep in the tree's bark. They all cheered, especially Cal because that meant it was his turn again.

His goal was to beat Drake and stick it in less than three throws. It was not a realistic goal. Just when he felt like he was making progress, the darn axe would clang off the tree in a bad way and make him look even more incompetent and unskilled.

In order to relieve a bit of his tension, after about ten throws, Cal proposed, "You're so good at this, Drake, next time there's a thief at the store, you can just throw something at him instead of running him down. It would be a lot safer anyway!" he said with a laugh.

After an abundance of reassurance and support from Drake and Joe, Cal tried about five more times and gave up. Axe throwing just wasn't fun at that point, and he was ready to do something else.

"I think I've worked up an appetite," Cal said with a weak smile to hide his defeat. "How about dinner?"

The suggestion triggered hunger pangs in Drake and Joe, and they realized how hungry they were as well; the day had gotten late while they weren't paying attention.

In the morning, Drake found Joe cozy on the tire swing and Cal practicing his axe throwing again. Without a distracting audience, he was making better progress, but he was still not nearly as accurate as Drake. As for Joe, he was so relaxed that he almost fell back asleep with the slow sway of the tire through the air and the creak of the tree branch with every change in direction. This was all perfect to Drake, as time seemed to stand still again; he was disappointed that he'd slept later than his buddies, as, for once, he saw it as a waste of time.

"Hey guys," he addressed his friends cheerfully. "How's the axe treating you today, Cal?"

Cal smiled at his now risen friend and affirmed his success, as slight as it was. He wasn't sure if he wanted Drake to take a turn and shake any solid progress he felt he'd made. But Drake wasn't interested in axe-chucking today. Since the evening had flown by when they'd actually found something to do, he hoped going back to doing nothing would be the best way to slow up the clock. His goal was to get really good and bored so he could reminisce of this calming time when he was stressed and busy at work.

"Here, you want the swing?" Joe asked Drake. "I've been on it enough. It's making me sleepy. I gotta take a leak anyway." Drake had been hoping he would ask; taking on a get-bored challenge might be the optimal way to guarantee slow-moving hours. Joe gave Drake a push once he was settled in, and Drake just melted into the swing as if he would never be getting out. Drake gazed up at the trees above as they slowly waved back and forth while he hung almost weightless in the air.

Suddenly, the tire was roughly attacked, and he heard laughing. Realizing he hadn't heard the thud of the axe in a while, he knew the onslaught was Cal on a mission to ruin his serenity.

"Come on, man," said Drake, "I was in a special place!"

"Haha," laughed Cal. "You? A special place? That's a new one." And he coarsely pulled again at the rope above the tire to jostle Drake around.

"That's it, you're done," Drake said, returning the playfulness by jumping out of the swing and tackling Cal to the ground. He had been totally jerked out of his peaceful state with no hope of regaining it. Joe reemerged and pretended to be both the referee and commentator in one. In the end, when both wrestlers were dirty, sweaty, and tired enough, Joe announced a tie.

"Let's go down to the creek. You guys can wash off," Joe recommended. The two warriors thought that sounded absolutely refreshing, so they raced to the shores of the cool, revitalizing water.

"Next time we come, we should build a fire down here," Drake suggested while splashing in the water, "to make it feel more like camping. We have such a good setup in the fort that it doesn't always feel like we're roughing it."

Joe agreed, standing on the sidelines watching his friends, "Yeah, good idea. A fire in the fireplace just isn't the same." He was apprehensive about getting wet since he didn't get sweaty and dirty.

"I'll make sure we have hot dogs and marshmallows!" Cal offered and then dunked his head under the water.

Drake wasn't sure all this planning was helping him not be disappointed about their regulated time out there now, but it was fun anyway. Something fun to look forward to was definitely a benefit more than a detriment; maybe their next trip wouldn't be as long of a wait as he was dreading it would be.

CHAPTER 24

Ryan, Joe's older brother, was back from his first year at college, and the Hart family was holding an entertaining game night, per his request. Leslie, being a teenager and the only female sibling, was not so keen on the idea, even if it was her cool older brother's wish. She would much rather be chatting about boys and gossiping about girls with her friends. But they were only twenty minutes into charades, Gail's favorite game, and there had already been plenty of fun and laughing to go around. The carefree evening was definitely needed and way overdue for all of them.

The six of them were split into two teams: mom and dad had to be split of course, and the oldest and youngest were on the same team, leaving Joe with Leslie and their dad Henry. Sometimes they would draw names, but from experience, they found that this arrangement was the most fair no matter the game, from sport to intellectual. Gail, Ryan, and Sammy were not making it easy on them; the match was hot and playfully competitive.

As fun as the night had become, the undeniable underlying goal on everyone's minds was to prevent Gail from overdoing it. She was deep into chemotherapy treatments, and as much as laughing and positive energy was good for the soul, there was a limit to the human body. She was a strong, independent woman, so sometimes, it took the whole family to convince her against something that might risk her health and safety. She had never been limited in her physical or mental abilities before, so it had taken some getting used to; having her family reminding her constantly was helpful but aggravating too.

When it was Gail's turn to act out her given phrase or word, she would do what she could from a seated position on the couch, and that seemed to work well enough. However, when it was her team's turn to guess, she would get so worked up, jumping around, flailing her arms, all while "sitting" as much as she could without getting scolded.

Unbeknown to Gail, her family was greatly more cognizant of her depleting energy level as a day would go on. Some days, she hid it better than others, but her struggle with fatigue could be quite apparent at times; nevertheless, what her husband and children feared the most was for her to know they noticed the change in her and how it affected them. Like most families, issues were only discussed when someone's patience or temper broke, not beforehand to prevent an explosion or increasing misunderstanding.

Henry was similar to many men in that he was so typically more unobservant than most women, particularly his remarkable wife. However, he felt, having been a teacher for so many years now, that his experience aided him in being more conscious of others' feelings and accurately interpreting their actions. Seeing the recent drastic changes in his children due to them watching their mom deal with the awful disease had prompted him to call up his oldest son in an attempt to have him convince his siblings that he wanted to come home for a fun, old-fashioned family game night in hopes to raise everyone's spirits. Even though its sole purpose was to prevent his wife from fully realizing the effect the dreadful disease had on her family, his efforts were satisfactory.

Ryan had been so busy with his major life changes of moving out of the house and starting college that he hadn't been as affected by the worrisome and confusing transformation in his mom as his siblings were. Being gone from the house, he hadn't witnessed the resulting consequences. Leslie, Joe, and Sammy's eyes were definitely not as bright and carefree as kid's should be. Their laughter was different, less relaxed, and more cautious.

Ryan found it touching to see how careful they were with Gail – no talking back or arguing, making sure she was comfortable, fighting over who got to sit beside her, helping around the house without being asked, and so on. As he watched them all playfully interact while Henry and Leslie anxiously attempted to guess what Joe was portraying, part of him felt like he was missing out. He had to live his life, but if time with his mom was limited, he really was missing out, and he felt foolish that it had taken his dad to call him for him to come home for a visit. He only lived thirty minutes away. He knew he needed to make more of an effort. Now that the initial shock of the disease was over, coming home shouldn't be so scary; his siblings had to live with the reality of it every day. And during times he couldn't come home, he vowed he would find a way to still be supportive from afar.

Leslie was still in partial denial about her mom's cancer. There were so many emotions she didn't understand, and she was unable to deal with them. The two of them had obviously bonded differently than a mother-son bond would be. She was the only daughter; they shared girly things and thoughts. She was upset that her only female family bond was being threatened. She was extremely sad and scared at the thought of being left alone. It was distressing to see her strong mother weak at times now. Being seventeen, much like ordinary teenage girls, she would, from time to time, take her anger and unsteady emotions out on her mother, who was an easy target,

228

not comprehending what she was doing and why.

The horrible, life-threatening illness was even more confusing to Sammy, who had recently joined his siblings in the teenage club. Gail found he was the one with the most questions, and repetitive questions as well. He didn't understand the fragility of life well enough yet to be angry or too scared; death wasn't a reality to his young mind. Perhaps puberty had something to do with that, involuntarily captivating his thoughts and actions.

Being the caring, protective soul Joe was, he felt he had to take care of everyone, to be there when needed, help them deal with their emotions, be a reassuring presence, etc. especially since Ryan wasn't home much anymore. Though emotionally draining for him, accompanying Gail to her chemotherapy appointments gave him a much better understanding of the disease as well as provided him deep, heartfelt conversations with his mom. Eliminating the unknown from something makes it a lot more bearable. Having taken on this heavy role, however, he probably needed this carefree, uplifting night more than any of them.

The score was tied, Sammy was struggling to persuade Gail or Ryan to guess "Batman," and time was running out fast. His persistence and tension caused Gail to leave her allowed seated position on the couch, and she was flailing her arms and jumping around, believing that would jar the correct clue from her brain. It was too much. The next thing the family knew, she was slumped in a heap on the couch, silent and unmoving.

After the initial shock and disbelief wore off, the family sprang into action. Ryan grabbed his car keys while Henry gently picked up his wife to transport to the car. The look in his eyes as he gazed down at his wife's blank face was something Joe had never seen in him before, and never wanted to again. A

229

vulnerable dread had replaced the jovial spirit that was there just moments ago.

As badly as Joe wanted and needed to go with them to the hospital, he knew his responsibility right now was to stay with his sister and little brother. They needed him more right now than his mom did. He knew it, but also couldn't help feeling slight resentment because of it. The rest of the night was going to be long and agonizing for all of them.

The front door closed, and Joe, Leslie, and Sammy stared at it, not moving a muscle, listening to the sound of Ryan's car become more and more faint, until there was silence.

"This can't be happening," Leslie softly whispered, not taking her eyes off the door, mentally pleading with it to reopen and reveal the rest of her family right on the other side like it was all a joke or dream. "She's going to be fine, right? She has to be fine." Her voice cracked from her throat tightening up. Reality began to hover heavily over them, allowing raw emotions to surface.

"I wasn't trying to get her excited," Sammy began to sob, innocently taking all of the blame.

The shock of how quickly the evening went from fun and laughter to fear and uncertainty prevented Joe from immediately consoling his little brother. The three of them who were so abruptly left behind each had to individually deal with their own emotions until some sort of sense of what happened was determined.

Joe felt like crying too, besides cursing and hitting something, or blaming anyone or anything including himself for letting this happen. And now he couldn't even be there for his mom for comfort and support. He wanted to be there with her when she woke up. It wasn't fair he was stuck at home with his siblings wondering what was going on and naturally imagining the worst.

Sammy's wailing became too much, overpowering Joe's inward reflections, and if only for his own sanity, not responsibility, he went to his little brother to console him. Once the noise subsided, Joe realized Leslie was no longer in the foyer. He assumed she was in her room, where she spent most of her time, especially when she was upset. He considered going to check on her but thought it best to give her some time alone to sort things out, not trying to presume he understood a thing about how the female mind worked.

"How about some ice cream?" Joe asked Sammy, feigning enthusiasm. "That always makes everything better."

Sammy apprehensively nodded in agreement, and they warily ventured to the kitchen. Joe hoped the insignificant act of scooping ice cream would help calm his nerves and anxiety. Moving between the entryway to the kitchen, the house was so extra quiet and vacant that it was eerie to him; the only sound was their footsteps.

"Hey, can you do me a favor?" Joe requested of his little brother. "Go find a good show on TV; maybe we can watch something funny too, so we're not so worried and sad." *And they better call soon so we know what's going on,* he finished in his own head. The unknown was almost worse than bad news.

Before long, a red-eyed, moping Leslie entered the living room with her own heaping bowl of strawberry ice cream in search of some company-comfort to relieve her sadness as well. It took them all a lot longer than usual to allow the comical people on the screen to pull smiles and laughs out of them, but it did eventually happen. Joe was pleased with himself; not only did he feel better, even if somewhat guiltily, but his siblings were not nearly as upset as they had been. He had successfully gotten their minds off the terrible, unfortunate event, for now.

An hour into the movie, instead of the expected phone ringing, the front door opened and closed, making the three of them jump from their seats and hustle to the front of the house. It was Ryan, and no sign of their mom or dad. Joe's heart skipped a beat.

The wide-eyed and nervous looks on his siblings' faces reminded Ryan that they needed an update ASAP. The last time they'd seen their mom, she was unconscious. He was so exhausted that he forgot they had been waiting with no word of what happened after they'd left.

"She is stable," he said, figuring that was the best statement to immediately relieve the tension, and the resulting sighs from all three confirmed that notion.

Joe felt so much better that a bit of anger arose, and he questioned why they had to wait so long, suggesting that Ryan should've called a long time ago, at least before he'd left the hospital. Ryan apologized, admitted his lapse in judgement, and proceeded to disclose the timeline of events from when they left to now, once he'd corralled them back into the living room.

"You don't even know how long of a drive that was to get to the hospital, you guys," Ryan began, shaking his head. "The longest fifteen minutes of my life. I dropped them off at the emergency entrance, parked the car, and then had to just sit in the waiting room just as uninformed as you guys were. Every beep that went off or nurse that ran by hurriedly made me worry, and it didn't do any good to try to ask anyone questions."

The three audience members sat in awe, realizing they hadn't had a worse time than their oldest brother. Both were bad, but they'd at least gotten ice cream and an entertaining movie, and had also had each other's company for support.

"Dad finally came walking down the hall towards me," Ryan continued. "I had mixed feelings because it was a huge relief to finally see someone I knew, but from his expression and demeanor, I couldn't tell if it was going to be good news or bad. He looked so spent. And I probably looked like you guys did when I got home.

"He slumped down in one of the waiting room chairs and started by telling me she was sleeping. They had stabilized her, and she eventually woke up only for them to ask a few vital questions, get some answers, and then give her something to sleep and some liquids through IV.

"They still weren't sure of the combination of things that caused it, but probably no more games where she can get competitive anymore," Ryan finished, attempting to ease the mood with a reminder of how much they loved seeing her get excited when she was having fun.

Leslie, needing some more information, asked, "So when is she coming home?"

"She'll probably just stay there through the night, they said," Ryan replied. "I don't think it was as bad as we felt it was. Just overdoing it, nothing seriously wrong."

Sammy asked if they could go see her, and Ryan had to remind him that she was sleeping, and that disturbing her might be detrimental, so maybe in the morning, depending on how long they planned on keeping her after she got some rest. He suggested they all settle in, finish their movie, and try not to worry about anything. Joe agreed, as he knew how well it had worked the first time, and now that they knew she was ok, it would be easier to relax.

Once Leslie and Sammy were snuggled in, Joe and Ryan excused themselves with some vague reason to talk in the kitchen. In a sort of venting session, they discussed each of their roles in the night's trying incident. Ryan complimented Joe on his ability to keep the others calm, while Joe confessed that he was grateful Ryan had been there to be able to drive their parents to the hospital. They each realized the other hadn't especially wanted to be in their unassigned role; it just had to happen.

Ryan started heating up some popcorn while they presumed to foresee what the future now held for their family. The older brother vowed to be more present for them, which resulted in a smile of gratitude from the younger brother. Joe felt the freeing release from a great deal of pressure coming off his shoulders that he didn't even know was there.

CHAPTER 25

A picnic was planned this time. Johnny loved his specially set-aside mother-son days. His devoted, loving mom would take the time to think of the most fun and imaginative things to do with him, so he knew it meant a lot to her to spend time with him too. They were celebrating him finishing his 1st grade year of school, and he couldn't wait for everything she had in store for their special day together.

Francine had asked her son for a list of what favorite foods he craved for the picnic, and since she had a few treats of her own, they had a full basket of deliciousness for their city park adventure. With her son's help, they successfully transferred their belongings: a blanket, the picnic basket, a kite, and the current children's book they were reading together, from the car to the easily agreed upon, perfect grassy spot to bask in the sun and take in the invigorating fresh air.

Little Johnny Jr. filled his mom in on his favorite, and least favorite, parts of the school year while they enjoyed their goodies and people-watched. When Francine asked him how the last day of school was and what the teacher had done to make it special, his eyes lit up in excitement.

"We didn't do any work at all," Johnny responded eagerly, sitting on his heels, "We just got to play games and stuff. And we had more recesses too, so we didn't have to be inside the school even. *And...* she gave us popsicles for a treat in the afternoon. We never had those before, ever. It was a really fun day. I wish every day could be like that at school."

His eye caught a bunny dashing across the lawn, and he pointed at it enthusiastically; his mother smiled at his innocence. Francine wished too that her days could be filled with endless recesses and popsicle delights. It filled her heart to see her little boy so thrilled about such simple things, and the concept of how the responsibilities of adulthood would way too soon be pressuring her son made her briefly melancholy.

They had been done with their meal long enough for Francine to need a little something more, so she pulled out a little bag of salty sunflower seeds to keep her mouth busy while they lounged and chatted.

"What are those, Mom?" Johnny asked, eyeing the interesting plastic bag. He had been lying on his back on the blanket to watch the birds fly over and make interesting assumptions about the shapes of the clouds.

After spitting out a shell, Francine answered, "Sunflower seeds. Want to try one?" She picked one out of the bag and handed it to him.

"What do I do with it?" Johnny asked while inspecting the little capsule.

Francine giggled, forgetting that the idea behind sunflower seeds wasn't clear to someone who had never tried them.

"There is a yummy seed inside," she explained. "You gently crack it open with your teeth, scoop out the seed, spit out the shell, and eat the seed."

Johnny's eyes widened at the thought. "No way. A seed inside this little thing? You sure would have to eat a lot to get full."

More laughing from Francine.

"Here, let me show you," she said, and she proceeded to follow her own instructions up until the eating the seed part. Between her thumb and index finger, she then revealed the tiny treasure that seemed to magically transform from shell to seed inside her mouth. Reinserting it back into her mouth, she chewed it up with a smile on her face.

Now he really wanted to try it himself. Johnny popped the small morsel into his mouth and found the initial saltiness preventing him from wanting to open it just yet. His taste buds were in overload searching for more seasoning.

Once he had sucked it bland, with his tongue, and using his cheek as a barrier, he positioned the sunflower seed between his teeth to crack it open. *Crunch*, it was over, and the whole thing was in tiny pieces all mixed together. Johnny was surprised at how quickly it had smashed under the force of his jaw, and his disappointed face was easily noted by his mother.

"Oh, dear, that'll happen," she comforted him as he spat the mixture from his mouth. "Here, try another one. It might take a few times to get the hang of it." She handed him another kernel.

Johnny was wholly determined. He wanted to see what the seed tasted like, but more so, he desired to succeed in the magic of breaking the shell while leaving the seed unharmed. Francine observed her son as his mouth and lips twitched from one angle to another since his complete focus was on what was going on in his mouth. His eyes were glazed, and his hands were moving around like they wanted to help but knew they couldn't as the action was inaccessible and off limits.

"Ow!" Johnny exclaimed shortly after the second crunch. He had been so focused on the seed that he'd forgotten to move his tongue out of the way before biting down.

Francine's amusement turned to concern, and she feared she would see blood with his second spit out. What was she thinking letting him eat sunflower seeds?

Johnny reassured her, "I'm ok, I need to try it again; can I, please?"

"Are you sure?" his mother checked. "Are you bleeding?"

"No, Mom," he answered nonchalantly, "it wasn't that hard of a bite. It just surprised me." His only concern was winning this battle with the little encapsulated sunflower seed.

On Johnny's third attempt at coordinating every part of his mouth to do what he wanted, he was, at last, successful. The small pop, followed by the discarding of the shell and the sweet victory of the tiny prize, brought a smile to the little boy's face.

"That was fun!" he roared in enthusiasm. "More please!" and he bounced up and down until he was given another treasure chest to break open. More concentration, another fruitful result, and Johnny was hooked.

"And when you get really good at it, most people do a mouthful at a time," Francine stated, just before depositing multiple seeds into her mouth. "But let's wait until you've had more practice. I don't want you to choke. Ok?" And she proceeded to work on her own mouthful of sunflower seeds while he contentedly worked on one at a time.

After the sunflower seed introduction and practice, the duo decided to stroll around the park and head toward the pond to watch the ducks. Once their belongings were secured back in the car, mother and son moseyed through the grounds without a care in the world. The multitude of nature they witnessed was enlivening for Francine and fascinating to Johnny. Squirrels, birds, more rabbits, ants, butterflies, and other animals big and small went along with their day as if humans weren't around, or tried to anyway.

Not in any hurry whatsoever, just enjoying their day and each other's company immensely, the mother-son duo eventually reached the duck pond after several welcomed wildlife distractions. Johnny was feeling generous and

238

supposed the ducks would like sunflower seeds as well; he wanted to share his newfound entertainment with them. Throwing a few seed into the water, he watched for the ducks to respond, expecting immediate action. Since the closest ones were quite a distance away from them, most of the way across the small lake, they were oblivious to the offering being presented to them. This discouraged Johnny, as there wasn't much he could do to entice them to come closer. If he shouted, it would only scare them further away.

"Just wait, dear," Francine suggested. "We have to be quiet so they feel safe and comfortable coming toward us. Let's practice patience."

Johnny was confused. "But I'm not going to hurt them. I'm just going to share with them."

"They don't know that, sweetie," his mother explained. "All wild animals are used to having to protect themselves, from whatever might threaten them."

"But we're just being nice," Johnny reasoned back. "People wouldn't do anything to them."

Francine took a few minutes to figure out the best way to educate her son that not all people are nice without causing lasting damage to his psyche, besides not wanting to spoil the delightful day they were having.

"Son, unfortunately some people are accidentally hurtful and some are intentionally cruel," she softly generalized, hoping he wouldn't ask too many more questions.

Still not comprehending the concept, Johnny continued, "What does that mean?"

"There are some people who are just not nice, and they don't care about other people, animals, or anything," Francine spoke frankly. "It's not ok, and they know that, but they just don't make good decisions. So, we have to show the birds we are good people by not scaring them."

Johnny looked at the ground with a sad expression. He just couldn't fathom why anyone would choose to be a bad person. That was enough gloomy talk for Francine, and she quickly changed the subject, knowing her young son's attention would quickly shift and he would easily forget about the bad people of the world, at least for now.

"Hey, look, I think they're coming this way," she said, pointing toward the ducks swimming in the water.

Johnny's head lurched up to see, followed quickly by him rising from where they had perched themselves alongside the shoreline to talk and wait. He cautiously neared the water's edge, goodwill seeds at the ready.

"They are coming!" he loudly whispered back to his mom. "They are, I can see them!" He smiled and turned his attention back to the approaching waterfowl.

"Maybe if you squat down, you won't seem so dangerous to them," Francine recommended, still comfortably seated in the grass several feet away.

Just as Johnny reached his lowest level of a crouch, his mother heard him announce, "Hey, there's a frog right down there in the water."

Before she could warn him to be careful, his arm outstretched too far for his lack of balance in a crouched position, and into the water he went, head first. Up Francine jumped to save her son from what she figured was a likely death of drowning, though the water was only a foot deep at the edge. By the time she reached him, he was standing, dripping wet, with a scowl on his face. The shock of going from dry to wet in a split second was upsetting for a child.

He looked so helpless and adorable that Francine couldn't help feeling amused, but considering her son's woeful expression, she dared not distress him even more by showing her initial feeling. As she put out a hand to assist him out of the water, she put her other hand to her mouth to cover a smile that was just refusing to obey her mind that was telling her it was not ok to reveal itself at that particular time.

Yet her efforts to conceal her state of mind were entirely unsuccessful, as Johnny could still see the unmistakable grin in her eyes, but instead of growing more troubled as his mother had guessed he would, he broke out into laughter. The hard giggling made him so wobbly he had to rely more on her to support his efforts of reaching dry land, and he eventually was forced to give her a big hug to regain his composure, thus getting her just about as wet as he was. Surprise from the wet sensation easily gave way to humor for the woman, and they both plopped down on the warm, dry grass, rolling in laughter at the comical incident.

The ducks and frog were, not surprisingly, long gone, wanting nothing to do with the senseless antics of the silly humans. The mother and son did not care; it was a memory that would last a lifetime.

CHAPTER 26

It was the last game of the season, and every one of the town's crazy high-school football fans were in the stands surrounding the playing field, ready for a great game between the two rival teams. Cal and his crew were boosting each other up in the locker room, about to take the field. He couldn't help reminiscing about how unforgettable the season had been, good and bad.

Once the coach and school learned the truth behind the locker room misunderstanding, they were overjoyed and grateful, maybe not as much as Cal himself, or his dad, but very glad to hear they were not mistaken about his character after all. Aside from not having another student fall victim to drugs, a good kid was hopefully saved from it too. It was quite Cal's pleasure to inform them all that they had made a huge mistake about him and, moreover, about Brent's sincerity to sober up. There was a lot of apologizing and hand-shaking that ensued; Cal felt like a star.

Mr. Hannover softened his demeanor enough to admit that he had not been fair to Cal and confirmed he would be more careful and understanding in the future with other students. Cal was kind and mature enough to state that he could see how it would be hard to trust kids, especially when a particular situation looked pretty clear. The incident had been wiped clean from existence, and Cal was back to his life as normal.

Shortly after the mix-up and revelation, Richard and Cal had another deep, respectful, adult conversation over it, with both of them left feeling even better about their growing relationship.

"How do you think you would have done things differently?" Richard asked for his son to analyze.

Cal thought for a minute. "Well, first I should have questioned why Brent didn't just tell the coach himself that he was going to be missing practice. That should have been a big clue. I was just so happy to be asked to help him out that I didn't think about it."

"I understand that," Richard agreed. "Now you see how tricky trust can be. Unfortunately, most people are just out for themselves, intently selfishly or not. I'm sure he didn't expect you to get into trouble, but he knew you wouldn't question him either."

"I really looked up to him, so it wasn't even a thought in my mind that there was anything shady going on," Cal continued, shaking his head. "I can't believe people can be so selfish."

Richard added, "I think the drugs have something to do with that, but I also think that the quality has to be in a person's character somewhere, on some level, to use people so easily too." He felt this was a good lesson for his son, but he also felt bad that he'd had to learn it in such a hard and unfair way.

"I sure hope he has learned from this and stays off drugs," said Cal; his concern for Brent was genuine. "And I hope he hasn't already ruined his chances of playing football for a college." The doubtful expression on his face was evident as he spoke. "That would be a real shame."

"I'm glad he has you as a good, solid friend to help him through it," Richard said, complimenting his son. "And he'll probably need your recommendations when he applies for jobs. You might just be the eraser to his bad deeds on paper."

Cal laughed. "Ok, Dad. That's a lot of pressure," he said

teasingly. "I've never been compared to an eraser before." He knew what his dad was intending but decided to give him a hard time. Richard smiled back and assured him he was the man for the job.

Moving on, Cal continued to dissect the situation. "I think the toughest part of it all was not being listened to by Mr. Hannover. That was so frustrating, not having a voice, not being heard one bit."

Richard nodded, and a sadness overcame him. He didn't like the thought of his son struggling like that, made to feel worthless, especially when he hadn't done anything wrong, quite the opposite, in fact. The vice principal should feel lucky that Richard hadn't gone in to his office to give him the "what's what" for treating his son that way. He realized that the vice principal was just doing his job, and he was probably tired of all the student's excuses day in and day out – goodness knows Richard got it enough himself from all the perps on the street – but just taking one second to listen to his son could have prevented all of this.

Then he stopped. He himself had done the exact same thing, and he wondered if his son was trying to hint towards that fact. He couldn't feel more horrible about how he had treated Cal, especially after the mistreatment by the school. They had already talked about it, but he was compelled to rehash it just in case.

"I don't recall if I've ever been in that situation before, where someone wouldn't listen to my explanation," Richard began. "I can't even imagine how that felt for you. I know I told you, but I'm saying it again, I'm so sorry for causing you more pain of adding to your frustration, stress, and helplessness by not giving you a chance to explain yourself either. That was very wrong of me. Even if you had been guilty of doing drugs and skipping out on practice, I should have been respectful enough to listen to you."

Cal's sudden emotional throat blockage almost prevented him from responding, but he quickly swallowed his feelings and replied, "I appreciate that, Dad, more than you know. I'm not sure I would have done anything differently if I was in your shoes. Besides, for life in general, now I know for when I have kids."

"Oh, dear," Richard exclaimed. "I'm not ready for that yet! Don't you go getting yourself into that kind of trouble now." He laughed nervously, but more freely than skeptically.

Once Cal was done giggling and blushing, he assured his dad that wasn't an option yet anyway.

"Really? No smart ladies out there who want a date with my handsome son, eh?" Richard teased. He found himself quite relieved. His son would have plenty of time for that later; now was way too soon for his comfort level.

Blushing a darker shade of red, Cal confirmed, "I think I've been too busy with football. No girls, Dad. I think I still believe they have cooties."

Richard laughed. "Son. They do, and they never get rid of them. What happens is you stop being scared of their cooties. But enough about that, just know I did land your mom, so if you ever need advice or anything, I do know a thing or two."

"Thanks, Dad, I'll keep that in mind." Cal was more than ready to get off that subject. He was grateful his dad verbally opened that particular door, even though he felt a lot more comfortable talking about anything with him lately.

"Teamwork, on three!" shouted the coach. Cal hadn't realized how far into his reminiscing he had gotten until he was suddenly shocked back to reality by coach Steed's encouraging yell.

Cal always searched the crowd for his parents as soon as he ran onto the field. There were so many people there that he could not find them this time, but he knew they were there, and that was enough. Drake had made sure to get the night off from work, so Cal was sure his buddies were there supporting him as well. Now the goal was to make them proud; this was his one last chance this year to show them what he could do. Generally, he made good plays and was definitely a significant asset to the team as a whole, but he really wanted to do something to stand out, end it on a grand note.

The teams were very evenly matched; each had speedy players who could run circles around and past others. There was an equal balance of heights and weights, and the quarterbacks shared similar stats. Brent "The Man" Jackson had gone through his required three weeks of therapy and was cleared to play the last game, so the team was extra excited to crush their opponents.

The score bounced back and forth as the first half played on, and neither team led by more than a touchdown at a time. One side of the field hooted and hollered when their team would score or put on a spectacular feat, and the fans on other side would respond even louder when it was their turn to celebrate. Cal was certain he could specifically hear his parents and friends now and then above the crowd.

Halftime arrived and allowed the tired teams, as well as the electrified fans, a cooling off period. Both the concessions and restrooms were bombarded like a cool oasis in the sweltering desert during the short break. No one wanted to miss a minute of this game, or they would hear about it on Monday.

Cal and his team came out of the break well-rested enough to hit the other team hard right away. The fans and coaching staff could tell the members of the team were familiar with each other's moves, as each play was completed perfectly. Unfortunately, the other team was experiencing similar second-half success.

At last, it was finally near the end of the fourth quarter, and Coach Steed opted to run a new play; he was striving for something different in an attempt to throw off the other team, pull ahead, and seal their fate once and for all. It would either pay off with high reward or result in disaster, but he was willing to, and needed to, take the risk. The players lined up, the tension grew even higher, and the trash talking became louder and nastier.

The ball was hiked and grunting quickly ensued, followed by the sound of bodies crashing together. Cal didn't even see it coming. With a short groan, his world suddenly and unexpectedly became black. The play changeup had been a success, but just for the home team, not Cal. Resulting from the play modification, the largest player on the opposite team found himself head-to-head with one of the smaller players on the other team and took advantage of his new fortune by wiping him out, hard.

From the stands, Diane gasped and nearly fainted. Disbelief prevented her from moving. The scene on the field was exactly what she'd dreaded from the moment Cal had come to them requesting to join the football team. Her son was lying motionless on the ground. And then she started to shove people out of the way and run. She swore she was running in sand; she could not get out there fast enough. Richard passed her up just before reaching their son. The team's physical therapist was already attending to Cal, so all Richard and Diane could do was watch and wait.

The ringing in their ears from hours of loud cheering added to the irony of the contradictory deafening silence on the field.

What seemed like hours had only been minutes; the stillness of the boy lying on the ground coordinated with the stillness and blackness of the evening. Finally, movement. One of Cal's feet swayed to the side and back. Diane begged for more. Just moments later, his eyes opened, and the physical therapist, who had been anticipating this, prevented him from making any sudden movements, out of confusion and unawareness, that could increase the risk of lasting injury. Basic vitals were taken, and specific questions were asked until the professional was comfortable moving the young lad. The stretcher was called out to the field, and Cal was very carefully placed in a neck immobilizer, loaded onto the stretcher, and wheeled off the field to the waiting ambulance.

Diane was allowed to ride along in the aid car while Richard drove with Drake and Joe. If she sat any closer to her son, she'd have been on the stretcher with him. All she could do was hold his hand in hers to stay out of the paramedic's way while they were performing their duties. Cal was asked similar questions to the ones he was asked on the field, but this time, the paramedics had to remind Diane to let her son answer. She was so used to being the parent and taking control of situations like these that it was very unnatural for her to not the be source of the information. Besides the "this can't be happening" feeling, all she was thinking was how grateful she was that he was conscious and alert, and moving.

Drake and Joe were very worried about their friend. But since they weren't in his presence but in Richard's instead, their concern was diverted. Cal's protective father was in such a ranting daze they regretted getting in a moving vehicle with him. He was blaming the other players, the coach, and of course himself and his wife for allowing this to happen. The two passengers fearfully noticed Richard's focus was not on the traffic around them but solely on the ambulance in front of them; nothing was going to stop him from losing that vehicle. Nothing.

The hospital waiting room was unoccupied when they arrived. After Diane filled the men in about Cal's condition, the majority of the communication between them was not through words but concerned and agonizing looks now and then. The mutual fundamental hope was that, since he had been alert and able to move his body, his outcome would be a full recovery, but they all understood that head and neck injuries were not an insignificant matter. Even if Cal walked out of that hospital, that wouldn't be the end of it; he would be closely monitored, by all four of them. The two companions were just as protective of Cal as his parents. Diane, Richard, Drake, and Joe waited.

Finally, an optimistic female, dressed like a doctor, walked toward them, and Diane jumped up from her seat, followed quickly by Richard. The encouraging smile on the physician's face was promising, but until they heard the diagnosis verbally, they still feared getting their hopes up. She confirmed that the small group was there for Cal, introduced herself, and proceeded to give them the information they so greedily craved.

"It is a concussion," she said respectfully, "as you probably could have guessed. We ran some preliminary tests and are pleased with the results. From what we have so far, we expect Cal to come out of this just fine. There shouldn't be any permanent damage."

The sigh Diane exhaled could have probably been heard back at the football field miles away, and the subsequent tears were ones of mass relief. Hugs went around, and Diane asked if she could see him.

"I want to point out that, since your son was unconscious for a time, he is not out of danger just yet," the doctor continued. "We will be keeping him overnight at least, to run a few more tests, monitor him, and ensure his condition continues to improve." Then she agreed to allow them to see him.

Diane and Richard confirmed with Drake and Joe that they would be ok until their parents came to get them, thanked them for being there, and disappeared to where the doctor had emerged just a few minutes prior. They wished they could go see their friend too, but tomorrow was another day, and he was in good hands.

CHAPTER 27

"That was so nice of you guys," Cal said, his face beaming. "I still have the deflated balloon you brought me the next day." The three friends were reminiscing over the football accident a few weeks ago and subsequent events.

Cal laughed. "*My Little Pony* was just the right touch too. You guys know it's my favorite. All those pretty pastel colors brightened me right up! The nurses were giving me weird looks after that," he said, and they all doubled over in laughter.

Drake was driving the three of them around in his new car, showing off his skills. Of course, it wasn't a "new" car, but to them, it just as well was, and his "skills" weren't much to brag about. This giant step between childhood and adulthood was a fresh, exhilarating feeling of being grown-up with the freedom to do what they wanted and go where they wanted without someone looking over their shoulders for once.

The trio had been warned, by each of their parents, how crucial it was for Cal to take it easy. And also reminded them how easily their freedom would be taken away if they heard of any misdoings whatsoever. Drake and Joe didn't need reminding; they were pretty stern on Cal regardless. The last thing they wanted was for him to have a relapse while under their care.

There was no destination, just the open road, wind in their hair – even if more metaphorically, it was the best day ever for all three of them.

"I'm so jealous. I can't wait until I'm driving," Cal stated.

"This is second best for sure, though."

Drake nodded. "It's a little scary – other drivers are nuts, seriously – but I love it. And Mom is sure liking not having to take me to work and pick me up anymore. It has been a bit tricky coordinating our work schedules sometimes, but so worth it."

"My parents aren't as anxious to have me driving because of Ryan and Leslie already driving and helping out," Joe chimed in with a pouty face. "Stinks for me. Seems like it will be forever before I get to drive… maybe once I get a job. Good thing I have you guys!"

Drake continued, "As much as I like driving, though, it seems she always needs an errand done. This is only my second time taking the car out just for me! Driving my little brother and sister around is getting old already too, even though I knew I was going to have to. I know they just find things for me to take them to, I just know it."

"Maybe that will calm down eventually," Cal suggested. "It's new to them too, and they probably like you driving them better than your mom."

Joe inquired, "Do you have extra spending money, or is it all going toward the car and helping your mom out?"

"I have a little," Drake confirmed, "but it sure disappears quickly. Mom hasn't asked for anything; she's been really good about that so far. She knows I've been working hard to earn my wages. But I know the day is coming, and then she'll probably expect it more and more. Sure makes me angry at our dad."

The sad, disturbed look on his friend's face made Joe regret asking, but he didn't know the topic was going to lead to that. He quickly changed the subject.

"Hey, where are we headed?" Joe asked excitedly. "We don't need to use up all your gas. Maybe we should think of somewhere to go and let the car sit for a while."

Cal thought quickly. "We should get a burger and root beer at the drive-in. Then we could still be in the car but not using gas."

Drake agreed, "Great idea, I am hungry. And that'll be fun too," he continued, as his stomach grumbled at the mention of food and he altered the car's direction toward that destination.

Joe and Cal dug out their allowances and odd job money to pay for Drake's food in return for the gas being used to haul them around for entertainment. When they pulled up to a spot at the drive-in, they felt like kings, as this was another very pleasing, new experience. All three young men were fairly nonchalantly looking around to see who noticed how they were now adults, in their opinion, and should be respected as so.

Waiting for their ordered food, they caught up on recent events.

"That's so scary about your mom," Cal stated. "I would've been freaking out."

Drake agreed, "How did you even get through those hours? I would have died from worry."

"Maybe having Leslie and Sammy there to focus on kept me from losing it completely," Joe admitted. "As much as I resented them because I didn't get to go along with my mom," he finished with a sour look.

Cal cautiously ventured to say, "At least it was more just a scare than anything really serious."

"Yeah, things have been back to ok since then," Joe agreed. "We have been even more careful keeping her calm, so no more emergencies, but she is always weak and tired seems like." Drake and Cal weren't sure how to comfort their friend.

The food arrived, brought to them by a young lady on roller skates and dressed in an old-time uniform, and Joe was thankful. He appreciated his friends' concern, but he was ready to stop talking about his mom's illness. All three boys' attention quickly shifted to the employee, who was attractive enough to make them blush and stammer through what should have been simple conversation. Nothing was said to embarrass or tease anyone when she left, as they were all in the same silly discomfort, not having dealt much with the fairer sex in their young lives.

"So, no lasting effects from your accident, Cal?" Joe inquired with a mouthful of warm, crunchy fries.

Cal swallowed his salty bite of mushroom burger to respond, "I had a few checkups, one a few days after and another the following week, and I've been cleared. It is kind of scary knowing something could creep up, but the doctors are pretty certain I'm fine." He washed down his last bite with his root beer float.

"Well, that's good to know!" Drake exclaimed. "Medical professionals are so smart. They didn't ask us; we know you're not fine!" He chuckled at Cal's expense.

"Haha," Cal giggled. "I'm finer than you. Didn't you see how that girl was looking at me?" He was proud of himself for thinking of that comeback so quickly.

Drake countered, "You need your eyes checked, man, she was looking at me the whole time, dude. The ladies love a man with a license." He lightly placed one wrist on the top of the steering wheel and tilted his head, trying to look cool.

"What do you know about what the 'ladies' love, Drake?" Joe said, joining in the banter. "Oh, please fill us in! Where's my notebook, I need to write this down..."

"Yeah, a license for crazy talk." Cal's jibes were coming so easily that he was immensely enjoying the lighthearted, playful conversation. "Go ask for her number, I dare ya."

Drake recoiled at the terrifying thought of putting his words to action by actually talking to a girl. "You started it, you go do it. I'm not finished eating," he said, and he chomped on his cheeseburger looking too terribly busy to bother with a female at the moment.

Both Cal and Joe laughed heartily at his shy reconsideration and retreat from the front lines of the dating game.

Bellies full and content, the trio hit the open road again before falling into a food-induced calm in the warm car. Once again, they had nowhere in mind to go; it was just thrilling to not be walking or riding their bikes. Just a few blocks from the diner, Drake stopped at a red light. Cal was fooling around with the radio, seeking the perfect music station for a carefree day. Joe was the first to notice a car full of young men pull up next to them at the stoplight and begin taunting them.

Drake knew better than to allow them access to his feelings, because having a car was a privilege not a right, and that the freedom could be taken away from him in a second. However, he was still a young man learning the ways of the world, and there was no way he was going to let them get away with provoking him, or his friends, without some kind of retort. The three buddies would not be bullied; that was just the way it was.

However, a good old-fashioned fist fight was not in the making. All the instigators ended up wanting was to see who could beat who off the line and down the street. Another new experience for the three adventurers, this racing game relieved the boys by how the male-measure-up had changed to something so simple and less threatening to their well-being, in their opinion anyway. No longer did they have to physically stand up for themselves and risk bumps and bruises, both literally to their bodies and figuratively to their egos. They naively didn't consider the risk of a car accident from the dangerous activity.

Drake revved up his engine, at least, as much as he could get the old heap of metal on wheels to rev, in affirmative answer to the joust invitation, and smirked and nodded to the other driver. This resulted in another, louder engine roar from the adjacent vehicle, which if Drake, Joe, and Cal hadn't been so new to the driving scene, would have told them the age difference between the two cars so that they could foresee their impending fate before embarrassing themselves. No one would have bet on them winning, but they didn't know that. Lack of life experience, as well as excitement, blocked them from that realization.

Joe's grasp clutched tightly to the back of each of the front seats while he was barely sitting on the edge of his own. From the front seats, Drake and Cal stared at the red light in front of them, anticipating its change to green. Drake's foot was barely on the brake, ready to punch the accelerator in a split second. Time stood still.

Since none of them knew how to predict the switch by watching the opposite light posts, the troublemakers in the opposing car jumped ahead with plenty of seconds to spare, leaving Drake, Cal, and Joe behind without a chance. Regardless, Drake had stomped on the gas as soon as he got the go-ahead green light, and before they reached the other side of the intersection, the old car jerked, sputtered out, and died. Its limits had been greatly exceeded, and without much effort by the young driver.

Drake had not done lasting damage, however. The vehicle started right up when he turned the key, which allowed the boys a little less embarrassment than being stuck in the middle of the road and having to push their means of transportation instead of it carrying them. The other vehicle was long gone, so they were free from that ridicule as well, unless the other boys saw them again on the road, of course. They would probably not be as easily forgotten as they hoped.

"They sure had our number, didn't they?" Cal said, feeling foolish. They were back traversing the streets, though apprehensively now, as the wind had been taken out of their sails.

Drake nodded. "That was stupid." He wasn't sitting as high up in the driver's seat as he was previously.

"Well, now we know," Joe added. "Besides, that kind of stuff is dangerous anyway. We were lucky there wasn't a pedestrian or cop around."

"Someone could have been trying to beat the red light from the other way too," Drake agreed. "I sure am glad we didn't get into an accident."

Cal backed them up, saying, "I guess as embarrassing as the result had been, we got off lucky, actually."

"Maybe if we were outside of town," Drake concluded as he slowly controlled the car, turning it from an avenue to a street. "It sure was fun, and would've been cool if we could have been actual competition for them!"

Joe reigned him back in, saying, "Don't get too excited. I don't know if that's such a good idea either. You don't want your license taken away, by either the cops or your mom."

"I know," Drake pouted. "But you can't deny how exciting it was. Maybe I should look into being a racecar driver."

Cal huffed a bit, and then said, "Oh no. That would be dangerous, you operating a machine that races at high speeds. Oof!"

"Why don't you stick to your grocery store job for now and worry about your career later," Joe encouraged. "How's that going, by the way?"

Drake actually smiled. "It's been great, besides not having as much free time anymore. I'm learning a lot, meeting new people, getting more responsibility… and Mr. Riley is so smart and funny. We joke around a lot, but I make sure I get to business when I need to. I really respect him."

"Wow, that's cool, almost makes me want to get a job too," Cal said. "Almost. I hope I have a cool boss when I get a job."

Joe asked, "What kind of things does he have you doing?"

"Mostly just cleaning things up, the backroom and if there are any spills or anything," Drake informed them. "Stocking the shelves and heavy lifting in the backroom too."

"Are you going to be learning anything more?" Joe asked.

Drake nodded. "There's been talk of me learning how to check. Sometimes it gets busy and they need a hand up there."

"Would you like that?" Cal inquired.

"I wouldn't want it to be my main task, but it would be a nice change from the other stuff I do," Drake answered. "How's the job search going for you guys?"

"Ugh." Cal couldn't get an actual word out before expressing his initial opinion. "I'm trying to put it off as long as possible. I like not having that responsibility!"

"Agreed," Joe stated plainly. "I don't want to have to work. Besides, the jobs we can get are so lame anyway."

Cal said, "I know the money would be so nice, but having to be tied to a job sounds horrible. I can't use the head injury excuse much longer; the parentals are pressuring." He rolled his eyes.

"It is kind of a crazy thought," Drake added as he braked for a slower car in front of them, "if you want more freedom, you have to be tied down and accountable to something. In order to have a car and money for things, you have to earn it; well, most people do anyway. Wouldn't that be awesome if you just inherited money? If your family was rich and you didn't have to work?"

In complete opposition to their daily, somewhat subconscious, goal to prove they were adults, the naturally growing, maturing teens temporarily stopped their complaining and fight to grow up to live in that care-free dream for a moment.

CHAPTER 28

Drake was back to the grind, performing the kinds of tasks that still allowed his mind to wander. He was still far from obtaining any kind of job that was too thought-provoking. The big boss man, Clement Riley, had him start his shift at the grocery store that day by organizing and stocking a big order that had come in. He reckoned his whole shift would be spent in the back of the store, which was fine with him as he was in a mood and wasn't in a hurry to get the order done and venture out front and see if there was any other work to do.

The last couple of evenings, he had been stuck being babysitter to his siblings, again, so the solitariness of his current task was more than welcomed. And, here he was, compensated and appreciated for his hard work, where at home it was expected and without such reward. Clement also let him turn a radio on, as long as it wasn't heard beyond the walls of the storage room.

He was be-bopping away, singing when he knew the words, humming when he didn't, and letting the rhythms pace his work flow. It leisurely turned into the ideal remedy as his quick irritation and surging impatience were dissipating with each crate or pallet he unloaded. It was surprising to him how he was finding the orderliness and productivity a release, unlike how untidy he kept, and liked, his bedroom at home.

Just when Drake was as engrossed into his assignment as possible and proudly making it his own, a co-worker, James Taleroux, surprised him with his presence. James had been employed there for a few years now, and he knew the ropes. He took advantage of the fact that Drake was new and learning and teetered between being bossy and being helpful, at least towards Drake, and especially when the boss wasn't around.

"Hey, what's this?" James' voice echoed over the soft music, causing Drake to jump and turn towards the sudden, unexpected noise.

"What's what?" Drake asked, craning his neck to see. He wasn't feeling too accepting of the interruption, so he didn't rush right over. And it seemed odd to him that James didn't know something.

James was all for letting Drake know the reason for his confusion. "Well, this isn't supposed to be here." He was pointing at a large stack of paper towels that Drake had finished with an hour ago. "Why in the world would you put these here? Now I have to move them. You created more work for me." He put his hands on his hips to increase the "very put out" look he was portraying.

"I didn't know," Drake said with a shrug. "That's what my map says. That's where they go." He was thoroughly confused, first, as to why the paper towels didn't go there, and second, as to why James was so overly upset. He could move them himself if need be; it had nothing to do with James.

James would not let up. "You must be using an old map. You have to know which maps to use, which ones are current." He ripped the back stock organizational map out of Drake's hands with a sigh that could cause a hurricane and an eye roll that made Drake wonder if his eyes were ever going to come back to normal. He was being so dramatic that Drake would've laughed if his temper hadn't been rising for being made to feel stupid and incompetent.

"Fine. Where are the current ones?" Drake demanded. "And

how do I know if I have a current one or not?"

"You have to pay attention to when new ones are drawn up," James replied, delivering as unclear of an answer as he could.

Obviously, that information did not help Drake in any way. He stood staring at James, silently urging him for more facts to work with; he was so dumbfounded by what useless material he had gotten so far that he couldn't think of a question to get the answer he needed. James stood staring back at him.

"Everyone just knows," James finally stammered, shaking his head. "It's just… it is unacceptable not to know."

That didn't work for Drake. Everything he had learned from Clement so far was clear and logical; this was far from that.

Instead of going straight to the boss to clear up the apparent misunderstanding, Drake unintentionally made things worse, saying, "That's outrageous and stupid." He pointed directly into James's face, almost touching his nose with the tip of his index finger.

James's face flushed hot red, and not knowing how to respond as no one before had stood up to him, he remained silent, allowing Drake to continue.

"Why wouldn't that be communicated *to* the staff when new maps are created?" Drake probed. "Or just dispose of old maps altogether. Wouldn't that eliminate the risk of things being put where they don't belong, thus creating more work?" He felt he had come to that easy solution so quickly that he just knew James's reasoning wasn't sound.

Drake persisted, "But you come back here, obviously looking for trouble, making stuff up, and criticizing my work."

"I wasn't looking for trouble," James responded, defending himself from that specific comment. "I just want things done right, and you clearly weren't doing it." James retaliated the finger pointing toward Drake as he emphasized the word "you."

"Well, now I know, and I'll fix it. It won't take me long. Why would you assume you'd be redoing it anyway?" Drake asked. "I did not create more work for you, it has nothing to do with you, so you don't need to lay that on me too."

Drake walked away from James; he saw no need to converse with the guy any longer. Even if he had heard James continuing the argument, he would not have given him the respect to turn around and listen. He was on a mission to find the correct storage map, fix the apparent issue, and get on with his task.

He found Clement in his office, knee-deep in paperwork. Drake noted his bifocal eyeglasses were barely hanging off the tip of his nose, and he had a pencil in one hand and a piece of paper in the other. The lamp on the corner of the large wooden desk was the only source of light in the small room, but it was more than sufficient lighting for the tedious work in front of the boss man.

The gentle knock on the door from a patiently waiting Drake caused the big man to look up from the papers to unmask the identity of his visitor. Through the shadows, Clement's eyes focused on the young man, and he smiled as he put down the document and pencil to welcome him in.

"Just in time," Clement recited gleefully, "I needed a break from this monotony. What can I do for you, Drake?"

The positivity was easily contagious, and Drake's temperament instantly started to return to its content pre-James situation level. The greeting was a one-eighty from what had just happened in the store room, and he was not surprised, knowing Clement's personality well enough, but he was much in need of the encouragement.

"Hi, Mr. Riley," Drake courteously began. "I was just wondering where the updated, current storage maps are. I guess I put the paper towels in the wrong location and would like to remedy that mistake as quickly as possible."

Clement became a bit confused. He didn't mind being interrupted, and he welcomed Drake's company, but he wondered why he didn't ask another staff member instead of coming all the way up to his office. Once his puzzlement subsided, he sensed a tension and aggravation coming from the boy, and an unfortunate inkling grew in his mind. He wasn't blind to the troubles James caused in his store, and he knew Drake was still respectfully not in his office to tattle-tale.

"Let me guess," Clement supposed, "you had some unkindly business just now downstairs?" He sighed, removed his eyeglasses from his face, set them on the papers in front of him, leaned back in his office chair, and folded his arms across his chest.

Drake felt foolish. Maybe James was right after all. He must've been instructed about the maps early on and forgotten; there was so much to learn that it was a possible explanation, though not an excuse. Now he had gotten himself into more trouble by talking back to James, a trusted, valued employee of Clement's. And the darn paper towels were sitting in the wrong location, proof that he messed up.

He nodded his head in shame. "I'm sorry, I should've known about the updated maps. And I should not have lost my temper with James. I know he was only helping, it's his job, but he was so condescending that I couldn't help standing up for myself, but it was the wrong way..." He realized he was rambling and that it was likely making the situation even worse. "The last thing I want to do is make more work for anyone, including myself," he finished quickly.

"Oh, dear boy," Clement said with a chuckle, "you are mistaking the direction of my disappointment. I know how

James is, and I'm getting to know you pretty quickly too."

Drake's attention shifted from despair at the floor to hope at his boss's entertained face.

"You aren't the first one to have some trouble with James," he explained, "but I'll talk to him about that." And seeing Drake's face turn to worry, he added, "He will know you didn't come here to get him in trouble."

"Now," the boss said, moving on to the actual matter at hand. He sat back up in his chair, placed his forearms on the desk, offered Drake to take a seat, and proceeded, "first off, there should only be current maps on the backroom clipboards, so there shouldn't be any confusion.

"Second, storing the 'wrong' item in the 'wrong' place for a cycle isn't a big deal," he advised. "We will just swap what was 'supposed' to go there until new shipments come in. No need to waste time moving things around. It's not the first time this has happened, James knows this.

"Now, lastly, tell me what happened with James. I need your side of the story so I know how to proceed with him. How badly did you lose your temper?" Clement asked, concluding his instructional, investigative part of the impromptu meeting with an assumption.

Drake recounted the recent awkward and regrettable backroom brawl. No matter how it made him look, he was honest about everything he had said and how he had acted, and to the best of his ability, he accurately portrayed James's role in the encounter.

Clement hesitated to say anything once it was clear that Drake was finished with his own account of the confrontation. He was relieved the altercation hadn't nearly been as bad as he'd imagined, but he needed Drake to know that no level of hostility was acceptable in his store. He was proud of his business, he had worked very hard to make it successful, and he wasn't going to let young boys' rampant testosterone ruin that. He knew that customers saw and heard a lot more than they let on, and if he let it go he would soon be out of business because he would have lost them all due to unpleasant vibes.

"How would you handle it differently next time?" Clement asked his newest employee.

Drake contemplated for a few seconds. "Well, knowing how James is now, I would listen to his instruction and then ask another employee or come to you for confirmation or additional information if something seems off. I guess that would go for any co-worker."

Clement nodded. He was pleased that Drake was intelligent and mature enough to see the error and solve the problem on his own instead of having to be told, and multiple times.

Drake was genuinely thanked by his fair boss, given the current storage maps, instructed to dispose of any old maps, and asked to return to the store room to complete his task. As much as he appreciated his boss and enjoyed spending time with him, he was more than happy to get back to work and forget about the stressful event.

CHAPTER 29

Life around the Hart residence had been back to normal since the hospital scare for some time. Or as close as it could be to normal with cancer's rude intrusion of making itself at home there too. Ryan kept his word and had been coming around a lot more often, and additionally, making more phone calls. Sometimes, he would call just to talk to one of the family members, and sometimes the phone would be passed around.

Gail had learned her lesson and was much more careful in her active duties. It wasn't good for her to just sit around, but she definitely had a limit, and she stayed far from that line. The family found great ways to help her feel like she was still a useful contributor instead of another chore they had to cross off their list.

From folding laundry on the couch to making out the grocery list, and from being in charge of the finances to light dusting and helping with schoolwork, the kids felt as though their mom was somehow even more evident in the house than she was before. Gail experienced her outlook improving as well; having assigned tasks made getting out of bed in the morning easier, and the kids understanding her restrictions relieved much of the guilt or resentment that came with her debilitating disease.

It was Joe's turn again to accompany his mom to another chemotherapy treatment appointment, and he was all too pleased to be the chosen one, aside from the circumstance. The one-on-one time with his mom was a necessity for him, even before she got sick.

They had struck up quite a friendship with little Peter and his mom Rachel. And without a doubt, they both very much looked forward to his entertaining and uplifting positive attitude and wondered what jokes or talents he was going to share with them today.

As Joe and Gail walked into the cancer treatment facility, they looked around for their friends as they normally did. Not seeing them, they proceeded to a station that had an empty one beside it and "reserved" it for when their friends did show up.

"I was going to research some magic tricks but didn't get around to it," Joe informed his mom once they were settled in. "I wanted to impress Peter for once," he said with a smile. "Maybe next time."

Gail grinned back. "He usually has more than enough to entertain us. I don't know if he would share his 'stage' with anyone anyway. It might have been a waste of time, but it is a nice thought." Still smiling and thinking of Peter's cute attention-getting antics, she put her head back on the chair and closed her eyes.

"I should have brought a book and read to you," Joe commented. "I guess I wasn't prepared to be the entertainer today."

"That's ok, dear. Tell me how school is going," Gail suggested without lifting her head or opening her tired eyes. "Anything exciting or interesting lately?"

Joe thought about it. On average, school wasn't anything stimulating to talk about.

"How about Cal? Is he all healed up?" This new inquiry was enough for her to open her eyes and lift her head back up to observe her son's face.

She found Joe's expression to show concern and relief in one. "Yes, he is doing very good. That was sure scary, Mom, seeing him just lying on the ground not moving."

Gail patted her son's hand. "It is not something you see every day, even on the news."

"I'm glad he doesn't have any more games. I don't know if I could watch him play anymore," Joe added. "I think his parents feel the same way too. He's really been taking it easy, and his last checkup they still didn't see anything wrong."

With that report, Gail felt comfortable resting her weary head back on the chair and closing her eyes again. "That is great news, Joe. I should give Diane a call soon. You are a great friend to him, and Drake too."

"Yeah, they are great friends to me too." Joe felt proud to say that. And remembering their latest excursion, he filled his mom in on their fun day out with Drake's new car, sans the failed racing part of the story.

Joe had done such a great job keeping them occupied that the session was over before they knew it. When the nurse came to release Gail, she realized what had happened, and worry set in because Rachel and Peter never showed up. They had told them that they would see them next time; maybe they'd had a conflicting engagement that just came up. She wasn't sure, legally, how much the facility could divulge to them, but she had to ask.

"Did little Peter not have an appointment today?" Gail asked politely.

The nurse shook her head and attempted to hide her solemn expression but failed. They both knew there was nothing else to say. It was understood that the sweet, petite young boy was no longer suffering through his tough struggle. He was done just putting on a happy face when he was confused as to why he was imperiled with the deadly disease.

Joe hadn't caught the emotions between the two adults at

first and wondered why the nurse wasn't answering. Once he saw his mom's face, however, he went into denial. No. It couldn't be; Peter was too cute, smart, funny, and encouraging of a little soul for him to be taken. He was supposed to get over it, not let it take his life. Too many times, his eyes had filled with tears in this room – less since he'd met Peter – but this was going to be another teary-eyed day added to the list.

Gail and Joe's eyes locked, and neither could say a word. The waterworks were on, the floodgates fully open. They slowly embraced each other, and standing in the middle of the treatment room, they mourned together over a bright, innocent soul that had so positively touched many people and should not have been taken so soon.

This was quite a loss for humanity, and Gail needed to give her condolences to Rachel and their family. The cancer center would have to understand that. They agreed to give Peter's family the Hart's contact information, and Gail requested to write a note as well in hopes of urging a response. She didn't care if she was crossing any ethical or personal lines; she had to let them know they cared and to offer any help they could.

Mother and son were quiet on the drive home. All Joe could think about was how fragile life was. Since his mom had been doing so well since her episode, he had forgotten how deadly of a disease it was she was still fighting.

After dinner, Joe and Gail found themselves at the kitchen table finally discussing the sad news.

"It makes me scared," Joe said with a quiver to his bottom lip. "We could lose you just like that."

Gail agreed, saying, "I know, me too. I can't imagine not being here for you, your dad, and your brothers and sister. It is a very scary thought."

Joe continued, "It makes me angry too. Why don't the mean

people get diseases and die instead? Why do such great people have to suffer? It's not fair and doesn't make sense."

"I agree it doesn't make sense, but that is life. We're not supposed to know everything. It's probably better that we don't know everything. There would be no surprises and mysteries; life would be pretty boring," Gail softly rationalized. As upset and scared as she was about having cancer in the first place, she had to be a parent right now and be there for her son. It hurt her heart to see him like this.

"What's worse is that we can't do anything about it. We can't just fix it or ignore it. We just have to live with it and deal with it," Joe complained.

Gail fully understood and replied, "We need to learn from Peter and not get ourselves down. He would not have wanted us to pout and be negative."

"I know, but it's just so hard," Joe said, his voice wavering. "Can I just be mad for a bit and then find something to be happy about? I'm not ready to be happy about anything yet."

Gail found herself suppressing a laugh at how cute that statement was. "Yes, son, you can take time to grieve and think things through. We all need that time." His stubbornness was just what she needed to start the process of coming out of her own depression. Leave it to her caring, thoughtful son to succeed where she was failing, and he wasn't even trying.

A few days later, Gail received a call from her doctor's office requesting her to schedule a checkup and consultation appointment as soon as possible. She was looking forward to the update and seeing if there had been any progress, but with the recent sad news still fresh in her mind, she decided to ask her best support buddy Joey along too.

The vibe between mother and son was upbeat and positive

on the drive to the doctor's office. They discussed getting a bite to eat after the appointment at their favorite little spot. That was almost more enticing than possibly hearing good news about Gail's progress. They just hoped it would be a celebratory meal instead of a comfort food meal. Gail sensed it was going to be a good day, as they had had too much disappointment and sadness lately to take any more.

Joe waited patiently for his mom while they did their tests and examinations on her. The sports magazine he picked up was not captivating enough for his mind not to wander, and the page turning was simply automatic, not from his use and subsequent ending need for the information it reported. As energetic as they had made the day, the chance that the whole atmosphere could change in a minute depending on the test results was in the forefront of his mind. Either way, he was glad he was the one to be there for her, good or bad.

His mom, with her smiling face and bouncy gait, eventually emerged from a back room, and she joined him in his paused waiting position where time seemed to stand still. Joe couldn't help but think they should call it an eternity room instead; he had been in too many waiting rooms lately. He thrived off her energy but was still worried. They were doing everything they could and followed every instruction explicitly for her to get better, but the Hart family knew too well that cancer cannot be controlled. It does what it wants to whomever it wants, for no reason.

"Do the tests hurt that they do?" Joe asked with a worried look.

Gail shook her head and smiled at her son's concern. "No honey, just some bloodwork and x-rays, doesn't hurt a bit. What have you been up to?" Though she liked him being there with her, she tried to distract him from her unpleasant journey as much as she could.

Joe didn't want to reveal that he was solely focused on her welfare and return, so he generally replied, "Oh, just looking through magazines." He hoped she didn't ask for more detailed information as he had no clue what material the magazine he held had reported.

"What should we do after lunch?" Gail asked. "I know my options are limited, but I feel good today." She was practically jumping around in her seat.

"Maybe we should wait to see what the doctor says," Joe answered, trying not to sound negative. It just made sense. Why plan something fun if they wouldn't be able to do it after all? Her vitality was infectious yet confusing. He wanted to put his hands on her shoulders to quiet her apparent rear end springs. If she had another relapse, this was the best place for it, but he wasn't going to let it happen regardless.

She looked as though someone had just taken her new pet kitty away: confused and hurt. Joe felt bad but was also amused by this new childlike behavior in his mom.

"I'm sure we'll think of something, no matter what news we get," he rephrased, and he could feel her attitude shift back to happiness again. Their roles had momentarily changed, and Joe felt like a responsible, reasonable adult talking to his child. The shift was an odd feeling, but it gave him a sense of comfortableness and maturity too. He realized he was capable of being in charge and taking control of situations, regardless that his mom wasn't much of a challenge.

A soft-spoken, amiable nurse approached and requested they follow her. Gail addressed her by her first name and thanked her as she rose to her feet. Joe left his eternity seat and followed the two ladies down a warm, quiet hallway. The doctor's office they each took a seat in opposite a large desk, had a mixed atmosphere of pristine and spotless, and cozy and welcoming. This confusing aura impressed upon Joe an even more unsure feeling of what the outcome was going to be.

The doctor's initial expression did not disclose one way or the other what the mother and son were going to hear. The nurse excused herself, quietly closing the office door behind her.

"We never completely rely on preliminary, immediate tests for several reasons," Dr. Emory began. "The worst thing we can do for any patient is give them false hope."

Gail and Joe looked at each other skeptically and dreadfully. Joe took his mom's hand, patted it, and looked back at the doctor with courage, hoping his strength would support her to do the same.

"That being said," the physician continued, "what I have reviewed today, which astounds me quite honestly, is that you have reached remission."

Gail jumped out of her seat and squealed. Then she covered her mouth, regained her composure, and resumed her seated position. Her hands covering her mouth did not, and could not, conceal the grand smile that was beneath them. Her cheeks almost hurt from the wide grin. Joe grabbed her hand again as she sat back down, but for a much different reason. They could not believe their ears, and Gail asked the physician to give them more information to confirm what they heard was indeed true.

"How certain are you?" Gail inquired. "I mean, how excited can we get here? You seem a bit apprehensive."

Dr. Emory could not remain impervious to the Hart's irresistible positive energy, and he smiled at them before he could respond.

"I want to make it clear that remission does not mean cured," he stated. "This is a very good sign, one that not many cancer patients get, but the chances of your cancer coming back are much higher than in someone who never had cancer. I just want you to be aware of that fact. You will still be coming in for checkups and such, but definitely no more treatments for now. So go celebrate! But take it easy until you have had some more time in between having cancer and showing no signs of cancer cells."

Joe released an enormous sigh that he hadn't been aware he'd been holding in. Both he and his mom stood and then hugged each other. His mom pulled him in so tightly that he could hardly breathe, and she was trying to jump up and down while he bobbled around in her arms.

"Mom, don't overdo it already," Joe said, laughing. "Besides, I can't breathe." She let go, put her hands on his shoulders, kissed his cheeks like they were in an Irish bar dancing around, and recommended they go eat now, announcing she was starving.

Gail thanked the doctor, but before he let them leave, he made sure she knew to call if anything seemed out of the ordinary, if anything seemed out of place, no matter how insignificant.

The mother and son sat enjoying their ooey-gooey food almost as much as each other's company. As lighthearted as their emotions had been before the appointment, they were immensely overjoyed with life now. They couldn't wait to get home to share the great news with the family, but it was mother-son time for a bit longer, and they were both taking advantage of it. They shared lots of laughter and joking as well as a non-healthy but most excellent meal.

Near the end of their feast, Joe's face suddenly transformed from pure joy to curiosity as his head tilted to the side and his eyes narrowed. Gail could tell he was onto something deep.

"Mom…" he said, "do you think this good news could have anything to do with Peter being gone now? Can it work that way?"

She found herself not fully comprehending what her son was implying at first, so she didn't answer, which gave Joe a chance to continue his thought.

"I mean, isn't it odd," he went on, "or more pretty darn coincidental, that you have been cleared of the same disease as someone who just recently died from it? Your last checkup wasn't bad, but it wasn't necessarily good. And it hasn't been too long since your emergency room scare either."

Gail's arms and legs then grew pronounced goosebumps. Somewhere from deep within her, she remembered a Bible verse from the book of Peter about how Jesus had died so we could live, and she instantly experienced the most humbling feeling she had ever felt.

CHAPTER 30

The driver of the Blue SUV in the lane next to John nearly collided with his pickup truck when the jerk quickly, and without warning, decided to join John in his lane on the freeway between work and home. Luckily, John had noticed the incompetent driver's intent with just enough time to simultaneously swerve slightly and stomp on the brakes to avoid a situation that would have more than ruined his night.

After quite a few cuss words, hand gestures, and honking, John realized his road rage was getting out of control, even though the imbecile deserved worse. He should not let others have this much influence on his feelings. He had been feeling more and more constricted and bored lately, his normal scouting locations for events were failing to excite him anymore, and he was also sensing suspecting eyes looming closer as well, and that was just way too risky. Maybe local fires should cool for a while. He needed an adventure. A road-trip to somewhere new sounded like the cure for his dull life as of late. His boss at the magazine had just suggested he get creative and think of a different, unique idea for a shoot – the freedom to do what he wanted couldn't have come at a better time. Getting paid to get out of town was like sweet, buttery icing on the delicious cake of an epic event somewhere undiscovered. His imagination canvas was clear and ready for a masterpiece. He hadn't done this in a long time. He felt refreshed already and couldn't wait to get home to plan his next event.

First, John got out a map, even before deciding what he

wanted for dinner, and laid it out flat on the dining room table. He sat down and gazed at every road, followed them to random ends, and paid attention to the surroundings of possible locations. He was looking for a smaller town on the outskirts of a city. The city was for his article. Otherwise, he would easily be tied to the small-town event. The small town gave him a better chance of making the news, well not him directly of course, just his brilliant events. Though riskier, his events were much more devastating in a small town. His heart skipped a beat at the thought of all the chaos he was going to create. People screaming. People crying. All asking dumb questions like, "Why us?" and "How could this happen?" And all the stunning photos he was going to get of the brilliant, lifelike blaze that would be added to his collection.

John realized he had stopped looking at the map and was blindly staring at the blank wall above his sofa in the living in front of him. Back to work; he could revel in the marvelous outcome after the excursion was finished. He found four promising towns near bigger cities, one in each direction, and opened his laptop to start researching their webpages for possible locations to destroy. John didn't intend on spending much time researching a city for his article. There was always something that interested his readers in a bigger city, and unique topics to write about always had a way of finding him. But for the small-town event, maybe a historical site because the townspeople would probably be more upset about the destruction of something that meant so much to them and that they would not be able to replace. He felt a little butterfly in his stomach. The anticipation was almost too much to handle, and he was growing more impatient with each clever thought he envisioned.

The first town John cyber-visited was pretty ordinary;

nothing about it was teasing his creativity enough to spark an idea of where to create an event. The community page hadn't been updated in months, so he wasn't clued in to any social happenings where mass people would be gathering. He couldn't find anything with noteworthy historical value that would cause excessive uproar. And the area looked to get a fair amount of rainfall each year. Maybe this research was going to be more grueling than he thought. He remembered why he stayed local, so he could personally scout out his next location.

Feeling a bit discouraged, and disappointed in people that they weren't more proud of their hometowns to post all pertinent information on the internet, John got up from the table and went to his fridge. His stomach had started to grumble as he was working, and he thought it a good time to address the issue. He was surprised to see that an hour had flown by since he'd started; no wonder he was hungry. He didn't want to take the time to make anything from scratch, so leftovers it was, as long as there was something decent. With one arm resting on the open refrigerator door, he leaned over to peer inside for good review at his options and spotted a decent helping of spaghetti sitting in a Tupperware container waiting its return. There was also a half-eaten steak and some vegetables he had grilled up a few days ago, but he was really craving pizza, so the spaghetti was going to have to be a close second. He decided it wouldn't take long to make some cheesy garlic bread to make up for not getting exactly what he wanted. He stuck the spaghetti in the microwave after preparing the cheesy bread and putting it in the oven.

To use his time wisely, while waiting for all that to heat up, he moseyed to his bedroom to change out of his work clothes and relieve himself. By the time he got back to the kitchen, the smell of the garlic bread toasting up in the oven made his stomach even more impatient, and it reprimanded him with a loud growl for making it wait. One more thing to make his meal complete, he poured himself a big refreshing glass of milk. His feast was finally ready, so grabbing his food and drink, he moved back to the dining room table, sensing the nourishment would help regain his focus and energy to get more suitable results from his analysis.

John placed his meal beside his laptop, sat down on the simple brown oak dining room set chair, and deposited a forkful of spaghetti and a bite of bread into his watering mouth and moved onto the next little town on his list. The homepage showed a very nice park with brick bridges over little streams, park benches, and well-manicured grounds. Now this town looked like the kind that its residents were proud of. *Perfect, good start, keep it coming,* he thought as he took another healthy bite of spaghetti. Further inspection revealed plenty of notifications of upcoming goings-on around the quaint town: the county fair, neighborhood clean-ups, city park information, an open house for the remodeled library, the next high-school football game and fundraiser, etc., and multiple links to other areas of the site.

As if that wasn't gift enough, the best news of all might as well have been wrapped in a bow; he couldn't believe his luck when he read, *"The Fire Department will begin flushing hydrants around town this coming Monday through Friday..."* Preoccupied firefighters. It was like Christmas. He wouldn't have to create a diversion himself, and he would have more time to enjoy the result of his hard work. He was so thrilled that he almost spit out the gulp of milk he had just poured into his mouth. He didn't even consider looking at the other two towns he had listed; this one was the one.

The time John was investing virtually exploring this town

was nothing compared to the options he was finding to plan his deadly display of disaster. He was having a very hard time deciding which site was best: one would create a larger inferno, another would harm more people, while another would cause more irreparable financial and economic damage. It was truly a shame he couldn't plan more than one location at a time, for two major catastrophes in one small town might just finally give him the ultimate fulfillment he was always craving but never quite accomplished.

But for now, he had to settle on just going back someday. If he did some scouting while he was there, he might be able to pull off the feat the next time. John decided on his first idea of the Historical Society & Museum building. Handmade craft exhibits, various pieces of antique farm equipment, priceless memorabilia, countless vintage photographs of significant historical eras, displays of old clothing and household items depicting long-forgotten ways of life, and a roomful of timeworn reels of documentaries were more than enough to entice John to "take care" of it all. The thought that most of those things would not be able to be replaced once he was done gave John a complete, comforting feeling that made him a little sleepy. He smiled; this was going to be fun.

Next, John used his computer's virtual map and geographical information program to survey the entire expanse of the town. In slowly and meticulously examining the town and outskirts, John noticed a small, dark building in the woods. He zoomed in as far as the program would allow to look closely at the little dwelling; from what he could see, it was a bit worn and dilapidated, but the structure looked sound, and the roof was intact. Since he could not discern any roads or trails to the shack, it was pretty clear it was not being occupied. His luck just kept getting better; he had found the absolutely perfect setting to hunker down and not be bothered or questioned by anyone. This also ensured he would not have to check into a hotel and give investigators any easy clues, for even when using aliases and fake identification, the risk always worried him some. You never could be too safe.

Camping out in the woods instead of staying in a hotel would alter John's packing list, but he welcomed the change immensely. This was his whole reason for doing this: to get out of town and try something new, to continually develop his repertoire of events. To effectively plan any event, he, first and foremost, needed to take stock of what supplies he did and didn't have; there was nothing worse than going out on a mission only to find he'd overlooked a vital component, because the mishap would most likely thwart his whole operation, and that was simply not acceptable.

John opened the icon folder on his laptop that he had titled "Backpack," which held the file lists of his gear and provisions that were essential for a successful trip. He'd named the folder that in honor of his first event, where everything he needed was in his trusty backpack, but things had changed a lot since then. Things were more complicated now, so he now had separate files in that folder for distinct phases of planning an event: packing checklists, a risk-reduction checklist to double-check his plan, separate ingredient checklists for different types of fires, years of notes he had taken of his successes and failures (or learning experiences as he liked to call them), generic blueprints for improved understanding of structures, extensive research on materials – more specifically, simply what burns and what doesn't, and a variety of chemical compound sketches.

His cell phone rang sharply just as John was getting deep into his research and planning, causing him to jolt at the abrupt noise. Rubbing his eyes from all the computer screen straining, he answered with a raspy voice, "Hello?"

"John, Carl here, I've got an emergency of sorts," his boss curtly started without any type of customary pleasant lead-in.

John quickly turned his wholly focused mind away from his now hours-long planning party to mumble, "Ok, what do you need?"

Carl proceeded very quickly, "Peterson can't do the article on the endangered pygmy owls of Arizona and Texas because of the bad weather down there right now. It was due to print next week, so I know this is asking a lot, but I don't have anyone else. I know you are capable of coming up with something remarkable like you usually do. You're my go-to guy. Thanks, John." Then there was a click, and John realized his boss had hung up before he could respond in any way. This wasn't necessarily a surprise, however. He had found Carl to be quite brusque since the moment he'd met him twenty-one years ago when he'd walked into the magazine's conference room for his job interview, but the discourtesy still got under his skin a bit for being cut off. *Good thing I'm a nice guy*, he thought. It would have been nice to know if he was expected at the office in the morning.

Knowing Carl the way he did, John easily understood that he wasn't being intentionally rude, and John was also pleased that he was being counted on with obvious complete faith that he would do the job and well. Fortunately, he had already gotten a good start tonight on his strategy for an article, and event, but this did change things. With even less time to plan and the trip being in unfamiliar territory, he was going to have to be extra careful to ensure this wasn't going to be his last event due to being caught, but with how the evening had gone so well so far, he wasn't too concerned.

He presumed he was going to need more than just his laptop, as he was rather certain the cozy old shack would not provide him with the modern marvel of electricity. John grabbed his dirty dishes, set them in the kitchen sink, and ambled back to the spare bedroom to his four-drawer file cabinet, which contained numerous files and folders of old newspaper clippings of his former events, photos, and more sketches of chemical compounds and building blueprints that he had been meaning to scan into his computer. He felt another sense of "everything is right with the world" that he hadn't scratched that off his to-do list because now he would have enough examples of his previous work to refer to that he most likely would not be able to access from his computer on-site. John had everything fairly well organized, so it didn't take him long to rifle through and find what he presumed he would need.

Again, due to the probable absence of electricity, he most likely wouldn't be able to access the internet, so he also made sure to grab his sacred "bibles" – a few of his favorite books on thermochemistry and explosives. The first ones he had acquired, he had actually stolen from the library; he'd been so enthralled by the complicated information and awed by the limitless options that he just couldn't bring himself to return them. The books showed signs of extensive wear on the covers, bindings, and pages. After collecting those and most of his papers, photos, and files he arranged them neatly in carrying cases, bags, and briefcases to put out in the truck.

Next he used his materials checklist to compile ingredients for the supreme event. Without having an actual location picked out, he would have to bring a variety of accelerants, materials, and igniters, as it was nearly impossible to predict now the exact formula he would be utilizing later. With each step of preparation, John grew increasingly anxious for the upcoming event; working with his materials was by far the most fascinating and pleasurable part of preparation anyway, so being more enthusiastic and eager during this phase was not a shock. He actually found the new process of preparing for the unknown a refreshing change, on top of the challenge of having to be even more cautious and diligent due to the higher risk of being caught. Everything was going better than he could have hoped, and therefore, his spirits were high.

John then filled his special containers with an assortment of materials: gasoline, matches, paraffin, cotton, lead azide, and his lucky butyl acetate, various types of cloth, paper, and cardboard, coal, electrical wire, blasting caps, and various incendiaries and detonators. Looking over his collection, he felt confident he would have what he needed to create his next event, and then some. With the extra left over, he might even consider a quickie at a stop on the way home; that would be a new one as well. With the way the night had gone, he was up for anything at this point. It didn't seem like anything could go wrong.

Once he was done packing up his clothing, which was over quickly, that was the easy checklist, he was torn whether to do more small-town inspection or settle down for a good night's sleep, but once the thought of possibly obtaining some more great destruction ideas through dreams revealed itself, it was off to bed he went.

CHAPTER 31

It had been way too long since the boys had been to their hideaway in the woods; it seemed like to them anyway. They had made a quick afternoon trip not more than two weeks earlier to update their supplies and get some fresh outdoor air, but they were itching to get back for a full weekend. With jobs, families, and after-school functions, the young men were finding it harder to schedule time off together. Finally, they were able to make a fishing weekend out of it again and were at Cal's house on a Thursday evening preparing so they would be ready to just head out after school Friday. The three of them were sitting at the kitchen table planning their trip. Joe was perusing their list of what was already in stock out there, and Cal was making a list of what they still needed. By now, all of their parents were fully aware of their vacation home and were ok with it, partly because they knew their kids weren't out causing trouble, but mostly because it was real life teaching them how to survive and get by.

"We need to get fresh bait on the way out tomorrow," reminded Cal, "but other than that we have everything we need still out there, except for food. You guys still have some extra clothes there, right?"

Joe looked up from his paper and replied, "Yes, I do, plenty for now, but I know I'll need to bring them back for a good washing this time."

"Yep, I'm good too," confirmed Drake as well. He was busy picking on a scab on his arm from a cut he'd gotten the other day, making it red and swollen. It was his way of suppressing his impatience of one more day of school before some freedom from rules and restrictions. He didn't feel like looking at lists and being organized; he just wanted to go, now. He knew his disinterest wasn't fair to his friends, but they didn't seem to mind. They quite enjoyed taking charge of all the preparation. He also knew he would regret it if something got forgotten that he could have prevented, but he just was too anxious to get out there to concentrate on remedial things, besides the fact that Joe and Cal never forgot anything before, so he wasn't worried. This was why his crusty scab now got all the attention it was receiving from his fingernail.

Joe got up from the kitchen table and started making some peanut butter and jelly sandwiches. He packed the rest of the loaf of bread, some crackers, apples, jerky, potato chips, granola bars, jiffy pop, and trail mix into a couple of plastic grocery sacks. "Do either of you remember how much frying oil we have left? I know we're going to need a lot because I'm feeling lucky!" smiled Joe.

"We might want to bring extra just in case," responded an excited Cal, smiling back, "because I'm feeling it too. I see us emptying that creek for sure. Those fish are doomed." He proceeded to write down the items for the small cooler that they couldn't pack until last minute: ice, water, juice, soda, ketchup, mustard, and hot dogs – just in case their plan for catching fish didn't pan out.

When the lists were finished being compiled and the provisions packed up, Joe and Drake said, see you tomorrow, to Cal and left his house for each of their own for one more night. They would see each other at school tomorrow and could talk more about things if need be. Drake couldn't leave fast enough, not that he wanted to leave his friends, but he just figured tomorrow would come sooner. Joe and Cal just laughed as they watched him scurry down the street in the dark. They knew their friend well enough to not be offended. Once they were out in the woods, Drake provided more than his share of work, and that was fine with them.

"I got a call from my boss last night," said Joe when he finally found Drake and Cal in the hall near their lockers at school the next morning. They noticed he looked stressed and knew this wasn't going to be good. "He needs me to work tomorrow. I can't go this weekend, or at least until Sunday, but that still just ruins everything."

Drake became almost irate. "He can't make you work. You weren't scheduled to. You don't have to." He almost stomped his foot with every part of his statement.

"That's right," agreed Cal. "It's not your responsibility to do it if you weren't scheduled. Did you tell him that?"

Still looking utterly depressed, Joe answered, not wanting to glance up from the floor and look them in the eyes, "No, I didn't think of it. I was in shock that it was happening in the first place, so I just said ok. Oh, man, what am I going to do? I've wrecked our plans." He put his hand to his head as if it were aching.

"Are you sure there is no one else who could work? Maybe you were the first one he called. Can you call someone?" asked Cal.

"Or just call in sick. Come on," urged Drake stubbornly, "you're not going to work. We'll fix this somehow."

Joe turned a bit more optimistic with the thought of trying to find someone else to work. "Yeah, I'll start calling now. Actually, there are some kids here at school who I work with. Maybe I can find them and talk them into it." Without even a goodbye, he started off down the hall with such intent it was like his friends hadn't been standing there at all.

Drake and Cal found each other in the hall again after suffering through two whole agonizing class periods, the longest class periods they had ever been in. With every minute that went by, the more discouraged they became that they were going to have to postpone their outing to who knows when. With their busier lives, this was just not acceptable; it was such bad timing for Joe to pull this absence-of-mind move.

"Where is he? He must really be working it, which might be a bad thing, meaning he can't find a replacement," rationalized Cal. Drake looked exhausted. Cal couldn't remember a time he saw him looking more stressed. "What happened to you? You don't look so good," said Cal, holding back a snicker; he was surprised Drake was that bothered by this snag in the plan.

Drake responded, "I've been racking my brain trying to figure out a solution to getting Joe out of working, plus just being worried we won't be able go at all. I know if he got caught by his parents or his boss for calling in sick, it would be over for him, but this sure isn't fair. And this waiting is killing me. You know how impatient I am."

"Let's go to his locker; we'll at least get some kind of an answer," suggested Cal, seeking a way to ease his tension. Sure enough, they found him there quickly exchanging textbooks in and out of his locker, much to Drake's relief, but he still hoped he wouldn't be hearing terrible news.

"Sorry, guys, I haven't had time to find you; Susan Mattson is checking with her mom, but I think she's going to be able to do it," an exhausted Joe finally informed them. "She said she'd let me know as soon as possible. I suppose I need to call my boss too and make sure that works for him. Man, this growing up and being responsible thing isn't fun at all!" Joe finished and slumped down on the floor next to his locker.

Cal grabbed his arm to pull him up, knowing the bell would be ringing soon. "Get up. Only one more class until lunch. We're almost there, and this was just a hiccup. We're going, I know it. Cheer up guys." He smiled a reassuring smile at both of them and trotted off to his next class.

"He's sure in a good mood. I can't wait until I know we're for sure a go so I can stop worrying about it," said Drake with Joe nodding and watching Cal traipse off. "See you at lunch; I hope this class doesn't drag too." With that, he started off in another direction to his class.

Joe stood in the hallway for another minute watching his fellow classmates slowly dwindle from his presence and disappear into various classrooms. He was disappointed with himself for making his friends go through this; they were being so cool about the unfortunate news and not making him feel bad or anything, just helping him figure out a solution. Replaying the conversation in his head, he remembered being caught off-guard when he got the call from his boss and completely forgetting about their weekend plans for that split second when he consented to his boss's request. He wanted his boss to be able to count on him, and he couldn't bear the sound of desperation in his voice, so he said yes before really thinking about it. The sense of pride that swept over him when he could hear the appreciation in his boss's voice overwhelmed him at first, only to then be replaced by opposite and just as strong feelings of guilt and regret when he hung up. Next time, he was going to handle this much differently for sure. He didn't want to put himself, or his friends or co-workers, back in this situation again, ever.

The three young men finally made it to lunchtime and were standing in line in the cafeteria when Joe felt someone tap the back of his arm. He turned to see a smiling Susan standing there holding her tray of what the lunch ladies had selected to serve that particular day.

"Hi, Joey. I just wanted to let you know I can work tomorrow, no problem," she verified.

Joe beamed back at her after hearing the good news and replied, "That's great, Susan! Thank you so much, I owe you big time. Seriously, anytime you need something, I'm your guy." He almost wanted to hug her; thank goodness their trays prevented that awkward scene.

"I might just hold you to that," she countered, "but who's going to work for both of us if we're both *busy*?" she hinted, and with a wink, she turned on her heel and strode away to a table of girls who were not being shy about watching the show.

"Oh man, I did not see that coming," Joe muttered through the fog clouding his brain as he turned back around. "She is kind of cute, though; I guess I wouldn't have to be too nervous to ask her out since she's flirting with me. That is what that was, wasn't it?"

Taking a step further down the line, Cal shook his head and laughed. "Come on, Joe, come back to us. Now that that's over, we need you to focus on our guy's weekend. You can think about her all you want Sunday evening." He nodded to accept a helping of lumpy mashed potatoes to his tray from the server.

"Yeah, Joe, after what we just went through, don't let a woman ruin our outing now, and did you hear her call you Joey? What's up with that?" Drake added with a scrunched up nose, but when he looked back at Joe behind him in the line he could plainly see his friend's mind was somewhere else far away.

Only a few short minutes after the final bell of the day rang, Joe, Cal, and Drake had converged outside the school at their usual spot in what had to have been record time. The sky held only a few wispy clouds, the temperature was warm, and a light breeze barely tussled their hair. Nothing else mattered; it was all they could do to get out to their fort as quickly as possible. The plan was for each of them to go home, drop off their school supplies, change clothes, and grab whatever few things they needed before reconvening at Cal's house and then heading to the grocery store. Even though this part of the preparation was way better than waiting for the school day to end, it still wasn't the fun part for any of them. Since they lived in the same quadrant of town, they took off in that direction while excitedly chatting about the possibilities of the weekend as well as laughing about the close call that had threatened their plans. Drake didn't want to dwell on that too much because, whenever the stressful circumstance and solution were mentioned, Joe's eyes would glaze over a bit.

Cal sat on a hallway chair near the front door of his house in anticipation for his friends to arrive. He had everything ready to go, and it had been about five long minutes before he heard Drake's little car puttering closer to his house. In that time, he recalled the incident in the lunchroom just hours earlier and how the presence of a female actualized how their lives were changing and going to change even more drastically soon enough. Not only would they be going on to college but eventually getting married and starting families. The three friends had been so preoccupied by each other all their lives that they didn't think much about how their carefree childhoods together would be ending someday. They weren't going to be kids forever. He felt melancholy. Maybe that was why Drake was so upset about their weekend possibly not happening; he had already realized their time together was coming to an end. They were just going to have to make this trip extra special.

Drake and Cal didn't wait too much longer for Joe to show up, and they loaded up the car with the food and a little gear and took off to get their cooler supplies. Once at the grocery store, they had a hard time resisting all kinds of treats, as they were getting quite hungry. If not for their limited budget and the difficulty of transporting certain things to the shack through the woods, they might have allowed for a royal feast. They packed the cooler with the perishables, added the few extra snacks they'd grabbed to the existing stash, and started their short drive to the remote, forgotten road that would lead them near their private home for the next few days. The sense in the atmosphere was completely carefree, especially since they all knew how close their boy's outing had been to not happening at all. They were taking advantage of every minute together.

"Hey, get out of those chips. We need to save them for when we're out there!" exclaimed Joe to Cal after he opened a bag of corn chips they'd just bought; he was sitting sideways in the backseat, munching away like his buddies weren't there. "Or at least send them up here so we can have some too," he said with a laugh, and he grabbed at the bag only to catch air instead as Cal swiftly slumped back out of his reach.

Cal laughed as well and played along. "Nope, they're mine. All mine, and they're going to be gone before we even get there," he muttered with a mouthful of crunchy, salty goodness.

"I'm starving. Hand them over. I can smell them, and it's driving me crazy," Drake stated in agreement with Joe. "I'll stop this car right here!" he teased while tapping the brakes a bit and swerving slightly to the side of the road.

"Alright, fine, but I'm eating the first fish that each of you catch then," advised Cal. "Up to you, still want them?" He swayed the bag back and forth from them back to himself until it was quickly snatched by Joe. "I've got more back here anyway," he said, and with head down, he proceeded to ruffle through a couple of the grocery bags, only to make some noise to get a reaction. Joe's head turned so fast that Cal thought it might swivel right off, and the look on his face was priceless, Cal chuckled so hard that he grabbed his stomach and leaned back so quickly that his legs came up enough for his feet to hit the roof of the car.

Drake barked, "Hey be careful back there, don't be denting my beauty." And with that, they all roared, because even though they appreciated the independence of having their own ride, they all knew there wasn't much they could do that could make his dump on wheels much worse.

Soon they were parked at the farthest spot they could go on the old grassy road nearest the fort and commenced grabbing their gear as they climbed out of the car. Cal grabbed the cooler from the trunk and started down the narrow path toward their shack. Joe snatched a couple of backpacks with a few supplies that they don't like to leave there. The dark of night was closing in, so he made sure to retrieve a flashlight out of the pack before securing it to his back and set out after Cal. Meanwhile, Drake took the grocery bags of food out of the backseat, locked up the car, and pursued his friends, anxious to get there. They probably would have jogged there if they hadn't had the cooler to carry, but the distance to their vacation home was only about a half of a mile, so it didn't take too long anyway, and with their joking and carrying on, the jaunt flew by rather quickly before the little old cabin was in their sights and making each of them smile with delight.

CHAPTER 32

John was sleeping so soundly that it took him a while to come to enough to remember his plans for the day. It must have been his busy, tedious evening that he needed the recovery from. Initially, he wondered why his alarm didn't go off to get him up for work. In the short time it took him to stretch, rub his eyes, and open them, he was reminded by the travel bags on his bedroom floor what his itinerary was, and he was up and out of bed in a blaze to prepare the final items for his departure. He had done the majority of all the physical packing and preparation last night, but he wasn't sure he was completely prepared to head toward a foreign location, so he wanted to go online to search the area again before possibly losing all internet connection until he returned home. He was not going to rely entirely on Wi-Fi accessibility in a place he had never been either. He had his GPS navigation tool but questioned whether the territory the remote cabin was located in would be on it, so he planned to pick up a paper map once he got to the town.

Seeing as how he was going to be out of town for a few days, John decided to make an egg scramble for breakfast with various leftover items in his refrigerator so they wouldn't spoil. He did not like wasting things, especially food. The steak and vegetables that didn't make the cut for dinner last night would be just perfect. After he chopped up the steak and added everything to the nearly done eggs in the skillet to re-heat, he fired up his laptop for one final review. Scouring the roads and land again, he felt confident of where he was going and how to get there, including specifically where to go once he arrived. Just as he was about to close up, he zoomed the webpage in closely to the old structure and noticed a barely visible grassy old road leading close enough to the shack to not have to carry his supplies and such too far. He could still park his truck under cover at the end of the no longer used road for ultimate security and safety from being discovered.

John sensed the content feeling he aimed for on every outing and decided it was time for action; now that the preliminary planning was complete, he was bursting with anticipation to get on the road. He could not gulp down his makeshift breakfast quick enough, and the following kitchen clean-up seemed to take a lifetime. Every minute that ticked by added to John's energy level, and he practically carried all his gear out to his truck in one load. It wasn't a matter of strength that he could not accomplish the feat, it was a matter of not having enough arms.

With his belly full from a warm meal, and his truck full of his favorite things in life, John was feeling incredibly spry and invincible as he drove down the freeway on that bright sunny morning. He sort of wished that terrible driver from last night would reemerge so he could have another chance to not let the man's lack of driving skill or consideration get to him. With about four hours to drive before reaching his destination, there was sufficient time to go over his plan as well as brainstorm other ideas for absolute destruction.

The radio was switched off to provide him uninterrupted reflection, besides the fact that he was not fond of the selection of music out there nowadays; he considerably preferred silence to nonsense lyrics and melodies. Generally, on long trips, he would listen to an audiobook, as he loved a good story to nurture his imagination, but he had been so rushed that he didn't have time to purchase a new and interesting saga to take him away. This trip was different anyway. He quickly surmised he was not in need of anything to occupy his mind, and he kept catching himself smiling like a fool visualizing random results he could get with each alternate ending of his current mission. Those entertaining thoughts reenergized him again, and with the sun reaching through the driver's side window and warming the left side of his face, he switched the vent blower from notch one to notch two to regain comfortableness.

Halfway through his drive, John decided to make a quick stop to stretch his legs, top off the truck with gas, and relieve himself. He favored 7-11 stations, as they held a special place in his heart, but they weren't always available, nor did they always supply gas pumps, like this time, so he settled on the cheapest, most convenient one instead, scouting out the dumpster to see how full or empty it was out of habit.

Just as he was finishing filling up his gas tank, an irresistible urge to cause damage came over him. Maybe it was because he couldn't find a 7-11, or perhaps it was from the sweet smell of gasoline, or maybe from the excitement of what was to come, but whatever the reason, he craved some havoc. John then took a more careful look around the area, taking into account the amount of people around and nonchalantly looking for security cameras. Since he had been so oblivious and lost in his own thoughts when he'd first pulled up to the station, he questioned whether it was smart to create a scene here. He had always been more than careful with his number one rule, don't get caught. That was first and foremost, even to creating the perfect event, because if he made a mistake, his fun would be over. One way or another, he would either be behind bars or dead. Therefore, any time he had the slightest inkling that things were not right, he would move on, and he was beginning to reckon this was one of those times. Even small events should be permitted a certain amount of prep time.

John finished his task at the pump and relocated his truck to a parking spot nearer the station building. Once inside, he found the restrooms and discovered it was the usual single-person type, so there was no chance of the blame of something suspicious to not be on him. Disappointment led him to buy an extra treat before heading back to his truck for the second half of his journey; the sweetness of a chocolate bar and the saltiness of some sunflower seeds would do much to aid his patience.

Back on the road and munching on his snacks, the urgency for an event gave way to impatience to just get there; he didn't usually grow tired of driving, but this time he just wanted to get out of the vehicle, and the sooner the better. John was excited about a change of pace, and the privacy of the shack in the woods too. He couldn't wait to get his hands on his supplies and start devising his plan.

John absolutely loved his life. He could not comprehend the need or want to marry and have a family. The thought of being tied down and responsible for others made him shudder. He was free to do what he wanted, every single day, and answered to no one. He was grateful for how lucky he was to have a life where he could do what he enjoyed all the time. John figured it was his payment for losing his mother when he was so young and having a father who didn't care one bit for his welfare. He was proud of himself for making his life what it was.

The eager arsonist finally started seeing the road signs counting down the miles to his destination, and before long, even with his impatience, he had arrived. It was a small town, so he knew getting around and getting what he needed wouldn't be a problem. First stop was another convenience

298

store for a map or two and the restroom again, then he would explore the town a bit and swing by the Historical Society and Museum building to get an initial feel for its setup before heading out to his personal lodging. He was more than excited to get out to the little shack, unpack, and do some preliminary preparation and research.

The worker at The Historical Society and Museum building greeted him with a pleasant welcome before he even fully emerged though the front door. She looked up from the desk she was sitting at just inside the doorway and displayed a wide smile; her oval glasses covered warm hazel eyes, and after welcoming him in, she urged him to be sure to ask if he had any questions while visiting the pride of their town. The place was just what he had hoped and pictured. There was no entrance fee, just a box on the desk labeled "Donations" with a handwritten smiley face on the sign. Beside the donation box was a small bowl of wrapped hard candy pieces. He picked up a butterscotch button, unwrapped it, and popped it into his mouth. The sweetness of the hard candy stung his salivary glands and made him pucker for a second. In the time it took his glands to calm down, his eyes focused on a flyer on the wall behind the desk advertising that weekend's 95th Annual Craft and Fundraising Bazaar here in this very building, Saturday and Sunday. Well, only he knew there wasn't going to be a building left, or hopefully near as many people to attend, on Sunday.

While walking through the old brick building, John quickly noticed the displays were neatly arranged and the different sections led him easily through the timeline of the town. He got a good feel for the history, and he could tell the townspeople were immensely proud of their heritage. These things were not going to be able to be replaced for sure. And with the generous townspeople unknowingly assisting him in his plan by hosting this wonderful fundraiser, he anticipated an even more momentous outcome. Who would have thought that the firefighters would schedule their hydrant draining the same weekend?! He felt all warm and cozy inside and felt pretty sure the sensation wasn't due to the friendly neighborhood feel of the Historical building.

As far as John could tell, there was only one worker in the building; the not-for-profit business was reasonably quiet for a late Thursday afternoon. This made his mission even easier than he originally figured it would be to go anywhere in the building he wanted without being watched; he had yet to spy a single security camera anywhere in town. It didn't take him long to locate the unlocked door that led to the basement, and with continued caution, he quietly descended the steps to the bottom floor of the building. It greatly pleased him that these people were just the right amount of trusting for his liking. Upon arriving at the basement, he found it chilly and a bit musty, and just as with the works of art upstairs, even every piece of storage had its place, and he was going to have plenty of room to work in the middle of the large room.

Having gotten a more than satisfactory scope of his new canvas, John discreetly left the old building and used his recent map purchases to get his bearings of which direction his new vacation home was. He counted on there being a grocery store on the way out of town; he would need some sustenance for sure since event planning always increased his appetite.

After obtaining all the food and drink that he suspected he would need and want, which was a bit tricky as everything had to be non-refrigerated, John headed out of town. The old grown-over road was barely noticeable, but he preferred it that way. There was less of a chance of being followed and discovered. He turned his truck onto it and, about a mile down the road, came to a dead-end. But, to his delight, there was enough space to keep his truck off the road and under cover; he didn't need any hunters, kids, or environmental surveyors foiling his plans. He pulled his cell phone out of his jeans pocket and noticed he didn't have any messages, or reception, which was fine with him; he gladly powered down the electronic link to the real world. Another peek at the more detailed map of the two revealed the general direction the hut would be in, so he grabbed his first load and started his hike. He was looking forward to a little exercise after a day of sitting on his rear end and eating treats.

Once John came into view of the old shack, he quietly dropped his cargo to sneak up on the building and peer inside. He was always fully aware of his surroundings, listening, looking, feeling for any sense of danger. Lifting himself to his tiptoes, he slowly peered through a small window and discovered that the room was not empty as he suspected it would be, and it was not as if the things were left long ago, it actually looked a bit tidy. He didn't like the feeling he got from something he wasn't expecting.

Again, relying on his senses until he was sure he was alone, he ventured inside. He first spied a lantern and deck of cards sitting on a rickety old table in the center of the room. *The table will sure be handy*, he thought. Three sleeping bags were rolled up in one corner of the room with three bags of clothes beside them. The clothes were not quite adult-sized pieces. A few fishing rods leaned up against the opposite wall with a tackle box sitting at their handles. The cozy fireplace had a bucket full of dry pieces of wood, so they had to have been inside for a while now. There were dish-washing items on the far counter as well as other sundries, and a decent selection of dry food stashed underneath the counter. It was hard to tell how long it had been since anyone had been there or how often they came, but John decided to take temporary residence. It was his home now. Most likely, he would be long gone before anyone came back anyway. His feeling of success and hominess helped boost his energy to get the rest of his belongings.

It took John four heavily loaded trips until all his gear was safely in the fort and his truck was locked and hidden. With map in hand, he scoured the area around the shack for other buildings, animal dens, or any other threat to his existence there. There was a nice stream a short distance away that was going to be very useful for cleaning and freshening up. He could see why there were fishing poles in the shack, but he wouldn't have time, or the interest, in catching his own meals. He was pleased with how secluded the whole area was, and it was clear how easily he'd be able to come and go unnoticed with the townspeople not knowing what happened. Only second to the cravings of creating destruction was seeing the ultimate shock and disbelief on victim's faces.

Only once John's stomach started growling did he realize how long it had been since he had had his treats in the truck on the way there and how long he had been combing the area. He closed his eyes, took one last deep breath of fresh air, and ventured back inside his new temporary home to find something satisfactory to fill his belly before starting to configure his exciting strategy of disintegrating the old Historical building.

Mr. Hackett had bought some of his favorite crackers, and he guessed they would go great with the tuna he'd bought that came in a pouch. In between each bite, he started tacking up photos on the wall, before and after pictures of buildings and vehicles, burned bodies, shocked faces of survivors and rescue personnel, and his favorites – the glorious blazes themselves.

Once the pouch of tuna had been consumed, John grabbed a Honeycrisp apple, rubbed it on his flannel button-up shirt for a not-so-thorough cleansing, and took a big bite. The crack and crunch led way to the sweet juiciness that then filled his mouth. With the second part of his gourmet meal underway, he began rifling through old newspaper articles of his events. Ones of particular importance and similarity to the event at hand, he sat out on the floor underneath the picture wall. It always was fun reminiscing; he compared it to families looking through their photo albums of years of memories made together, but his was much better. His events were his family. Next he got to review his notes and sketches to find the most suitable combination of fuel, oxidizer, and ignition options from his available stock. To finish his meal, he took a container of vanilla pudding out of one of the grocery sacks and spooned himself a helping while still reviewing his past for the perfect near future.

John wasn't sure if it was the nourishment or the fresh air, or the combination of both, but with his head clear now, it didn't take long after getting all his possessions organized that he concluded this was going to be a job for his trusty colorless, odorless, and flammable chlordane liquid, as well as detonation boxes of gasoline. As he sat in one of the old wooden chairs next to the table, he pictured three or four containers of gasoline in the basement with blasting caps. From liquid-soaked fuses out of the containers, he would lead a healthy trail of the chlordane up the stairs, and then, while feigning interest in the crafts and displays, he would use a briefcase filled with the flammable liquid and a small hose at a bottom corner to administer it to multiple wall/floor elbows with long, thin doses. Ultimately, he would lead one trail out the backdoor where he would ignite the liquid and quickly take cover, waiting to take pictures and take in his grandiose event. Just like that, it was a magnificent plan! And literally right under people's noses. He was really falling in love with this town.

Finally, John was ready to prepare the gas boxes with the appropriate non-electric fuse blasting caps; he would wait until the last minute to fill the briefcase, as that was not the proper way to store chlordane. The long day was developing into night, so when the gas boxes were complete, he unrolled his sleeping pad and set it up near the wall opposite his work display. On top of that, he laid out his sleeping bag and pillow, and like a cherry on a sundae, he placed his fully-loaded Beretta PX4 on the floor next to the bed. Taking a step back, taking in the whole setup, he thought his temporary home looked rather inviting. He took off his boots, changed his clothes to shorts and a t-shirt, much more appropriate attire for sleeping than jeans, and climbed into his soft, makeshift bed. With no more planning to do, he became sleepy quickly, and once his head hit the pillow, he was happily beyond consciousness.

The next morning, John awoke feeling very refreshed. The night had been uneventful; no animals or humans disturbed his sleep, a bittersweet fact. Still lying in bed, he could see the sun shining through the small windows of the shack, so he got up, put on his boots, obtained an orange and granola bar from his food stash, and journeyed outside for some fresh air. He found a nice rock beside the creek and sat to ponder his plan once more to ensure he had thought of everything. He listened to the babbling water and watched squirrels and ants scurry around minding their business and ignoring his existence. Soon, he grew tired of the nothingness and decided he desired a warm meal. Moreover, since his event-planning was complete, he thought he might get his actual work out of the way by traveling to the nearby city to do his article. After checking his maps, he got dressed, grabbed his cameras and miscellaneous photography essentials, along with a container of mixed nuts to snack on along the way, and started the hike to uncover his truck. While walking up the trail, thoughts of getting his work done so that he could wholly focus on his play time, pleased him entirely.

It was nearing dusk by the time John finished shooting for his article and began his long drive back to the small town and remote fort. He remembered seeing a roadside diner between the two towns, so he thought he'd enjoy another warm meal before being back to resorting to dry goods. He had had a successful day, and his article was well on its way to being a knockout, much like his previous work, so he was in an exceptionally upbeat state of mind. He switched on the radio to some old-school rock and roll. He got a half an hour's listening in to The Doors, Aerosmith, The Eagles, and ZZ Top before getting to the diner. After eating, he drove the rest of the trip in silence again, as the food put him in a rather comfortable lull. Another forty-five minutes, and he found himself back at the end of the now familiar grassy old road, but this time his truck was not the only vehicle there.

CHAPTER 33

The three buddies were still laughing and playing around as they entered their dark hideout. As he opened the old screen door, Joe turned around quickly to prevent Drake from getting some easy smack or hair tussle or the like in on him while his back was turned. Before Joe was able to transition between flashlight to lantern, their sense of lightheartedness changed instantly to unease for all three of them. Someone was there; there was a different smell than the familiar "boys in the woods and old house" smell. Eyes wide open, trying to scan the almost pitch black room, the trio stood in the doorway, absolutely quiet, listening for the smallest sound that would give away the intruder's location, or any movement to defend themselves. The plastic grocery bags Drake was carrying seemed to take forever to quit their crinkling sound from being swished around upon entering the house, but eventually they heard nothing, no safety-impeding noises or movement came from inside the old house.

Feeling a little safer, Joe shakily shone the flashlight around the room, particularly in the dark corners. The amount of light from the flashlight, which was usually more than enough, was now more than disappointing as they strained their sight to make out anything threatening. Even in the dim light, they could all see the place had been taken over by someone else, and who knew when they would be back.

Drake whispered, "I don't think anyone is here." Suddenly, they all sprang into action as if they had practiced a million times. Cal put the cooler down and quickly lodged one of the rickety old chairs under the doorknob of the front door and then the same to the backdoor. Drake dropped the food bags and pulled the dirty old sheet curtains over the windows while Joe got the lantern going.

When they all converged back to the center of the room, backs to each other, and looked around at all the unfamiliar objects cluttering their safe place, all they could hear was their own heavy breathing and hearts beating rapidly. There were stacks of paper on the table and floor, photographs on the walls, and all sorts of gear, which they didn't know what half of it was for, along the edges of the floor near the walls, draped over the chairs, and on the table with more stacks of papers.

Even though they all knew they weren't safe and maybe had little time before the evident threat returned, Cal expressed the overpowering curiosity they were all experiencing, "Maybe we should look around," but he didn't move quite yet.

Drake was a little more proactive thinking, *I'll feel a lot better snooping with a weapon in my hand,* and he escaped the security of their triangle and grabbed his trusty small hand axe from the storage area. Cal followed suit and promptly armed himself as well with a hammer. As Joe took a step towards their arsenal to grab the biggest utility knife they had, he heard a crunch underfoot; removing the obstacle to detect the culprit of the sound, he found a couple of now crushed sunflower seeds.

Feeling much safer, however ignorant the decision may have been, they split up to investigate. Joe found some of the stacks of papers to be so old that they were yellowing. Some looked official, like police reports, while others were newspaper clippings, and then he found lots of scribbling and note-taking documents as well. A quick perusal of the notes revealed detailed plans of sorts on specific dates, as far back as twenty years, and unfamiliar sketches of gadgets and lists of hardware-type items. The newspaper clippings were of fires that destroyed buildings and claimed innocent victims. There were tons of them, some recent and some very old as well.

Drake starting looking through the gear and found an array of photography items: straps, lenses, memory cards, all types of cords, tripods, and bags. There were also boxes and books of matches, and cigarette and butane lighters. He found ropes and fasteners. Jugs of what appeared to be gasoline but other jars of liquids as well, and many hand towel-looking cloths in plastic packages.

Cal decided to take a look at the collage of photographs covering the south wall. Even with the heavy ominous feeling that filled the room, he was curious and anxious to see the art. Before he got very close, he could pick out that a lot of them were of fire and flames and burning buildings. Then he got sick. He had never seen pictures of burned living beings, so he wasn't sure, or didn't want to believe it, at first. But once it became clear how real what he was seeing was, he quickly kicked the chair out from under the back doorknob, opened the door, and ran outside just before his dinner decided to reemerge on its own. Down on his knees, hands in the dirt, he couldn't get the pictures out of his head, and he had to stay there for a while before he was able to regain safety with his friends.

The other two boys, instantly alarmed by Cal's sudden, loud move, and once fairly sure of his safety outside, decided to see what had triggered the unwell feeling. Knowing that they were probably going to see something unpleasant, they were both able to keep their stomachs in check, but it was still overly disturbing to see what someone, who'd been in their "home," was capable of, and once again their security senses were heightened to the fullest degree. They quickly got Cal back into the house. They were still more comfortable in their safe haven than trying to make it all the way to the car just yet, at least until they had surveyed their surroundings a little more.

They sat down and shared what each of them had found and their preliminary assumptions and conclusions. First, they needed to understand a little more what level of evil the person they were dealing with was. Then they could decide what action to take to get out of there alive, whether they left or stayed, they might very well have to defend themselves.

After sharing their findings and analyzing every detail, they soon determined the threat that had invaded their space was an arsonist. And a very deadly one. Suddenly, they didn't feel very comfortable in a dry, old wooden building.

"Do you really think the same person started all those fires and created all that destruction and killing? Is anyone really that malicious?" Joe just couldn't believe how in the world someone could be so evil.

"And whoever it is seems pretty proud of themselves too," added Cal with a disgusted and confounded look on his face, refusing to glance back at the trophy wall.

Drake just shook his head. He felt bad that his friends had to see this; he should've been the first one in the door and stopped them from coming in. Now they could be in very great danger; he knew he needed to act swiftly and cleverly. "I think our best chance is to get out of here and make our way back to the car with our weapons to protect us. We have no idea, the guy could be well enough away that we'd leave and he wouldn't even know we were here. We can't just sit here and wait for him to get back." There were hard decisions to make, as they felt safer in their shack than the eerily dark outside. The unknown was almost unbearable for the friends who'd never wanted or expected to be in this situation.

"I'm not sure our weapons will be very effective," revealed Joe as he looked at the utility knife in his hand. "Who knows what this guy has equipped himself with." For all they knew, they could be holding nothing better than toothpicks and rubber bands compared to whatever real weapons their possible assailant would most likely have.

"We're going to have to make it work," Cal piped up. "There's no other option. It's better than being out there using only our bodies to defend ourselves. And there's still hope we just get out of here unnoticed. But before we leave, we should see what else we can find of his that might help." They all got up and repeated going through the foreign items in the room but with a different intent this time than last.

"Well, hello there, boys. What's got you so busy in here?" a slow, deep, gruff voice came from the now open back door. Standing in the doorway was a large, rough-looking man in dirty clothes and boots. He held a shovel upright in his left hand. He stomped the handle down on the wood floor and leaned on it while crossing his right leg in front of his left and setting his toe on the floor. He looked absolutely and completely comfortable. Unfortunately for the boys, they were not experienced in doing harm to others, even to protect themselves, but they knew the trespasser was.

John was not surprised to find the intruders; besides the car back at the "parking spot," when he had arrived at the old building the day before, the place hadn't looked lived in, but it was clearly not totally vacant either. He had been hoping this would happen so he could have some more entertainment, and these three boys looked like precisely the prey for his type of fun. With his mind racing with what to do with them, how to scare them, how to play with them, he made sure he didn't look surprised or angry to see them. He wanted to portray a calm demeanor to unsettle the young men. However, he had never had to think so much on the fly before. This was not his comfort zone, and he didn't know how to proceed because he hadn't thought this all out over and over like his usual events. But that wasn't going to stop him; he wasn't going to waste this ideal opportunity.

John needed to take control of the situation before the boys got any wild ideas, so smiling, he stated, "First off, don't get any funny ideas that those ridiculously measly tools you each have are going to help you in any way. You might as well all toss them towards me."

The three boys, who felt a significant drop in their phase of new adulthood by the presence of this man, nervously and apprehensively relinquished their weapons after silently checking with each other that conceding was the best plan for now.

Once all the tools were in front of John on the floor, he took a powerful step towards the young men, pointed at each of them separately like he was poking them hard from a distance, and he ordered, "The three of you need to get in the center of the room and lay face down. Now. Hands behind your backs."

The boys looked at each other with terror and displeasure in their eyes. Did they dare not listen and try something? They didn't have anything to fight with anymore, though. How bad was this guy? Temporarily surrendering, they made their way to the center of the room and proceeded to get down on the floor. None of them had ever felt so vulnerable, and Drake had an overpowering sense of protectiveness, but he knew he could make this all much worse if he did something stupid. He had to bide his time if they were to have any chance at all of getting out of there.

John grabbed a chair and sat down at their heads, his right elbow on his knee and the shovel still in his left hand standing erect on the floor. "Did you like all my trophies, boys? It's quite a collection, isn't it? I suppose you're really questioning your decision to come up here tonight. Well, you should consider yourselves lucky. You know why? You are the only three people who have seen some of my magnificent work... *and* met the maker. That, my boys, is an unprecedented event."

He sat back smiling, admiring the evidence of his extraordinary events all over the room. It was quite a blissful feeling, and he wondered why he had never thought of it before. He could have been showing people his work for years now, and then burning them after of course, but he had been depriving himself of the close-up and personal looks on their faces all these years. Suddenly, the contentment was replaced with anger for robbing himself of a previously unknown pleasure of life.

From the floor, the boys stared at the man in horror as they watched his wicked smile fade to a nasty scowl and his eyebrows turn downward sharply. They were not sure which they were less comfortable with, so they each slowly looked away.

John quickly stood up and kicked the chair he was resting on backwards, hard. It bounced off the wall behind him and settled on the floor sideways. The boys all jumped at the sudden loud ruckus and resisted the urge to look up for fear they would get a shovel in the face.

Using the shovel as a walking stick, John started pacing back and forth, his clunky boots vibrating the old creaky floor with every step. *These boys need to be tied up. Then I can think better*, he thought. Cal heard the man's boots get a little closer to him and then felt a sharp kick in his ribs. "Get up, you!" He was on his feet in seconds, though he wasn't sure how he managed to stay standing; counting on his legs to hold his weight seemed an absurd notion at the moment.

"You two stay where you are. You, boy," the man said, motioning to Cal, "get that rope over there." Drake was fuming, he couldn't let this man cause any more pain to Cal. He knew he didn't have much time, but he felt quite helpless on the floor. He couldn't even get a good view of what was going on or what their escape options were. Joe could see the look on Drake's face and shook his head just enough for Drake to see but not the man. He knew Drake's impatience; it had gotten all three of them in trouble more than once. He tried to look at Drake with as much "let me handle this, I've got a plan" intent as he could.

Cal walked slowly to where the gear was because he knew that, the sooner he got the rope, the sooner the man would do something with it. He fumbled with the long line, acting like it was all knotted. Joe knew they would have to run, but they would need to get to the door with enough time to open it and get all three of them through unharmed. The man was so big, there was no way he could catch them if they could just get out.

While the dangerous intruder was watching Cal get the rope, Drake noticed Cal purposely taking his time, and he just knew this was his chance. So he rose as quietly as he could, and with one quick swoop, he grabbed up one of the big mason jars of liquid and swung to hit the man in the back of the head. There just wasn't enough time; the man ducked with a millimeter to spare and swung the shovel around, hitting Drake in the stomach, and he was knocked to the ground, gasping for breath and holding his midsection.

"Now that wasn't very nice. You didn't listen very well, boy," grunted John as he looked down at Drake, who was barely holding on. "How is that feeling, you idiot? Serves you right to try to attack me. I guess I don't have to worry about telling you to stay down again."

Turning back to Cal, he yelled, "Get me that ROPE!" Cal understood he couldn't play around anymore, and he hastily did exactly what he was told. He grabbed the rope that he had dropped during Drake's assault and, turning back to the man, Cal saw that Joe was thinking it was his turn to be the hero, so he purposely tripped getting back to the man with the rope. He figured it would either buy time, draw the man's attention, create more frustration for the man, or, he hoped, all three. The trick must've worked because as the man instinctively bent over to pick up the rope, instead of letting Cal get it, Joe tried Drake's move but with a lot more time to accomplish the task. The heavy glass jar came down on the man's head with so much force it broke, spilling the smelly contents all over him as he went down limp.

The three boys stopped and gaped wide-eyed at the evildoer on the floor, surprised that the plan actually worked and wondering what the extent of the damage was. They hoped he wasn't dead, even though their own lives could then still be at stake. They were quite exhausted, and the now silent, unmoving man gave them such a false sense of security that they foolishly overlooked their need to leave. Joe and Cal went to Drake on the floor to help him regain composure; he was still having a hard time catching his breath and was in a lot of pain.

"I'm ok," Drake said, barely able to get the words out. "We should leave now."

"Agreed," said Joe and Cal simultaneously. They had just gotten Drake to his feet when they heard a noise behind them, John was almost to his feet already too but, luckily for the boys, not very steadily or quickly moving. How had they not heard him?!

"GO!" yelled Cal, and he pushed his two friends toward the back door. They didn't need much of a push. They ran, and Cal followed quickly, slamming the door behind him. He heard a bang and assumed the man had run into the door, not expecting it to be suddenly shut in front of him.

The boys only got about twenty feet from the house before they heard the man loudly yell in agony and anger. Instinct made them stop in their tracks and look back at the house. They were pretty hidden in the trees, and the night was so dark out that they felt safe enough to linger just a moment. They could see flickering light in the windows, and for a second, everything was silent.

Squinting, Cal asked, "What is that?"

"We need to go," Drake whispered. But just before they turned to run again, the back door opened, and a fire monster of a man appeared in the doorway. The huge man was even bigger, engulfed in flames and lumbering through the door to get outside. His arms were outstretched in their direction as if he was looking for returned affection.

Stumbling down the stairs, "Aggghhhhh," John yelled again. He was definitely really beginning to suffer from the flames. He couldn't take the heat anymore. He dropped to his knees without any energy to even roll in an attempt to smother the flames that surrounded him.

Joe ran back into the house and grabbed one of their old sleeping bags and tore some curtains off the windows. The other two boys promptly caught on to what Joe was up to and were ready when he reemerged from the house. They doused the burning man with the improvised extinguishers as carefully as they could, only concerned with their own safety still, but they couldn't just watch a man be tortured and not do anything at all.

"Ok, stop," said Joe when they saw there were no more flames coming out from beneath the scorched fabrics. There was no movement from the pile on the ground, but all three boys backed up a good length anyway while they waited for any sign of life.

Quietly Cal spoke, "It's too late. We did what we could. I don't think he's getting up this time."

They stood near the man for a few more minutes to be sure, and then Drake ambled back towards the house. Now that they were safe, he needed to sit down. The other two followed. Drake found a flashlight, clicked it on and set it on the table, and slumped down in one of the old chairs closest to the door. He was in pain, and it was still hard to breath, especially since he had just run some. Standing in the doorway, carefully touching his ribs from the boot kick, Cal continued to study the lump on the ground outside. Joe chose a chair at the table, his back towards the photo wall. Nothing was said for a long while.

CHAPTER 34

The little old house in the woods was all over the local and national news for days; it was by far the top story, and reporters were having a field day.

The cause of death for Mr. John Hackett Jr., as far as the crime scene investigators initially surmised, was due to a lantern being knocked over as the arsonist was trying to get out the door to chase after the boys. Once they found the burned remnants of what looked to be pieces of a lantern, their assumption was nearly confirmed. And since he was drenched in "a smelly liquid" per the boys, assumed to be a highly flammable substance by the police, he instantly became his own personal inferno.

Contrary to typical criminal investigations, not much effort was put into discovering the particular reason behind John's death. Much more time and effort was put into solving the man's crimes and putting closure to them. John didn't have any family or friends worried about his well-being, so there was no one to pressure the police for definitive answers. The boys were never really accused of the accident, but were officially cleared of the death only a few weeks after the incident.

Luckily, the majority of the lantern had been extinguished after engulfing the victim, or all the evidence in the shack would have been lost. The police also discovered, once locating his residence, that John had kept every scrap of documentation and plans of every event he was responsible for, so between the evidence at the crime scene and the abundance of what they uncovered at his residence the next day, they were finding it quite easy to solve countless past arson and murder cases. Some stories came together quicker than others, but with the profile similarities, they were finally able to connect what were previously random clues to unsolved cases. Though this massive discovery might have reopened old, healing wounds, countless families finally got the closure they needed and deserved.

The extent of this evil man's repertoire was unbelievable and hard to fathom. He had been committing these crimes for so many years without getting caught. Why did he do these things, and how did he get away with such evil for so long? For so many questions being answered, there were just as many new ones that needed explanation. Since there were no living relatives, most of their questions were to remain unanswered.

The three boys were interviewed by multiple venues and were considered heroes for inadvertently stopping what would have been a major catastrophe in their quaint town, and for preventing all the subsequent arsons and murders that would have followed, but they would rather they had not been. They just did what they had to do and were grateful to be alive, especially after hearing how evil of a man John Hackett actually was.

Drake, Cal, and Joe never returned to their fort.

54381200R00191

Made in the USA
Middletown, DE
13 July 2019